SALVATION

Salvation

Stephanie John

This book is a work of fiction. Names, characters, places and incidents are either the product of the author's imagination or are used fictitiously. Any resemblance to actual persons, living or dead, is purely coincidental. The author does not own the rights to any products, names and song titles mentioned in this novel, which have all been used without permission.

A Cataloguing-in-Publication entry for this novel has been lodged with the
National Library of Australia
ISBN-13: 978-0994261427
ISBN-10: 099426142X

Cover design by Amygdala Designs
Interior designed and formatted by

www.emtippettsbookdesigns.com

To those that have graced my life and left it too soon, and to those who continue to bless me with their presence every day. This is for you.

Chapter 1

"Wish I had a best friend as awesome as me."

My good friend stood in my private office doorway. Deep chocolate brown eyes twinkled with mischief, and a huge self-satisfied smile adorned her pretty face. It was a look I often saw when Mai Harvey was interfering in my non-existent love life. I was sure it was her favourite pastime. "What have you done now?"

"Just hooked you up with a meeting on level fifteen." Making her proud announcement, she tottered in on sky-high tangerine stilettos that added at least four inches to her five-foot frame, the skirt of her yellow fifties-style dress swishing as she moved. "You can thank me later."

"Shouldn't Michael attend that?"

"The sleazeball's been called elsewhere, so I volunteered you take his place."

Slipping off my glasses, I raised a disapproving brow. Michael Cole was the Finance Director and our inconsiderate boss. Married, mid-forties and slightly overweight, he had a roaming eye for the younger ladies.

"What?" she moaned with a flick of long poker straight hair that matched her eyes, "He's pervy."

"He isn't that bad. I've never had any issues with him."

"You intimidate him. He knows he doesn't stand a chance, but thinks us less-blessed in the looks department are grateful for some attention."

Mai was half-Hawaiian, a sensual and exotic beauty who received more than her fair share of attention. According to my father, I was the quintessential English rose—creamy skin, large green eyes and caramel blonde hair with a natural wave that gave Mai serious hair envy.

"Anyway," she continued, hopping onto the corner of my desk and knocking over my photo, "level *fifteen!*"

"Is that supposed to mean something?" I returned the picture to its upright position. It had been taken in the garden of the family home in Oxfordshire six years ago on the day I moved out. A moment of great sadness for my parents, but great excitement for me.

"The top floor, Kara!" Mai clapped her hands and did a little wriggle in childlike excitement. "You might see *him*!"

"Ah, Blake," I said. She was referring to the founder and owner of RED, the leading brand management consultancy in North America, and the man we both worked for.

"Hell, yeah!" Mai swung her legs, all distant and love-struck. "You say you've sworn off men, but wait 'til you see him up close."

"He's that good?"

"Well, I sure as hell wouldn't kick him outta bed in a hurry."

"Are there many you *would*?" I shot back.

"I'm a happily engaged woman," she exclaimed, wafting her left hand in front of my face as a visual reminder. I pushed it away. Mai was engaged, but nowhere near as happy as when we first met. With an encouraging grin, she went on. "Remember that photo I showed you on the company website?"

I nodded. It had been Mai's warped way of persuading me to apply for my job. Wavy, dark chestnut hair, immaculately groomed back off an angular face, highlighted eyes the most vivid shade of electric blue. Corporate profile photos rarely made people look good. *Except him.* He looked sinfully good—not that I ever admitted that to Mai.

I'd seen him once, albeit from the rear across the marbled lobby one morning. Every female employee unashamedly lusted after him, and judging by the heavy flirting going on between him and the main receptionist, Blake was arrogant enough to know it and not afraid to take advantage of it.

Definitely *not* someone I should waste my time on.

"If he doesn't get you tingling between the legs you may as well turn lesbian," Mai stated emphatically, strolling back to the door.

I rubbed my temples, trying to soothe a headache, and put my glasses back on. "What time's the meeting?" I asked, not wishing to engage her further in this conversation.

"Two. I've updated your schedule with the details." Mai was employed as Michael's PA but insisted on keeping me organised, too. It was greatly appreciated. She accepted my weak smile of thanks and wobbled out of the office.

I pulled the relevant files off the server and created a new folder on my computer to store them all in one place. Luckily, it was a project I was familiar with. With my tablet syncing, I spun my chair to face the window.

Associate Finance Director, West Coast, USA – my job title sounded far grander than it was. RED handled some of the most recognised corporate brands across the globe. No two days were ever the same and I thrived on the variety. I could be involved in the upfront assessment of a prospective client's brand value one day, then preparing budgets and forecasts for a Marketing campaign being implemented another.

Deciding the late July California sunlight streaming through the tinted windows was too much for my delicate head, I stood and drew the cream blind shut.

"Take these," Mai insisted as she returned, "you look like shit." She set two Advil and a glass of water on the desk and dropped into the visitor chair opposite.

"Well, thanks," I retorted, finding her straight-talking as endearing as ever. "Exactly what I needed to hear before heading upstairs."

"K, I'm kidding. Even with a hangover, you're still gorgeous." Ignoring her flattery, I sat down and took a tablet. "Sooo," she began, leaning forward, "Jay was *seriously* into you last night. Lemme give him your number."

"Do *not* give him my number." Last night, after yoga, we'd belatedly celebrated my one month anniversary of full-time employment at the bar Mitchell—Mai's fiancé—worked as Head Bartender. Their friend and roommate, Jason, had popped in and ended up keeping us company. Thanks to his trust fund, which covered the rental payments, he was the sole reason they could afford to live in their serviced building.

"But Jay's cute," Mai whined. She was insistent I needed a good lay to get me over my drought, but I disagreed. Meaningless sex wasn't the answer to my problems.

"Honestly, I don't recall much of the evening. If I were interested, I'd have taken more notice."

With a defeated sigh, Mai muttered, "Shame. He can go *all* night long. I've heard him through the walls…"

I pursed my lips at her wiggling eyebrows. “I’d better prepare,” I said, checking the time. “Thanks for the Advil.”

AT a quarter to two, I made my way to the top floor. Standing in the empty lift, I fussed with my hair, wishing it wasn’t tied back in a ponytail that drew attention to my tired face.

At least I was wearing trousers. Paired with a black polka dot blouse, I was comfortable and professional, someone to be taken seriously—more appropriate for dealing with a group of businessmen than a skirt or dress.

When the metal doors opened, I stepped out into a small bright vestibule with the word *RED* sandblasted onto double glass doors. A young man with jet black hair styled into a high quiff peered up from behind the reception desk. He reached across it and the doors swung open. I was hit with the fragrance from the extravagant lily display on the glass table in front of me as I entered.

“Hey.” He pushed to his feet. “Can I help?” His smile was confident, his manner easy-going. I introduced myself and waited patiently whilst he verified my attendance on his computer. His style was slightly quirky, a pale lemon shirt, patterned tie and taupe slacks. The light shades set off his Hispanic skin and dancing brown eyes.

“This way, Miss Collins.” He stepped from behind the desk and led me to a waiting area. Jonathan Booth, Chief Finance Officer, sat engrossed in the latest edition of business news streaming from a huge wall mounted plasma television. The sound of my heels on the cherrywood floor announced my arrival.

He nodded and gave a curt, “Hello,” before going back to his programme. Thankful he wasn’t much of a talker given my delicate disposition, I sat opposite on a cream, suede sofa, with burgundy coloured soft furnishings in line with the company branding. There was so much natural light up here it renewed the dull ache in my head.

“Can I offer some refreshments?” the man from reception asked. “Tea? Coffee?”

“Espresso please, Ramón.” Jonathan rudely didn’t take his eyes from the television, but Ramón maintained his cheery manner and switched his attention to me.

“I’ll have some water, please.” I’d had enough caffeine for the day. Ramón nodded and disappeared behind the partition wall.

At the far end of the suite, open double doors framed an executive desk and revealed plush white furnishings inside…*his office.*

An unwelcome wave of disappointment washed over me upon seeing it empty. Enlightened by the knowledge that maybe I wanted to see Blake more than I cared to admit, I turned back to Ramón, who was placing our drinks on the glass coffee table. I offered my thanks and took a sip of chilled water.

A flurry of activity distracted me, drawing my attention to where some people were exiting a Boardroom, their animated chatter breaking the relative quiet. I was about to turn away when I caught sight of the magnificent vision emerging last from the room…

Striding elegantly through double cherrywood doors, wearing a navy two-piece tailored to fit his lean frame in *all* the right places, a white shirt and pale blue tie finished his stylish look. Effortlessly charming both the men and ladies surrounding him, his lips pressed together as he smiled politely and shook their hands. Mid-conversation, he glanced over in my direction, and when those intensely bright eyes locked onto mine, his eyebrows rose subtly. Tilting his head to one side, his lips parted before the ghost of a smile teased the corners.

Keen to avoid his gaze, I looked away, anywhere but at him as I squirmed in my seat, embarrassed at being caught staring. I heard his associates make their goodbyes and peeked up briefly to see him address a young blonde now joining Ramón at reception. The hair at my nape prickled with anticipation, my heart rate accelerating when he started making his way over.

"Jonathan." A smooth, polished voice flowed through the air. Mr Booth stood and shook hands with the man who honestly looked like he'd stepped straight from the catwalks of Milan.

"Mr Blake! Your gift was very generous." Jonathan proceeded to talk about Marcus—his partner—and their recent wedding and honeymoon. Blake listened, but he wasn't paying attention.

His gaze had snagged on me, as if I were a far more interesting subject.

"How's everything with you?" Jonathan asked once he'd paused for breath.

"Well, it appears my afternoon has just taken an unexpected turn for the better," Blake answered. I sat enthralled, blindly placing my water back on the table as he leisurely weaved his way around it towards me, smoothing down his tie.

"I don't believe we've met before?" He offered his hand, exposing a simple, but expensive watch on his right wrist beneath the French cuff of his shirt.

“This is Miss Collins, our new Finance Officer,” Jonathan muttered behind his back.

Ignoring that dismissive introduction, I stood and nervously took the long-fingered hand still extending out to me. There was no denying the jolt of electricity that sparked through our fingertips, nor the tightening of his grip as his left hand closed around mine a second later.

I sucked in a breath as the aftershock bubbled through my veins. Heat slowly radiated up my arm, spreading throughout my body, reawakening something dormant low in my belly. His grip was strong and firm, yet somehow possessed a reassuring quality with its caress.

“Nate Blake,” he offered as an introduction, regarding me shrewdly. “It’s a pleasure to meet you.” The entire tone of his voice had altered, quietening to a soothing, sexy whisper. It was so…*intimate.*

Blake definitely had a voice for sex.

“And you,” I murmured, all breathy and weak. It was all I could manage, rendered speechless by this impossibly handsome man standing in front of me. It was rare to find a man much taller than me when I wore heels. Given the few inches he had over me, I’d guess he was around six-three.

I found myself staring into clear blue eyes as deep as the ocean and likely just as dangerous. Unaware of what hid in their depths, I found them strangely calming.

Then—they darkened.

I felt the impact right between my legs. I licked my dry lips and turned my focus to his mouth, now slightly quirked at the corner. The sudden urge to touch the dimple presenting itself in his cheek had me clutching my tablet tight to my chest to stop myself.

“Are you okay?” His smoky voice broke through my daze. “Do you need your water?”

I blinked and raised my eyes back to his amused ones.

Jesus. *Those eyes.* That photo hadn’t done them justice at all. They were even more breathtaking in reality.

I couldn’t look away. Had I been thinking straight, his smirk would’ve told me he knew the effect he was having on me. But I wasn’t, because I’d been blinded by the gorgeous man in Prada, who still had a firm hold of my hand.

The arrival of two Brand Managers brought me crashing back to reality. Abruptly, I withdrew my hand, flustered I’d held his for longer than was politely acceptable.

With a cocky raise of his brow, Blake adjusted the knot of his tie. "We'll talk soon, Miss Collins."

Evidently unaffected by our encounter, he strode confidently towards his office. His shoulders were broad, waist trim, and his legs long and lean. He moved with such an easy, sexy swagger, I couldn't take my eyes off him. When he glanced back over his shoulder, a small frown marring his exquisite features, I knew in that instant he *had* felt that strange charge between us.

"Kara," Jonathan urged, pulling my concentration back, "Room 2?"

I got the impression he'd been talking to me. I quickly greeted the gentlemen who had joined us, keen to return my attention to the office in the far corner. When I did, Blake had removed his jacket and was sinking gracefully into the black leather chair behind his desk. Leaning forward, resting both elbows on the desk, he brought his hands to his mouth thoughtfully.

Piercing blue eyes found me again, and as I dragged my own away from him, was conscious of his lingering stare, following me as I walked into the meeting room next door.

AS expected, the meeting was relatively straightforward. I ran through the revised financials and was pleased the budget amendments were accepted without argument. Once all parties were satisfied, I took a back seat whilst Jonathan discussed other matters.

It gave me time to think about things I shouldn't. Like a certain gentleman I'd met some forty minutes ago. I made an absolute fool of myself, barely stringing two words together, gaping at him like a smitten teenager rather than the mature, professional woman I was. The only consolation—I suspected he received that reaction all the time and wouldn't have taken any notice—but it didn't lessen my shame or humiliation. I rubbed my palm, recalling the feel of his smooth skin, and the heat that flooded my body when we'd touched.

Mai warned me Blake was good-looking, but *damn*, up close he was a work of art. One glimpse of those sculpted lips told me he'd be a great kisser. And the way he moved suggested there was no way on earth he'd be crap in bed. I fumbled with my stylus pen, fidgeting in my seat at my errant thoughts, whilst the conversation around me faded away. I couldn't help glancing behind me, conscious he was sat the other side of the room.

Finally, the meeting concluded.

"Miss Collins?" a warm, masculine voice demanded behind me as I made my way to the lifts. My steps faltered, thus causing the Brand Manager following me out to stumble into my back. Muttering my apologies to him, I turned, and was greeted with the sight of the man who'd sent my pulse soaring again.

"I need a word. In my office." Blake stepped aside in his doorway, gesturing inside with one hand. What did he want to talk about? Perhaps he had one-to-one chats with all new employees, though nothing had been mentioned to me before.

"Um..." With a panicked glance over my shoulder, I noticed Jonathan and the two gentlemen disappearing into the lift. They hadn't given me a second thought, abandoning me here with possibly the most beautiful man I'd ever laid eyes upon. I was hit with his fiercely expectant gaze when I turned back. "...Okay."

With my stomach spinning nervously, I moved towards him. He wore an expression I imagined him using when he was about to negotiate the terms of an important business deal. Focused, determined, not willing to budge until he was satisfied with the outcome. I tried ignoring the fact that, as I stepped into his expansive office, he moved forward, causing my arm to brush across his rock hard abs.

"Take a seat." He pointed to a modular sofa on his right as he closed, and *locked*, the door behind us. I sat, feeling edgy and slightly awkward as I balanced my tablet on my knees and quickly hid my glasses under the leather cover.

The external décor flowed seamlessly into his office, and the rich wood furnishings added warmth to the light, airy space. The walls of windows, with unobstructed San Fernando Valley views, must ease the isolation of being the only person, aside from his assistants, on this level.

"How was the meeting?" Blake asked, making his way to a built-in dresser spanning the length of the wall. Standing with his back to me whilst he organised drinks, I couldn't help but admire his pert backside. Two splendidly rounded globes of delicious taut flesh, the thought of running my hands over them made my skin heat.

Blake glanced over his shoulder and caught me drooling, enhancing my embarrassment ten-fold. I tried occupying my mind with something else, but struggled to ignore him. *As if I could.* Being in his presence, just the two of us, I was extremely aware of the strange, unseen energy between us once more.

"Good...I think," I managed to say. "I didn't contribute a lot, actually."

The sound of ice hitting glass ceased as Blake stilled. "You're English?"

He didn't turn so I answered, "Um...yes?" to his back. "Is there a problem? I have all the necessary paperwork and visas."

"No." He cleared his throat. "No problem."

Without another word, he finished making the drinks then made his way over. He set a tumbler of clear sparkling liquid in front of me and sank into the sofa opposite, draping an arm casually along the back, appearing unfairly relaxed. I eyed the square crystal glass, resisting the urge to gulp whatever it was down. Blake didn't need to know how uncomfortable I was in his presence.

"I'm sure you made a valuable contribution," he offered. "You impressed those gentlemen, judging by the contented smiles on their faces." His mouth twitched as he fought his amusement. "Never underestimate your worth, Miss Collins. I only employ the best."

He looked away, towards where his fingers stroked the back of the sofa. After a brief moment of silence, he sat forward and clasped both hands together, elbows resting on his knees. Those brilliant blue eyes fixed onto mine.

"Have dinner with me."

Chapter 2

My mouth fell open, stunned by his words. "Dinner? You mean like a business dinner?"

"No." A small smile teased his mouth as he kept his curious gaze upon me. "No business talk."

"A date?" Panicked, I pressed my fingers to my lips to prevent any more ridiculous presumptions from pouring out.

"That's what I'd call it, yes. Do they call it something different in England?" He still had that sexy half-smile tempting his mouth, whilst his eyes burnt into me expectantly. Somehow, I broke free from the inexplicable hold he was having over me, and took a much-needed gulp of what I sadly discovered was only sparkling water.

"Dating the boss isn't really my thing." Thank God my head was talking, gratefully overruling any irrational ideas my heart was having. Because, for a split second, I actually wanted to say yes.

"You don't work for me. Well, you're not directly beneath me. Which is unfortunate..."

The arrogance of his smirk made my skin bristle with irritation. I tried thinking of a smug response to his blatant innuendo. "You know what I mean," I muttered, failing miserably.

"We can do lunch if you'd prefer?" Blake stared at me with interest, like he found our conversation utterly fascinating.

I laughed and shook my head. "I don't think so." Drawing my eyes over fine, symmetrical features, I noticed his jaw working beneath the contours of his clean-shaven face. He rose to his feet and turned, giving a close up view of that arse. *Jesus.*

"It's only a date, not a proposal," he stressed, sauntering away. "We'd have a great time together. Wouldn't you agree?" When he reached his desk, he turned, and locked eyes with mine.

His words were arrogant, but the suggestive way he purred them made my skin flush. I wiped my damp palm down my thigh as X-rated images replayed in my mind. I couldn't ever recall being so turned on.

"I want to discover everything about you," he declared. "How do I make that happen?"

"Are you always so forward?"

"I don't play games." He started coming towards me with more than an alluring edge of confidence. "If somebody has something I want, or need, I'm prepared to make sacrifices in order to get it." *What the hell was he sacrificing by coming after me so blatantly?*

"And you think I have something? Why, exactly?" I raised a brow, challenging him to come up with something more inventive than breasts and a vagina.

Blake shrugged noncommittally, stopping just short of where I sat. "Something in your remarkable eyes tells me you could be good for me."

I lowered my gaze, crossing my legs. The roguish glint in his eyes told me he'd be really *bad* for me. "Well, I'm not interested."

"I think you are, Miss Collins."

His overconfidence was fully justified. I had to end this somehow, but the force of his will had knocked any coherent thought from my brain. I stood, and sidestepped towards the door. It happened at precisely the same time he moved around the sofa.

Standing not two feet in front of me, one hand tucked casually into his trouser pocket, Blake asked, "What do you say?" in that muted, sexy tone.

Sexual attraction charged the air between us, the draw towards him stronger than anything I'd experienced before. I dragged all the air I could into my lungs, my heart racing in my chest. Whilst extremely tempted, I wasn't about to back down anytime soon. This situation was a disaster waiting to happen.

"Thank you, but I don't think it wise to mix business with pleasure." I rushed to the door, desperate to get out.

"You're saying no?" he scoffed behind me.

"I'm saying no." I rattled the door handle, remembering too late that he'd locked it. "I don't really have that big an appetite." I cursed under my breath at how obvious my discomfort was in my voice.

The sound of his luxurious brown wingtips moving across the polished wood grew louder as he shortened the gap between us. Then, a light outdoorsy fragrance, woody and clean—not as heavy as cologne—swept over me. Blake was right behind me. Feeling his breath tickle the back of my neck, and the light touch of his left hand at my hip, told me exactly *how* near he was.

"Well, then," he murmured, his lips brushing my ear, "it seems I'll be satisfying my hunger alone this evening." A wash of heat ran through me, but I still shivered under the weight of his magnetic presence. He reached around me, his powerful frame pressing into my back, and unlocked the doors.

I yanked one open, swallowing the unexpected knot of yearning blossoming from our far too intimate interaction, and fled to the safety of the lifts. Blake was beside me, his one stride matching my two, guiding me with one hand at the small of my back. I tried ignoring him, and the heat surging to my groin from his touch, but the shock on Ramón and the blonde's faces as we reached reception made it impossible to keep up the pretence.

The lobby doors were both propped open. I slammed the call button, relieved when a lift arrived immediately. I rushed in and hit the '8' button.

"It's been a pleasure, Miss Collins," he murmured in that seductive tone.

With a twinkle in his eyes and the hint of a smirk on his lips, it was clear he hadn't accepted my brush off. Unnerved by his expression, I stepped back, not uttering a word whilst I fixated on my shoes.

As the doors began closing, I peeked up and was greeted with an utterly disarming smile. I sagged against the cool metal interior walls, all the air rushing from my lungs in one huge breath as they shut.

What the hell just happened?

SHORTLY after five, I packed up, eager to get home. My head still throbbed, my body dehydrated from the after effects of last night. Making a mental note never to drink so many tequila shots again—at least not during the week—I took my bag and went to collect Mai. She'd been unusually quiet since I'd returned from my meeting, so I was dreading the car journey home because I knew a Mai Harvey interrogation waited for me.

I found her bent over her desk drawers, rummaging around as though she'd lost something. "Ready, Mai?"

Her head bobbed up. "Just have to find my cigarettes. They're here somewhere…"

"Again?" Mai was great at organising other people, but her own life lacked the same discipline. She had to be the most disorganised person I knew. "Meet you by the lifts."

I slipped my sunglasses on my head, offering goodbyes as I passed my colleagues. When I reached the foyer, I called the lift.

"Got them!" Mai cried, scurrying through the glass doors, waving the packet in the air. "They were at the bottom of my bag."

"You should give those up. Disgusting habit."

"Yeah, yeah. One day." She shoved me into the half-full car, wedging herself between me and another woman. "Now, tell me what the *hell* happened earlier. You've been antsy ever since you got back."

The last thing I wanted was to discuss my encounter with Blake in front of other colleagues. "I'll tell you in a minute," I whispered.

Thanks to secure Basement parking, I'd left my black VW Golf overnight so I could enjoy a few drinks. "Are you going out tonight or having a romantic night in?" I asked, pulling my keys from my tote.

Mai sighed heavily. "Mitch is working. *Again*." She checked the time on her phone. "I should catch him for a bit before he leaves."

I raised my brows. "A bit of what?"

She groaned. "I should be so lucky."

We didn't even get as far as the parking exit gate before I was bombarded with questions. I had all the time in the world to fill her in as we crawled along in the heavy traffic heading through the canyon.

"Why the hell didn't you say yes?" Mai cried after learning Blake had invited me to dinner.

"Be realistic, Mai. He didn't want to eat, he wanted to get laid."

"God, could you imagine…" Mai's eyes misted dreamily. "I'd have him as a friend with orgasmic benefits any day of the week."

"We certainly *aren't* friends. I don't even know him." I swerved to avoid the bus pulling out at the crossroads just as the lights changed to red. Driving an automatic on the opposite side of the road was still something I was getting used to.

Mai snickered. "No strings sex with a rich CEO, not to mention one who's gorgeous. Not many people get that offer every day."

"I'm sure they do if Blake has anything to do with it. You've seen for yourself how flirtatious he is."

"You've got balls, Kara. I bet he doesn't get knocked back often. Not sure I could, and you know how much I love Mitch." Mai's voice softened at the mention of her fiancé.

"You're probably one of few women in this world he hasn't slept with—*yet.*"

"I've worked there three years, and never heard a single rumour about him sleeping with the staff. Flirt? Possibly. Fuck? *Never.*" Mai tapped the cigarette she was desperate to smoke on the packet clasped in her lap. I refused to let her fill my car with the stench of cigarette smoke. "You, girlfriend, are the first confirmed case."

"Yeah, I'm a real trailblazer," I scoffed, not believing a word. "He's probably thrown money at them to keep quiet."

When we came to another standstill, I glanced across at Mai. She was chewing the inside of her mouth, her neatly plucked brows drawn in, revealing her contemplation. Her silence forced me to continue talking. "I admit he's extremely charismatic and could easily charm his way into any woman's bed. But it's more what he didn't say that got to me."

I jumped at the sound of honking horns and pitied the homeless man pushing his trolley full of rubbish bags sluggishly across the road, the target of everyone's frustrations. "Most women would've caved," I continued, finally moving again. "If I wanted instant gratification, I'd have probably jumped into his lap without hesitation."

"You're definitely not interested then?"

"Why would I be?"

"Um, lemme think." Mai raised a hand, using the cigarette as a pointer to count her fingers as she reeled off her reasons. "Apart from the megabucks and the drop-dead face, I bet there's an awesome body inside those fuck-me suits. Those glutes could crack nuts." She paused for a minute, distracted by her observation. "And without doubt, he'd do you hard and dirty, leave you completely sated, yet begging for more. You're right, Kara—can't think of any good reason why."

Mai was the little devil on my shoulder, voicing my own inner thoughts I was too timid to express. We arrived outside her complex in Hollywood. As usual, she swore when she couldn't open her door; my habit of locking us in for safety drove her mad. I unlocked it and twisted to face her, leaving the engine running so the air-conditioning didn't cut out. "You know I want more than that. I need it. Getting my life back is happening slowly but surely, so I don't need another man screwing it all up again."

"I get it." Mai air-kissed me goodbye and climbed out. Before closing the door, she leant back into the car. "Consider it, though. Imagine having *him* as a fuck buddy." She smiled sweetly and shut the door before I could reply, lighting up as she skipped to the front doors.

Travelling the short distance to my apartment, I became conscious of how strung up I was. Since crossing paths with Mr Blake, an ache had developed inside of me; a flame of sexual frustration, gradually on the burn. One now licking through me until I felt feverish and desperate to find some relief. My black driving flats pressed harder on the accelerator, wanting to get home faster.

I needed an orgasm.

Chapter 3

I barely made it to my office before Michael offloaded an enormous pile of data onto me Wednesday morning. Dread filled my stomach when I saw precisely how much information I had to plough through, so I took a minute to savour my skinny cappuccino before getting started.

My head was thick thanks to the few hours' sleep I'd managed last night. Fantasy mixed with actual events as the embodiment of everything male, currently residing on the fifteenth floor, took the starring role in my vividly realistic dreams. I'd tossed and turned well until the early hours of this morning. Now, my limbs were weary, as though the explicit scenes that took place whilst asleep had actually happened.

Add to it the shocking orgasm I had in the shower, and it was no surprise I'd barely slept a wink. The fact I masturbated thinking of Blake confused the hell out of me. *Why was I thinking of him that way?* Intense blue eyes haunted me as skilful hands touched and caressed me. Even recalling the melodious, rhythmic flow of his voice had brought me to an explosive climax.

I managed to put all disruptive thoughts aside and focus on my work. By lunchtime, I was ready for my meeting with Michael. As I passed Mai's desk on my way to Michael's office, she held up her hand. "Please hold," she said into her headset, then pressed a button to silence the caller. Her eyes twinkled. "This one's for you, K."

"Can you take a message? I'll call them back."

"Think you should take it now," she smirked. Then she mouthed, "*It's Mr Blake,*" and wiggled her eyebrows.

Crap.

I'd half-expected him to get in touch again, but not so soon. I hadn't recovered from yesterday's encounter and wasn't sure I could handle being confronted with him again. "Tell him I'm in a meeting." I began edging away.

"Too late. Already said you're here," Mai called after me, halting me in my tracks. Sighing in resignation, I turned back towards my office.

"You owe me." I glared at her as she gleefully put the call through.

I let the phone ring a few times whilst I took some calming breaths.

"Are you hungry for me now, Miss Collins?" Blake asked smoothly before I could utter a word. That hint of a whisper in his voice made my stomach flurry wildly. I leant my hip to the desk to keep me steady.

"Dining alone not much fun, Mr Blake?" I teased, recalling my own experience in the shower.

The velvety rasp of his laugh travelled straight through me to the spot at the top of my thighs. "I'm sure you'd agree, it's so much better when another person is involved."

My mouth went dry. It was plainly obvious he wasn't talking about eating either. Blake apparently *wasn't* used to rejection and was coming back for another shot. I sipped some water, smiling at his tenacity. "Last time I checked, you were still the boss."

His sigh was audible. "Listen, I don't normally do this. In fact, I *never* do. But, I want to take you to dinner. And to clarify, I'm not actually your boss."

"Well, actually, you are. You own the company."

"Well, *actually*, you're right. But, we're all simply people at the end of the day." There was a slight pause and a hint of humour when he added, "And everybody has to eat sometime."

Hmm, he would say that. Blake was ruler of his empire, answerable to no one. "I don't think dinner would be appropriate."

"So suggest something else instead."

I breathed a sigh, quietly flattered by his persistence. Obviously someone of his position wasn't going to give up easily. I recalled the insane way my body reacted to his touch, making the idea of us going to dinner dangerous for my health. I knew it might lead to other things.

"I'm free tomorrow. We could meet for a drink?" I grimaced as the words tumbled freely from my lips, not believing what I was saying.

"Perfect. Be ready at six." The triumph in his voice increased my annoyance at being so easily won over. "There's a wine bar two blocks south, *Estrella de*

Mar. Let's meet there at six-thirty." It wouldn't be wise to meet here where everyone could see. I didn't want to become the latest office gossip.

After a long minute when I thought he might've hung up, Blake quietly warned, "We will happen, Miss Collins."

A shiver ran through me. I suspected he might be right, judging by how aroused I was.

"WHAT'S he want this time?" Mai demanded when I returned from Michael's office and found her loitering in mine. Having no interest in my work, I knew she was referring to my earlier telephone call.

"The same as last time—a quick fuck." I rarely swore aloud unless I was sufficiently outraged about something. Mai found it hilarious to hear. She said it didn't sound dirty enough coming from a *plummy* English mouth.

She stifled a snigger. "God, he must really want you. He could easily have someone else satisfy his *needs*." Mai pinched two fingers in the air on either hand to emphasise the word.

"I agreed to meet him."

"*What?*" she spluttered.

"We're meeting at Estrella tomorrow for a drink."

"Finally!" Mai grinned. "You've been off the scene way too long." I gave her a *don't go there* look. "I'm not surprised. He could easily handle a hottie like you. And let's face it, you need a good handling, K," she insisted. "What changed your mind? You were certain it wasn't happening yesterday."

"I still am. The bar is neutral ground. I can make him see sense there without feeling like he has some hold over me here."

Mai frowned. "How? I know you're not that strong."

As usual, Mai was right. I was going to need all my strength to carry this through and escape unscathed tomorrow night. "I've told him once, I can do it again."

"Blake's exactly what you need. Sleeping with him has gotta give you some confidence back."

"Maybe." Admittedly, someone like him wanting me had given my fractured ego a minor boost. Then the hammer of self-doubt slammed it down again, mindful I was merely one of a long line of women and nothing special at all. "But, he's our boss for God's sake."

"Well, *he* doesn't care."

"Why should he? He won't be trying to climb the career ladder with everyone assuming they've slept their way to the top." I picked up a paper clip and started bending the metal into one crooked line.

"We both know this is nothing to do with that, and everything to do with your past. Go have some hot, steamy fun with the man." Mai covered my hands with hers. "You deserve some happiness, Kara. It's time to move on."

I smiled uncertainly as Mai retreated to the safety of the doorway. "Wear something sexy tomorrow," she called over her shoulder as she strolled out, "oh, and your raciest underwear."

BY the time I parked outside my building, I was miserable. My gym workout had done nothing to lift my mood either. I sat in the car, staring at the palm fronds brushing the window of my neighbour's apartment. At only five storeys high, it was small compared to the newer high-rises surrounding it. There wasn't a communal pool or garden, but it was the only place I'd lived on my own since arriving here, and I loved it.

Wearily, I climbed the stairs to the fourth floor and let myself in. I placed my keys and glasses on the kitchen counter, and carried my bags the short distance across the open floor plan to the bedroom. I flopped onto the bed, my limbs weighted with memories of heartbreak and deceit. I moved here with hopes of finding myself again, desperate to rediscover who I used to be before my world crashed down around me. *Bastard.*

After a long, thought cleansing shower where I scrubbed the pain from my skin, I threw on my satin camisole and shorts and had a light bite to eat before selecting my outfit for tomorrow. Having a well-paid job meant I could afford the occasional luxury item and indulge in my passion for vintage accessories. Half of my built-in wardrobe was crammed with clothes I loved but seldom had the nerve to wear; the other housed more conservative tastes that I habitually gravitated towards. That was my ex's fault, and I hated that I still allowed his perception of my body to influence my choices.

I dug out some unsexy black La Perla underwear. Who was I kidding? My appreciation for nice clothes extended to enjoying wearing good underwear, too. Even my sports bras were pretty. I tossed them back in the drawer and shoved it shut.

I brushed my teeth and climbed into bed with my iPad to check my emails, eagerly opening the message from my father first. With him in England, time zones restricted when we talked. I missed him terribly, especially when I needed a hug, or some words of wisdom only a parent could offer, like now.

When I first informed him I was leaving London, he'd worried, insisting I was emotionally unstable and needed people close to support me. I suspected he also knew I was running away. That made me more determined to prove him wrong. In six weeks, I was returning home for the first time since leaving, when he'd see firsthand I was coping well.

I plumped my pillows and shifted onto my side, preparing for sleep. My thoughts returned to Nate Blake. We would never work. He exuded confidence, was borderline arrogant with it, and oozed raw sexuality. Any self-confidence I once had got shot to pieces years ago.

And I was far from sexy.

Hooking one leg outside the sheet—my favoured sleeping position—I shut my eyes. That impression of command and success, combined with his wealth and good looks, would be a heady aphrodisiac to some. He'd probably found a willing dinner companion, and by now was enjoying *dessert*.

That disheartening thought weighed heavily on my mind as I gradually drifted off.

AFTER A restless sleep, Thursday dragged forever. I'd spent most of the night awake, regretting my decision to meet Blake. After the failure of my last relationship, I'd made it a rule to never date someone I worked with again, let alone the boss. There were too many complications when it all went wrong. Too many people who knew your business and were all too willing to pass judgement.

A short run in the cool of early morning helped put our meeting into perspective. This wasn't a date. We'd meet for a drink, I'd politely tell him he was wasting his time pursuing me, and that would be the end of it. Blake might see tonight going differently—drinks, possibly dinner, followed by some hot sex—but that was his problem.

Mai had gone home, but not before imparting some words of wisdom—"do what you want, have some fun." Then, as she discreetly slipped a packet of condoms in my bag with a wink—"don't let a hot date become a due date." I powered down my computer and headed to the bathrooms to freshen up.

I'd decided against an entire outfit change, opting to wear the simple cap-sleeved black shift dress I'd worn for work to maintain a purely business approach to the evening. That was an act of defiance—a subconscious rebellion to my past—to prove I could wear a dress and feel confident about it. Last night I'd felt brave, but now, as I swapped my work shoes for crimson suede peep-toe heels, I was regretting my impulsive decision.

I retouched my make-up, hiding the lack of sleep well with a little concealer, and tidied up my French twist. My berry red lipstick was bold, but not too harsh, and drew out the natural pout of my lips.

I walked to the bar, deciding I needed some air. When I spotted the familiar hedging shielding the bar from the road, my stomach flipped, churning with a mix of nerves and excitement. It was a dangerous blend of emotions. I didn't want to feel this way about a man—but Nate Blake wasn't like any other man.

I shyly avoided eye contact with the valet man as I passed and made my way up the path. Exposed red brick walls and dark floorboards complimented the long mahogany bar greeting me when I pushed open the heavy glass doors. Keeping my head down, I squeezed through a group of businessmen crowding the floorspace between me and the quieter lounge area. When I looked up...

...*Nate Blake.* I wanted to arrive first, but he'd beat me to it.

Chapter 4

Wearing black trousers and a white shirt, the top couple of buttons undone, he sat tucked away near the back wall staring right at me. The sight of him caused my heart rate to quicken and a storm of butterflies to flit around my stomach. He was even more glorious than I remembered.

Piercing blue eyes slid over me, seductively drinking me in, his lips slightly parted. In a drawn out action, his tongue licked over his upper lip before he dragged his eyes to meet mine.

It was so sexual. My sex clenched, heated desire running all over me. Nate Blake wanted me.

Naked. In his bed. Tonight.

Drawing every bit of strength I could muster to my now skewed intentions for the evening, I fixed a confident smile to my face and tried to refocus as I approached. Blake stood, squaring his shoulders, and ran a hand through his thick hair. It made me want to tease my own fingers through the glossy, luscious lengths.

"Kara," he murmured. *How did he know my name?* And how could he make it sound so provocative, like it meant so much more than a simple greeting? "It's a pleasure to see you again." He pulled out the other burgundy leather wingback chair, gesturing for me to sit down.

"Hello." I placed my bag beneath the drinks table, then sat and crossed my legs. Blake's eyes drifted hungrily to where my dress had ridden up my thighs. *Damn.* What had possessed me to wear a dress? I tried, unsuccessfully, to tug it back down. "How are you?"

"Getting better by the minute." He sat, angling his body towards mine. His face glowed with humour, eyes dancing with pleasure. "How about you? How was your day?"

"Distracting…" In fact, the entire work day had interfered with my building anticipation of this exact moment.

"Oh?" Blake tilted his head and pursed his lips, clearly confused by my response.

"Busy," I rushed out, trying to conceal my thoughts, "but good."

A light growth of trimmed stubble covered his strong jawline, and because he'd recently run a hand through it, a few strands of hair had fallen sexily over his forehead. It gave a slightly roguish edge to an otherwise well-groomed appearance.

"The wine list is impressive," he noted, offering me the menu. "Anything in particular you like?"

You. The word came unbidden to mind. "Red's fine, thanks," I flushed, without taking it from him.

Mischief swept across Blake's face. He caught the attention of a male server who came rushing over. "The 2002 Lonely Oak Cabernet, please."

The server nodded, glanced briefly at me, then stumbled on a chair leg as he made a hasty retreat to the bar. I winced sympathetically. The poor man could probably feel the pheromones emanating from Blake as much as I could.

Blake lounged back into his seat, amused. "You always have that effect on people?"

Me? "Do you?" I countered. "He was obviously intimidated by you. You're very disconcerting."

Blake looked puzzled as the server returned in record time. He was desperately trying to concentrate, flushing as red as the wine he poured with his trembling hand. I knew how he felt. I wanted to sit on my hands so Blake couldn't see them shaking.

Taking pity on him, I smiled and said, "Thank you." The server mumbled incoherently, placed a bowl of pistachio nuts on the table, then scurried away with a harried smile. I glanced at Blake. The index finger stroking rhythmically back and forth across his top lip as he watched me was very distracting.

"*You* intimidated him, not me. Not to mention the heads that turned when you passed the gentlemen at the bar." He calmly sipped his wine. "You're exquisite."

Unsure how to respond to his compliment, I laughed uncomfortably and smoothed my hair around my face.

"Tell me about yourself, Kara." A frown flit across his face, then he relaxed. I hated talking about myself, so decided to have some fun with him.

"Well, you already seem to know my name." I raised a brow. "I'm twenty-four, five-nine tall, green eyes…" I hid my smile with my hand.

Blake smirked. "That's not what I meant. You're more than just a beautiful face." His eyes scanned the length of my body. "And unbelievably long, long legs."

My tongue darted out to wet my lips. His gaze darkened as he leant closer and murmured, "Those luscious full red lips are begging to be kissed. Keep licking them? See what happens."

The enticing promise of his kiss made me lightheaded. The sensual scent of his cologne smelt like a drug I could quickly become hooked on. He settled back and casually took a sip of wine, whilst I felt like I was going to pass out from sensory overload. Without realising until it was too late, I licked my lips again. His eyes narrowed. I dived for my glass and brought it to my lips, not believing for a second it would deter Blake from carrying out his threat.

"Why choose LA?" he asked, balancing his glass on the arm of the chair. "Not that I'm complaining." His left hand brushed my arm, the tiny bit of contact enough to cause a buzz throughout my body.

It took a second to compose myself before I could reply. "An old school friend lives here. I needed a change, she invited me to stay, and…here I am." Millie had been my lifesaver when I needed it most. I'd jumped at her offer without hesitation.

"A fresh start?"

"Something like that." Blake didn't need to know about my baggage. I straightened, determined not to sink into another self-pitying moment, here of all places.

"Were you alone?" he asked cautiously.

"Yes, my brother is currently on a gap year travelling. New Zealand, last time we spoke. Our father still lives in the village we grew up in." I smiled fondly, thinking of them both so far away.

He waited for me to fill in the glaring omission of my mother, but when I offered nothing else, asked, "How long have you lived here?"

"Ten months," I answered, sipping my wine.

Blake frowned. "That's pretty fast to get a visa."

"I have a US passport. My father worked for Steelman Group back in the day."

"The architects?"

I nodded. "He took a secondment to Chicago. We returned to England after Liam was born. We both have dual citizenship." Setting my wine back on the table, I asked, "Have you always lived here?"

"I grew up in the Canyon, studied in Rhode Island." Blake topped up our glasses as he talked. "I've spent the last five years between here and the East Coast, but all my family live here…" With the bottle suspended mid-air, he stared outside towards the patio, entirely consumed by his thoughts. Suddenly, he snapped back to the present. "Sorry." He cleared his throat and set the bottle back on the table.

I considered his mood switch strange but chose to ignore it. "Locally?"

"Except my brother. My parents own a vineyard in Sonoma. Will lives there."

I cringed. "Just my luck to pick a wine bar."

Nate smiled. "I don't claim to be knowledgeable about wine. Will's the expert, he manages everything now they've retired."

I took a minute to allow the velvety red to run through me and loosen me up some more. "Any other siblings?"

"An older sister. She's an attorney, family law. Happily married, got four kids, a great home." He spun the stem of his glass distractedly, lost in thought once more. "The happily-ever-after."

I found it intriguing hearing he viewed her life as ideal. His seemed pretty perfect to me. When Blake smiled shyly, a strange sense of ease came over me, as though part of me was being washed away. I knew it was a little piece of the barrier surrounding my heart cracking. I re-crossed my legs, holding the hem to prevent the dress riding up again.

"She's a little overprotective," he continued with a shrug, his jaw clenching.

A man so driven, with all that focused intensity, who never gave up until he'd succeeded in achieving his goals, was so *not* like someone who needed protecting. For some reason, nerves perhaps, I chuckled.

"You seem to find me amusing," he noted dryly.

"Sorry, but I can't imagine you allow people to take advantage of you."

He titled his head, weighing up my observations. "She doesn't have to worry about me anymore. Will's the one to watch."

"Why?"

"Let's just say, he has an eye for the ladies," he muttered, "the wrong type of girl." He lifted a shoulder in resignation. "But, he's only young. Maybe he needs to experience the harsh realities of life first-hand."

"Must be a family trait," I mumbled.

Blake shifted in his seat, his expression unreadable as he reached for his wine. He remained silent when the server reappeared and asked if we wanted another bottle, preferring to keep his attention on me.

"No, thank you," I replied on our behalf. I couldn't allow alcohol to cloud my senses around this man. The feelings he stirred inside me were enough to give me a slightly merry impression all on their own. My mind was already racing down the twisted road of recklessness and wild abandonment, of scorching hot uninhibited sex, when it needed to be driven steadily on the straight sensible one where it belonged.

"What do you enjoy doing? You look quite fit."

I felt my cheeks redden at the English meaning of his choice of words, though I don't think he understood the double-meaning. "I love running, outdoors preferably. I go to the gym and I practice Vinyasa Yoga."

"Interesting." Blake smiled seductively. "You must be supple, pliable…" he murmured, rubbing the scruff on his chin with careful deliberation, "…*flexible*."

My skin flushed, imagining all the positions this man could manhandle me into. The darkening of his eyes unsettled me. He was having the exact same thoughts. I quickly cleared my throat. "What about you?" I asked, breathlessly. "Do you have much spare time outside of running your empire?"

"It's a tough job running an empire." Those blue eyes appeared to laugh at me. "But, I always make time for other pursuits, if they're important enough."

"Like?"

Blake opened his mouth as if to speak. He licked his lips and deliberated his response with a small smile. "I go to the gym to blow off steam. Otherwise, I prefer the warmth of the sun on my skin when I'm working up a sweat."

I tried not to visualise tanned, slick skin, but it was pointless because it came to me as clear as if it was right in front of me. "What about friends?" I managed to ask, fumbling with my earring.

"Yes, I have friends." His lips curled upwards.

"That isn't what I meant," I pouted. "Do you socialise much?"

"Sure. I'm just a regular guy."

With designer clothes and extraordinary good looks, Blake was as far removed from a regular guy as you could get. Men in his position were usually out enjoying themselves, hitting the bars and taking advantage of the many willing girls keen to provide company for the evening.

I could feel his eyes on me, studying my profile. "What?" I asked, nervously spinning my mother's ruby eternity band on my finger.

"How do you do that?"

Having no idea what he was talking about, I shrugged.

"I've told you more about myself in the past hour than I've told any woman in the last two years," he admitted, his brow furrowed.

"What do you talk about then—the weather?" I scoffed. When he continued to hold my gaze so sincerely without reply, it dawned on me. "Ah, I suppose there's no time for small talk when you're luring them into bed."

An utterly disarming grin flashed across his face. "I've always found bed a great place for talking, Kara." His tone had switched to that seductive whisper once more. Lust heated my blood, his words chasing over my skin.

His expression darkened, his eyes firmly fixed on me, like he was brooding about something. "Is there a boyfriend I should be concerned about?"

I was taken aback by the directness of his question. Incredulous, I replied, "You honestly believe I'd be sitting here with you if there was?"

What kind of woman did he think I was? Or maybe it wasn't a reflection on *my* morals and more his. Arrogant enough to think no woman, no matter what her relationship status, was immune to him. Blake's expression was unfathomable as he waited for my answer.

"Not that it's any of your business," I relented, "but no, there isn't."

The killer smile that flashed across his face floored me. *Whoa.* My breathing shallowed as my heart rate shifted up another gear. Against my better judgement, I was curious to know what he called his current state of play regarding relationships. "Do *you* have a girlfriend, Mr Blake?"

"No, I don't," he bit out, as pissed off as I was about the question. "I'm sorry if I offended you. That wasn't my intention." His mouth set in a straight line as he eyed me warily. "I haven't had one in a while. Nothing serious, anyway."

"Really," I sneered.

"That surprises you?"

"Not in the slightest. I imagine you've had many...*acquaintances*." Blake brought his glass to his mouth, hiding a smirk. "You probably have a different woman in your bed every night," I stupidly went on, cheeks heating with my blunt observation. "Rest assured, tonight it won't be me."

He choked on his wine. "Excuse me." He straightened, thumping his chest, and set his glass down. "You suggested a drink, Kara. It's telling that *you* were thinking about taking me to bed. But, if you insist…"

"No!" I shook my head. "I—" Nothing came out of my mouth. "That's not…I wasn't."

Blake lowered his head, tilting it to the side. One corner of his mouth lifted into a half-smile as he gradually raised his gaze to meet mine.

He looked as sexy as hell.

"What I have, and what I want, are two *very* different realities," he murmured cryptically.

Attempting to regain my equilibrium, I grabbed my glass to steady my racing pulse. "My expectations from relationships usually differ from those of the women I meet on a daily basis," he stated, sounding resigned to the fact. "Therefore, I don't engage in one with them."

I glowered at *him*, but I was more annoyed with myself. I'd started to fall under his spell and think he might actually be more than solely a walking advert for sex. Now, he'd basically confessed to only wanting women for one thing, and wasn't interested in anything meaningful.

The tiny sliver of hope that he wasn't the serial one-night-stander I'd accused him of crashed away. Even the satisfaction of being right couldn't lighten the odd sense of disappointment filling me.

"Are you sure I can't tempt you," Blake leant forward, eyes glinting with indecent intentions, "with dinner?"

"You're wasting your time with me," I said quietly.

Blake turned my hand over and slotted his fingers between mine; my own instinctively curled around his. I drew a deep breath when that surge of energy flashed through our fingers again. His thumb stroked the underside of my wrist, somewhere that inexplicably felt incredibly intimate.

"Why suggest this date if you're not interested?" he asked softly, his eyes unwavering in their gaze.

I swallowed hard. "I wanted to see if you were still hell-bent on just fucking me, or if you had more to offer?"

Blake's brows shot up. "What else do you want?"

"More than an orgasm or two."

"Well, that's a relief." His mouth curved, his eyes gleaming with sexual dominance and certainty. "Multiples are my speciality."

God. If he fucked as good as he talked, I had no doubt that statement was absolutely true. Why did I keep feeding him these lines? I pulled myself together. I'd veered off track, sidelined by his cocky arrogance and the hint of something lingering behind the sparkle in his eyes. He seemed almost hopeful, as though what I said next could have the ability to change his world.

Not wanting to waste any more of either of our time, I refrained from going into further detail. "Lust is great, but it doesn't last." I shrugged. "I want more."

Blake's grip tightened. I stared at his face, battling against the flicker in his eyes confirming he'd just heard exactly what he'd been waiting for. His eyes grew larger and darkened as they scanned my face. Releasing my hand, leaving me strangely bereft, he stroked some hair behind my ear. His fingertips felt like lightning against my skin. My eyes closed briefly, my breath hitching as I fought the urge to nuzzle into his caress.

Suddenly, all warmth vanished from his eyes. He became guarded and distant as he withdrew his hand. "I don't tolerate the inevitable drama that follows commitment, Kara." Avoiding any eye contact, he sat back, staring blankly at the glasses on the table, somewhat pained by his revelations.

"So you do just want no-strings sex?" I asked quietly.

"I want—" He glanced at me with pensive blue eyes, then gave a small shrug. "I want you."

There was no point pretending his brutal honesty didn't excite me. But, I'd never been one for one-night stands, and just because the epitome of male sexiness was offering it on a plate, didn't mean I was about to start having them now. "I should go." The legs of my chair scraped across the floorboards as I shoved it back, reaching into my bag for my purse.

"I've got this." Blake tucked some notes under the empty wine bottle, giving the server a hefty tip.

"Thanks." I hung my bag in the crook of my arm and started for the door. Blake steered me through the now much busier bar by my elbow, the innocent touch sending a thrill through my body. Holding the door open, he allowed me to step out first. The old-fashioned gesture was unexpected. It made me think less playboy, more respectful gentleman.

"I assume you're not driving?" he asked when we reached the valet. A small group of women stood waiting for their cars. Unsurprisingly, Blake snagged their interest as more than one jaw dropped and glances were furtively cast.

"No, I left my car at work." I moved a few steps away from them then faced him. "I'll get a taxi."

God, he looked good in this light. Passing car beams bounced off his face, casting shadows that enhanced his chiseled features. Behind him, the group of women were still eyeing him up, even though their cars had arrived.

"I'll take you," he insisted, removing his phone from his trouser pocket. "I have a car coming." He briefly concentrated on the screen then dropped it back into his pocket.

"No!" The fresh air made me realise I'd had more wine than I wanted to drink, and I couldn't trust myself to be around him much longer.

"It's no problem, Kara." Blake eyed me with curious interest, his eyes slightly wider than before. I wasn't sure if my rejection had impressed or entertained him. I realised this was it—he really was expecting me to go home with him.

"I'd prefer a taxi," I stated, as firm and assertively as I could manage under his close scrutiny. I was actually the complete opposite, and given some gentle persuasion, knew my decision could easily be swayed. I needed to get out of here. Fast.

I stepped to the kerb and hailed a taxi. I didn't know whether to be mad or relieved when one stopped straight away, pulling up as a luxury car arrived.

Blake studied the two vehicles. He looked thoroughly baffled, at a loss as to why I'd opt for the city taxi over his own private transportation.

"Thank you for the wine," I said, shuffling awkwardly. "Sorry tonight didn't end as you hoped."

He turned to me. "On the contrary. It's ended *exactly* as I'd hoped."

I had no idea what that meant, but the sincerity in his tone tugged at something buried deep inside of me.

When I met his gaze, the change was there, in plain sight. His frown showed his perplexed state of mind. Gone was the need to screw me into unconsciousness—which I'm sure he could. In its place, a yearning for something much deeper. It went against everything he'd just told me.

"Get home safely." Blake placed a hand on my upper arm. I flinched, wary of his touch. No man had touched me since…

My painful memory was forgotten when Blake dipped his head forward, close enough so I stared straight into darkening blue eyes. They lowered to my mouth and stayed there for what seemed like an eternity. Then, with the same leisurely pace, they returned to my eyes.

A satisfactory smile curled his lips as he angled his head and kissed me chastely on the cheek. He hovered there briefly, then released me and opened the taxi door.

"Goodnight, Nate." After helping me into the back seat, he stood watching from the pavement as the driver pulled into the streaming traffic. His eyes blazed, his sense of accomplishment evident in the smile dazzling over his face.

Shit.

I wanted him to kiss me. And he knew it.

Chapter 5

I stroked my cheek, recalling the stubble that briefly grazed my now flushed skin. I sighed heavily, clutching my bag to my chest. I wanted to feel that stubble with my fingers, my lips. Hoping to relieve the pressure at the top of my thighs, I pressed them together. I wanted to feel it there, too.

The way Blake undressed me with his eyes when I arrived? I'd seen that enough times before to know it meant *I want to fuck you.* I'd expected him to pursue me far more aggressively than he did, and now, his easy going approach had thrown me. If he wanted me in his bed, it didn't make sense to let me leave with a cursory kiss on the cheek. Talk about sending out mixed messages.

I was just as guilty. Pleased with the assertiveness I showed in the bar, I'd succeeded in telling him we were *never* going to happen, albeit more directly than planned. One look outside the bar later, and all my bravado had been blown apart.

My mobile chimed with an incoming message. I fumbled in my bag until I located it. It was from Mai: **HAS HE ROCKED UR WORLD YET** ;-)

Even *she* assumed we'd end up fucking. I sent a quick reply: **NO** then tossed my phone into my bag.

After analysing everything far too many times, I climbed into bed, mentally drained. I squeezed my eyes shut, desperate to ignore how I could still feel Nate's lips on my face, his scent on my skin even though I'd showered. He was everything I wasn't, and could have any woman he wanted. It was baffling to think he wanted me. A shy girl, all too accustomed to her flaws and failings in life, and a far cry from the stunning women he undoubtedly attracted with his lifestyle.

Yes, the sexual chemistry was there, a strong, powerful attraction, the extent of which I've never experienced before. But Nate was wrong for me. He couldn't give me the emotional commitment necessary with sex.

With the sheet high around my neck, I snuggled into the pillows, certain I wouldn't hear from him again. He'd gone home alone, or at least, not with *me.* It wouldn't be a surprise if he'd picked up one of the eager women ogling him outside. I doubt I made as big an impression on him as he had me.

ARRIVING AT my desk the next morning after a long taxi drive in, I found my usual strong skinny cappuccino waiting for me. After tucking my belongings beneath the desk, I sat, dragging the mug towards me. Craving the hit of caffeine, I took a long savouring gulp.

Whilst the PC came to life, I watched my colleagues arrive through the internal windows, mentally preparing for another day at work and the inevitable inquisition I'd endure from Mai. As if on cue, she appeared in my line of sight, waving eagerly. I groaned inwardly as she headed towards me.

"You're pissed off. What did he do?" Mai dropped into the chair opposite, all concerned and worried.

"Nothing," I sighed.

"What do you mean *nothing*? Did you blow him off," she asked, crossing her legs and grinning, "or just blow *him*?"

"Seriously?" I cried, scrunching my face. Mai always had to lower the tone.

"What? I'm bummed I couldn't give you a ride this morning, 'cause *something* happened between you two." Scooping her hair to one side, she sat forward. "Blake screams sex. No woman could be immune to him. One look from him and—bang, ovaries destroyed." Over-dramatically, she fanned her face, like the temperature in the room had increased significantly.

"That makes no sense whatsoever." If that were true, I was never having children. That stare he'd fired at me when I walked into the bar made sure of that. I sank into the chair with my cup cradled in both hands. "Actually, he was nice."

"Nice?"

"Okay, he was warm, engaging, chivalrous…not what I expected." *He didn't try and jump my bones,* is what I wanted to tell her. But I didn't.

Mai leant her elbows on the desk, supporting her chin in her hands, and raised her brows. "What happened at the end of the night?"

I sipped my coffee. "I went home." Mai's eyebrow lifted another notch. "*Alone*," I reiterated.

"What?" she shrieked. Her palms hit the desk with a loud slap. I shrugged, having nothing else to say. "I bet the goodnight kiss was *uh-ma-zing*."

"There wasn't one," I said wistfully, stroking my cheek and recalling the delicious feeling of Nate's skin against mine.

"Okay, now I'm really confused." Mai frowned, her head tilting. "He can't be gay."

"Definitely *not* gay, Mai."

"Are *you*? Because, you know, I would—if *you* wanted to." I gaped at her, dumbfounded and exasperated. And slightly amused, but I tried not to show it.

"Nothing happened because I told him I wasn't interested."

"Jeez, I never thought you'd actually go through with it!"

"Believe me, I'm pretty shocked, too. I don't know where it came from." In truth, something about being in Nate's presence made me feel fearless. That knowledge alone unnerved me.

"Wow, you're stronger than I thought, Kara. I really expected you to get laid last night." Mai smirked, clearly tickled by a thought she had. "I bet he was pissed off. Turned down twice by someone as gorgeous as you? His ego must be seriously dented."

I chuckled feebly, a stab of regret flashing through me. I set my mug down and typed my password into the log-on screen.

"What did he say when he figured out he wasn't getting any sweet lovin'?" she asked.

"I didn't give him the chance to say much. I just jumped into a taxi and left."

Lowering back into her seat, Mai crossed her arms, the smirk from earlier gone. "He didn't even drive you?"

"He offered, but I had to leave..."

My vagueness was enough to spike her attention. She leant forward and narrowed her eyes. "You *do* like him, don't you?"

I exhaled slowly, fixing onto the gradually disappearing company logo on the screen. If I lied, Mai would see straight through it. We hadn't known each other long, but she read me well. Pleased with this titbit of information, even though I'd admitted nothing, her face split into the biggest grin.

There it was—the meddling face.

"It's not happening," I warned. "I could never trust him. Women fall at his feet. They did last night, even with me there. He won't be short of company for long. I called him out on it, too." An image of him with another woman caused a sharp stab of jealousy in my chest. That reaction irritated me.

"You called him a man-whore?" she snorted.

"He doesn't want commitment, he wants some fun and thought I could be his latest plaything."

"Thought he didn't try it on?" Mai frowned. "Blake must've known if he wanted, he could've gotten in your panties."

"Mai!"

"Guys like him know if a woman's interested. If he really needed a fuck, those stupidly long legs wouldn't be walking straight this morning."

"That's what's baffling. I know he wanted to..."

"You told him no. Don't be pissed he respected that." A reasonable explanation. Blake had definitely begun the night with sex on his brain, but during the course of the evening, something had altered his way of thinking. Mai stood, shaking her hair so it fell around her shoulders. "Think he'll call again?" she asked hopefully.

"I doubt it," I snickered. "He went home alone. That should've told him all he needed to know."

Mai eyed me dubiously, as I regarded my own thoughts with the same uncertainty.

A couple of knocks on my open door announced Michael's arrival in my office. Honestly, I was glad for the interruption because there was nothing else to say.

"YOU didn't have to get me this you know," I told Mai as she set my lunch down on the desk in front of me. She twirled around so her red skater dress flared out, unable to keep still she was that excited. I laughed. "I assume you're leaving now?"

"Soon as Mitchell gets his sexy ass here." She was like a schoolgirl giddy with the first signs of love. They were going on a much needed weekend break, hopefully to put the spark back in their relationship. "If I don't get me some this weekend I'll explode!"

I pursed my lips. "Three weeks is not that long to go without sex, Mai."

"How the hell do you cope?" she carried on. "Soon you'll know how long it's been by the length of hair on my legs, never mind other areas. Vibrators are good, but nothing beats a man."

I shook my head, speechless.

"Seeing the girls later?" Mai asked, checking her mobile impatiently.

"Only for the one." I first met Mai during one of my gym trials a month after landing in LA. For some reason, she latched onto me, taking me under her wing and adopting me as her friend. I was introduced to Robyn and Jenna a week later, and we've been close ever since. Both pretty brunettes and both single, Robyn works as a PA in Marketing at RED, Jenna a Recruitment Consultant for a Nanny Agency. We rarely crossed paths during the working day, so I enjoyed our Friday drinks.

The phone clasped tightly in Mai's grip rang. "Hey babe, be there in a second." She hung up as fast as she'd answered and dashed to the door. "Gotta go, K!"

I followed and stood in my doorway whilst she gathered her belongings. "Be gentle with him, Mai."

"Where's the fun in that?" she called back with a massive grin, waving as she disappeared.

"Enjoy Carmel." I adored Mai. Hilarious, scatty, yet often wise beyond her twenty-three years, she was annoyingly astute and right, especially when it came to men.

We were complete opposites in many ways, yet similar where it counted. We bonded over a shared love of fashion and a strong work ethic. Under my guidance, she'd begun studying for her professional accounting exams and was flourishing. She always had my back, was full of encouragement—often misdirected—but I considered that part of her charm.

Most of all, I admired her honesty, an attribute I valued greatly.

MY LUNCH date with Millie turned into somewhat of a celebration after hearing that finally, after three years of trying, she'd signed her first recording contract. Her showcase at The Mint in a couple of weeks had two tickets with my name firmly stamped on them.

As I strolled home along Sunset Blvd, I was still very much the tourist. I always got a kick from people watching as I passed restaurants on the Strip, window shopping at overly expensive shops and soaking up the crazy sights and sounds of my new home.

Aside from initially struggling to secure permanent employment, I'd settled in well. With a great place to live and a few good friends, the vibrant city—with endless traffic, fantastic weather and shopping to die for—was a far cry from the sleepy village I'd grown up in. And very different to London where I'd lived since attending university.

Just as I dashed across the road, my mobile rang. Keeping an eye on where I was going, I dug it out from my bag, careful not to spill my grande cappuccino, and answered the unknown caller.

"*Kara.*" The dulcet rasp of Nate's voice swirled its way down into my core, dragging all my concentration to the warmth now spreading up to my chest.

"Hi," I spluttered, shocked to hear from him again.

"Hi," he replied softly. I could hear his smile. "How are you?"

"Good…thanks." I shook my head, hoping to clear the alcohol fuzz.

"I'm glad you're all right. You should've let me take you home the other night. I worried about you." His concern made me unsteady on my feet. After a beat, with his voice low and teasing, he added, "Taking a ride with me would've been far more enjoyable."

"I imagine so," I replied dreamily, forgetting to engage the slightly inebriated brain as an image of a very *different* ride came to mind.

"How's the weekend so far?" Nate asked cheerfully.

"Fantastic!" I giggled at my over-enthusiasm.

"You sound happy." I stopped and squinted up at the Chateau Marmont hidden behind the trees opposite. I *was* happy. Because I was talking to him.

"I've just had lunch with a friend. It usually entails alcohol." With another sip of coffee, I headed towards home.

"You're not driving are you?" he demanded.

"Of course not!" I was startled by the authority and concern in his voice, unsure why he deemed it necessary to ask.

I heard him sigh with relief. "Good. Any plans for tomorrow?" he asked in a tone far too composed for my liking.

"No. I might spend all day in bed." I rolled my shoulders, realising how tiring the past week had been. Right now, I could think of nothing better than not getting out of bed for the day.

"Sounds like heaven. Let me keep you company," he murmured gruffly. The tone rippled through me, my skin breaking out in goose bumps.

"You're very persistent."

"Do I strike you as being easily deterred?"

I remembered the steely determination in his eyes from before. "No."

"So let me pursue you." An image of his face from Thursday night flashed through my mind, reminding me of how, with one momentary lapse in composure, he'd appeared so bare and susceptible. As much as he wanted to bed me, I'd seen a glimpse of something deeper hiding beneath the surface. The pounding of my heart confirmed I liked what I'd seen.

"What are your plans? Apart from trying to gate-crash my private slumber party?" I grinned, unable to resist flirting.

"That depends."

"On?"

"You. You've turned me down more times than I care to admit, but I hoped you'd reconsider my offer?"

"What offer?" I tossed my empty cup into a bin and pushed up the sleeves of my white shirt.

"Of dinner."

I damn near fell over my own feet. "Are you serious?"

"Kara, never doubt me. I mean every word I say." The seriousness in his tone reinforced his statement. My stomach twisted desirously, as I imagined his inexorable gaze sliding over me. "If not dinner, maybe something less formal instead?"

"Like what?" I asked, nervously.

"If tomorrow afternoon works for you, I'll pick you up at one-thirty."

"I need to know what to wear." That sounded pathetic, as if I cared more about my appearance than what we could be doing. *Together.*

Nate laughed quietly. "Casual's good." Was he expecting whatever I wore to end up discarded on the floor?

Two men passed me, holding hands as they walked a beautiful Schnauzer. They flashed me matching mega-watt smiles. I sighed. Why did everyone make being in love seem so easy?

"C'mon," he coaxed playfully, "no dinner. I promise."

"Why do you want to see me again?" Over the past year, I'd been racked with insecurities, concluding I wasn't good enough for anyone, let alone someone like Nate Blake.

"You really have to ask?"

"Yes, I told you I'm not interested in what you're offering."

"I know, but..." He sighed quietly. "I can't keep away. I have to see you again to know if what I felt the other night was real."

Hearing that he'd sensed the odd connection too made my pulse race. Neither of us could walk away from something that wasn't what either of us was looking for. I wanted him, more than I'd wanted any man in a long time, irrespective of what he could or couldn't give me. A small smile curled my lips as victory swirled low in my belly. He wanted me just as badly.

"So long as it's casual," I found myself agreeing. If Nate could hear the slight fluctuation in my voice, he'd have his answer as to how badly he affected me.

"This is my private number," he confirmed. "Add it to your contacts."

"Okay." We both stayed silent for what seemed like forever, and it was strangely comforting. Eventually, I said, "See you tomorrow."

Staring in bewilderment at my phone after I'd hung up, Mai's words returned to haunt me. Maybe Nate *wasn't* used to being rejected. Perhaps this was all simply a game to him?

Deciding a slightly merry, alcohol laced disposition wasn't the right time to dissect the inner workings of his puzzling actions, I swapped my phone for my keys and let myself into my building.

It didn't even cross my mind to question how he'd obtained my number. Or how he'd know where to find me tomorrow.

Chapter 6

"It's Nate."

The sultry tone of his voice over the intercom sent a charge of excitement rushing through me.

"I'll be down in a second." I replaced the handset and returned to the bedroom to finish up. He was ten minutes early, but I was pretty much ready. In keeping with the natural look of my make-up, I'd left my hair loose and wavy.

I sat on my bed and buckled up my black leather sandals. After accessorising with silver jewellery, I put on my wide-brimmed sunhat and headed through the lounge, collecting my tote and sunglasses off the kitchen counter. With shaking hands I locked up, trying to calm the butterflies in my stomach as I carefully took the stairs. *Breathe, Kara.*

Nate was leaning against the wall outside with his back to the doors. Stone coloured long shorts displayed etched calves, and the hem of his white cotton shirt sat on the curve of his pert arse. Clearly it wasn't only suits that made him look amazing. He wore the casual look equally as well. I opened the door and startled him into turning around.

"You're early, Mr Blake," I teased. He scanned me appreciatively up and down, his mouth parting slightly. My pulse quickened as his gaze lingered, his iridescent iris' sparkling in the sunlight.

"And you, Miss Collins, are stunning."

I sensed my cheeks flush at the compliment. I was only wearing white skinny jeans with a loose charcoal v-neck t-shirt.

"After you." Nate indicated for me to lead the way down the path.

"Nice car," I smirked, eyeing the gleaming convertible Bentley parked at the kerbside. Dark grey with a hint of smoky blue, it was the colour of a stormy sky. Sporty, sleek and exquisitely honed—much like its owner.

"Thank you." He smiled graciously and opened my door, waiting whilst I slipped into the cream leather passenger seat. Nate rounded the car and climbed in beside me. I watched avidly as he smoothed his hands around the stitched leather steering wheel, imagining them running over me with the same admiration. His shirt allowed a glimpse of muscular, sun-kissed forearms and a quietly understated Bremont watch on his right wrist.

"British designs are visually stunning." Nate glanced sideways, a smile teasing his lips. "I haven't found an exception to that rule yet."

"My father would love it," I said, quickly buckling up my seat belt, hoping to hide my no doubt flushed cheeks.

"What does he drive?" he asked, starting the engine. *Damn.* Even his car purred sexily.

"A 1970s Aston Martin."

"Ah, a man after my own heart."

I slipped on my sunglasses as Nate did the same, hiding those glorious eyes behind a pair of Ray-Ban Aviators. They only served to accentuate the features I could still see. Cut jawline, covered once again with a light dusting of stubble, and unruly windblown hair from the drive over. He flashed a boyish smile, shifted the gearstick into drive and pulled into the road.We drove through the city towards the coast and it was a good twenty minutes before I asked where we were going.

"I thought we could go to the beach." He smiled uncertainly. "Sound good?"

"Sounds lovely." The beach wasn't too formal and perfect for such a sunny day.

We didn't talk much more for a while. I watched, dazed as countless SUV's and sports cars swarmed around us. The volume of traffic on the roads, even on a Sunday afternoon, never ceased to amaze me.

Eventually, we reached the Pacific Coast Highway and headed north. The car accelerated with a surge that pushed me back into the seat and had me holding onto my hat. Nate's carefree laugh made me smile. The ocean stretched out to our left as far as I could see, glinting as the sun caught the rolling waves. I took a sly glimpse of Nate as he concentrated on driving. Young and relaxed, his thick hair blowing in the breeze, so different from the slick, polished image portrayed at work.

We pulled off the highway onto a side road, following its twists and turns past increasingly opulent mansions. Nate swung the car through solid wood opening gates, up a sweeping driveway and straight into the double garage nestling beneath three-storeys of million dollar modern beach house architecture. A mountain bike hung on a whitewashed wall, and a couple of surfboards on another, but otherwise it was empty.

Nate silenced the engine and removed his sunglasses. He appeared nervous, giving me a tight smile before climbing out. He moved gracefully around the front of the car and tried to open my door.

"Sorry." I quickly unlocked it, blushing furiously as I stepped out, mentally chastising myself for my OCD safety issues.

Nate smiled but said nothing. I removed my sunglasses and tossed my hat back into the car whilst he took a brown paper grocery bag out the boot. Had he actually brought me to his home? *To his bed?* The idea was as unsettling as it was thrilling.

"Follow me," Nate said, brushing past and heading through a door at the rear. I waited in a small hallway whilst he switched off the alarm then followed him upstairs.

The vast open layout I found myself in spanned the entire length and width of the house. It was pleasantly cool, a welcoming respite to the sun that had beat down on me during the journey. The distressed white oak floor and off-white painted walls gave the spacious room a clean, bright, airy feel. There was an abundance of natural light streaming in from a double-height window to my left, and skylights in the soaring vaulted ceiling over the dining area.

"Come on in." He made his way to the contemporary galley kitchen and set the bag on top of a large island. A grand timber dining table faced the kitchen, and in the centre, a huge fishbowl filled with shells and pebbles.

"These photos are fantastic." Twelve assorted sized black and white images of inanimate objects hung in coordinated frames on the wall behind the table. Arranged in no particular order, the randomness created a stunning visual effect.

"Thanks." Nate offered a shy smile as he removed two wine glasses from one of the high gloss wall units.

I headed to the sunken lounge, leaving my belongings on the table. A large sofa faced a giant flat-screen television fixed above an open fireplace, with built-in shelves on either side stacked with books and a few family photographs.

The cool blues, whites and silver of three large canvases hanging behind the sofa picked up the furnishings and accents. Two oversized armchairs faced out towards floor-to-ceiling bi-fold doors offering panoramic views of the Pacific Ocean.

"Is this your home?" I called, not taking my eyes off the view. The immaculately manicured lawn lined either side by tall cypress trees that ensured total privacy, stretched to the cliff edge before disappearing into the dramatic backdrop of the ocean.

"I have a place in the city that suits my needs during the week. I like to escape here on weekends. It's more me."

I turned and found Nate watching me from the top of the few steps. "It's breathtaking."

He made his way down and slid the doors open the width of the room. My breath caught on a gust of salty sea air, whilst the sound of crashing surf joined the rush of breeze in my ears.

"Let me show you around." Nate smiled proudly, his hand settling on my lower back and guiding me to another curved staircase. He glanced up, his wayward thoughts written across his face. "Go ahead."

Despite my reluctance to head upstairs with him, I couldn't stop myself from sashaying my hips as I climbed ahead of him.

"Behave," he gently admonished with a smile when I let him pass me. I grinned at being proved right. He was checking out my arse.

"Guest bedrooms." Nate pointed at two closed doors off a mezzanine hallway then opened a door directly in front of us and walked in. "That's my closet…bathroom…and this," he said as the room opened up, "is my bedroom." An inviting huskiness now laced his voice. He propped against the wall, ankles and arms crossed, observing me keenly as I cautiously stepped further into the master suite.

The colour scheme extended throughout the house, making a seamless transition from space to space. Vintage framed surf magazine covers hung on the far wall, their muted tones of green, blue and white drawing the scenery from outside into the room. An armchair and matching ottoman sat parallel to the windows with a sky-blue blanket neatly folded over the back. It looked the ideal place for lazy daydreams.

I glanced across at his huge bed, draped in a slate grey cover and positioned on a stunning hand-woven rug to face the windows. The light grey button back headboard gave it a classic, masculine feel. I found myself blushing as I imagined Nate in it, and tried not to think of all the women who had joined him as I edged to the windows.

"What an incredible view to wake up to." I flattened my palm on the warm, tinted glass.

"*Absolutely.*" The mesmerising tone of his voice captured my attention. His eyes glistened, watching me intently, his mouth hinting at a smile. I got the distinct impression we weren't agreeing about the same thing. I stepped away from the window and pressed my palm to my cheek, feeling it heat again.

"Shall we?" he asked, shoving off the wall towards me.

"Shall we what?" I squeaked, panicking as my eyes darted to his bed without warning.

"Head back downstairs?" Nate nodded to the door, my panic amusing him. "What did you think I meant?"

"Nothing." I hurried past and dashed downstairs to safety.

In the kitchen, Nate grabbed the bag and an ice bucket. "Let's go outside."

"Here," I offered, collecting the wine glasses. I followed him through the lounge, down a set of wooden steps off the deck to the garden below. Nate hoisted open a retractable canopy, providing some welcome shade to the patio.

I made my way across the lawn to the edge and was rewarded with the most breathtaking vista. Stretching across the entire bay area, all the way round to rugged cliffs on the right, I could only gaze in awe at the view.

"What do you think?" Nate appeared by my side.

"It's incredible."

"Isn't it?" He took the glasses out of my hands and strolled back to the patio.

As I followed, I noticed something in the far corner of the garden. "Is that a spa?"

"Yeah." He paused, glancing back over his shoulder, a naughty glint in his eyes. "You wanna use it?" It was asked so innocently, but I was certain his thoughts were far from pure.

"I don't have my bikini."

He sat on the large outdoor sofa. "And that's an issue…*how*?" A wolfish grin curled his lips.

My eyes narrowed. "This is supposed to be a casual *non-date*, Mr Blake."

"Call it what you want, Kara," he shrugged, "but it's only the two of us here. I won't tell if you don't." Grinning at my pursed lips as I joined him, he unpacked some crackers, a selection of antipasto, cheeses, and a platter of grapes and cantaloupe melon on the table.

"This looks delicious. Thank you."

"It's not dinner." He cocked his head to one side. "Help yourself." He stood and took a bottle of white from a drinks refrigerator beneath the decking. "Wine?"

"Please." Nate poured me a glass of Pinot Grigio and a smaller one for himself. "I can get a taxi later if you want a drink," I offered, realising he'd have to drive me home.

"I know my limits," he murmured. "I'm taking you home tonight. You're not running away from me again."

It was a warning. One that irritated me until I conceded in a sense, I'd done precisely that. Hesitantly, I raised my glass to meet his.

"Cheers," we said in unison as we touched glasses. The wine was delicious, crisp and refreshing. I accepted the cracker topped with a wedge of cheese Nate handed me with a shy smile. My stomach had settled, hunger pangs now replacing the nervous butterflies.

"Have you lived here long?" I took a bite and moaned as the cheese melted in my mouth.

"Almost a year. It was the first and only place I viewed. I bought it immediately." *As you do when you're a millionaire.* "The peace and privacy sold it for me." He tipped his chin towards the ocean. "You can't get to the beach unless you live here."

I could see why he'd fallen in love; it really was stunning, and a great place to relax from the stresses of life.

"How about you," he asked, "you get to the beach much?"

"Last weekend I went rollerblading along the track at Santa Monica with a friend." My backside still hurt from the sprawling fall I had on the concrete as Mai and I fooled around. "She gets these crazy ideas sometimes."

Nate laughed, popping an olive into his mouth. My eyes were drawn to his lips. His mouth was very enticing. I rubbed my stomach, hoping to settle the butterflies as I watched his cheekbones accentuating with each movement. I recalled the other night, and the yearning I had to feel his stubble brushing against my cheek again.

"Living in London, I never really got to the beach very often," I said, reaching for my glass.

"I hear there are some nice ones. I've only been to Newquay."

"Surfing?" I asked, casting my mind back to the boards in the garage.

His smile was shy and unpretentious as he nodded and picked up the bottle to refill my glass. "I love England," he stated. "I visit our office two or three times a year, inevitably returning with far too many pieces. I can't resist. The art, history, music…women." I took a large breath of air, unable to break away from his hypnotic gaze. "One in particular has definitely captured my attention…" his soft voice trailed off as he faced the ocean.

With my heart in my throat, desperate to escape my body, I coughed and gulped down half the wine in my glass. For the next hour, we shared stories about England, discovering what we enjoyed and missed. It highlighted how alike we were and how similar our tastes were.

"You have some stunning artwork."

Nate lounged back into the cushions, tucking both hands behind his head. "You're into art?"

"Some." I shifted so he wasn't talking to my back and tucked one leg under me. "I love stills and candid pictures, images that stimulate your imagination. It's fascinating how two people can see the same image and interpret it in completely different ways."

Nate flashed a broad smile. "Now I understand why my pictures captured your eye."

I flushed. "I have to confess, my real passion lies in vintage fashion."

"Fashion is an art form, Kara."

"I suppose." I shrugged, stroking the curve of my hoop earring. "I enjoy scouring the thrift stores and markets and unearthing hidden gems."

"Indulging in pursuits that bring you pleasure is good for the soul." He smiled a secret smile, one that had me wondering what he was thinking. "You've got a great sense of style. Classic, sophisticated and elegant," he continued, straightening. Hearing that from him, the most sartorially blessed man I'd ever met, was a real compliment.

"You've got great legs though." He grinned. "You should definitely get those out more."

I rolled my eyes playfully, fighting a smile. After spending time with a man who succeeded in making me view my body as nothing to be proud of, I was unaccustomed to hearing it praised.

Nate reached for his glass, inadvertently brushing my bent knee with his arm. A tremor ran through me when he sipped his wine, never breaking eye contact as he lowered the glass and licked his lips, collecting the remaining drop with his tongue.

"What's keeping you busy at the moment?" Nate brought the direction of the conversation back to safety, for which I was grateful as I found my skin heating with embarrassment and some other warmth that definitely wasn't coming from the sun.

"I've recently finished the brand valuation for the Galaxy sponsorship, and I'm nearing completion on the amended business case financials for the Star Airlines work."

His bright expression morphed into one of displeasure, as though I'd mentioned something I shouldn't have, yet I had no idea what. "Have you always worked in Commerce?"

"No. I graduated, got a job with Morgan Sanders in London, and qualified with them."

His brows shot up. "They're one of the most prestigious accounting companies in the world." Even though he seemed surprised, he sounded quite impressed. Feeling awkward, I shrugged in agreement.

Each year, only ten places were available for the highly respected graduate programme. I was ecstatic when I got one of them. So it was double the guilt when I handed in my notice two weeks after gaining my professional qualification.

"Why give up a promising career in the financial sector to come here?"

Crap. I walked into this one. "I just fancied a change."

Nate studied me, intrigued. "Intelligence *and* beauty—that's a lethal combination." His eyes clouded, narrowing as they ran over me, his lips parting to allow for his deep inhalation of air.

The sultry perusal made me feel naked, like he'd scorched all my clothes off with the glow from his eyes. That warmth I'd previously experienced seemed like a chill compared to the heat now blazing throughout my body.

Abruptly, Nate stood. "Let's go for a walk."

WE kicked off our shoes and made our way down a narrow strip of sand weaving through a sloping scrub embankment to the beach below. It was quiet, with only a few people enjoying the late afternoon sun.

I glanced sideways, watching Nate take lazy strides along the wet sand, leaving footprints waiting to be washed away by the foam occasionally lapping at our feet. I was too wrapped up in the moment to care if my jeans got wet. He appeared happy and content, comfortable in his own skin. Something I hadn't been for a long time.

Gentle slopes gave way to higher cliffs the further we went along the waters' edge, until a point in the distance where the rocky terrain stretched out and met the ocean.

"There are some great hiking tracks up there." Nate's voice startled me from my daydream. He pointed ahead to the headland I'd been admiring. "The view from the top is unbelievable."

"I can imagine. Do you go up there often?" I curled a strand of windswept hair behind my ear.

"Sometimes. It's a great place to clear your head," he said wistfully.

We stopped and sat, partly shaded by the massive boulder. I stretched my legs out and leant back on my hands. The beach was a place I always found soothing, somewhere to sit for hours daydreaming, letting time pass me by.

"You're very quiet," Nate said, mirroring my pose. His fingers grazed mine, but neither of us moved.

"I think I'm being seduced by the view."

His lips curled, as though thinking of a private joke at my expense. "I had a feeling you'd like it here."

I smiled wryly. "I'm sure I'm not the first you've brought here to impress."

Hurt flashed across his face, and I instantly felt guilty. "It is wonderful, though," I quickly added. "Thank you for showing me."

He smiled softly. "Ever surfed before?" He nodded to a small group of people bobbing up and down on boards in the ocean, trying to catch a wave.

"No, I don't like going too far from shore."

He tilted his head as his lips turned downwards. "Can you swim?"

"Yes," I nodded, shielding my eyes from the sun's glare. "I'm just scared not knowing what's swimming around me."

Nate's genuine laughter prompted a wry smile through my embarrassment. "Don't let fear of the unknown hold you back," he reasoned. It was an apt statement, considering our circumstances.

"Would you let me take you out there?" He bumped shoulders with me. "I'll keep you safe."

I giggled at his playful nature. "We'll see."

"If Mel lets me take my little goddaughter out there, I must be trustworthy, right?" he grinned. "Though, come to think of it, that's our secret. She'd probably kill me if she knew."

It was difficult reconciling the ruthless businessman with a carefree young man, a doting uncle with a strong presence in his family's life. It was another layer of normality I hadn't anticipated.

"I can't believe how quiet it is." I lowered onto my forearms and tipped my head back, savouring the warmth from the setting sun.

"It's a great place to escape from unwelcome attention or prying camera lenses."

Nate quickly turned away when I caught him studying me intently. Tucking my chin into the nook of my shoulder, I watched him survey the ocean, blinking in the sunlight. "Do you get that a lot?"

"Occasionally. I like to keep my private life exactly that—*private*. Being photographed at events and so on is all part of the job. So far, I've managed to keep other stories out of the spotlight." Nate moved into an upright position, folding his arms across his bent knees. His voice roughened. "The interest in my personal life pisses me off at times." He shrugged his broad shoulders, his loose shirt rippling in the breeze.

"You've been labelled one of the most eligible bachelors in the country." I sat, brushing sand off my hands. "What, or *who* you're doing has to make for some interesting stories for the tabloids."

Nate turned sharply, examining me with questioning eyes.

"Plus, I bet you take a great photo." I smiled nervously back at him. *Well, that's one way of telling him how hot he is.*

Nate scanned my face suspiciously, then nodded in the direction of his house. "We should head back."

He stood, offering both hands to help me up. That familiar spark spurred through our fingers, scattering the same rush of heat up my arms and across my skin as the first time we touched. Nate hauled me up a little too heavy-handedly and I stumbled forward. My hands went out, fingers curling around solid biceps that flexed at my touch. I blinked up, taking a deep breath as I met his gaze.

Standing in his arms, close enough to see the fire blazing in his eyes, caused a riot of sensations to weave through every part of my being. He was just so… *there.*

"*Kara,*" Nate whispered, reaching for my face.

"Don't." I shook my head, pushing him away. I started off back to the house, needing the distance to clear my thoughts.

"You okay?" he asked softly when he caught me up.

"Give me a minute. I'll be fine." I smoothed both trembling hands over my neck, trying to ease the imaginary pressure. Even though I'd panicked, I longed for Nate's touch on my skin. Gentle fingertips that could banish the last of my demons. There was no explanation for my body's reaction to him. The more I tried fighting the attraction, the stronger it became.

The stroll back was in silence. The rolling swell of the ocean was therapeutic, lulling repetitively back and forth, easing my mind. By the time we reached the path I'd regained my composure.

Nate cautiously slipped his hand into mine to help me back up, and I accepted his silent reassurance without a fight. The rush I got from that tiny connection—our fingers entwining together—made me reluctant to let go as we crossed the lawn. He was taking control, luring me in, and my resolve was weakening.

"Look at this." Nate turned me to face the ocean. Dusk settled across the sky as the sun melted into the water, the lights of a plane taking off from LAX twinkling in the distance. Streaks of orange and gold blurred into the blue haze of the ocean in the most spectacular sunset.

"Wow, it's so pretty." A shiver of excitement ran through me when I caught the darkness in Nate's eyes. My hand gripped his harder as the effect of his command surged through me.

"Fuck, I can't hold back any longer." Nate tugged me closer, cradling my face as he angled his, and pressed soft lips to mine. They were warm, burning me, pushing heat through my body and setting me on fire for him. I let out a small moan when he grazed his teeth over my lower lip. "More," he rasped, exerting a little more pressure. "Give me more."

My hands went to his hips as I surrendered, unable to resist him any longer.

He tasted divine, his mouth sweet, his tongue hot and tender as it licked into mine. One hand came to my lower back, pressing me into his solid frame until there was nothing between us. His heart raged against my chest, the same frantic rhythm as my own.

This was what I unknowingly needed. What I'd been waiting for all afternoon.

He kissed confidently, skilfully, and took his time not to rush, knowing there would be plenty more chances to discover me again. Lost in him, I found the hem of his shirt and without thinking, slipped my hands beneath it. The tensing of his torso and the small shudder and groan that moved through him had me wanting to explore more. With fingertips either side of his spine, I slid my hands up, feeling the defined muscles of his back, picturing it in my mind.

Nate's hand moved over the curve of my arse and gently squeezed, pushing me into him so I felt his erection.

"No!" I jerked away, lowering my eyes to the ground.

"What's wrong?" he rasped, barely audible through rapid breaths.

"I can't do this." I covered my face, mortified by my actions. Nate peeled my hands away, forcing my eyes up to meet his. My heart was pounding furiously as I took some steadying gasps of air. "God, I'm sorry."

"For what?" Nate anxiously ran a hand through his hair. "Doing what you've tried denying you wanted from the moment we met?"

This had to stop now before we both got carried away in the heat of the moment. "I'm not sleeping with you."

The corners of those enticingly blue eyes creased as his smile reached them. "Have I asked you to?"

"No, but—" I felt stupid standing here in front of him, conscious of the mixed signals I was giving. Having my hands all over him and kissing him back so responsively—he must know I wanted him.

"I'd be lying if I said I didn't want to. But if that's all this was about," he murmured, eyes gleaming mischievously, "we'd have tangled up my bedsheets hours ago."

The way he stared at me with such conviction, along with his sureness of himself, and us, excited me.

"You can't deny the attraction, Kara." His fingertips grazed my cheek as he tucked a lock of hair behind my ear. "You want it, too. Otherwise you wouldn't be here."

Nate was right. I *had* come back for more. I was lost, struggling with my emotions. "Everything about you is so…overwhelming." For the first time in almost a year, I'd found someone I was actually interested in. But Nate wanted nothing beyond sex. "You know this can't work. We're expecting completely different outcomes."

His expression softened as he ran a thumb along my jaw. "You took the words right out of my mouth."

I frowned as I scanned his face, noting his own bewilderment. Why continue the pursuit if he didn't think we'd work out?

"I don't want to become a woman whose face you won't even remember in a few weeks' time."

"You never could be," he assured quietly. "You're the only woman I've considered having more with in a long time. I know I came on strong at the beginning. It was a mistake, I realise that now." His expression saddened his eyes. "But, uncomplicated is all I've known lately, all I've allowed myself to have. It's difficult to change that overnight."

I turned, wondering why Nate believed he was so unworthy of emotional intimacy, and faced the ocean. His hand crossed my back and settled on my hip, his head nuzzling mine. The breeze blew over me as I shut my eyes and took a deep breath. The salty sea air blended with the woody hues of shower gel from this complicated man beside me.

"Listen, I'm away on business the next few days. Use our time apart to really think about what you want."

I'd do nothing *but* think about him. "I do like you, Nate."

"That's good to know," he said playfully, tucking me into his side. "Hate to think you kissed men you *didn't* like that way."

I was grateful we had the long drive back to the city before having to say goodbye.

"Are you still okay with the top down?" Nate asked as he climbed into the car.

"I like it," I told him, clipping up my seatbelt, noting he locked the doors.

"Say if you get cold. I'll put the seat warmer on."

"Heated seats?" I don't know why I was surprised. The Bentley was top of the range; of course it had all the latest mod-cons.

"Second thoughts, don't want you getting sick." As we drove away from the house, a stream of warm air steadily emitted through the seat cushion around my neck.

"Hmm, this is nice," I murmured, snuggling into the seat. "It makes me sleepy."

"Be my guest." Nate's eyes glinted mischievously to match his smile. There was no way I'd be falling asleep. "There's a built-in massager if you really want to relax."

"Are you talking about yourself, Mr Blake?"

He laughed loudly as he concentrated on the road and shook his head. "No, though ask me nicely," he purred, "I'll be more than willing to oblige."

I grinned. "You keep your obliging hands on the steering wheel, thank you."

Nate reached over and squeezed my knee, sending a thrill up the inside of my leg. I clenched my thighs together, hoping to appease the throbbing. His fingers were long, and I was certain they would be exceptionally talented. I covered his hand with mine and switched them to the armrest between us because I couldn't stand having it on me, imagining it creeping up my thigh and doing all sorts of naughty things to me.

Old Motown music played quietly in the background. When a particular song started, I burst into laughter. "Let's Get it On?" I snorted. "Did you choose that on purpose?"

"No, it's on shuffle." Nate glanced sideways, grinning. "I swear." Slipping his hand from beneath mine, he went to change the music.

"Leave it. It's good."

We settled into a comfortable silence. Occasionally, Nate removed his hand to drive, but always placed it straight back into mine. Once or twice I caught him peering across at me, a shy smile on his face. My heart soared every time.

It was dark when we arrived at my apartment. We walked up to the glass doors of my building hand in hand. I stopped on the step and faced him. "Thank you for keeping it casual today."

"My pleasure."

The force of his stare made me look away as my gaze dropped to our feet.

"Hey," he said, cupping my face, forcing my eyes back up, "don't over complicate this. Go with what's in your heart."

I laughed quietly. "My heart and head never listen to each other."

The concern in Nate's eyes abated as his thumbs gently stroked my cheeks. "So don't think, just feel."

Right now, I wanted to feel those lips on mine again. Tentatively, I placed my hands on his waist and let my eyes drift deliberately to his parted lips, willing them closer as I offered up my mouth.

He obliged with a kiss as tender as the first, only this time there was a reverence, a level of affection in it that blew my mind. "See me again," he pleaded quietly against my ear, "let me take you to dinner."

I hugged him harder, the only way to demonstrate how much I wanted him to. Nate breathed me in, then all too quickly released me from his embrace. I dug my keys from my bag and swiped the fob to unlock the doors.

"Goodnight." I glanced sideways and saw his glorious face now marred with concern.

Nate pushed the door and held it open. "I'll call you Wednesday."

I locked my apartment door and slid to the floor, my mind racing with a million unasked and unanswered questions. Nate was great company, so much so, that for a while I forgot myself. Forgot my fears and inhibitions and allowed myself to live. I touched my lips, reminded of his gentleness, and drew my knees to my chest to calm the scattering butterflies in my belly.

His kisses were designed to tease, a hint of how good the sex would be. I longed to feel him all over my body, his sinful mouth exploring every piece of flesh. And I was desperate to do the same to him.

After showering, I sank into bed. Antique furniture filled the room, and the Baroque wrought iron king bed was my favourite piece. The dusky pinks and champagne tones gave the sense of calm and serenity I'd been hoping for when I chose the accessories for my haven.

My phone spun through my fingers for a good five minutes whilst I debated whether to text Nate. Finally, I caved: **THANK U AGAIN. SAFE TRIP X**

I lay there, listening to my own steady breaths until the buzz of my phone startled me: **TRUST YOUR INSTINCTS X**

What were my instincts saying? I was undeniably drawn to Nate. His sexy smile reeling me in, daring me to discover what was hiding behind those smouldering eyes.

What happened with Stuart was the result of a weak man. He'd let his own insecurities and jealousy take over our relationship until it destroyed us. *Destroyed me.*

Nate was strong. Even if I hadn't known him long enough to trust him, I knew enough to trust my intuition.

He was different.

Chapter 7

Being from England, the unusual torrential rain greeting me the next morning didn't bother me. In LA, however, everyone freaked out at the slightest downpour and forgot all knowledge of how to drive. Nearly an hour after leaving home, with nerves slightly frayed, I drove into the car park.

"Typical." I moaned at the sign kindly informing me the underground parking was full. I found a space as close to the building entrance as possible and switched off the engine.

Whilst I swapped my driving flats for mid-heels, I admired my place of work through the rain splattered windscreen. It was only a few years old, purpose built for RED, and served as head office for the NTB Group of businesses. The fifteen-storey rectangular structure was constructed from recycled glass and steel, and equipped with all the latest technology. It was impressive yet understated.

After dropping my bag in my office, I went to make my own coffee. Mai had taken the day off to study, but at yoga this evening, I knew she'd want the full run down—*with details.*

I focused all my energy into work, using Mai's absence to my advantage and actually making progress without her frequent interruptions.

By 5 p.m., I'd broken down the revised expenditure for Star by division and projected revenue return by market segments, and commenced the brand valuation of a recently acquired modest supermarket chain in Portugal for an existing client. On top of that, I'd negotiated an earlier deadline to receive estimated costs for an international hotel chain's rebranding, enabling me to produce a first draft budget before my holiday.

With my productive day, I hadn't time to think about Nate. Now, as I left, it didn't take long for him to creep back into my thoughts. I allowed myself that small indulgence as I drove to the gym in the driving rain that hadn't eased all day.

Being away, no doubt in the company of far more attractive women vying for his attention, all willing to give him what he wanted, could make Nate realise I wasn't worth the effort. I was making a lot of assumptions, but how could I trust someone who had temptation put in front of him everywhere he went? A man who had explicitly told me he didn't do relationships?

"THE wet look, it suit you, huh?" My yoga instructor, Marco, appeared from the gym office, a lusty grin on his tanned face as he scanned my drenched body. The short distance from my car to the entrance of the gym had been enough to get thoroughly soaked.

"Not happening," I teased back, shaking the rain from my clothes as I pushed open the changing room door, giving him a backwards glance.

"Bella ragazza—one day you'll gimme your heart," he called after me, pulling black chin-length bangs back into a stubby ponytail. From Italian descent, Marco was blue eyed, leanly muscular, and his broken Roman nose and cleft chin made him ruggedly handsome.

I'd never been one for exercise, but I arrived here with a new outlook. I took up running as a way to familiarise myself with the city I'd chosen as home, with the added bonus of enjoying the Californian sunshine. Then I joined the gym and signed up for yoga, eager to get an all-round workout and sweat away my woes. Marco ran my induction and we hit it off immediately. I thought he was gay until he asked me on a date. Had the timing been better, I might've said yes. But it was too soon.

"Don't even ask about my day," Mai grumbled as she arrived with Robyn. She dropped her bags on the wooden bench and collapsed in a heap beside them. "I'm so behind on my project."

"Do you need some assistance?" I asked, hanging up the last of my damp clothes. "I can take a look at it if you like?"

"You're the best, K," Mai gushed, starting to undress. "I'll bring it in tomorrow."

"Tell me about the weekend." I took her hot pink sweatshirt and hung it in an empty locker.

"And there's my cue to leave," Robyn said, heading for the exit with our yoga mats. "Only so many times I can hear this. See you out there."

Mai's mood lifted instantly. "Kara, it was the best. We spent all weekend in bed."

My nose wrinkled. She loved Mitchell, but lately his busy work schedule meant they hadn't been getting much alone time which was causing arguments. "So your legs are hair free now?"

Mai laughed. "Shaved, waxed and lasered. Don't know how I'm gonna make it through class though. I can hardly move I'm so sore."

"Ew! T.M.I!" I secured her locker and tossed her the key.

"What about *your* weekend, Miss Collins," she asked slyly, gathering her hair and twirling it into a bun as we approached the door, "how was that?"

"Good." I held the door open, using my water bottle to wave her through with a grin.

"How's every person tonight?" Marco asked cheerfully in broken English as we joined Robyn and Jenna outside the private studio. Our resounding groans made us giggle. "That a good, huh?" Marco let us in and set his water down in front of the mirrored wall.

Poor Marco. Having to contend with four women carrying shitloads of emotional baggage between them must be a drag. I think he secretly enjoyed our hour sessions, though. What straight man wouldn't?

Invigorated and relaxed once the class was over, I went to collect my belongings from the changing rooms. "I'm not eating tonight," I said, gathering my bags. I'd shower when I got home as my clothes were still damp.

Mai whispered, "Where you sneaking off to?"

"Nowhere," I slung my bags over my shoulder and tucked my mat under my arm, "just getting the groceries for tomorrow. Are you still coming over?"

"Unless you've made other plans?" She wiggled her brows.

"No other plans. See you tomorrow." I kissed her cheek and called, "Bye girls," to the others in the showers as I disappeared out the door.

TUESDAY BEGAN with a *very* detailed run down of Mai's weekend over coffee. I managed to fob her off about Nate, promising to tell all this evening. Mai had kindly brought me lunch so I could work through, and was busy dissecting the latest issue of People on her tablet. She lived in the social media world and followed the celebrity culture like a religion.

Her shrill squeal alarmed me as I jerked up, peering over the rim of my glasses to see her making a beeline straight for me.

"OMG, Kara! Look!" The tablet was thrust into my face, her acrylic nail tapping on a grainy photo of Nate and me beside a taxi.

"What the f—?" I rubbed my brow and read aloud:

> *"Nathan Blake, CEO of NTB Group, was seen last Thu. 24th with a mystery blonde outside a wine bar in Studio City, CA. We have no idea who the lucky woman is that has caught the mega-rich tycoon's eye, but we'll be keeping watch on this hot love affair as it heats up!"*

My fists clenched around the screen case. "Hot love affair!"

"Don't sweat it." Mai brushed it off, like seeing me online was the most normal occurrence in the world. She sat in the chair opposite and snatched it back. "You do look very cosy…thought there wasn't any lip-smacking?"

"There wasn't." Only, the angle of the photo suggested less fleeting embrace, more sensual clinch. "Nate's going to freak." We were in a state of limbo; neither of us sure what was happening next. Dealing with this intrusion only added further strain to an already complicated situation.

"Relax, K. Take a Valium."

"Why am I in People magazine? There are far more interesting nobodies to snap than me."

"You two make one *seriously* sexy couple. I could see you both towering above Sunset on a huge billboard. Blake brooding in his underwear…you draped seductively around him…" Mai talked with her hands, artistically arranging the photo-shoot in her head.

"Whatever."

"Is it vegetable fajita's tonight?" Mai asked with a grin. I served that every time she came for dinner. It was the only meal I made vaguely edible, and I never added meat for fear of poisoning her.

"Yes," I smirked, appreciating her effort to take my mind off things.

"Thought so. Got the margarita mix in my bag, so we're good to go." Mai insisted it was to create a Mexican authenticity to the meal. Secretly, I think it was so she could stomach the food. She said they tasted good, a compliment considering her own talent for cooking, and they usually did after a few of her cocktails.

"Let me get back to this work otherwise we're going nowhere tonight."

"PHEW, after that scorching kiss, it sounds like Sunday was much better than the first date," Mai concluded, barely containing her delight from where she sat on the other side of the lounge. I'd spent the last ten minutes giving her a not-too-detailed rundown of our date whilst preparing dinner. The windows were open, and Mai's choice of Mariah Carey was playing in the background loud enough to drown out the helicopter circling in the sky a few blocks away.

"Estrella wasn't a date." I threw some chopped vegetables in the pan and took a gulp of the strawberry mix, with extra tequila thanks to the bottle Mai found in my cupboard. "Neither of us knew where we stood after that."

"So, now you have him by the balls, whatcha gonna do with him?" She stuck her head out the window and took another drag on her cigarette.

"I'm foolishly considering giving him what he wants." I took the tea-towel off the counter and wiped my hands.

Mai pursed her lips and scowled. "Nothing wrong with that. Casual's what you need right now, ease you back into the scene."

"It's not. Nate could make me fall in love with him. Then what?"

"We deal with that if it happens." Mai stubbed out the end of her cigarette and flicked the tab into the small ashtray I left on the windowsill for her visits. She got up from the bench window seat and joined me in the kitchen.

"I have to give him an answer tomorrow." I leant back on the counter and sipped my drink.

"I think you already know the answer."

I shook my head. "Nate's got obscene amounts of money that could buy his hearts' desire. We move in entirely different circles. I don't want to be a forgotten number in a long line of many."

"Money can't buy love," she announced, pushing up her sweatshirt sleeves and giving her hands a quick wash. I rolled my eyes at Mai's cliché and returned to the cooker.

"You're gorgeous. He'll be the one falling in love, not you." Mai brushed me aside and took over the cooking as she usually did. "Mitch works in a bar surrounded by women. If I suspected him every time he went to work, I'd destroy us and myself along the way."

"I know you're right, but I can't help it. Do you honestly think I want to be on my own forever?" After getting the plates and cutlery out, I set two places at the breakfast bar.

"So do something about it. This is ready now," she said, resting the spatula on the pan and settling on a stool opposite. "Blake's a busy guy. If he's prepared to make time to pursue you, I'd say he's interested in more than just a fling."

I served up dinner and pushed a plate in front of her. "All I want is a normal man. He doesn't have to be the most handsome, *definitely* not the richest, but kind, responsible, someone who loves me. Above all, he needs to be honest and trustworthy."

"In the meantime, all fairytale crap aside, go fuck Mr Sexy 'til Mr Boring comes along."

I think I'd been drawn to Mai's frankness from the beginning. I always knew where I stood. By the time I'd done a brief tidy and sat beside her, Mai was already eating, deep in thought. "Has he got many close friends?"

"How is that relevant?" I asked, assembling a wrap.

"Someone in his position, who has time for good friends, is someone who can forge a long-term relationship." She sipped her drink. "What about serious girlfriends?"

"I don't know! We haven't discussed the ins-and-outs of our pasts." *Thankfully.* I grabbed my drink, taking a healthy gulp to calm down.

"I'm only trying to help you see the situation more clearly," she snapped, tossing her food onto her plate so the entire wrap fell apart. "You don't want my opinion? *Fine.*" She got up and stomped to the fridge like a sulky child.

"Sorry." I wiped my hands on the napkin and nodded at her offer of a refill. "Nate mentioned not having a relationship in a while."

"At least he's had one." Mai returned the pitcher to the fridge. "Looking like he does, I'd be worried if he hadn't. Shows there's potential, we can work on him."

I agreed it would be disconcerting to think he hadn't experienced at least one serious relationship in his life. "According to him, commitment equals drama," I mumbled through a mouthful of food.

"So be drama-free." Mai shrugged. "He'll be eating out of your hands."

I snorted. "Easier said than done."

"You know as well as I do, most guys would've given up by now." Mai returned to her stool and wiped the last of her wrap around the plate, scooping up guacamole. "You have all the control, Kara. Do something empowering with it."

"How do you work that one out?" I felt the exact opposite. Nate's enigmatic presence and charisma charmed me to the point of losing all sense when he was around.

"You set the time and place for the bar. You told him you weren't jumping his bones—of which I'm still impressed, by the way," she added, smiling. "If he had his way, you two would've fucked by now. Give him a chance." Pleased with her summation of events, she wiped the corners of her mouth and set her napkin on the counter.

"What kind of woman starts seeing a man who she knows is wrong for her, who's had enough heart*ache* to last a lifetime, yet is considering hooking up with a certain heart*breaker*?" I sagged into the low back of the stool.

"The kind who needs someone to bang the hell out of her and remind her what she's missing." Mai raised her brows as a smile crept across her face. "Go have dinner, enjoy the evening. If you still think he's wrong afterwards, I won't push you anymore." She lifted her glass to make a toast. "Agreed?"

I raised mine hesitantly from the counter, still not entirely convinced.

"To future happiness." Mai clinked her glass to mine as the meddling face appeared. "Beginning with hot sex."

I WOKE much more optimistic, but with a slightly fuzzy head. Tonight, I would endure an extra tough gym workout as penance for the over-indulgence of a litre tub of ice-cream Mai and I demolished between us.

My eager friend had insisted she handled all my calls—just in case. All morning, I'd seen her field call after call and shared her sorrow when each one wasn't Nate. Then I received a vibrant bouquet of mixed tulips, wrapped in green tissue and hand-tied with green raffia. The message, artfully handwritten on a simple white card:

Thinking of you. Nx

"Now you have an excuse to call him," Mai stated. "Thank him for the flowers, see where the conversation goes."

"I can't." Full of anxiety, I stood, deciding that making the coffees might distract me. My mobile rang just as I reached the door. I froze, knowing it was Nate.

"Answer it then!" Mai picked it up, shoving it at me impatiently.

"Can I have some privacy?" I motioned to the door. She backed away, huffing and puffing her indignation. My mind slipped into gear and I answered before it went to voicemail.

"Hello." I rounded the desk and sat down, noticing my hand trembling.

"Kara." Nate's soothing voice instantly calmed me. "I'm so sorry I haven't called sooner."

"It's fine. You must be busy."

"I've missed your voice. It's so good to hear it again." I let his confession sink in as I noticed Mai loitering outside my now closed door. "You haven't left my thoughts since I saw you last. Did you receive my flowers?"

"Yes, they're beautiful, thank you. I wasn't sure if you still—"

"If I still what? Wanted to see you?"

"Yes," I mumbled. I could give him many reasons why he could've changed his mind about us.

"Well, I do, so have you made a decision?" he asked nervously.

"I have."

"Are you going to put me out of my misery and tell me?" There was humour in his tone.

I smiled. "I'm starving."

The relative silence accompanying our conversation was unexpectedly interrupted by a blast of car horns and screeching sirens, making me think he'd stepped outside. Then it quietened again after the sound of a car door slamming shut. "Interesting choice of words," he murmured.

"Thought you'd appreciate them." I grinned, swivelling my chair side-to-side.

"Oh, I do," he said smoothly, "and I'm ravenous." Warmth spread rapidly through my body, my nipples tightening, my skin misting. "What do you like to eat, Kara?" he asked, his voice suddenly husky.

"*Everything.*" I panted, unbuttoning the top button of my cotton shirt. I heard a muttered expletive and my smile widened.

"What's going on?" Mai mouthed, eying me curiously with a smirk through the glass. Then, she put her hands together like she was praying and begged, "Let me in." I shook my head and swivelled my chair around, needing all my focus on the conversation happening on my phone.

"Be ready at eight Saturday evening," Nate stated boldly. "I'll pick you up."

Never one for patience, Mai allowed me all of five-seconds after I'd hung up before barging in. "Well?"

I spun to see her wide-eyed expectant expression. "Saturday," I confirmed.

Mai shrieked and fist-pumped the air. "I'll clear your schedule." With much excitement, she danced back to the door. "Time for some sexy clothes shopping!"

I collected my thoughts, tapping my phone on my chin as I flopped back into my chair. I'd done it now. No going back. I was agreeing to more than dinner.

I was giving him permission to take me to bed.

Chapter 8

This was it. Never had I been more nervous about a date than right now. My skin flushed, my core stirring expectantly with nerves and excitement. I drained the last of my wine and placed the glass in the dishwasher, careful not to chip my newly French manicured fingernails.

The pearl earrings my father gave me when I left matched the minaudière I'd purchased at a house clearance a few weeks ago. My eyes were smoky grey, my lips glistening with the sheen of pink gloss. A few strands of hair curled around my face, the rest twisted into a loose chignon at my nape.

The outfit Mai persuaded me to buy during Friday's lunchtime shopping trip was beautiful, if a little more daring than I was used to. The embellished golden 1920s style flapper dress was sleeveless, with a scoop neckline and a deep 'V' cut back, showing a serious amount of flesh. The dropped waist gave way to a ruched skirt that hung above the knee.

If I had carpet, my metallic ankle-strap heeled sandals would have worn a hole in it from all the pacing I was doing in the lounge. I stopped to admire them for the umpteenth time and the co-ordinating shimmering bronze varnish on my toes. Mai called them "fuck me" shoes. They lengthened my legs and revealed the arches of my feet—an extremely erogenous zone. I heard a car outside, the sound of a door closing, then a few seconds later my intercom was pressed.

"Hi." My voice was breathy when I answered.

"Hey, it's me." Nate's tone was warm and inviting, if a little breathless, too.

"I'm on my way down." I grabbed my clutch and exhaled a large breath of air as I locked my door and made my way downstairs. My steps faltered on the last step when I saw Nate staring back at me from outside. He looked good. *Really good.*

I opened the door and stepped into the muggy night air.

"*Wow.*" Nate's voice hitched and he quietly cleared his throat. He stepped forward, lips grazing mine. I breathed in his cologne—a sensual exotic scent, reminiscent of a stroll through a Moroccan marketplace—allowing it to weave into my senses. "You look incredible."

"So do you." It had been such an unexpected kiss, I temporarily lost the ability to think or speak, fumbling with the clasp of my bag instead. Nate's mouth twitched. He was dressed in black trousers and matching shirt. The undone top two buttons hinted at smooth tanned skin underneath. Effortlessly handsome, sensual eyes and smooth skin, never had I seen a man look so good. Or maybe it had been so long since I viewed one with as much admiration as I did Nate.

"Shall we?" With his hand at the small of my back, he guided me down the path. As his fingers skimmed the open cut of my dress, a soft sigh escaped my mouth.

A tall, burly man, mixed race and possibly mid-thirties, wearing a white shirt, dark tie and trousers, stood next to the rear door of a black Mercedes. It was the same car that had appeared at the wine bar. Nate opened my door and gestured me inside.

Settling beside me, Nate nodded up front as he buckled his seatbelt. "That's my driver, Ross."

I smiled shyly at Ross, his eyes acknowledging me in the rearview mirror. Nate lifted my hand to his mouth, kissing the back before lowering our joined hands to the seat between us. His lips sent a tingle up my arm, straight down my core, finally settling with a flutter in my stomach.

That sexual charge of tension hung in the air between us. I swallowed, my mouth suddenly dry as my eyes drifted appreciatively over him. The shadows dancing over his face, combined with the inky black of his attire, gave him an extremely captivating, yet almost dangerous aura.

Dangerously beautiful—the perfect description. I didn't stand a chance.

THE car stopped outside Cleo, a restaurant nestled beneath The Redbury in Hollywood. Nate joined me on the pavement and led me inside. As we walked across the checkerboard tiled floor of the subtly lit lobby, I began to relax. I knew Nate has chosen this establishment with me in mind. It was classy, but not ostentatious. It wasn't somewhere to flash the cash and intimidate.

Nate guided me past the few patrons enjoying pre-dinner drinks at the bar. A sharp-suited maître de greeted us and led us through a large archway, an illuminated image of an actress from the golden era of silent Hollywood films dominating the wall in front of us.

Candles replaced the subdued mood lighting, flickering in red and blue tea lights on the tables. The hub of noise from the other diners chatter brought a different ambience to the place; it was vibrant and fun, yet remained intimate and romantic.

I slid onto the tan leather studded sofa and tucked my bag beside me. Nate sat, close enough so our legs touched beneath the table. After handing us menus and informing us of the specials, the waiter agreed to bring water before disappearing into the darkness.

"Have you eaten here before?" I regretted the question immediately. Nate bringing other dates here was information I didn't care to know.

"Never," he quickly reassured, smiling guiltily, "but I've had takeout enough times to know the food's great."

I scanned the dozens of dishes on the menu but could barely read it. Too self-conscious and not wanting to put on my glasses, I said, "It's going to be tough choosing, everything sounds delicious."

"I can order for us if you like, baby?" The tenderly spoken term of endearment made my already rapid pulse leap.

I exhaled in a rush, relieved. "That sounds perfect."

The flick of his tongue over his lips drew my gaze to his mouth. I remembered how great they were to kiss and how badly I wanted to do it again. Gently, Nate teased my bottom lip from my teeth with his thumb. I hadn't appreciated I was biting it. "Dinner will be over before we've even eaten if you keep looking at me like that," he muttered roughly.

The waiter interrupted, so whilst Nate ordered, I took a large gulp of chilled water. The whisper of his words still vibrated through me, the question of how the night would end never far from my thoughts. Nate squeezed my hand, then trapped it between both of his.

"I'm so glad you said yes, Kara." He spoke quietly, his eyes fixed on our hands, drawing my own to the same place.

I wasn't sure if it was Nate or the atmosphere, possibly both, but I was being seduced in the most unassuming way. "You're hard to say no to." In this intimate setting, I was incredibly turned on, and rubbed my leg intentionally against his.

His head jerked up. He studied me without a word, yet his eyes screamed of his hunger for me. It took a minute for us to acknowledge the sommelier presenting a bottle of vintage Veuve Clicquot.

"Champagne?" I asked Nate as two flutes of my favourite celebratory drink were poured.

"We're celebrating." He handed me one then raised his. "To finally having dinner."

I took a welcome sip, unable to take my eyes off him. My mind raced with thoughts of kissing, touching and feeling him against me. Skin to skin. It was so unlike me. Yet when Nate pierced me with a focused gaze, it was easy to forget the woman I thought I was. In that second, I was all he could see, all he noticed. And I was everything I wanted to be.

An array of dips in bowls, with flatbreads wrapped in brown paper bags, arrived at our table. I sat forward for a closer inspection, tearing off some bread whilst deliberating which to try first. "This looks good, you chose well."

Nate's mouth curled at the corners as he did the same, diving straight in and spreading a generous amount over his. "Try this one," he said, offering it to me.

My hand curved around his and brought it to my mouth, catching his thumb as I ate it. "Mmm," I swallowed, "delicious." Nate's eyes dropped to my mouth, his glazed expression as he sucked the pad of his thumb afterwards making all the muscles low in my stomach clench.

I sipped my champagne, keeping my eyes on him as he attempted to regain his composure. "How was your trip?"

"Good," he said, preparing some food for himself, "we resolved a lot of issues."

"Where did you go?"

"New York, mainly." His lips pressed into a tight smile as he grew distant, consumed by his thoughts.

"That's on my bucket list." I'd explored the West Coast, but the East was still unknown territory. I had been in line for a possible secondment to Morgan Sanders' New York office upon completion of my exams, but it all got royally screwed up when I left.

"Unfortunately, this was all business. There was definitely no pleasure," he stated harshly. With his lips to his glass, he went on. "I had a brief visit to Rhode Island to meet some students at RISD, then spent two stressful days brainstorming with Star."

Star Airlines were the No.1 domestic airline in the US and top five internationally. They were revamping their image, expanding into the Asian domestic market, and wanted the leading brand consultants to undertake the daunting task. "Securing that contract must've been a real coup."

"Trust me," Nate said grimly, setting his knife down, "it wasn't."

I wasn't sure why he was playing down his success and achievement. "Rumour has it they specifically wanted you and RED, and that our competitors never got a look in. It should be very lucrative for you. I'm impressed."

An uneasy laugh escaped his mouth as he sat back, draping an arm over the back of the chair so his fingers touched my shoulders. "Spoken like a true accountant. You probably know more about my financial affairs than I do."

His presumption made me uncomfortable. "I'm sorry, I meant impressed by your revered reputation, not by how much money you'll make. I wasn't being personal." Shrugging off his touch, I drained my glass. "Just to be clear, I don't have access to any of your private accounts. I have no idea how wealthy you are."

"Hey," he said, sitting forward, "that information is common knowledge, give or take a few zeroes." He cocked his head, his lips curling. "I can't control public information. It's why I strive to keep everything else private." His smile faded. "It can be expensive sometimes."

The sommelier had poured a Sancerre, and the waiter was back to clear the table before another array of tempting delicacies were placed before us. Some sizzled on hot plates, sending steam into the air, leaving behind a pleasant spicy aroma. I drank my wine whilst the waiter dished couscous into bowls followed by some sort of hot broth.

Talk of privacy reminded me of Mai's internet discovery. I twisted the napkin laying across my lap, wondering whether I should raise it with Nate, but not wanting to spoil the evening.

"What's wrong?" he asked as he dished some meat into our bowls and passed one over.

"There was a photo…online." I pushed a piece of chicken around with the back of my fork. Nate deliberated my words, his demeanour giving nothing away. “We were…together.”

I dropped my fork and sank into the chair, searching his broad back, trying to gauge his thoughts. Calmly, Nate reached for his water.

“I know,” he said flatly, taking a sip.

“I had nothing to do with it,” I quickly reassured him.

His eyes shot to mine. “Why would I think you did?” He scanned my face, attempting to fathom something out. Then he cupped my nape, urging me forward until our mouths collided in a fervent embrace. Lust flamed my body, any concerns over this very public display of affection disappearing, overtaken with the way I was responding to his decadent exploration of my mouth. I wanted more, but he broke away, leaving me panting. A devilish grin played over his face as he nudged his nose against mine.

“They can have as many pictures as they want if we get to kiss like that again. Let’s give them something to talk about.” He caressed my cheek. “C’mon, you have to try this food.”

“It did taste good,” I admitted with a shy smile.

Grinning, he handed me my fork and waited until I started eating before resuming his meal. He guarded his privacy fiercely, so the fact he appeared unperturbed by this and understood I wasn’t out to benefit from it, spoke volumes of his opinion of me. But I needed more reassurances before taking this further. *Damn my insecurities.*

With my bowl almost empty I broached the subject, but not before taking a large gulp of wine for courage. Nate relaxed, one hand on my leg, the other holding his wine. He smiled contentedly, his thumb stroking back and forth across my knee.

“So…what are we doing here, Nate?” I waved a hand through the space between us.

His brow creased. “Having a *long* overdue dinner date?”

I was suddenly bold, perhaps it was the wine talking, but I had to know if he thought this was going anywhere. “If we end up sleeping together tonight—what then?”

“Then we’d be two *very* satisfied people in the morning,” he rasped, curving his hand around my knee with a gentle pressure that resonated at the top of my legs.

“You’re that confident in your prowess?” I crossed my legs, snaking my left arm through his right and cuddling into him.

"And yours." Nate's eyes held a predatory gleam, his smile full of sexual promise. "*When* we fuck, you know it's going to be good."

And I did. *Explosively good.* It was all I'd thought about since agreeing to this. "But I want more than that. I want the drama. I want all the impossible guarantees no one ever has in a relationship. You don't."

His voice deepened. "Don't be so sure about that."

"It's what you said." I twisted his platinum cufflink between my fingers. "I know what you want, and I could easily give it to you. I just—"

"You *want* to." Insightful eyes met mine. Feeling like he could read my soul, I dropped my gaze to the flickering candles on the table.

"A man like you isn't interested in dating exclusively or anything long-term."

Nate nodded his approval for the waiter who'd returned to clear the table, waiting until we were alone again to resume the conversation. "But that's what you want?"

As much as I desired him, in a stark moment of clarity I realised I couldn't go through with a one night stand. Sexually, Nate was arrogant without being cocky, an attribute I surprisingly found alluring. My body responded to his touch in ways it never had before, inspiring me to test my boundaries, take risks, be a better, bolder version of my old self. Nate drew it out without even realising. But it was better to be upfront and save myself the suffering in the long-term.

"Yes," I replied simply.

"Do we really need defining right now?" He set his glass on the table with a frustrated sigh. "Let's just enjoy ourselves, see what happens."

"I like you, Nate. More than I have anyone in a long time. But I *deserve* more. I'm putting myself out there, but I can't go through it all again…" My whispered voice trailed off to nothing.

Nate studied me closely, his mood impalpable, for a long time before responding with unwavering certainty. "I'm a red-blooded male who thinks you're sexy as hell, with a firm belief we'd be great together. And I'm damn sure *after* we've slept together, I'll want to do it again. And again."

I shook my head, astonished he saw me that way. Nate laced his fingers with mine and raised them to his mouth, warm lips grazing my knuckles. "If I thought I could have a fulfilling relationship," he continued, his voice softening, "I'd take it in a heartbeat."

"You would?"

He nodded and blinked away, avoiding eye contact. I was so engrossed in him, I hadn't appreciated how hard I was squeezing his hand until I felt his fingers flexing in mine. When he faced me again, his expression was deathly serious. *Crap.*

"I love my family, have great friends, and a career that has surpassed anything I could ever have imagined." Nate paused, regarding me pensively. "I'd say I've had my fair share of good fortune, considering." All the lightness in his voice had gone, his jaw clenched tight. "That's no consolation when I'm alone at night in my bed…"

I was transfixed by his eyes. They were so big, the window to his soul wide open and spilling from his mouth. My free hand cuddling his arm bunched in the Italian cotton of his shirtsleeve.

"Everyone aspires to that one all-consuming love," he said earnestly. "Love that overwhelms you, takes your breath away, drives you insane. I'm no exception."

His response was unexpected, leaving me unsure what to say. After a minute, he straightened, forcing me away from his side. From his rigid body language, it had caught him off-guard as well. Unaware I'd been holding it, I released my breath and tried processing what just happened in my muddled thoughts.

Slowly, Nate ran a hand through his hair and exhaled, causing the few strands falling over his forehead to lift in the breeze. "You did it again." He glanced sideways, catching my puzzled expression. "Why can't I engage my brain to mouth function around you?"

"I'd be happy simply engaging my brain," I said, beginning to smile. "You make me lose all common sense."

Nate laughed quietly as he shifted to face me. Tilting my chin up, he gazed at me for a long minute before pressing his lips tenderly to mine.

"Your entrées." The waiter cleared his throat when neither of us acknowledged him.

"We won't need those," Nate told him, eyes never leaving mine, "just the check."

Chapter 9

We were driven back to my apartment, which was completely unexpected. Nate hadn't asked where I wanted to go, in fact, he'd barely spoken the entire journey. For twenty minutes, one leg had tapped restlessly whilst he focused on where we were heading through the front seats. Now, alone in the car, as he released my hand and unclipped our seat-belts, my already heightened level of anxiety grew.

I twisted to face him. Nate edged closer so our thighs pressed together and moved an arm to the back of the seat. My breath stuttered and my palms grew damp.

"You seem nervous." Nate's voice was low, hoarse and uneven, revealing his own nerves. He twirled the few strands of hair framing my face in his fingers, his eyes flickering to my mouth before closing as he neared.

His kiss fluttered across my lips. Then it was gone.

I blinked, dazed and unsure why he'd stopped. Nate's eyes, merely inches from mine, worked over my face, deep in troubled thought.

With a timid hand, I touched his face. "Kiss me again."

At first it was tentative, before gradually deepening into a more heated embrace. A low groan escaped from Nate, reverberating right through my body, and I felt him shudder. I wrapped my arm around his neck, urging him closer. He tasted heavenly, his tongue expertly moving with mine, teasingly licking and stroking. Nate's kiss had the ability to wash away my fears and worries. Everything became right with just one touch.

"No," he gasped, tearing himself away. My heart felt like it could pound out of my chest. For a minute, I couldn't open my eyes, wasted and almost unconscious from the delicious taste of his scorching kisses. "Not here." His right hand went into his hair, fingers flexing as he raked through it. Taking a deep breath, he straightened. "I'll walk you to your door."

After our frank conversation in the restaurant, I presumed we were spending the night together, so I wasn't quite sure what to make of that. Nate opened the door and tugged me onto the pavement. I sensed the spark between our fingers once more and my body heated. I wanted him to make love to me. Needed his touch to return some light into my darkest memories.

On the doorstep, his worldly eyes assessed me, hesitating to give me what I wanted. That added to the chaos in my head because Nate wasn't the type to hold out. Virility oozed from every pore of his skin, in every step he took, the way he moved and the cockiness of his outrageously charming smile.

I knew if I let him leave now, I'd regret it. Cautiously, I ran my fingertips over his cheek. Nate's eyes closed as he leant into my touch.

"Come upstairs," I murmured.

When his eyes opened, they were almost black, hooded, revealing a hunger that sent a shiver down my spine. I swiped my fob and opened the door, reaching for his hand.

"Kara—wait." There was no denying how much he wanted this, but the indecision glimpsed in his eyes was incredibly touching. I tugged his arm again, a physical response to his unspoken uncertainty. His expression softened instantly. "Hold that thought."

Nate disappeared and spoke to Ross, who had returned to the car. They chatted briefly whilst I leant against the doorframe, not quite believing what I'd done. After a few minutes, he returned. "Lead the way."

With every stair we climbed in anticipated silence my heart rate accelerated. I fumbled with my apartment key, trying to get it in the lock.

"Don't be nervous." His hand covered mine, his whole demeanour suggesting calm and authority. "Allow me."

I entered with some trepidation and placed my clutch on the dining table, all too aware this would be the first time I'd had sex in over a year. Nate emptied his pocket contents onto the kitchen counter and led me into the lounge, lit only by the orange glow from the lamp posts outside. Without warning, he spun me forcibly into his arms so my palms hit flat against his chest.

"I need you to be sure, Kara, because when I kiss you again, there'll be no going back. I won't be able to stop until I've heard you scream my name as you come."

The firing shot of his words hit their intended target, right between my legs. *God.* He was outrageously confident and I was beyond turned on by it. A shard of light shining through a gap in the blinds highlighted dark, intense eyes full of lust and longing, and waiting for an answer.

Spiked with courage, I did the two things I'd wanted to since first laying eyes on him. I brushed one hand through the long, thick hair on top of his head. It was exactly as I imagined, silky and soft. Holding him at the nape, I traced a finger along his full, hot lips with the other. "Don't stop," I agreed, breathlessly.

The touch of his lips on mine was so delicate my knees buckled beneath me. I gripped his arms, fighting to stay upright as his grip on my waist firmed. Every curve of muscle tensed with my touch as unhurriedly, both hands slipped back to his nape.

Against his steadfast frame I could feel myself trembling, and when Nate tugged my lower lip between his teeth, I gasped.

"I want to savour this, prolong the experience, but you make me so hard," Nate growled. He grazed along my jaw, then sucked on the sensitive spot below my ear, sending a shiver across my skin.

"Take your time," I whispered, my attention-starved body enjoying the seduction. I tipped my head, allowing better access to my neck and shoulders. His lips gave way to teeth, small bites and teases, hands sliding over my body as his arousal built.

"I want to rip off this dress, bend you over the couch and fuck you 'til you can't walk."

"I rather like this dress," I sighed, running my hands over his shoulders. "And walking comes in handy."

Nate's laugh against my shoulder made me smile. "Tell me how you like to be touched, Kara."

What? No! A man's touch had been absent from my life for so long I half-imagined I'd forgotten what to do. His gaze returned to mine. "It's okay."

"I can't," I whimpered.

"You can. Don't be ashamed to let me know what your body enjoys." Nate prowled behind me, his body heat making mine hum with anticipation as I blindly awaited his next move. He stroked a finger lazily down my bare back, scattering goosebumps across my flesh. "So creamy and soft," he murmured.

"I've longed to taste your skin for weeks." His lips grazed my shoulder, working up to my ear and whispered, "But I imagine you knew that already."

My breathing shallowed, my body swaying as Nate played this tantalising game of seduction. The straps of my dress fell down my arms, his hands leaving a trail of fire on my skin as he eased it off. His breath hitched. "No underwear?"

"No bra," I corrected. He eased the dress over my hips and down my body, and tossed it to the side.

"Your legs are spectacular." His breath tickled the back of my knee. Warm hands and soft lips mapped their way leisurely up my thighs until Nate regained a standing position. Taking both my hands, he wrapped them around the back of his neck and deliberately trailed fingertips down my arms, making my skin tingle.

"Feel what you do to me, Kara?" he rasped, both hands splaying above and below my navel, urging me flush against him. His erection strained against his fly, pushing against my arse.

Unable to respond coherently, I whimpered and nodded. Realising Nate was so hot for me was enlightening. I arched my back, moving both hands to his hair.

"So incredibly sexy." His thumb skimmed the lace top of my panties, then he slipped his hand inside, moving down until his finger found my clit. My body jolted and I gasped. "I can't wait to bury myself inside you."

His breathing changed, growing heavier and uneven next to my ear as he began circling the sensitive bundle of nerves, making me moan. "You like that?" he asked, drawing the delicate skin of my neck between his teeth.

"Hmm." My head fell back, my hips swaying of their own accord.

"Shall I make you come?" His lips brushed my ear, the pad of his fingers dipping into the wet at my opening then gliding back up.

"Not yet," I begged. I didn't want to come at the mercy of his fingers. I felt too bared.

With the familiar swell of an impending orgasm building, I turned to him. Scorching lust burnt in his blackening eyes. He was a man on the edge, struggling to maintain the steady pace. He wanted to fuck but was giving me the slow seduction I requested.

With shaking fingers, I unbuttoned his shirt. I prised it from his waistband so it hung open loosely. "Wow," I muttered, awed by his well-cared-for body. Hesitantly, I pressed my palms to his muscular chest, feeling it rise and fall in time with his heavy breathing.

Nate's hands came to my hair and started meticulously removing the pins. The feel of his fingers sifting through my hair was exquisite.

I kissed over his chest, trailing a finger down the groove in the middle of taut abs, sculpted and firm as they rippled with my touch. The unique scent of *him*, heightened with lust, made me squirm. I continued past his navel, down the light trail of dark hair disappearing into his trousers.

"It's fucking too much." His kiss was hungry, urgent as he took back control, eating at me like he'd starve if he didn't. Holding the collar of his shirt, I hastily pushed it off, yanking it over his wrists so cufflinks scattered across the hardwood floor.

I cupped his arse and urged him against me, grinding into him. "I want this," I panted, need and impatience flooding me.

"I want *this*." My breast filled his hand, his thumb rubbing my hardened nipple before being sucked into his hot mouth. I groaned. His teeth grazed the tender bud, then his tongue soothed the bite. Every touch was experienced between my legs. It was borderline painful but insanely pleasurable.

He moved lower, circling my navel, sending chills through my body. I shifted restlessly, grabbing fistfuls of his hair, getting wetter as the sensuous torture of my body continued, unsure how much more I could take.

Nate slid off my panties, following their path until he was crouched by my feet once more. Only this time I could see him.

"Mmm," he murmured appreciatively, "let me put the lights on." He blinked up through impossibly long lashes and licked his lips.

"No!" I was standing completely naked in my lounge, exposed and vulnerable. Self-consciously, I wrapped my arms around my waist.

"Don't hide." Nate stood and opened my arms. "Your body is stunning, made for sex and sin. Be proud of it. Use it." He swept my paranoia away with a tender kiss. His hand found its way between my legs, fingers parting the slick folds before one slipped inside.

"Yes." I panted, clenching around him, greedily wanting more.

"You're so turned on, baby." Nate's words disappeared into my mouth as he pushed another finger inside. His palm found my clit, and with measured circles whilst his fingers slipped in and out, he coaxed my orgasm closer.

My hands trembled as I began undoing his belt. I tugged at the button of his trousers, swiftly followed by the zip. I pushed inside his trunks and found his swollen cock, hard as steel yet silkily smooth.

"Fuck!" Nate strained, throwing his head back. I fisted his thick shaft, lightly squeezing as I pleasured him. He was losing control with every stroke.

Abruptly, he removed his fingers from their sweet ecstasy and hoisted me into the air, urging my legs around his waist. Nate moved us across the room until my back hit the wall, pinning my hands above my head as he lowered me back to the floor. The coldness of it was a stark contrast to the heat flaming my body.

Being restrained like this should've frightened me. But I wasn't scared. All I could think about was how badly I wanted him to fuck me.

"I want you. Here—*now*," Nate growled through ragged breaths that matched my own. He released my hands and took a condom from his trouser pocket. My chest pounded furiously, my hands flexing impatiently against the wall. The man was so sexual I thought I might come merely watching him roll the condom down the long length of his cock.

When his eyes returned to mine, there wasn't a trace of blue left. I'd never seen someone so hungry for something, so wildly aroused, yet so controlled. Nate encouraged one of my legs back around his waist, nestling between them. Steadying myself with a hand on his shoulder, I reached between us, desperate to have him inside me.

"Christ, Kara," he muttered roughly, easing the first inch inside. Nate's eyes lowered to where we were intimately connecting. I tried moving, needing more, but he stilled me, taunting me with small rolls of his hips. He leant his forehead to mine. "You're so tight. I need to be careful." He nudged my leg wider with his knee and steadily went deeper. I moaned at the invasion of my body, my muscles clamping tight around him.

Nate stilled. "Did I hurt you?"

"No," I said breathlessly. I hadn't done this for so long I felt so damn full and stretched, it took a second to adjust to the initial sting.

"Here." Nate altered his stance, encouraging my other leg around him. Then he started to move. Slow at first, but the pace soon quickened. My mind fogged, my body tingling as an orgasm built. Taking my weight on one arm, he brushed the hair from my face. "Baby, you feel so good."

With hands clasped at his nape, ankles locked behind him, we faced each other, both lost in the moment. The sex was raw and animalistic, his hips driving a hard, fast punishing pace, shoving me up the wall each time he slammed into me. But the eye contact, being face to face with no option but to watch each others reactions, was crushingly intimate.

"Lean back," Nate urged, stepping back to alter his angle of penetration, moving from stimulating my clit to rub the hidden spot deep inside. Pleasure surged from my core.

"Right there…" I pushed my shoulders to the wall, head back as I gripped his shoulders for support. Thrusting harder, Nate took complete possession of my body and mind. My grip started slipping as sweat misted his skin. Feeling too wide open, I pulled him close and buried my face into his damp neck, tasting his salty skin and scrunching my fingers into his back and hair.

"Come for me." His fingers dug into my arse. Somehow he went deeper, hitting the spot that sent me over the edge.

"*Nate.*" My orgasm shook through me, my cries growing louder as the pleasure overwhelmed me.

"Fuck." Nate's hand slammed against the wall by my head. He came hard, hips grinding into me, rubbing the last of his orgasm out, his body shuddering. The only sounds in the room were our ragged breaths, gradually abating and levelling out to normality.

Nate raised his head from my neck, a broad smile spreading across his flushed face. "I couldn't wait."

"I noticed."

His laughter set flutters off in my belly. He lowered me to the floor and eased out. I was still shaking as I tried to regain some strength in my legs, using the wall for support. Nate took care of the condom and restored order to his clothing. Then I was in his arms. "Where's your bathroom?"

"There," I said, nodding to my bedroom door.

Nate carried me with ease and laid me on the bed before switching on the bedside lamp. "Finally, I get to see you."

I sat, drawing my knees to my chest. I was fully naked compared to his half-dressed body. The bed dipped as Nate sat and started unbuckling my shoes.

"What's so funny?" Nate cocked his head, questioning my wide grin as he slipped them off.

"It's my shoes, I just realised I kept them on." I shoved up the bed and removed my earrings. "My fuck-me shoes."

"Yeah," he snickered, standing up, "it was all because of the fuck-me heels."

Desperately aware of my naked body, I darted to the en-suite and jumped into the shower, not caring if the water had time to warm. When I re-entered the bedroom wrapped in a towel, Nate was setting his phone on the bedside table. "I've set some fresh towels out," I said, as he rounded the bed towards me. "Feel free to use my toothbrush."

He caught me by the cheek and gave me a sweet lingering kiss. Then, without uttering a word, disappeared into the bathroom. I climbed into bed, relieved to cover up with the sheets.

Chewing my lip, I shut my eyes, recalling the passion that exploded in the living room. I relished the slight soreness when I rubbed my thighs together.

When Nate came out a few minutes later, he looked simply breathtaking. The just-fucked freshly showered glow suited him, and his proud posture and dazzling smile suggested he knew it without being arrogant about it. I suspected my own expression was the same because I felt amazing.

"Tired?" he asked, noticing the yawn I failed to stifle. He climbed in beside me, plumping his pillows so he was slightly upright.

"Hmm."

"Then close those beautiful eyes and sleep, gorgeous girl."

I switched off the lamp and snuggled into his arms. I thought he might've whispered something into my hair, but I couldn't be sure as I fell into a very satisfied sleep.

Chapter 10

The brightness of dawn threatened to wake me. I shifted in bed, hoping not to properly wake, but something was weighing me down. Or rather, *someone*. Nate's breath tickled my nape as he slept behind me, his arm at my waist securing me to him. I stretched lazily. As consciousness returned, memories of last night flooded back.

What gave me the courage to invite him in? I've never been that forward. But some sort of primal instinct kicked in and I had to be with him. Wanting Nate so badly shocked me—giving in to that urge even more so. All along I'd been under the assumption he just wanted sex, yet when it came to it, *I* was the one who succumbed to those carnal desires and took us to another level. The line had been crossed now. There was no going back. Last night was purely about lust and two people desperate to fuck.

And it was seriously hot.

Smiling, I hugged his arm closer. All my instincts were right. The man knew how to kiss. He knew how to fuck even better.

Careful not to disturb him, I rolled onto my back, taking the chance to admire Nate without fear of being caught. The suits gave him an air of authority that made him seem older. Now, beside me, he looked younger than his thirty years. Enviably long lashes curled and occasionally fluttered as they reached below his eyes, overnight growth beginning to cover the fine contours of his face.

Nate blinked open one eye, then the other. The biggest smile of accomplishment gradually beamed across his face. Heat flushed my cheeks, but I couldn't help returning his infectious smile. "Morning."

He brushed hair from my face and kissed the tip of my nose. "Morning," he replied, examining me with questioning eyes. "You okay?"

"Yes." I trailed fingers up and down his upper arm as it crossed my chest.

"No regrets?"

"None." Before I could return the question, Nate rose onto his elbow and scissored one leg between mine. My breath caught when his erection prodded my thigh.

"Wanna do it again?" The once beaming smile grew into one of pure wickedness, his eyes flaming with lascivious ideas.

I grinned. "Thought you seemed pleased to see me."

"If I'm not mistaken, you were enjoying the view, too," he drawled.

He'd been awake the entire time I was studying him. I shoved his shoulder. "You're good at faking it."

"Hope you're not," Nate countered dryly, grinning as he peeled the sheet down until it bunched on the curve of my hip.

"Nate, no." My hand went to ease it back up, but he stilled it.

"Don't be shy, let me see you."

Last night, his scrutiny had been fairly painless given the subtle lighting. I'd even go so far as saying I felt desirable. But now, in the dappled sunlight, knowing he was purposely checking me out made me desperately want to hide.

Nate's gaze slid over my bare flesh, drinking me in as his fingers traced the contours of my body. "I want to explore every curve," he murmured, pressing his lips to my shoulder, "and I will." Goosebumps skittered across my skin, my nipples hardening when he caressed beneath my breasts. "I'm all for wild, passionate fucking, but I wanted to experience you without hurry."

His lips moved along my jaw to my ear, where he tugged my lobe between his teeth. "I'm a man of my word."

Drawing his head back, the glazed look of lust in his eyes was the same one glimpsed last night. I stroked an unruly strand of hair from his forehead, silently telling him yes. I was already aching for his touch, beyond aroused by his words alone. Thinking of him inside me again was a real aphrodisiac, fuelling my passion. Shoving my hands into his hair I kissed him, languidly luring him deeper, ready for so much more. I savoured the heat of his firm, naked body covering mine, cradling me beneath him.

"Your eyes…" Nate murmured, "…so unusual, so wise." He lay a trail of kisses down my neck. "I want to taste you."

My hips undulated, rising to meet him, my body showing how much I wanted him to. Cupping my breast, he rolled the nipple between his thumb and forefinger, watching his deft fingers move. A shockwave of pleasure darted to my core as I arched my back, needing more. Then his mouth was on me, covering my nipple and sucking gently, switching between both breasts.

"Oh." I dropped my head back, absorbing every bit of pleasure Nate was giving me. As he moved down my body, I tilted my hips, willing him to kiss me in the most intimate place. I was aching to feel his tongue on me.

The anticipation was killing me, my body a tangle of energy and sensation as I waited, my breaths coming fast and heavy. Nate straightened and sat back on his heels. Lifting my foot and placing it on his shoulder, he worked both hands leisurely up my calf.

"Your legs drive me insane," he said hoarsely. "Having them wrapped around me last night was too much." His mouth followed his hands all the way to my knee then on to my thigh. He was a master of seduction, deliberately making me wait, heightening my need for him. He did exactly the same with the other leg. Moaning my appreciation, my hips bowed off the bed when he reached my apex once more.

"I can't wait any longer. I have to taste you." Nate's voice was gruff as he hooked my legs over his shoulders. His thumbs moved softly over me, parting me until his hot breath blew on my clit. "God," he murmured, "you're just as lovely down here."

Any shyness over what he was about to do went as I gripped the pillow beneath my head, my mouth dry with anticipation. Strong hands held me still as his tongue slowly ran the length of my cleft.

"Yes," I moaned, the feeling unbearable in the most satisfying way. Clenching the pillow tightly, I bit my lip to stifle another moan but couldn't stop it when Nate sucked gently on my clit. My body took over, shamelessly grinding against his mouth, lost in his languid exploration as I chased my orgasm. Teetering on the edge, I grasped his hair and pulled, deliriously not knowing if I wanted him to stop or carry on. It was *so* good.

Nate groaned, and the erotic sound vibrating against me sent my orgasm soaring through me. I was helpless, crying out with the force of it, shaking uncontrollably. He worked his tongue over me, sustaining the rolling orgasm, relentlessly driving me to the point where I lost all sense of where I was. When he sucked again, I reached the peak almost instantaneously and climaxed with a shudder.

"No more," I whimpered, sagging into the mattress, utterly spent. Nate's chuckle rippled over my tender folds of flesh, causing me to moan again.

"You don't like?" he drawled.

"Too much," I panted, trying to push away from his mouth. "You're too good."

"Sweetheart." He dragged me back down. "You taste so fucking good, I may be here a while."

I raised onto my elbows and met his hungry eyes. Smiling salaciously, his thumb replaced his tongue and two fingers dipped inside. I was too sensitive and jolted when he began rubbing my clit back and forth. An elongated groan escaped my mouth as I watched him finger me, his face so close to my sex. Nate was watching me back, reading my face, seeing my reactions to him, and I let him.

Those eyes were hypnotic, encouraging me to be so expressive, making me feel wanton and sexy because I could read those exact thoughts in their stormy blue haze. See how much it excited *him*, how good it made *him* feel to see me like this, shedding my inhibitions. When his tongue joined in, it wasn't long before I was coming again, reaching for the iron bed-head to support my shattered body.

Satisfied he'd got me off enough, Nate made his way back up my body the same leisurely way he'd gone down it. "That's almost as good as fucking you," he said roughly, sealing his mouth over mine. "Almost."

The taste of my own arousal was still on his lips, and the muscles in his back flexed and tightened as I rubbed over them, unable to get enough of him and the way he felt beneath my hands.

"I need to be inside you." The nips on my shoulder became more insistent as Nate started rocking into me, the stiffness of his cock rubbing against my tender sex. I needed it too, shamelessly lifting my hips to meet him. I remembered the condoms I'd tossed in my bedside drawer and stretched to get them.

Nate was one step ahead of me, reaching in until he located one of the foil packets. He smiled—a lazy grin that unexplainably made me feel excruciatingly shy considering what he'd recently been doing to me.

I took it and ripped the packet open with unsteady hands. Nate hovered above me, watching my every move. "God, Kara," he groaned, biting his bottom lip when I rolled the condom down the length of his thick shaft and squeezed at the base.

He nudged my legs wider and eased into me. With hands either side of my shoulders, arms outstretched lifting his body high above me, Nate rocked back and forth, his movements practised and precise. I'd barely recovered from the earlier orgasms, yet another was building. I traced his face with hesitant fingertips, watching him make love to me, every move he made breaking me down, owning me.

The pressure on my clit was acute, his cock simultaneously massaging the tender spot deep inside. A sheen of sweat glistened his body, his mind lost in his own ecstasy.

Nate gazed at me through unfocused eyes. *"Kara."* There was so much unspoken meaning behind the reverent whisper of my name. My chest tightened, taking my breath away. Folding an arm beneath me, he raised my hips off the bed and held me there, pushing into me deeper and deeper. I clasped his shoulders, holding on and tilted my pelvis into him.

"Again…" I was on the verge once more.

"Let go," he growled, sending me over the edge. I collapsed beneath him. Shockwaves pulsed from my groin to the tips of my fingers and toes, and up to my head in a rush. His body tensed when his own orgasm took over, the cry of my name muffled against my neck as he weighted my body with his

Fuck, that was good. *Really good.*

We lay in a post orgasmic haze. Nate kept his face buried in the crook of my neck but stroked my hair affectionately. I dragged my nails up and down his back, soothing him as he held me tight.

When our breaths had calmed, Nate raised his head. He looked lost, equally as unsettled by our lovemaking as I was. He pulled out and rolled onto his back, disposing of the condom in the bin beside the bed. In a blissful state of elation, I sprawled across the bed, unable to move my limbs. They were deliciously heavy and tired.

"Come here." Nate tugged me into his side, draping an arm around my shoulders. I weaved a leg around his and rested on his chest, listening to his levelling heartbeat.

"I see what you mean about fucking and making love," I said timidly. Both of his hands had been drawing patterns on my arms and shoulders, but they stopped the second I spoke.

"Mmm," he replied disconcertingly, "think we both proved there's a definite difference."

I glanced up, wondering what was running through his mind when I saw his troubled expression. He smiled, but it didn't quite reach his eyes how it usually did.

"Which do you prefer?" Nate asked once I'd settled back on his chest.

"Both."

His chest lifted with a chuckle, bringing a smile to my own unsettled composure. "Me, too."

WHEN I opened my eyes a while later, the brightness hinted at late morning. I craned my neck to look at Nate and found him sleeping. Without disturbing him, I extracted myself from his arms and crawled out of bed to the en-suite, closing the door quietly behind me.

My cheeks were flushed and my eyes sparkled. My hair was all tousled and wild, my lips plumped and red. All in all, I was radiant. I took a hair tie from the cupboard and finger-combed the disorderly strands into a high ponytail. Then I brushed my teeth and splashed cold water on my face, hoping to take away the heat still radiating from me.

Back in the bedroom, I paused to examine the male perfection that was Nate Blake as I slipped on my silk robe. His upper body was leanly ripped—defined pecs, at least a six pack of sculpted abs—and the crowning glory was the deep *V* jutting down to his sheet covered groin. I sighed longingly as I drank in his wondrous body stretched out in my king bed.

Closing the bedroom door quietly, I padded barefoot across the lounge to the kitchen, collecting our discarded clothes on the way and hanging them over the backs of dining chairs. After measuring out the coffee beans and sticking my oversized cup in the machine, I took my phone from my clutch whilst waiting for them to grind and percolate.

I was shocked to find it almost midday. Sleep was a favourite hobby of mine, but I hadn't managed to sleep this late since my student days. A tiny voice in my head reminded me I hadn't been doing a lot of sleeping. It sounded very much like Mai's know-it-all voice. I put that down to seeing a missed call and two text messages a few hours ago from her, each with varying degrees of desperation for details. I tapped a brief reply, letting her know I was okay and I'd see her tomorrow.

The aroma of freshly ground coffee filled the kitchen. I removed the almost empty milk carton from the fridge and added a dash to my drink. Folding both hands around the mug, I blew away the steam and took a sip. Tomorrow, I'd be heading into work after spending the weekend having passionate sex with the boss. I wasn't sure where we went from here but was grateful we didn't actually work together. Past experience had taught me that got very awkward.

I set the mug down and returned the milk to the fridge. It was pretty obvious last night would end the way it did. There was an undercurrent in the air from the second we said hello. Using the open door for support, I stretched down, enjoying the soreness left from a night of great sex. Fucking Nate was electric. But we'd just made love, and now there was an entirely different exhilaration buzzing through my body. In the last twelve hours, I'd possibly had the greatest sex of my life. *Twice.*

"Why did you get up?" a gravelly voice asked.

I jerked up from the fridge where I'd been staring mindlessly at the empty shelves, daydreaming. Nate leant shirtless against the breakfast bar, running a hand sleepily through recently fucked hair.

"I…I needed the bathroom."

He leisurely moved around to join me, revealing he was wearing his trousers with bare feet. I had no idea why, but the look had me feeling hot.

I took another mug from the cupboard. "Coffee?" My voice trembled, mirroring how I felt, as I shoved it under the nozzle without waiting for a reply.

"Er…please. Long black, double shot, no sugar." Nate leant back against the counter, arms crossed, and watched carefully as I went about making it. My hands shook nervously as I half-filled the cup with boiling water. Then I pressed espresso twice and waited, restlessly, feeling the pressure of his gaze on my back.

"Can I get you some breakfast? Or lunch?" I asked, running the limited contents of my cupboards through my mind and hoping he'd say no. *Thanks for those mind-shattering orgasms, accept some dry old toast and a banana as my gratitude.*

"No." He glanced around with a frown. "Thanks."

Trying to keep my wits about me wasn't easy. Nate made it increasingly difficult wearing little clothing in such close proximity. It was very distracting—*he* was very distracting.

"Here." I handed him his mug. He took it with a tight smile and moved to the dining area, sipping it as he walked. It hit me then that his usual relaxed mood and happy face had been absent since getting up. I finished my coffee, watching him over the rim as he shrugged on his shirt. His silence unnerved me, the rigidness of his features as he fastened the buttons more so.

Having men in my apartment was a new experience, a situation I hadn't been in for a long time. I wasn't sure of the etiquette in terms of how long I should expect him to stay before leaving. Nate probably wasn't used to being in a woman's place either. His conquests were probably made to suffer the walk of shame.

"I like your apartment." He collected his coffee from the table and wandered towards the windows.

"Thanks." The small space had a neutral base palette. My bedroom was feminine and romantic. The living areas were modern and edgy, filled with bold, bright colours. "It's enough for me."

"The flowers still look good." His eyes fixed on the tulips taking pride of place on my desk, his thumb brushing the petals. "There's a significance in each colour. I took a long time choosing the appropriate ones."

Pleased he'd made the effort to select them himself rather than sending an assistant, I mentally noted I'd be hitting the internet later to do some research. I was consumed by my thoughts as I marvelled at God's gift to women standing barely twenty feet away, in *my* apartment, drinking *my* coffee, after spending the night in *my* bed.

"Are you sure I can't get you anything to eat?" I offered, mentally kicking myself for my good manners. "More coffee?" I rinsed my mug and set it under the nozzle for a second hit of caffeine.

"No, I'm good, thanks," he muttered distractedly. With his back to me, Nate faced the window. His shoulders were hunched, both hands now shoved into his trouser pockets. I pressed a palm to my chest, rubbing over my speeding heart. Something wasn't right.

I made my way over. He glanced sideways when I reached his side, lines forming across his brow. The foreboding knot in my stomach twisted again from the chaos in his eyes. Without saying anything, he moved in front of my desk.

"Is this your family?" Nate stared at the collage of photos in the large frame on the wall above it, but he didn't really see them, his mind working on other concerns.

"Mostly." I joined him and pointed to the one taking pride of place in the centre. "That's my parents."

He leant in for a closer inspection. "You're like your mom."

My father regularly told me I reminded him of my mother at this age. My height and eye shade had come from him, but the rest of my features were all her.

Before I got to agree, Nate moved on to another. "Who's this?"

The picture of Mai and I wearing Mickey Mouse ears made me giggle every time I saw it. We'd taken her nieces to Disneyland a few months ago, and eagerly participated in the silliness. "That's my friend, Mai. She works for you too, you know." Hoping to raise a smile and bring back the good-natured man I thought he was, I nudged him playfully with my hips.

The tiniest hint of one appeared when he faced me. I tried figuring out what had happened to the relaxed, playful man from earlier, but all I saw was a lost soul. As his eyes drifted over my face, his frown deepened. Then he let out a soft sigh and returned to the photos. "And this one?" Nate jabbed a finger at another picture taken on a beach. "You two look close." His arms crossed defensively over his chest, drawing further away.

"What?" I chuckled, surprised by the snarky tone in his voice. "You really have no reason to be jealous of him."

"I don't get jealous," he snapped, scowling at the photo. His defiance wiped whatever was left of a smile off my face. I wanted to let him fester and not explain, but my prevailing sense of honesty won out.

"That is my not-so-little baby brother, Liam." He was nineteen in the picture, taken three years ago. His interest in health and fitness was evident even back then, in his athletic muscular frame—a good advert for his personal trainer career if, and when, he got a job. I was tall, but huddled barefoot into Liam's six-foot-four bulky frame, I looked tiny. "Blonds aren't my type," I joked, trying again to ease the tension radiating off Nate that left me on edge.

"What is your type, Kara?" he asked accusingly, his face set and eyes assessing.

You. Tall, dark and unbelievably blue eyes—a deadly combination certain to make most women weak at the knees. Last night, before sleeping with him, I'd seen something that gave me hope he wasn't like the rest. At least I thought so; otherwise I wouldn't have handed myself so willingly to him. Now, the hint of suspicion in his question made me think he didn't quite trust my motives.

I didn't get the chance to reply before the intercom buzzed, snapping us from our daze. "That's Ross."

It took a second to process what Nate said, but when I did, the earth seemed to fall away from my feet. He was leaving, relegating me to the same scrapheap as the untrustworthy fickle women from his past.

Nate stalked to the receiver and answered curtly, "I'll be down in a minute." He disappeared into the bedroom, returning a few minutes later with his shoes on and his belongings clasped in his hand.

I gaped at him, trying to remain calm, but fury was bubbling inside of me. With every bit of strength I had, I fought back tears, blinking rapidly as I followed Nate to the front door. "I presumed you were st-staying?" I mumbled, my voice breaking.

He paused when he reached it, hanging his head. The longer strands of hair swung softly as he shook it. The same strands of hair I'd tugged as he gave me the most intense orgasms of my life.

"I can't stay. It wasn't meant to be like this." He turned but kept his eyes lowered and said quietly, "I have to go."

The harrowing pain in my chest grew stronger when he finally lifted his eyes to mine. When he let me see how torn he was, how much inner turmoil he was in, how *guilty* he felt. The anguish in the eyes that held me captive every time I looked into them was heartbreaking.

Nate caught me at the nape. The light touch of his forehead, as he lowered it to mine, forced me to close my eyes. To try and block out everything that had happened. That was happening right now. Nate had fucked me—now he was walking away.

In that moment, I think I hated him.

"I'm sorry," he whispered roughly, thumbs stroking the line of my neck.

I wanted to hit him, fist my hands and pummel them against his chest, scream and shout every bit of abuse I could in his face. More than that, I wanted to wrap him in my arms and stop him leaving. Make him talk and explain what was happening.

Nate pressed his lips to my forehead in a last goodbye, then disappeared without a second glance. I let him leave because I was too stunned to do anything else, and pride prevented me from begging him to stay.

As soon as the door latched shut I lost it. Feeling humiliated, pathetic and foolish over falling for his charms, I charged to the door and gave it the beating I wanted to give him. Why did I stupidly think I'd be any different? It was all about the chase. Now he'd captured me, I was worthless to him.

Needing to vent my frustrations on something else, I stormed to the bedroom and began stripping the bed. I had to erase all traces of Nate. I felt sick as I yanked off the sheets, tormenting me with the memories they held.

They smelt of sex. They smelt of Nate.

I let out a loud, strangled cry and flopped onto the mattress, scrubbing at my face. My chest was tight, aching with despair.

For the first time in a year, I cried over a man.

I don't know how long I stayed there, curled up in the foetal position on my half-stripped bed, hugging my knees and rocking. Through the window, clouds chased across the sky, the sun moved around ready to set on another day. The landline ringing was the only noise that penetrated my daze.

I stumbled into the lounge and answered half-heartedly, expecting it to be Mai and not wanting to discuss what had happened. So it was a big shock to hear my father's voice.

"Is everything okay?" I asked him, calculating through my haze it was almost midnight in England.

"Yes, darling. I couldn't sleep so I decided to call my favourite daughter."

"Dad," I laughed, "I'm your only daughter." I meandered to the desk chair and sat, relieved there wasn't anything seriously wrong. Hearing the rumble of my father's carefree joy brought comfort at precisely the right time. "What's the matter?"

"I dreamt of your mother again." George Collins had married Eliza Harris when she was twenty, after a four-year courtship. They were each others firsts and lasts. Their enduring love, tragically cut short, had kept me believing in the fairytale, long after I'd lost all hope that the happy ending would ever happen for me.

"I dream about her too, sometimes." I touched the photo Nate had pointed out fondly, homesick and grieving for my family. "Do you want to talk about it?"

"It was wonderful. They invariably are," he said mournfully. "I'm all right, you don't have to worry about your old dad. What's happening in your world?"

"Nothing much. Tell me your news instead." I decided the more I got him talking, the quicker his sorrow would lift, and the less likely he'd detect something wrong with me.

He was the greatest father in the world. Growing up, I couldn't recall a single time he'd disciplined me. I'd always been able to discuss anything with him, including relationships, and since my mother had gone, we'd grown closer still. I shoved the chair back and propped both feet on the desk, contentedly listening whilst he told me his plans for the garden. It brought a lump to my throat when he said how much I was missed, and how excited he was to see me next month.

"I miss you, too." Right now more than ever.

"Got a gentleman friend yet?"

"You're so old-fashioned," I told him with a quiet laugh, avoiding an answer.

He laughed. "One day, Kara, one day it will be your time. The man who deserves my darling girl will enter your life and change your world. He won't expect your love; he'll know he has to earn it, treat you how you deserve to be treated, as the most precious gift in the world. Don't ever settle for anything less than one hundred percent commitment."

I placed my hand to my throat, stroking the exact spot Nate had earlier. Stupidly, I thought he understood the sentiments my father was expressing. *Obviously not.* "I love you, dad."

"I love you." His voice shook with emotion, how it always did when he spoke from the heart. My unpleasant break-up with Stuart had affected my family more than I liked. George had always had reservations as to whether he'd been good enough for the apple of his eye. In retrospect, he was right, and I'd vowed to always accept his judgement on any man I met in the future.

Half an hour after ending the call, I snapped my laptop shut on my internet research, wanting to throw it out the window. I was even more pissed off and none the wiser as to what had gone on in Nate's head. I pushed my glasses onto the top of my head. In a fit of petulance, I picked up the tulips and carried them to the kitchen, all the while muttering to myself—"love and romance…caring and commitment…beautiful eyes…"—apparently what they were supposed to be telling me.

"Bullshit." I tossed them into the bin. Then I drew a deep breath and poured a large glass of red.

Yes, I'd fallen for his player lines. Yes, he'd managed to charm my pants off. But no, I refused to let Nate get to me anymore than he had already.

From somewhere, I gathered enough strength to block out the surprising amount of hurt coursing through my veins, and vowed not to give Nate Blake any more of my time.

Tomorrow was another day. And another day could only mean a step further away from the disaster that was my weekend.

Chapter 11

Monday morning I went about my usual routine with a heavy heart. Not only was I having to go to work, I would have to face Mai and all her questions when I got there. She wouldn't pass judgement on what I'd done. No, she would be more pissed off at Nate than I was. It was highly likely she'd head straight to his office and give him a piece of her mind.

I toyed with the idea of calling in sick but decided that would be a huge mistake. I couldn't avoid Nate forever. He owned the fucking company, for God's sake. I drank my coffee in silence staring vacantly at the wall. Then I took a long shower and spent forever deciding what to wear, having no real interest in doing any of it.

I didn't even care when I locked the apartment at 8.45 a.m.—the time I typically arrived at work. I trudged down the stairs and out the door, double-checking my gym bag contents as I headed down the path towards my car. When I glanced up to see where I was going, the last person I expected to see was in front of me. *Nate.*

My breath caught in my throat, my stomach lurched. Then my heart began to pound wildly. *What the hell was he doing here?*

Leaning against the Mercedes, ankles and arms crossed, he stared at me, his face expressionless. Those big blue eyes, however, burnt with passion, hunger, need. Wasn't he content with screwing me over once? Did he think he could commandeer me for another quick fuck before work?

For a long minute I glared at him, rubbing at the tightness in my chest whilst figuring out my next move. I was also irritated because even though I was mad, the rush I got from seeing Nate again caused me to feel unbalanced on my feet.

He pushed off the car and prowled towards me. "*Kara.*" The way he purred it so damn sexily got my attention. How his expression promptly altered, from unabashed lust to empathy, sorrow, even more so.

The dark shadows beneath his usually bright eyes made it clear he hadn't had much sleep last night either. With us both dressed head-to-toe in black, our outfit choices reflected our sombre moods.

"Why are you here?" I choked out. The unexplainable hold he had on me strengthened the closer he came. Nate waited until he was a few inches away before responding.

"I came to talk."

I snickered. "You walking out yesterday means there's nothing left to say."

"Me walking *back* means I have plenty to say."

I scanned him up and down some more. "Sorry, but you wasted a journey." I pushed past him, not interested in hearing his excuses. Nate grabbed my upper arm and urged me firmly against him. He smelt amazing.

"Give me a chance to explain," he implored. He may as well have shouted the words in my ear instead of whisper because the effect was the same. The softness rumbled through my chest and shook my soul.

"I'm already late, I don't have time to chat."

"Get in the car, we can talk on the way." Nate's cautious eyes held mine, quietly pleading.

"You've said enough."

He stood tall and lifted his chin. "We can do this here on the sidewalk or in private. Your choice. But either way, you'll hear what I have to say."

My brow arched. "Where do you get off ordering me around?"

He didn't reply, merely waited. He wasn't going to let this go until he'd said his piece, but I didn't have time to stand and argue. I peered over his shoulder at the Mercedes. There was no way I would be arriving at work in his car with him, providing the workforce with enough gossip to last for weeks. "I'll get in the car if you drop me a block away. I'll walk in by myself."

Nate cocked his head. "Am I that embarrassing?"

No! God no! "I don't want everyone knowing I've fucked the boss."

Nate's eyes widened. Then he leant closer. "We didn't just *fuck*, Kara," he snarled.

"Didn't we?" I stuttered, shaken by his menacing tone. It pained me to say it because I'd given myself to him wholeheartedly. Calling it a fuck didn't convey the intensity in the slightest.

"Don't pretend what happened was merely a convenient interlude for both of us. As much as it was raw and passionate, it went far deeper than that, and you damn well know it." He cupped my cheek, his voice softening. "We made love."

I looked into his eyes and that's when I saw it. Our time together had affected him more than he'd wanted it to. I swallowed past the ache in my heart left by his fear as it fluttered in my chest.

"Let me explain, Kara."

I gripped my car keys so firmly they dug into my hand. "After what you did yesterday, you're lucky I'm even considering a lift." I gave a nonchalant shrug and stared him in the eye. "Take it or leave it." I sounded assured and in control, but never had I been so terrified of walking away from something in my life.

Nate's eyes worked over mine fast, trying to read me. Eventually, he took a deep breath and sighed. "Fine." He relinquished his grip of my arm and opened the rear door. "Now get in the fucking car."

It was a good ten minutes before either of us spoke. I had plenty and nothing to say, but Nate needed to go first. Ross raised the glass dividing screen so we had some privacy. After fumbling agitatedly with my two bags, I set them between us on the seat.

Nate promptly removed them, placing them by his feet. Then he angled his body towards me and took one of my hands. "I'm appalled by my behaviour yesterday. I know how big of a deal it was for you, and—"

"Clearly not that much of one for you," I spat.

Nate winced. "I get you're pissed off, and I deserve everything you have to throw at me, but let me speak before you start accusing me of things that aren't true."

"I was stupid enough to fall for a line," I huffed, freeing my hand and crossing my arms. "I'm sure I wasn't the first. I'm *certain* I won't be the last."

"None of it was a line. I meant every word, I still do. Sex has been straightforward lately." Nate glanced up front to get his bearings, then checked his watch. "It's the only way that's worked. A fuck with no meaning."

"Gee, thanks," I muttered, "you make lousy apologies."

The half-smile lifting a corner of his mouth was his only reaction to my sarcasm. Nate reached for the few tendrils of hair hanging loose from my ponytail and stroked them off my face. I inhaled sharply at the intimacy before his hand went to rest on the seat back by my head.

Self-doubt flooded back into my thoughts. Stuart had broken an already fragile woman—I'd become a stranger to myself. I shuddered at the memory and turned to Nate. Yesterday, *he'd* shattered me again.

"Was the reality of sleeping with me that disappointing? You clearly had high expectations of me. Didn't I give you enough excitement? I mean, I know it's been a while, but was it really that bad? Was I frigid and—"

"Christ, stop it!" Nate thumped the headrest in anger. I scrambled away to the corner in fear. His face was ravaged with fury. "I *hate* that I've made you think that way. Stop degrading yourself. You did *nothing* wrong, it was—"

"You?" I finished his sentence.

"Yeah." Nate let out a sigh of defeat and sagged back into the seat. "Me."

"Wow." I shook my head, disappointed and disillusioned. "And I thought that cliché was only used in films…"

"Is it the English reserve that makes you appear all shy and reticent? Because you're not afraid to let me know how badly I've fucked up when it counts, are you?"

Rolling my lower lip between my teeth, I raised my eyes to meet his. The tiny sparkle of amusement in them tugged a little smile to my mouth. Nate didn't speak, watching me worry the ring on my finger; a nervous habit when I was agitated and upset.

"I don't like not having control," Nate went on after a few minutes. "Of anything, but especially my emotions. They complicate things. You made me—" His jaw ticked as he shook his head. "I'd willingly lose control of everything, but there's no way in hell I'm losing you."

What? Hadn't that already happened? I allowed Nate to watch me as I quietly worked over what he'd said. The man was giving me a headache. "You're not making any sense."

"I know," he said softly, stroking my brow to ease the worry. "I lost count of the number of times I picked up the phone to apologise. I even drove back to your apartment and sat outside for hours."

Hearing Nate's confession gave me hope. "Why didn't you come up?" I asked quietly, reaching for his hand. I turned it palm up, and rubbed my thumb along the base of his long fingers that talked to me with their caresses.

"I didn't know what to say, how to make it right. I was too scared I'd fuck up again. I couldn't risk that happening."

"You could've brought me white tulips and begged for my forgiveness," I suggested with a hint of humour.

Nate's eyes flickered with surprise and joy. "You did your research?"

I nodded.

"Kara, I lay awake all night trying to understand how you'd gotten into my head so fast." Both of Nate's hands covered mine and squeezed gently. "I failed, in case you were wondering."

His arched brow made me smile. His worry had abated, but anguish still clouded his eyes. "I've *never* been so frightened by a feeling as I was when I gazed into your eyes as we made love."

My stomach flipped at the confirmation he'd felt it, too. I let my head fall back against the headrest and sighed. Was he scared of losing me or his own identity, the way I had when I tried conforming to another person's idea of who I should be? I had to be strong but wasn't sure if that meant giving us a chance or walking away. "You really hurt me, Nate."

"I know." Nate traced the shell of my ear, fingering the diamond stud in my lobe. "God, I know." I felt his touch in my breasts when the shiver hardened my nipples against my bra. Then he leant closer and whispered, "I'll do everything in my power to make it up to you. I need you to forgive me, Kara." He stroked his nose along my jaw. "Please accept my lousy apology. For both of us."

This time I felt it in my heart. I massaged the twinge in my chest and took a deep breath, hoping to slow my racing heartbeat.

How could I want him as much as I did right now? After what he'd done? I must have a death wish because the only place I could see us heading was to a major crash and burn. Yet despite all Nate's warnings, all my insecurities and driving need for commitment he knew I wanted, but we both feared wasn't possible, I chose to grasp hold of the tiny bit of hope he'd offered me. "Is there an us?"

"I hope so, baby. I really hope so."

The car stopped and Ross stepped out. When I spotted the deli I often used for lunch I realised we were only a block from the office. "But I still want a proper relationship and you don't," I said, facing Nate as I unclipped my seat belt.

"I'm not averse to the idea." He waited a beat, then said, "If it's with you."

Whoa. Where did that come from? The warmth in his eyes grabbed my heart and twisted it. His expression was gut-wrenchingly raw, but tormented. Like he was going way out of his comfort zone into a place he'd sworn never to go again. "I can't make any promises, other than I won't fuck you around anymore."

If Nate was prepared to go out on a limb for me and risk what he considered important, I had to do the same. "Okay then."

Nate brushed a thumb over my cheek. "Can I see you again? Tonight?"

"I have yoga," I said, pointing to the bag by his feet.

"What time?"

"Straight after work. We usually have dinner afterwards."

"See me instead," he urged. "I'll take you to dinner."

"Nate." I placed a hand over his. It would be easy to give in, but I wasn't about to drop everything. "I need some time to get used to this."

Nate's hand fell from my face, his brow furrowing. "Didn't we just agree this"—he gestured between the two of us—"is happening?"

The last couple of weeks had offered me a glimpse of the man behind the unbelievably handsome façade, but I wasn't stupid. Nate caught the attention of every woman he passed, even when I'd been with him. If he wanted, he could date a different one for every night he wasn't with me. "I think so, I just—"

"You *think* so?" His mouth etched in a thin line. "I'm offering you the commitment you've asked for. What else do you want?"

I took a deep breath. "Monogamy."

Nate's head drew back with a raised brow. "That goes without saying." He sounded insulted.

"You think you can do that?" I asked, surprised he agreed so readily.

"I don't share."

"I meant from you. I don't sleep around, Nate."

"Neither do I. Everything I want is here, in this car, right now." He tugged me roughly to him until our mouths collided. Every bit of my being sprung to life as his tongue worked in firm, insistent strokes with mine. Taking my hand, Nate placed it over his hardening cock and squeezed. "*That's* how much I want you. No one else gets me hard purely by talking. Only you."

Flustered, I drew my hand away. The road outside crowded with cars of people rushing late to work, oblivious to anything going on around them. I, however, was acutely alert to every little thing, my awareness of Nate heightened to the point where I could hear him breathing, feel his heartbeat, see the fortitude in his eyes.

"Let's get to know each other before we write this off." Nate's eyes pleaded with me.

"I'd say you got to know me very well."

"I did." He smirked. "I'd like you to get well acquainted with me, too."

Drifting over his sophisticated exterior, picturing how good he looked underneath, I longed to explore his staggeringly fit body the way he had mine. It meant a lot to hear he wanted that, too.

"I want to see you again, Kara."

"What about tomorrow?" I offered an alternative.

Nate ran a hand through his hair with frustration. "I have a prior arrangement early evening." Then his lips curled into a wicked smile. "We can meet afterwards."

It was tempting, but I wasn't about to become his booty call, confirming all my assumptions about him and us. "I'm sure you can wait until Wednesday."

"Two whole days?" The playful downturn of his enticing mouth made me smile. His finger stroked the bridge of my nose and down to the tip. "I doubt it, but I'll take it. I guess I have no choice."

"I guess you don't."

Nate leant forward and tenderly brushed his lips over mine. I was held captive by the wonder and gratitude sparkling in his eyes. "Shall I get Ross back in to drive us?"

"I meant what I said about keeping this between us. It's early days."

"I understand," he said evenly, straightening his jacket as he sat back, "but you can't hide us forever."

I had to maintain some self-preservation. This *us* was still unclear. I hadn't decided if I'd made a huge mistake or not, and needed to keep some emotional distance. Not acknowledging the truth behind Nate's words, I wiped the tiny smudge of pink gloss from his lips with my thumb, curious what state my own must be in.

"Bye, Nate. Enjoy your day."

"You too, baby." Nate's glorious smile lit his entire face and made me hesitate in climbing out the car. It was breathtaking.

Outside, I said goodbye to Ross, then stood on the pavement and watched the car drive away. Still dazed by the mornings unforeseen events, I slung my gym bag over my shoulder and stumbled in a dream to work.

I rushed through the security turnstiles and dashed to an opening lift. Unsurprisingly, given my lateness, it was empty. I smacked the button and glanced at the electronic time display as the doors began closing. I was five minutes late for a meeting and had missed my preparation time. A hand appeared, sending the metal doors opening again. Cursing under my breath, I silently willed them to hurry as I stepped aside to make way. I was met with the sight of Mr Nate Blake casually stepping in, his eyes shining with impure thoughts.

"Good morning," he said smoothly, maintaining a serious, unaffected expression as he positioned himself next to me.

"Morning," I replied, wondering where he'd appeared from. The scent of his body wash filled the air, bringing images of wet, naked bodies to mind. Desire pulsed through me, reaching my face to give away my sinful thoughts. I shifted restlessly as the car moved, blowing a wayward strand of hair from my face.

In such a confined space, the energy between us was magnetic. It was palpable, the spark from Nate's touch searing me when his arm brushed mine as he reached inside his jacket and took out his phone.

"I'm desperate to press you up against the wall and kiss you senseless," Nate warned, fixing on the screen of his phone. "I'm assuming you'd rather not put on a floor show for security?" He nodded up to the corner where a small camera flashed. "Did I assume correctly? Because I'll gladly let you prove me wrong if that's the case."

The car slowed and the doors opened on the Eighth Floor. I sighed with relief. "This is me," I croaked, focusing on the empty foyer ahead.

"Maybe next time," he said hoarsely, giving my arse a discreet pinch that sent me stumbling forward on shaky legs. *What the hell?* From the safety of the lobby, I faced him. He stood there with the smuggest grin and winked as the doors shut between us.

As my weak legs carried me to my office, Mai rushed alongside me clutching some papers. "Kara! You know what the time is?"

Still in shock, I couldn't muster a response. Mai tugged my arm and stopped me walking. I tried to normalise my breathing and calm down after my encounter in the lift. She inspected me closely, her eyes squinting. Then they grew bigger as realisation eventually dawned on her.

"Oh. My. God. You fucked him!"

Chapter 12

It was almost 1 p.m. when I returned to my office after the late start to my weekly planning meeting with Michael and began checking my Inbox.

Mai swooped in, kicking the door shut with a leopard print heel, her hands full of lunch and bottles of water. I set my glasses on the desk, eyeing her suspiciously, amused at the same time. "Hungry, Mai?"

"For details, yes!" She passed me a drink and sandwich and dropped into the chair opposite, big brown eyes begging me to reveal all. "Three hours is a long time to wait! Gimme the deets."

"Not much to tell really," I teased.

"Jesus K, you've been screwed outta your mind!" Mai shot me a narrow-eyed glare and pouted her full pink lips.

"Is it that obvious?"

"Only an orgasm or two could put that colour in your cheeks." She shrugged, balancing her sandwich on her crossed knee. "What's he like in bed? Bet he doesn't need a road map to find his way around a woman's body…" she sighed dreamily.

"Mai," I warned. We were discussing someone who's private life was of keen interest to many. It was imperative I didn't reveal too much. "Not discussing it."

Mai scowled and changed course. "Where'd he take you?"

I filled her in as we ate. She was impressed and cooed in all the right places. She was also notably in awe of Nate's straight-talking, gaping when I repeated the words that had basically sealed the deal.

"Where'd you do the nasty?" she mumbled through a mouthful of food. "His place?"

"Mine."

"Ooh, nice move." Mai nodded approvingly. "You made *him* do the walk of shame."

"I didn't have to. Nate walked himself out after admitting he'd made a huge mistake."

Mai sprayed water across the desk as she lowered the bottle from her mouth. "Are you *joking*?"

"Do I look like I'm laughing?" I grabbed a tissue to mop up the mess.

Mai set the remains of her lunch on the desk, then sagged into the chair. "Fucking shit. I hoped he was different."

I waited whilst she let it sink in. After a minute, she sat forward and clasped my hand. "Sorry chick."

"Mai," I snickered, "you're the last person who needs to apologise."

"You're right." She stood and brushed down her skirt. "Blake might be the boss, but no man uses my friend and gets away with it."

Before she went and made an utter fool of herself and got fired, I made her sit back down and told her all about my interesting car journey to work.

"That explains the lateness this morning," Mai muttered, still not fully satisfied.

"Was I wrong to ask for some dignity and arrive alone?"

"Hell no!"

I knew she'd get it. Then her lips curled.

"I, on the other hand, would've made him escort me, so everyone who saw us knew *exactly* what we'd done." Mai had fantastic self-belief and didn't care for others opinions on her. I both envied and admired her for it.

"He seemed genuinely sorry, I could see it in his eyes. You can't fake that, no matter what lies you can tell."

"Bet you didn't have to fake an orgasm." Mai grinned, her brows wiggling up and down. I wasn't surprised the conversation had returned to her favourite topic.

"No," I smirked, swivelling my chair side-to-side as I finished my lunch, "not even the fourth."

"Oh my God!" she cried, fanning her face. "I knew he'd be a good fuck!"

I choked on the last bite. She dismissed my shock with a wave of her hand. "If a guy gave me multiples like that, it'd be a sure fire way of getting my ass back in his bed again. You seeing him tonight?"

"No." I pursed my lips, eyeing her warily whilst considering how to phrase my next statement. "Keep this quiet for a while, please?" I implored, twisting the lid off my bottle. "Don't tell Robyn or Jenna."

"How the hell do you expect me to keep this quiet? This is, like, the most amaze-balls news ever. *Ever!*"

"I'm serious. It needs to stay private."

Mai wasn't happy, but eventually she held up her hands. "Okay, okay, won't breathe a word." She scrunched up the rubbish and stood. "I need some nicotine, you coming?"

"I better not. Michael knows I was late."

"Shall I bring some caffeine back?"

"Please." I reached into my bag for my purse and handed her some money. "Take this for lunch."

Mai earned significantly less than I did, yet she regularly treated me. Pleased she wasn't in an argumentative mood, she took it without a fuss and skipped out my office. I dropped my purse back in my bag, then went to the window.

People below were going about their business without a care, some running to refresh their over-stimulated minds, others meandering along with friends in the glorious sun.

By agreeing to give Nate another chance, I'd been handed an entirely new set of issues to worry about. He was certainly gifted when it came to satisfying a woman, and a man with his wealth of experience was admittedly a turn on, but too much experience became an instant turn-off. Exactly how many women had he slept with for me to be compared to?

I couldn't deny liking the way he made me feel, both in and out of bed. The old Kara had peeked through the layers of protective armour and insecurity in those few times already. Nate made that happen. And when he smiled at me?

God, that smile was fatal. It could do serious damage to me, because when it reached his eyes, it was so easy to trust him.

"Even with his monumental fuck up, you're still glowing," Mai said, heading back in with my cappuccino twenty minutes later. "I always said a Valentine's baby should never be celibate. It didn't suit you at all."

I often thought it ironic my birthday was February 14, considering how disastrous my love life had been of late.

Mai's smile grew impish. "I've just seen lover boy in the lobby."

"And?" I sat, noticing the heart shape in the chocolatey froth. Mai was becoming quite the barista.

"Looked like he was walking on air. Didn't even stop to flirt with me. Can you believe that?" she asked with mock disgust.

I let her get to the door before having enough courage to stop her. "Is Nate ever in your trashy magazines?"

She shrugged. "Tends to be pictured at social events, nothing scandalous."

I tipped my head, a little mollified. "Is he with people?"

"You mean women?"

I nodded, feeling stupid for not asking directly.

"Sometimes." Mai eyed me for a minute, then said, "If you want to know about his exes, why don't you just ask him?"

"Because then I'd be subjecting myself to similar questions I'm not ready to acknowledge."

We both noticed Michael approaching at the same time. I pretended to be working, but Mai stayed in the doorway. "Kara," she said softly. "I'm sure Nate's a good guy. Don't stress yourself out."

Mai's words placated me, but for the rest of the afternoon I fought the temptation to hit Google. Half of me wanted to know what I was letting myself in for, the other wanted to bury my head in the sand. *Ignorance is bliss.* I knew I'd end up comparing myself to his other women, and all my misgivings would immediately become apparent once more. Not quite ready to see him with other women, I packed my curious thoughts into a box to deal with another day.

"YOU seem different. Dare I say happy?" Mai probed as we descended to the main lobby shortly after five.

"I think I am." I popped a segment of orange in my mouth and handed some to Mai. It was our usual pre-workout routine and a great way to get some additional hydration.

"I'd be worried if you weren't after spending the weekend fucking *him*." Mai linked her arm in mine and nudged me to the left as we strolled through the cool interior.

Nate stood, hands in pockets, legs slightly apart, chatting to a security guard. The blonde from his office suite was there, too, and the raven-haired beauty who manned the main reception. Seeing her instantly got me suspicious, because she was the same woman Nate had flirted with the only time I'd ever seen him here before. It was entirely feasible they could have slept together in the past. She was very attractive.

His eyes found mine as he maintained their conversation but focused solely on me. He raked my body the same way he had at the bar.

"Wanna go over?" Mai asked, "Because he's looking at you like he wants to eat you alive." Luckily she still had my arm, otherwise I might have fallen over. What was happening to me? The way he looked at me had my stomach flurrying with yearning, my body wanting to be touched. *By him.*

"He's busy. Let's go or we'll be late." I picked up the pace and steered her to the doors.

A pretentious giggle bounced off the vast marbled lobby walls, managing to be heard amongst all other noise. I glanced back over my shoulder. The blonde had gone, but the other woman still had her head thrown back with a flirtatious giggle. Nate was still watching me, only now he looked aggrieved, scowling as he tilted his head, adjusting his cufflinks. I held his gaze, smiled briefly, then pushed through the revolving doors without looking back.

The heat outside was no relief to my irritated skin. Mai peered at me but stayed silent—so unlike her—as she lit up. I answered my phone when it rang without checking the caller ID.

"What's wrong?" Nate asked gruffly. "Are we okay? Why did you ignore me?"

"I didn't ignore you," I scoffed. "You were a little preoccupied, that's all." Mai flashed a grin when she realised who was calling.

"Preoccupied with thoughts of you," he corrected. That made the irrational stab of jealousy even harder to deal with. "I'm respecting your request for discretion, but finding it hard not to follow you out. Turn around."

I did as he asked. The building's reflective glass made it impossible to see inside. "I didn't get the chance to tell you this morning, but you look wonderful."

"Thank you." I kicked the gravel off the path, back into the decorative hedging lining the walkway. I was flattered and embarrassed, with a touch of guilt over my unspoken accusation. Trying to be rational, I told myself it shouldn't matter if they had history, so long as it wasn't still going on.

"Can I give you both a lift to yoga?" he asked. "Ross can drive us."

I turned and saw Ross waiting by the Mercedes. "I appreciate the offer, but we can walk. It's not far."

I wished I could see back inside, see who he was with, see whether he was flirting. I hated being this possessive already. "Why were you in Reception? Talking to those men?"

"There's been a few security breaches lately. My team need to be more vigilant until it's resolved. Plus," he added, his voice lowering intimately, "I hoped I might see you."

I exhaled in a rush, relieved. Mai was texting on her phone, then held it up to show me we were going to be late. "I have to go, Nate."

"Someone's got an attack of the green-eyed monster," Mai sang, relinking arms after I'd hung up.

I couldn't reply because Ross acknowledged us with a wave over. "Good evening, Miss Collins," he said, opening the rear door.

"Oh no, Ross, I'm not getting a ride tonight."

Mai sniggered. I glared at her, covering her mouth with my hand to stifle the rest of her laughter. "Mr Blake is inside, though," I told him. "I'm sure he won't be much longer. Have a good evening."

"And you." Ross straightened and clasped his hands in front of him again.

As we crossed the car park, Mai was still giggling between puffs. "You're so childish sometimes," I scolded, sharing the last of the orange between us.

"Sorry, it's just, your choice of words couldn't be more apt." I rolled my eyes as we headed to the gym. "Who was that guy anyway?" she asked.

I answered her questions, and by the time we arrived and met the other girls she seemed to have regained her composure.

THIS felt good. I let my head fall back to the damp white tiles of the steam room wall and closed my eyes on a contented sigh. The girls were dissecting Mai's weekend trip with a fine-toothed comb. I listened, offering an opinion occasionally, but memories of my own dirty weekend infiltrated my thoughts.

I remembered Nate's lips pressed against my neck, the words he spoke. And the way he made me feel…how he made love to me…

I blew out a large breath and wiped the sweat from my forehead with the corner of the towel wrapped around my body.

"Everything okay, Kara?" Jenna bumped shoulders with me and adjusted her bikini top. I was ridiculed every week for not wearing one whilst the three of them paraded their lean bodies in tiny two-pieces. "You're very quiet."

Silence descended and all eyes swung to me.

"She's probably a bit tired girls," Mai chipped in.

"Ooh, why's that?" Jenna asked. "Hot date last night?"

"Hot isn't the word. Sizzling might be close..." Mai blabbed as she poured water onto the coals, adding a sound effect to her unfiltered observation.

The excited squeals and clamouring for more echoed around the sauna. I managed to answer their persistence without revealing *who* it was—"we met a couple of weeks ago...been on a few dates...yes, I'm seeing him again...no, they won't be meeting him anytime soon..."

On the way home in Mai's car, I reprimanded her. She apologised profusely, whilst gleefully revelling in the knowledge that she was the only one who knew the biggest news that—according to her—would have the tabloids in a spin.

Later, as I drifted into a contented sleep, I hadn't forgotten the events of the past twenty-four hours or so, but for my own sanity chose not to dwell on them. Whether I liked it or not, Nate had stirred feelings in me that had been dead for a long time. And the tiny voice in the back of my mind that rarely made an appearance had chosen this moment to tell me I had to give him a chance, because I believed in him more than I was ready to admit.

EVEN THOUGH it was unusually cold, I breezed into work with a spring in my step and a sense of serenity absent from my life for a while. Drinking my cappuccino whilst waiting for my computer to load, a frisson of excitement rushed through me when my mobile rang and Nate's name illuminated the screen.

"Good morning, Mr Blake," I answered perkily, rolling the lip of the mug along my mouth and grinning inanely. He laughed, the mellow sound curling my stomach into a tight knot of desire.

"Good morning, Miss Collins," he replied in that sexy tone that sounded even more arousing first thing when he'd barely woken up. "How are you?"

"Fine, thanks. You?"

"Not so good." His tone switched from playful to serious. "I have to cancel our date."

"Oh..." I slumped into the chair, returning my mug to the desk. Warning bells started ringing in my head again. Had I made a huge mistake in giving him another chance?

"Sorry," he whispered.

"Whatever." Feeling way out of my depth and uncertain of where I stood, I went to hang up. I had to protect myself and guard my heart by not gifting him the opportunity to hurt it again. Nausea washed over me in waves.

"Kara?" he prompted after my weighty silence. With my finger hovering over the 'End Call' button, I swallowed hard and brought the phone back to my ear.

"I'm not interested in excuses," I managed, my stomach cramping. "Truth hurts, but at least it's honest."

Nate let out an exasperated sigh. "You want the truth? Call me arrogant but I cleared my calendar for last night expecting to see you. I agreed to tomorrow without appreciating I have a business function to attend."

Oh. "I didn't realise…I'm sure you'll have a great time." I hadn't intended it to sound as sarcastic as it did. I scrubbed at my face, exhausted by my own internal battle of wanting to have faith, but unsure if I could.

"Dressing up and walking the red carpet isn't as glamorous as it sounds," Nate said dejectedly.

"Believe me, I don't envy you one bit. I'd hate living in the spotlight." Nothing could be worse than being under constant media scrutiny. My hostility towards Nate dissipated when I remembered how uncomfortable he was with the attention, too.

"Having the same conversation repeatedly becomes tedious very quickly."

My brow rose. Was he indirectly letting me know there were only so many times he was willing to reassure me before he got pissed off?

"Be patient, Kara. The next couple weeks will be chaotic, but after that it should settle down." His tormented voice made my heart ache.

Resting my elbow on the desk, I spun the mug between my fingers. "We can do another time. Let me know when you're free, and I'll check my calendar." I didn't want Nate assuming I'd hang around, waiting for him to fit me in.

"I will. First, I have to go kick someone's ass. Talk later."

IT wasn't long after lunch when Michael rushed into my office, running a hand frantically through his greying hair, the other resting on his hip. He played squash every Tuesday lunchtime, and obviously hadn't been back long because his hair was still damp from a shower, and his face beetroot red from exertion. "Where are you with the Star business case projections?"

Pleased with myself, I said, "It's completed." Michael visibly relaxed. I began searching my folders on the server for the file. "Shall I send it to you?"

"No. Mr Blake wants to review it. He's called us upstairs for a meeting."

I choked at the mention of Nate's name. *"Now?"* Behind Michael, Mai sat at her workstation gaping. She'd obviously heard him. "It's all self-explanatory... he can review it...you can explain...answer his questions...you don't need me there..." I was rambling, talking wildly with my hands.

"Kara!" Michael glowered at me, shocked by my odd and thoroughly unprofessional reaction. I shut up immediately. "You did the work. Running Mr Blake through it will increase your exposure."

"You're right," I mumbled, clasping my hands to stop them flailing. "Sorry." This was all I needed, and proved my concerns over sleeping with the boss were entirely justified. How was I supposed to conduct a meeting with a man I'd recently seen nude? I'd heard the saying about overcoming nerves when dealing with people by imagining them naked, but really, this wouldn't take much imagination.

"C'mon, we don't want to be late." Michael's words disappeared along with him as he headed out the office.

With trembling hands and legs, I stood, gathering my tablet, and followed. I glared at Mai as I passed, wordlessly pleading to be rescued from this imminent calamity. All she did was shrug, quietly amused by my predicament, trying and failing to hide a smirk with her hand.

Travelling up in the lift, I fidgeted with my outfit, picking imaginary lint from my skirt and ensuring my blouse was straight. My hair was piled high on my head, and tucked on top of the loosely pinned tresses were my glasses. No avoiding it, I was going to have to wear them.

"You'll be okay," Michael assured me as we stepped into the vestibule, "he really isn't an ogre."

I smiled weakly, his assurance having the opposite effect as my stomach knotted. I knew exactly how tender Nate could be. The blonde sat behind the desk buzzed us through. She greeted Michael by name and asked us to take a seat, informing us Mr Blake would join us shortly.

I can do this. I repeated the mantra as we neared the seating area, taking deep breaths, my shoulders back and head held high. Before we could sit, Nate strode purposefully towards us from his office and I lost all focus.

"Michael, thanks for coming at short notice," Nate greeted him brusquely. He was without the jacket to his black pinstripe three-piece. A crisp white shirt and glacier blue silk tie were neatly tucked beneath the waistcoat, and the trousers draped over polished black wingtips. When I reached his face, I noticed his gaze had snagged on the black-rimmed glasses perched on my head.

Then they dropped to meet mine. A sensual smile crept across his mouth that lit his entire face. If I didn't know better, I'd say he found the idea of me wearing them exciting.

"This is Kara Collins. Not sure you've met before?" Michael introduced us. My eyes darted from Michael back to meet Nate's amused expression. Both his hands extended towards me and took one of mine.

"Oh, yes," he murmured in that tone reserved solely for me, "we've met before. And the pleasure was *all* mine."

Nate's suggestive smirk made my face flush. His bright eyes sparkled, waiting for my reaction. My body heated, my nipples hardening as his thumbs rubbed over the back of my hand, the same way they'd caressed my breasts.

"Ahem." Michael cleared his throat a little too obviously, causing us both to hurriedly let go.

"Let's use the meeting room." Regaining his composure, Nate pushed the door open and Michael strolled through. There were ten chairs around a large oak table. Michael went to the far end and I started to follow.

"Please," Nate said, pulling a chair out, "sit here." It was the opposite end to where my boss was now settling into his seat. I went from Michael back to Nate, who nodded encouragingly. Warily, I lowered into the leather office chair, setting my tablet on the table. I jumped when Nate's hands came around my shoulders briefly before he took the seat beside me.

Glancing over at Michael, alone the other side of the gleaming wooden table, he appeared nervous, which didn't inspire much confidence in me. He couldn't see my tablet at all, so I was going to have to do this alone.

"So, what do you have for me?" Nate asked smoothly.

I swallowed and flipped open the cover on my tablet. I hesitated for a long minute before finally relenting. Shuffling my chair closer, I lowered the glasses onto the bridge of my nose, clearing my throat as I took a discreet sideways glance at Nate.

His eyes flamed, but he gave nothing away to Michael. Composed and at ease, he stretched his legs, hooking a foot around the back of my right ankle and eased my legs apart.

Fuck. I squirmed in my seat. *I couldn't do this.*

Chapter 13

The next thirty minutes were the longest of my life. Sitting so close was a clever ploy on Nate's part, because I spent the entire meeting trying to remain professional and answer questions whilst discreetly restraining his wandering hand beneath the table.

Forecasts and variances had never sounded so sexy when they were being discussed by the influential male beside me with a voice dripping of sex. Not content with only massaging my knee, he'd tried progressively moving his roaming hand further up my thigh, getting the surprise of his life when he discovered what I was wearing.

I flushed with relief when the blonde interrupted the meeting and Nate had to leave to take an urgent call. It took him a moment to stand, and for the first time, I saw a slightly flustered side to the man normally so held together.

Michael was telling me of his dinner plans for his wife's birthday when the blondes soft drawl interrupted our conversation as we passed reception. "Excuse me, Miss Collins?"

"Yes?" I expected her to continue, but she said nothing else, preferring to tidy up instead. "I'll catch up with you later," I told an equally flummoxed Michael when the lift arrived.

He hesitated, before giving me a "Sure" and stepping in.

The blonde had a small elfin face, her edgy pixie cut suiting her perfectly. She smiled kindly though her grey eyes seemed bemused. "Mr Blake wants to see you in his office."

Oh? I touched my cheek as the blush started creeping from my chest.

“Go straight in, no need to knock.” She pointed to his office, nodding her head in encouragement.

“Er…thanks.” All too aware of my tremulous voice, I walked towards the closed door of Nate’s office. By the time I reached it I was breathless with expectation.

He was in the middle of a heated conversation when I entered, reclining in his executive chair with his back to me. One arm stretched behind him, rubbing his neck, the other tapped the knee of his crossed leg. He spun around when the door latching shut alerted him to my presence. “I believe we’re done here,” he said evenly into the handsfree earpiece.

Slowly, he rose to his feet.

“Kara.” Nate tossed the earpiece onto the desk and prowled towards me, loosening his tie and undoing the top button of his shirt. He stepped me away from the door, taking a moment to lock it. Lust clouded the determination in his eyes as they stayed on me.

“Hi.” A low hum of excitement swirled in my belly and down between my legs.

Removing the tablet from my hands and tossing it on the sofa behind me, Nate cupped my face and covered my mouth with his. I savoured the sweet taste of his tongue against mine, each stroke reminding me how much I’d missed him. How much I’d missed the reality of him, as I wrapped my arms around his waist and pressed my body closer.

“That last hour has been torture,” he said roughly. “I’ve been desperate to do that since I touched you outside the meeting room.”

Suddenly, I was in his arms. “What are you doing?” I yelped with a laugh.

Nate carried me to his desk and carefully lowered me onto the edge, pushing aside papers littering the polished surface. He sank into his chair and positioned it between my open legs. “This,” he said, sounding breathless.

I watched in silence as his eyes drifted ravenously over my legs, his hands curving above my knees then sliding higher beneath the hem of my fluted pencil skirt.

“Stopping me earlier,” he murmured, massaging my thighs as he glanced up through impossibly long lashes. “I lost concentration, picturing your legs in these glorious silky stockings, fantasising about how good you’d look spread across that boardroom table wearing them and very little else.”

Nate shoved my skirt up my thighs and sucked in a breath. He traced the lacy edge of each thigh-high, eyes fixed on every move his dexterous fingers made.

This time, I didn't stop him from exploring.

He dipped his head and nipped the bare flesh above the stocking, shooting a signal directly to the now damp spot between my legs.

"Now," I whimpered, as he moved to the other leg and did it again, "you get an idea. That persistence paid off again."

Nate lifted his head, pure lust blazing in his dark eyes. His mouth opened to speak, then his lips curled into a salacious grin. "Lucky me."

I wanted him badly. But we couldn't do anything here, not in his office with the blonde outside. I shut my eyes to banish the excruciating vulnerability washing over me when Nate spread my legs further. His face was so close to me it was unbearable. Every nip, each titillating lick was weakening me.

"Hmm, your arousal is intoxicating," he groaned, sliding his nose over my lace panties.

"Oh, God," I panted, gripping the edge of the desk until my knuckles turned white.

"If you didn't have to be decent the rest of the day, I'd rip this skirt off. I'm dying to taste you again." Nate pushed up my skirt until it bunched around my waist like a belt. He fisted my panties. "I'll settle for these."

The sound of them shredding made me gasp. A low rumble of yearning shuddered through Nate as he cupped my bare arse and slid me to the edge of his desk.

"Nate…no." I tried, weakly, to stop him, but I was too late. Leaning back on my hands for support, I shuddered as Nate licked up to my clit. *"Fuck!"*

"I want you, Kara. Don't try and resist me." His tongue was insistent, his hands pressing against my inner thighs, holding me open, immobilising any attempt I made to close them. He moaned appreciatively against my wet flesh, making my stomach clench and sending a wave of shivers through me.

"We're at work." I fought desperately to cling to the last bit of reason I had, but it was useless. My head fell back as I gave in, lifting my hips, offering more of myself to him. This man knew no bounds when it came to his accomplished oral skills, working me into a frenzy as skilfully, he brought me closer to the brink.

"I'm growing addicted to your sweet taste, baby," he murmured before gently sucking.

Spread wide on his desk, I was utterly defenceless. Desperate for some resistance, I pressed the soles of my Mary-Jane's against the armrests of his chair and pushed hard against his mouth when his tongue dipped inside. *"God…"*

Nate tasted me, licking, teasing me in the most intimate place. I shoved a hand in his hair, gripping tight, both of us moaning in unrestrained ecstasy.

Two hands came around my lower back for support, revealing Nate's intimate, and accurate, knowledge of my body as I teetered on the edge of an explosive orgasm. The sight of him between my legs was all I needed to detonate around him.

"Fuck!" I panted between stifled cries. *"Nate."*

His grip tightened, urging me closer, taking it all like he couldn't get enough, groaning wildly. My legs shook as the lone arm supporting me buckled, all my limbs weakened by the orgasm engulfing my body.

Dazed, I grew aware of Nate standing and folded into his soothing embrace. As I nestled against his chest, his heart raced, pounding loudly in my ear. Cocooned in his arms, my exhilaration was gradually replaced with content as I came down from my high.

Nate tipped my head back. His hair was ruffled, slightly damp at the roots, and his clean-shaven cheeks flushed a pale pink. "How's that for an apology?"

I lifted a shoulder coyly. "Not bad."

A smile threatened his lips as he traced a finger along mine. "For such an exquisite mouth, it can be extremely crude sometimes."

I bit my lip shyly, ashamed by my cries of pleasure. Apparently I swore aloud when I was mindlessly turned on as well.

"It's kinda sexy"—he lowered his voice—"as are these." He removed the glasses from the top of my head and carefully put them on me. "Why, only now, am I discovering you wear these?"

Embarrassed, I shrugged and placed them on the desk beside me. "I only wear them for computer work and watching TV. Sometimes driving if I'm tired."

Nate licked his lips and his concentration wavered slightly. When he let out a small murmur, I realised he was tasting me still. His head tilted. "Stockings, *glasses*, and not much else…"

Laughing, I hugged him. That's when I discovered he was hard. *Very hard.*

"Need some help with this?" I asked, worried about his response. Purposely, I licked my lips as I moved my hands from his back to cup him.

Nate's eyes flashed to my mouth, turning hot with want. "You have no idea how desperate I am to fuck that delicious mouth of yours."

Warmth flooded me. I took a deep breath before swallowing to moisten my dry mouth. Nate had no understanding of how reassuring those words were. Just as I reached for his belt, a timid voice crackled through the speakerphone on his desk behind me. "Mr Blake…um, sorry but, um…your next appointment is here."

"Fuck!" Nate raked a hand through his hair then pressed a button to answer. "I'll be out shortly, Riley." He stilled my hand over his zip. "I'm going to have to wait for that treat, baby."

I was disappointed, but the promise of tasting him, hearing he wanted me to, made me salivate.

"Here," Nate said, helping me off the desk, "come freshen up." He smoothed down my skirt and straightened my blouse.

He led me to a private bathroom off his office, complete with shower and closet, and left me alone. Floor to ceiling glossy white tiled walls, broken by a vertical strip of black tile running down the centre of the shower that wasn't massive, but definitely big enough for two.

My skirt wasn't too crumpled, and after adjusting my stockings I was reasonably presentable, but my hair was a mess. Behind me was a tall black shelving unit stacked with fluffy white towels and toiletries. I found a comb and hastily pulled it through my hair before tying it into a simple ponytail.

I shouted for Nate to come in when he knocked at the door. He eyed me curiously, with some amusement. "Got everything you need?"

"Um…sort of." I'd managed to restore my appearance, but it was my nakedness beneath my skirt I was more concerned with. I stepped out of his way to let him splash his face with cold water.

"What do you need?" he asked, taking the towel I handed him and patting his face dry.

With my back to the large silver ornate mirror hanging over the vanity, I set about unbuttoning his waistcoat so I could straighten his tie. Placing both hands on his hips, he let me dress him, watching fondly as I did.

"I don't suppose you have any spare underwear?" I asked. Nate's mouth curved the same time as my own. He let me finish then went into the closet.

"These do?" He wiggled his brows, shaking a pair of black Ralph Lauren boxer briefs in front of me.

I snatched them from him and shooed him to the door. "Out!" I smacked his perfectly rounded arse as he passed, laughing. Basking for a moment in this elation, I was happy and it showed. My body language was different. I stood taller, more confidently, and my eyes and skin were luminous. I glanced at the closed door, thinking of the man on the other side.

Nate had really got my head in a spin. Being with him made me feel things I thought I'd never feel again. Like a drug I was gradually becoming hooked on, I craved him when he wasn't there. I was falling far too quickly.

And that scared the hell out of me.

"All done?" Nate asked, striding to meet me when I joined him in his office.

"Yes, thank you." I took my belongings from him. "I should get back. You have no idea what I'm going to face when I get back downstairs." Mai would be filling her head with lewd ideas, having no idea how close to the mark she'd be.

"One more kiss before you go." He tugged my hand and pulled me into an embrace. As we said goodbye, I shoved a treat into his trouser pocket, then dashed to the door. "What the—?"

I peeked over my shoulder with amusement when I reached it.

"Kara," Nate groaned, scrunching the boxer briefs in his fist, "you're going to kill me."

I winked and left the office, walking triumphantly to the lift with the silliest grin on my face.

ON my return, I found Mai in the kitchen. "What have you been doing?" she asked, raising a curious brow as she inspected me. She stood on tiptoe to get another mug from the cupboard, but I still saw the smirk.

"Nothing." I fussed with the Peter-Pan collar of my blouse, checking it was straight. I leant into the unit and folded my arms, hoping to appear casual.

"That's a new word for it. Michael came searching for you half hour ago, so I know you've been alone with the Adonis." Mai noticed my fretful expression and said, "Don't worry, I covered. Your secret's still safe."

"Thanks, Mai." I touched her arm in appreciation and returned the milk carton to the refrigerator. "I had to answer some questions, that's all."

Mai sneered her disbelief and glanced up at my hair. "Next time, try remembering what hairstyle you came to work with." She spooned some sugar into her latte. "Pretty sure it wasn't like that."

I sifted my fingers through my ponytail. *Crap.*

"If I'm gonna cover your ass while the God in the suit screws your brains out," she said, handing me my mug, "I expect details when you get back."

"We didn't have sex!" I protested, lowering my voice as we exited the kitchen, passing some colleagues. "We only—"

What exactly had we done? Okay, there was no actual intercourse, but Nate had still gone down on me in his office. Not giving Mai the chance to probe further, I shook my head and hurried to my desk. "I've got work to do."

NATE called just before 5 p.m. I was surprised it had taken him so long to follow up from our encounter.

"Hello," I answered my desk phone with a smile.

"Baby." His breathy tone stirred the butterflies in my belly. "I'm going out of my mind up here."

"Why?" I feigned ignorance as I sank lower into my chair and crossed my legs.

"You know *exactly* what you're doing to me. It's taking all of my willpower not to come get you and drag your bare ass back up here to finish what you've started."

My mouth parted to accommodate a gasp, and my free hand trailed over my chest, coming to rest on the flat of my fluttering stomach.

"You're lucky I don't know where you sit," he said gruffly, giving away his own desire.

I scanned the office outside, checking our conversation wasn't being overheard, and lowered my voice anyway. "I'm sure you could locate me—if you *really* wanted to. It is your building, after all."

"Do you *want* me to?"

I closed my eyes to block everything out so I could concentrate solely on Nate's sensual voice and the wetness between my legs.

"Excuse me, Kara." Something distracted him, voices muffling in the background. The interruption brought me out of my reverie and back to reality with an unwelcome reminder. I straightened and gathered myself together.

"Sorry about that. Where were we?" Nate asked.

I cleared my throat. "You were about to say why you were calling."

"You sure," he teased, "because I'm pretty uncomfortable and won't be able to stand for a while."

"Nate! God, I hope the phones in this place aren't tapped."

He laughed. “Only telling the truth, sweetheart.”

He was, albeit entirely inappropriately given our location, and I had to respect him for that. Nate wasn’t afraid to express his feelings, and was more than willing to let me know what I did to him. It was a refreshing change compared to things of late. “Are you still free tomorrow night?”

I rubbed my brow, missing something. “I thought you had a function?”

“I do. Wanna walk that red carpet with me?” he asked, his tone playful and flirtatious.

My heartbeat ramped up. “I—We’ve barely defined what we’re doing ourselves. I’m not ready to face the media for them to tear us apart.” I’d seen gorgeous women cruelly ripped to pieces, judgement passed on everything—what they wore, what physical shape they were in—all because they didn’t fit into a particular stereotype.

One man had made my life hell in much the same way. I wasn’t ready for strangers to do it again.

“I knew that would be your response, which is why I scored two more invites.” He understood, but disappointment laced his voice. “Bring a friend and we’ll meet inside, it’ll be more private.”

Nate had no idea of the internal battle I faced in deciding whether to introduce him to my friends. Mai would kill to go to this type of event, and I knew if I turned him down, I’d be the one dead. When I saw her strolling happily back to her workstation without a care, I caved. “I’d love to, thank you.”

“I told you I’d find a way to spend time with you. Our meeting earlier was a welcome prelude to our next date. It was a pleasant surprise to see you.”

“You arranged that on purpose,” I accused, recalling how I’d told him I was working on that project.

“I did,” he admitted without shame. “What I hadn’t planned on was being tempted by every businessman’s fantasy brought to life. I couldn’t resist you.”

I knew he was smiling, and asked, “What do you mean?” with a smile of my own.

“In that outfit? Those stockings, and your hair piled sexily on top of your head? You rocked the naughty secretary look.” There was a short pause, then he murmured, “Those glasses tipped me over the edge.”

“Naughty secretary?” I laughed out loud. “In your dreams.”

“Baby, every thought I have of you is like a dream. I’ve asked myself many times if you’re real or simply a figment of my imagination.”

"A mind-blowing orgasm on your desk felt very real."

"Yeah," he laughed, "think you pulled half my hair out."

Embarrassment flushed my skin. I tried to reply but my throat clammed up, leaving me unable to form any words.

"I had to see you," Nate continued, more serious. "I'm determined to show you just how much I want this relationship, and I'll keep making amends until you understand what it means to me—what *you* mean to me. I won't let you down again, Kara."

"That isn't necessary. Just…" I didn't know what to say. I wanted a relationship, but one with Nate frightened me. I'd fall too deep, deeper than he ever would, and it would break me when he realised that.

"I have to go, my car's waiting downstairs. I'll see you tomorrow."

"Enjoy your evening," I said softly and ended the call.

Chapter 14

Whilst Mai had Jessie J and the remaining Rosé to keep her company as she made a mess of my spare bedroom, I had an empty glass and my frazzled nerves. Wearing a nude thong, glittery black painted nails and nothing else, I stared at the emerald green shantung dress draped across my bed. It was sexy, purchased on a whim, and *never* dared to be worn before.

Until tonight, when my ever helpful friend decided it was the only outfit to knock Nate off his feet. I stepped into the dress so I didn't disturb the loose flowing waves of my hair and zipped it up. The cool silk hugged my curves and stopped a few inches short of my knee. I was adjusting my cleavage in the strapless bodice when Mai walked into my room.

"Phew!" She added a whistle for effect.

"Will I do?" I asked, doing a little twirl.

"More than. Not sure I wanna go now with you looking all *glamazonian*." Mai's eyes dropped the length of my bare legs. "Jesus, those legs. What's it like living up there in the clouds?" Her arms waved manically in the air as she strutted to my dressing table in black suede heels. She was stunning, in a cream bandage dress that showed off her slim figure, olive colouring and hair, which she wore loose.

"Should I change?" I faced the full length faceted antique mirror and cocked my head to the side, assessing my appearance. "It's too much, isn't it?"

"Women pay good money for curves like yours. Go flaunt them!" Mai's smoking didn't suppress her appetite one bit, yet she didn't carry an ounce of fat regardless. I paid the price of overindulgence if I didn't workout regularly.

"I'm not used to wearing such bold, revealing outfits." I dropped onto my bed and put on my sandals.

"The dumbass didn't know a good thing when he had it," Mai insisted, referring to Stuart. "He wasn't man enough to have a gorgeous woman like you on his arm. Whereas, Blake…" She paused, taking a moment to daydream whilst putting on earrings. "He's *all* man. Now get your butt over here and do this up"—she held a statement necklace in the air—"so you can go blow his mind."

I helped Mai out and finished getting ready whilst she spritzed one of my perfumes on then smiled, satisfied with her appearance in the mirror.

"Ross will be here in a minute," I said when I saw the time was nearing 8 p.m.

"I'm so excited to finally meet Mr Blake—I mean Nate." Mai came to a halt in the lounge, slipping her cross body bag over her head. "Wait, what should I call him? Is he my boss tonight or my best friends lover?"

The intercom announced Ross' arrival. "Call him Nate." I held the door open, waiting for her to knock back her wine.

"How cool is it, having your own driver?" Mai pointed out, breezing past with a smile. "Cabs suck."

BARELY ten minutes later, the Mercedes stopped outside Andaz in West Hollywood. Searchlights beamed into the sky, and camera flashes popped incessantly at people posing their way up a plush red carpet. Mai squealed and bounced excitedly on the backseat.

"Kara, we *have* to do the red carpet."

Her enthusiasm didn't rub off on me. I shook my head, taking another peek out the window at the hordes of people. "There's no way I'm walking up there."

I thanked Ross when I stepped out the car and joined Mai on the pavement. She was deep in conversation with the valet who'd opened her door. That girl could talk to anyone.

She linked arms and tried steering me towards the carpet. "I'm not stopping, Mai," I repeated. "No-one will want a picture anyway, it's not like we're famous."

After being stopped and asked for ID by a woman in a little black dress, complete with headset and tablet, we were allowed through. The second we stepped onto the carpet we were faced with a blinding glare of flashbulbs.

Squinting against the brightness, I freed my arm from Mai's grip and rushed inside. From the shelter of the hotel, I watched Mai work it like a pro, until finally she joined me, giddy with the thrill of it all.

"Oh, Kara," she gushed, "I'm in love with your man. That was awesome."

We were escorted to the roof terrace by a male host who wasn't a day over twenty, if that. Walking through long, flowing black drapes billowing in the evening breeze was like being transported to another world. Fairy lights twinkled around large urns of grasses and palms, and tea lights floated on the surface of the shimmering pool. It was magical.

"We've hit the jackpot," Mai announced loudly, steering us towards the bar. We weaved through guests on the stone terrace, their chatter mixing with the heavy bass pumping not too loudly from a DJ booth on the other side. Mai ordered two dirty Martini's whilst I surveyed our surroundings. The bartenders and waitstaff were dressed in black, and the guests were the typical *'in-crowd'* I'd expect from this type of function.

"It's a free bar," Mai giggled, handing me a drink.

"That doesn't mean you have to drink it dry," I warned her. "Don't embarrass me tonight."

"When have I ever done that?" she whined with a sly smile. Mai spoke her mind at the best of times, but after a few drinks, she really got going. I cringed, imagining how easily she could show me up, or worse, Nate.

We found a spot at one of the tall bar tables. Mai excitedly pointed out famous faces she recognised from television, but I was none the wiser. The only face I did recognise was the twenty-something actress who'd been signed as the fresh face of Acacia, and whose endorsement had been given to the beauty book being launched. She was every bit as radiant in the flesh as on the big screen and was surrounded by men wanting her attention.

"Mai, this is the type of event covered in those magazines you read." I sipped my drink, moving behind the table, appreciating the shelter it gave me.

"Ooh, think we'll be in it?" she asked excitedly, clearing missing the point of my observation. "I saw E! outside."

"It's not really us, is it?"

"Why not?" Mai dug her phone from her bag. "We're way prettier than them." Smiling widely, she raised her near empty glass and took a selfie to post on one of her many social media profiles.

I sipped my drink but couldn't shake off my inadequacies as I watched the beautiful people preening themselves. "Look at them, Mai." I tipped my chin towards two women, possibly models judging by their waif-like figures and glamorous made-up faces. "That's the type of woman Nate is surrounded with. I don't stand a chance do I? I should just end it right now."

Mai glared at me. "Blake's chosen you. The sooner you fucking accept that, the better for all of us."

I felt scolded, like an errant child. Mai's unpleasant words were only appeased when she placed a supportive hand over mine and gentled her voice. "Don't let your crazy paranoia screw this up, Kara. I see how important he is to you already."

"Ladies, allow me to refresh your drinks." A blond haired man, early thirties, bright white teeth and sparkling hazel eyes, set two Martini's on the table. "That's an awesome necklace," he continued, lifting the black chain off Mai's chest. "It's the exact match with your hair."

I snorted. It had to be the worst chat-up line I'd heard in years.

"I'm sorry. Stephen Avery." He turned to me and took my hand without waiting for me to offer it. "You have the most wonderful eyes if you don't mind me saying."

"She might not, but *I* do." Nate appeared by my side and slid the Martini back to Stephen. His manner was calm and poised. The fierce glimmer of possession in his eyes suggested he was anything but. I snapped my hand away from Stephen and chanced a look at Mai. She was gaping, in as much shock over Nate's reaction as I was.

Stephen visibly shrunk, intimidated in Nate's presence. "The lady is with me tonight," Nate warned him, snaking a possessive arm around my waist.

"Hey." Stephen held his hands up and backed away. "Only a drink, buddy. No offence."

Nate settled between us, angling his body towards mine. "None taken. *Buddy*," he snarled over his shoulder.

Recognition unfurled through my body, carrying warmth through my now faster-pumping blood stream. When Nate faced me, his eyes shone almost an electric blue. The alpha-male standing in front of me was hot as fuck. Indigo jeans hung low on his waist, and the rich fabric of a dark navy slim-cut shirt, open at the collar and sleeves rolled below the elbow, caressed every muscle of his finely honed body. Casually half-tucked in at the front, it brought sex to mind. Wild, frenzied sex that had left him mussed and unkempt.

I drank him in, not quite believing how good he looked. He rewarded me with a lazy, sexy smile.

"Thought you didn't get jealous?" I raised a brow, referencing his small power exchange.

"That's an ugly word." Nate rubbed the small amount of growth gracing his jawline. "The man has nothing I want. Whereas I," he said quietly, running a fingertip over my cheek, "appear to have everything *he* wants. You look sensational."

His kiss, by my ear, caused a flurry of sensation across my skin. A current charged through my body from the brush of his fingertips over the bare flesh of my back when he pressed me into his frame.

My eyes closed, my head falling forward to nuzzle his, absorbing his longed for touch. Nate inhaled deeply before settling his hand on my lower back and stepping back.

Mai dug me in the ribs with a sharp jab of her elbow. Glaring at me, she nodded discreetly to Nate, hinting at an introduction.

"Nate, this is my good friend Mai. Mai, this is—" I wasn't sure how to introduce him, and settled for "Nate."

"Ah, Mickey Mouse," Nate lilted, extending his hand to Mai. As she took it, her expression dropped from a face-splitting grin to a frown as she turned to me for further explanation.

"He saw the photo," I explained.

Mai's normally olive skin turned crimson. I covered my mouth to hide a smirk and was rewarded with a mouthed "*fuck off*."

"I'm sorry. It's good to meet you, Mai." Nate covered her hand, patting it reassuringly, and dazzled her with a smile. Mai flicked her hair coquettishly, batted her eyelashes and visibly swayed on her feet. Her flirting made me uneasy and instantly possessive of Nate.

Stephen had long since disappeared. Nate's arm slipped around my waist and he struck up a conversation, mostly with Mai because I was too awed and overwhelmed. I wasn't sure how I was going to manage a relationship with Nate when he frequently rendered me speechless, but judging by his proprietorial body language right now, I needed to learn fast.

Party guests, mainly women, occasionally passed our table, all desperate to catch Nate's eye. Their scrutiny of *me* was unsettling. Some were curious glances, others more derisive. All in all, they succeeded in making me uncomfortable.

Nate tightened his grip on my waist and moved closer. "Ignore them, Kara."

I glanced over his shoulder at the small group standing nearby, who appeared to be talking about us, if the finger pointing and indiscreet glances were anything to go by.

"Don't let them bother you," he urged, moving so my back was to the crowd.

A photographer appeared, excusing himself for interrupting but readying his camera anyway. Nate angled towards me and locked me in a firm embrace. He gazed lovingly at me, whispering, "I want a picture with the most enchanting woman in the room."

Dazzled by his smile and overcome by his sincerity, I smiled back, just as the flash popped.

"Excuse me, Nate." A well-dressed, attractive middle-aged woman appeared behind him. Giving me a perfunctory nod of acknowledgement, she carried on. "There are some people I'd like you to meet."

Irritation washed over me as she ran her hand down his arm—the one still curled around me—seeming just a little over friendly with him. Practised in the art of managing people, Nate slipped gracefully out of the unwelcome contact without making her feel awkward.

"You going to be okay while I do this?" he asked me, irritated at being dragged away. He was referring to the moral-less women still making eyes at him even though he was clearly with me.

"I'll be fine. Go work the room."

"Be back as soon as I can," Nate apologised, eyes not leaving mine. They stayed that way as he stepped backwards, before the woman led him off to the other side of the terrace. The small gathering of women were quick to follow.

"Fucking hell, K!" Mai sipped her Martini, neck craned to watch Nate disappear. "He's a living, breathing, airbrushed photoshop! There's gotta be laws against looking that good in public."

"Weren't you the person telling me how hot he was in the first place?" I asked, following Nate around the room with my eyes.

Mai shook her head. "That was before."

"Before what?"

"He screwed you!" Mai handed me a fresh drink, courtesy of a waiter who brought them to our table. "Now I'm seeing him with entirely new eyes. I could cut myself on that jaw…" Mai blew out a breath and brought her glazed eyes from Nate back to me. "And, ugh," she groaned, "what I wouldn't give to hear *that* voice talk dirty in my ear as he fucked me into oblivion…"

"Mai!" I gave her shoulder a gentle shove. "You've got your own boyfriend. Stop lusting after mine!"

With a raised brow, she smirked as she supported her merry self against the table.

"Bad choice of words," I muttered, irked by my careless choice of noun. A couple of dates and a night of explosive sex hardly warranted Nate being given that label.

"All those honeys need to take a back seat, 'cause that man only has eyes for you." Mai yanked me down to her level and slurred in my ear, "*So* infatuated with you."

"Don't be silly!" I straightened, snickering at her outrageous comments. With the amount of empty glasses on the table, I could only assume she was on her way to getting drunk. "C'mon, bathroom." I gripped her elbow and steered her away from the table. She clearly had no idea what she was saying.

As we neared the exit, I heard my name. A hand seized mine and tugged me through the black drapes.

"I can find my own way," Mai announced when she spotted Nate and marched off before I could stop her.

"What are you doing?" I giggled.

Nate's sultry smile was the last thing I saw before I was pinned up against a wall by six foot three of hard, lean muscle. His hands were everywhere, roaming my body with a sense of urgency. He kissed like his life depended on it, getting his fix to keep him going until the next time. I was just as fervent, tangling my fingers in the glossy lengths of his tousled hair to hold him steady.

"I'm longing to make love with you again, Kara." Nate moved to my bare shoulders, breathlessly nibbling at the sensitive skin. "So much it hurts." Trapped between his solid frame and the wall, I was helpless.

"You're near-naked beneath this dress, and visualising how good that looks is driving me crazy," he groaned, cupping my jaw and capturing my mouth again. "Your beguiling nature could break the strongest of men." His hand curved my arse and pushed me into his erection whilst his mouth moved feverishly across any area of exposed skin. "You've wrecked me…"

I knew it was a sexy dress, but hearing what it did to him, feeling how I affected him, was eye-opening.

Nate paused for breath, resting his forehead to mine and cradling my nape. "You have no idea how alluring you are, have you?"

I shook my head. I didn't, but I was beginning to get an idea.

"That's such a turn-on," he murmured, his voice uneven. "It's all I can do to stop myself from fucking you, right here, right now, regardless of where we are or who we're with."

Nate's greedy mouth covered mine again, absorbing my gasp into his hot mouth. The thumping bass from the music vibrated against my back, a similar rhythm to the thudding of Nate's chest against mine. His hand skimmed my hip as it travelled up to my braless breast. His thumb brushed the erect nipple, his groan sending a shudder through his body as his lips touched my neck, collarbone then lower.

"Nate, stop!" I jerked his head away before he reached my breast. Scorching eyes flared back at me, whilst his chest heaved with rapid breaths.

"I can't stop this," he panted, closing in again. "Give me what I need."

"Excuse me?" I dodged his mouth. "You want to have sex here?" I cried. "In front of everyone? A dirty little quickie in the corridor!" I craved his touch like I needed to breathe, but I didn't want it here, not like this. I ducked under his arm and made for the gap in the curtain. "I knew this was a mistake."

"Wait!" Nate caught my wrist. Glaring at him, I couldn't make sense of anything. His eyes were still wild with lust when he closed them and quietly said, "Don't say that."

I deflated, upset at the way he'd made me feel. "I thought I was more important to you than that?"

"I didn't mean—" Nate folded me into his arms. "You could be so good for me, Kara, but you have to open up. I'm drowning in feelings for you and need a sign. Anything to show me you're feeling it, too. Give me something."

My indignation left me in a rush. The way Nate regarded me so adoringly with those gorgeous blue eyes made me ache. I brushed my lips over his.

"I feel it." My admission was so quiet I wasn't sure if he'd heard me. But the release of tension in his frame confirmed he had.

"Come home with me tonight," he suggested, tracing the line of my neck with his thumbs. "We don't have to make love. I just need to hold you, feel the heat from your body next to mine."

"I can't. Mai's staying over. It's not fair to abandon her." She wouldn't mind, but as much as I wanted to spend the night with Nate, I wasn't the type of girl that dropped their friends for a man.

Nate stepped back, keeping me at arm's length. "Do you want to be with me?"

"You know I do," I said shyly, running my hand down the buttons of his shirt until I reached his belt.

"I want this, so much. I can't stop thinking about you. Every goddamn minute I'm awake, you're in my thoughts. I can't sleep." He laughed quietly, tipping his head to the side. "Even in the few hours I do, I dream about you."

I trailed trembling fingers along his jaw, completely in awe of his honesty and openness.

"But you're hesitating," he added. "Why?"

"What happens when all this goes wrong? You'll be okay, you'll simply move on to someone else. Trade in the new girl from the office for a better model."

Nate's brow wrinkled. "You think I could forget you that easily?"

I shrugged. "More than I could you."

"You think?" he repeated flatly.

"Well, look at me." I gestured at my body, hoping he'd understand.

His gaze dropped the length of my body, then his lips curled. "Oh, believe me, I do. Every chance I get."

"I'm being serious," I tutted, batting his hand away as it slid over my arse.

"So am I. If I could, I'd spend every second of the day with you. I wouldn't let you out of my sight."

"A man like you couldn't possibly stay interested in me," I mumbled, sagging against the wall.

"You mean a man who's living and breathing?" He stepped forward and caged me to the wall, one hand either side of my head.

"I mean a man whose life is this." I pointed over his shoulder to the event in full swing the other side of the curtain. "Glitzy parties, and an army of pretty girls all vying for his attention."

"This isn't my life," Nate said despondently, "this is my job. Don't mistake them for the same thing."

I lowered my eyes away from his impassioned gaze. "I've made poor judgements of people before, laid myself wide open and suffered the consequences. You wouldn't understand."

"Hey." He bent down to my line of sight, tilting my chin up with his finger, drawing my eyes back up. "I understand more than you think. Trust me on this, I'm right where I want to be."

The arms that were already too familiar wrapped around me, holding me like they never wanted to let go. "This is all I want," he murmured into my hair, "you and me. Don't pay attention to anyone else."

And I believed him because nothing else mattered, was important, when I was safely in his arms, where I belonged.

I agreed to meet Nate back at the table and made my way to the bathroom. Being thoroughly well ravaged had mussed me up. Having unsuccessfully trying to locate Mai, I returned to the table and found the two of them deep in conversation. All the humiliating stories she could tell him flashed through my mind as I rushed over.

"Hey," Nate greeted me, placing a hand on my lower back. He slid a fresh Martini in front of me.

"Thank you." My eyes darted between the two of them, concerned by Mai's impish smile. "Don't mind me," I said, urging them to carry on.

"Oh, we're done," Mai said, sipping what must've been her sixth drink, "think he's got the message." She gave Nate a conspiratorial wink and picked up her clutch. "I'm going for a smoke."

I watched her stagger off. "She's scheming," I muttered under my breath, sliding the olive off the stick with my teeth.

"She's watching out for her friend," he corrected cryptically, rubbing my back reassuringly. "I like her."

"She can be an interfering pain in the backside, too, but don't hold that against her."

"She's enjoying herself." Nate took a sip of the iced clear liquid in front of him.

"Too much." I swept the table and took in five empty Martini glasses. "Getting a ticket to this party will be the highlight of her life. She's in her element that you and I are dating now."

Nate tucked me into his side and lowered his head to keep our conversation intimate. "Is that what we're doing?"

"I thought so." I glanced sideways. "Aren't we?"

His hand flexed on my hip. "Just wanted to make sure you understood that," he said, nuzzling my ear. "Tell me when I can see you again."

"I don't have any plans tomorrow." I found myself rubbing my face against his, the intimacy making my breath catch at how good it felt to be this close.

Nate's hand glided up my spine and brushed my hair aside, then settled at my nape. "I'm out of the office all day," he murmured, "and I can't cancel dinner with my sister again."

"Again?"

Nate laughed softly. "Mel needs managing appropriately. Cancelling because of you again will really piss her off. But," he said, turning me into a swift kiss, "I'm definitely seeing you Friday. No excuses."

My stomach fluttered, my entire body longing for his touch. I was missing him before we'd even said goodbye.

Mai returned, eyes gleaming brightly, the effects of alcohol and successful meddling agreeing with her. She took her ringing phone from her bag and said, "Fuck off, babe, you're a real dick with double-standards," in the sweetest, most insincere voice. The pent up resentment she held against Mitchell always came out when she'd been drinking. Hearing her snipe was our cue to leave before she humiliated us all.

"I should get Mai home," I told Nate, finding him engrossed in me and oblivious to Mai's rising voice.

His expression dropped. "You really have to leave?"

"You can do without her causing a scene." I kissed him, hoping to cheer him up. "Thank you for inviting us, I've had a great time."

"I'll have Ross bring the car to the rear." Nate made a quick call whilst I indicated we were leaving to Mai.

"Asshole." Mai abruptly ended the call and knocked back the last of her drink. Nate's brow rose at Mai's pleasant description of her fiancé.

"Everything okay?" I asked her.

"Everything's *awesome.* My fiancé's a two-faced jerk. My best friend's hooked the hottest bachelor for miles, ruining any chance I ever had. And I've just been hit on by a guy with more hair on his chin than his head," she said sarcastically. "What's *not* to love about life?"

"Bald men are supposed to be more virile," I joked, tucking her phone into her bag and taking her hand. I was the last person to encourage infidelity.

"Oh," she swayed, "in that case…" Mai tried feebly to go back as Nate helped steer her to the exit.

"If you're not happy with your fiancé, don't cheat," Nate offered sagely, propping her up as we waited for the lift. "Calling off the engagement and walking away is more dignified."

The wise words of advice hit a nerve and stirred something in my soul. That small insight into Nate's beliefs, standards, expectations, filled me with hope. How could he shred me so easily with a few innocent words? Nate glanced over, and when those smoky eyes latched onto mine, I knew he understood me more than I appreciated.

Nate came with us to the rear exit of the hotel. He held me back whilst Ross helped Mai into the Mercedes. "Don't ever feel like you're competing with any other woman," he reiterated, giving me one last delicious kiss goodbye. "Because believe me, you're gonna win hands down *every* time."

I was left to process his words from the back seat of the car. Mai didn't recover from her swooning until we were almost back at my place. "He coming over later?" she slurred, leaning into my shoulder.

"No, he wanted me to go home with him."

"S'cool. Ross can take me home." Mai lurched forward and smacked Ross on the shoulder. "You can take me home."

"Whatever you say, Miss," Ross replied politely.

Cringing, I apologised on Mai's behalf and distracted her with the contents of the gift bag we'd been given as we left.

KICKING off my shoes, I flopped into an armchair and tossed my clutch on the coffee table. Mai had found the bottle of Baileys, and was pouring generous measures into two glasses.

"I don't want one," I told her. "I'm going to bed."

"One for the road." Holding hers aloft, she knocked it back like a shot. When my mobile rang and I saw Nate's name, I took the call into my bedroom for privacy.

"How's Mai?" Nate asked. "Is she in bed?"

"I wish. She's started on the Baileys. Could be a long night."

"Ouch."

"Yeah," I laughed, switching on the bedside lamp as I perched on the edge of the bed. "Are you at home?"

"Still here. I'm hoping to leave shortly."

Since leaving, I'd tortured myself with thoughts of Nate still being at the event, surrounded by those stunning women keen to get noticed, all too happy to flaunt a relationship with him. Not hide it away like me.

I was peeved with Mai for not being able to handle her drink. "I wish I could've stayed." My voice was tiny, timid and wary. A few simple words felt like an enormous commitment.

"Kara." There was a pause and a small sigh. "I'd give anything to kiss you goodnight right now."

The sense of longing his words evoked in my soul was painful. "I'd be there if I could," I whispered, hugging a pillow to my chest, hating myself for turning him down.

"Friday," he said huskily, his voice catching.

"Friday," I agreed. Though right now that seemed too long to wait.

Nate cleared his throat. "Sleep well, baby."

I hung up and held the phone to my chest, silently processing the enormity of everything Nate had said to me tonight. It was all happening so fast. *Too fast.* It was crazy. The only comfort? I wasn't the only one feeling it.

"That Nate?" Mai asked from her stretched out position on the sofa when I returned to the lounge.

"Hmm." I took my drink and curled up into the armchair cushions.

"So what gives? You looked really uncomfortable around him." She removed her earrings and set them on the table beside the necklace. "Thought you were happy?"

"I am." I sighed. "I like him."

"No kidding," she said sarcastically. I threw a furry orange cushion at her which she caught and threw straight back, hitting me with surprising accuracy given her likely blurry vision. "Nate feels exactly the same. No doubt."

"Really?" I swirled the glass, letting the creamy liquid coat the sides. "Because every time I see him, all I see are reminders of why he shouldn't be with me." I sat as still as I could, hoping she was falling asleep. I didn't want to wake her. My bed was calling, and I was desperate to get some rest.

"You want more," Mai spoke unexpectedly, her eyes staying shut. *Damn.* "He's trying to give it. S'all you can ask for. Want him to become a monk?"

"Good God no! He's way too good in bed for that."

"I knew it!" she cried, leaping up and rubbing her hands together expectantly. "Details, please!"

"No." I laughed and went to the kitchen to get us some water, ignoring her grumbling. She knew how to play me, but I wasn't backing down this time.

Mai joined me. "Not all guys will jump into bed with the next slutty tramp who offers herself to them." Even though she'd never met Stuart, she hated him with a vengeance that rivalled my own.

“Thanks, Mai.” I pulled her into a hug and led her to the spare bedroom. “You going to be okay?”

“I’m great. Gonna sleep now.” Somehow she got out of her dress, leaving it in a pile on the floor with the rest of her discarded belongings. Then she crashed onto the bed, dragging the covers up, already half asleep and mumbling incoherently.

“Night, Mai,” I said quietly. “And remember, no sneaky cigarettes in here, please.”

Chapter 15

Even with my ironic choice of Taio Cruz blasting through the apartment on repeat whilst I jumped on Mai's bed to try and rouse her, it had taken nearly an hour for her to get up, making us both late for work. I managed to get through Thursday without any consequence. She, on the other hand, spent all day in sunglasses, complaining about how rough she was and swearing off Martini's for life.

Come five o'clock, I didn't fancy hitting the gym, so after I dropped Mai home I went for a run. Popping the buds of my iPod in, I started off down the pavement with the dance music as somewhat of an anthem to my current state of mind. En route back, I picked up dinner, then sprinted home, starving hungry.

The man with intimidating eyes that had sat in a parked car when I headed out was still there on my return, watching me creepily. In LA, I'd learnt to expect the crazy, no longer batting an eyelid at the strange sights I saw on a daily basis. But for reasons I couldn't fathom, he bothered me.

I showered, ate, and was about to crash in my PJ's and paint my nails a different shade when the intercom went.

"Open the door, Kara." Mai announced her unexpected arrival with an air of irritation. I buzzed her in, unlatched the front door, and had settled on the sofa by the time she barged in.

"Men!" she cursed, slamming the door. She hung some clothes on the back of a dining chair and dropped an overnight bag by the table. She didn't blink at the garish green beauty mask slapped on my face.

"What did he do this time?" I asked, lowering the volume of the TV.

“I can’t even waste my breath explaining.” Mai took some wine from the fridge, collected two glasses and made her way over. “I’ll go home tomorrow once he’s suffered a night alone. Jay can keep him company if he’s that desperate.”

“You’re staying?” I asked, nodding to her overnighter.

“That okay?”

I nodded. “Keep it tidy this time. I’ve only just cleared up the mess you made last night.”

“Okay, mom.” Mai unwound the fuchsia animal print scarf from her neck and pulled off a coordinating beanie, revealing hair scraped back in a bun. I had no idea why she was so wrapped up. It was early August and a pleasant temperature outside. With no make-up, she looked tired, drained, and still a little bit hungover, and her tiny frame was covered in worn jeans and a cream jumper.

“Why didn’t you use your key?”

“Wasn’t sure if you had company.” She filled both glasses, pushed one in front of me and took hers to the window seat.

“Nate has a family dinner tonight.” I picked up the bottle of nail varnish and started painting my toes.

“He coming over later?” she asked, kicking off her ballet flats and opening the window. She stole the TV remote and curled her legs beneath her, taking a large swig of wine.

“No.” I studied my foot, seeing how the aqua shade looked.

“Thank God. Couldn’t cope with you two going at it all night.” She changed channels until she found E! News.

I wanted to grin but couldn’t as the mask on my face dried out. “Thought you two were loved up after the weekend?” I mumbled.

“Same here.” She took a long drag on her cigarette as she lit up. “He had two nights off this week, and he’s gone out with friends tonight as payback for me going out last night.”

As well as I could, I lifted my brows in disbelief. Mai nodded and refilled her glass, eyes sweeping over my polish. “That new?”

“Hmm.”

“Cute.” She sighed, dropping her head back and closing her eyes. I felt sorry for Mai. For so long, she’d been my rock and supported me through tough times. Now, when my life was taking a turn for the better, hers was taking a nosedive. The only good thing was Mai had much more strength than I ever did and handled the downs far better than I ever could.

I switched legs and started on the other foot. "Want to talk?"

She snickered. "You can't move your mouth."

I pulled my lobe, miming I could listen. Mai laughed and shook her head. "Nothing to say. Mitch is a dick sometimes. A cute one, but still a big one." Suddenly, she sprang forward. "Shit, look!"

Mai increased the volume as I glanced up at the TV. A brief shot of the starlet posing on the red carpet quickly switched to an image of her and Nate outside the party.

"They look good together," I said mournfully, carefully slipping on my glasses. The glamorous couple posing on TV were far better suited.

"Ha! And you two *don't*?" Mai sneered, flicking her cigarette out the window. We heard the end of the voiceover: ***"...And ladies, prepare to have your hearts broken, as the man himself tells us he's off the market..."***

Shit.

"This should be interesting," Mai mused, rubbing her hands together gleefully. My heart pounded against my chest. I screwed the lid on the bottle and waited agitatedly through the adverts for the program to return.

Beginning with a montage of guests arriving on the carpet, I gaped in disbelief. The moving image of Nate, standing with a small, pressed smile for the photographers, appeared in full HD in my living room, accompanied by the female voiceover: ***"Our reporter was there to ask the gorgeous CEO the question we all wanted answering."***

Nate chatted eloquently with a female reporter about Acacia and gave some background on the project and design concept. He offered a vague reply when asked about his own beauty routine, quickly steering the conversation back to the new skincare range.

"God, his voice oozes sex." Mai shifted to the edge of her seat, wanting to get closer so she wouldn't miss anything. The volume was already loud enough Vicki next door could probably hear word for word. I nodded in agreement but didn't take my eyes off the screen, dreading what was coming next.

"One last question," the reporter asked with a flutter of her eyelashes, ***"can you address the rumours that there's a special lady in your life right now?"*** It would've gone undetected by the innocent observer, but Nate's usual controlled composure faltered. His head flicked down, skin slightly flushing as he laughed awkwardly, hands tucked into his pockets.

I waited with bated breath for his reply. Then it came. "Yes, there is."

Fuck.

"Holy shit!" Mai squealed, leaping to her feet, almost sending her wine flying across the room.

Nate tried extricating himself away from the reporter, but she called after him. ***"Is she here tonight?"***

Everything was so surreal as I balanced on the edge of the sofa, dreading his response. Nate laughed and diplomatically answered, "Tonight is about Acacia. Have a great evening." Then he was gone, lost in a blur of flashbulbs.

"Kara!" Mai dropped beside me. "He's just told millions of people he's seeing you!"

"Thank God he didn't mention me by name." I was so stunned I had no regard for the mask cracking over my face as I spoke. Nate had been put on the spot, caught off-guard. I wondered if, in hindsight, the private man had regretted his admission.

"Not yet," Mai noted, "but it's only a matter of time before someone finds out."

She was right. Nate must know the attention on him, on us, would increase thanks to that tiny tidbit of information.

"Definitely in it for the long haul, K." Mai drained her glass and refilled it before going to the bathroom.

Nate wanted us to be a couple. Properly. Unless I changed, I was in danger of making my biggest fear—the demise of our relationship—a reality. I picked up my mobile and sent him a text: **I'M THINKING ABOUT U**

His reply, two minutes later: **I NEVER STOP THINKING ABOUT U X**

WHAT U BEEN THINKING ABOUT? I sent back, curling my legs beneath me.

U REALLY HAVE TO ASK?

SURE I CAN GUESS ;-) I followed up, touching my face as the mask cracked further with my smile.

"Do you have to do sexting while I'm here?" Mai whined, disgruntled as she settled down beside me again.

My phone vibrated: **SURE U CAN…**

I took a careful swig of wine when Mai handed me my untouched glass, wanting me to join in the drowning of her sorrows.

HOPE UR READY 4 TOMORROW came Nate's quick follow-up.

A flush of anticipation rushed through me. I reasoned dinner with family might not be the most appropriate setting for Nate to have this flirty exchange of texts, and sent him a final one: **ABSOLUTELY. ENJOY UR DINNER X**

"There," I said to Mai, setting my phone on the table, "no more sexting. You have my undivided attention. Just let me wash this crap off my face."

"Thank you. I need some TLC."

As I walked to my bedroom, my phone vibrated again. Mai dived for it. "I will now," she read aloud from the locked screen. "What the fuck's that supposed to mean?"

"Nothing," I called back, mentally noting a change in my phone privacy settings was in order. The last of my face-mask cracked under the pressure of my enormous grin.

THE NEXT morning, I'd just sent ten copies of a thirty-page regulatory report to the printer in my office, and was busy reading my electronic version when I heard the ping of an incoming email. I switched programs and was surprised to see Nate's name in my inbox:

> *Thought you might like to see these. #12 is my personal favorite.*
> *Can't wait to see you tonight. Nate x*

I clicked on the attached link and was taken to a webpage full of photographs from the Acacia event. My breath caught when I found picture twelve. It was Nate and me.

He looked incredibly handsome, and I looked…actually not that bad. The picture itself was harmless, but the obvious level of familiarity between us shook me. Nate's hand rested lightly on my hip, the other wrapped possessively around my shoulders. My whole body was nestled against him, one hand pressed intimately against his chest. Both of us wore contented smiles, whilst our eyes met in a mutual show of affection.

"Whatcha looking at?" Mai strolled into the office. This morning, she'd breezed out of her bedroom wearing a pretty floral dress and black pumps. It was casual dress day, but Mai never adhered to rules.

"These." I angled the screen so she could see.

"Ooh, lemme see," she said, rounding the desk for a closer inspection. "Am I in any?"

"Not sure. I'll send you the link. I've only just received it."

Mai swatted my hand away and took over the mouse control, so I pushed my chair out to give her more space. She flicked through the thumbnails and enlarged the one I'd been scrutinising. She blew out a breath and peered at me over her shoulder. "Now *that* is the look of love."

"Rubbish," I snorted, chancing another peek at the picture and feeling a warm satisfaction.

"Look at the way he's smiling at you," she cooed.

Nate's smile, no matter how dazzling, how charming, was infinitely more beautiful when it reached his eyes. The way it did when he smiled at me. The way it had in the photo filling my computer screen. No other photos showed the glorious smile that made my heart leap each time I saw it. Mai twisted, perching on the edge of the desk, a smug grin on her face.

"Don't you have work to do?" I rolled my chair back in and tugged some papers from beneath her bottom.

"No," she said playfully, swinging her legs as she slid a drawer open and started rummaging inside.

"Make yourself useful then." I stood, shoving the drawer shut, and collected the pages from the printer. "Michael wants everyone to have paper copies of this report." I set them on the desk, indicating for her to sit in the chair opposite.

Keen to hang in my office, Mai sat without argument and caught the green highlighter pen I tossed her as I sat back down.

"He's such a dinosaur. Paperless is the way forward." Begrudgingly, she began marking off recipients names.

"He's old school. Likes to have a physical copy in his hands." I passed over the packet of Lifesavers she'd been searching for in my draw—a favourite afternoon pickup when we needed a sugar rush. Or when Mai needed to comfort eat. "Heard from Mitchell yet?"

"He called earlier to grovel," she said, eyes down. "He's picking me up from the bar later, I'll go to work with him for a while. We can chat before he gets crazy busy."

"I'm not coming for a drink tonight."

Mai peered up, frowning. "Why?"

"I haven't seen Nate since Wednesday, and we weren't really together then.

We have a date tonight."

Mai's displeasure vanished, her expression brightening. "From what I could see, you were *very* together. You should've sent him to the canapés if he was that hungry. They were delicious."

I shot her a glare. "What did you see?"

"Nothing"—her mouth twisted wryly—"except a *very* hot couple having a steamy make-out session in the hallway."

Unease settled over me like a blanket. I stared with wide-eyed panic at the photographic reminder of our night out. *"Shit!"*

"Don't worry, no-one else saw. I took a wrong turn to the bathroom, that's all."

I appreciated Mai's attempt to reassure me, but the reality was, he'd taken a huge risk that night. Thank God I'd retained some semblance of sense and stopped him before it got out of hand.

BY the time five came around, I'd had enough for the day and was ready to leave. Nate wasn't able to finish for another hour, so after arranging for him to call me when he was on his way, I joined the girls at the bar.

We got the last table outside on the busy patio and were steadily working our way through two bottles of wine. My mobile was on the table next to my glass so I didn't miss Nate's call. It was a little after six so I was expecting it to ring anytime now.

"What's with the dress, Kara?" Robyn asked. "You never wear them, especially on Fridays. Those unreal limbs are usually clad in denim."

I fussed self-consciously with my cappuccino jersey wrap dress. "I've got a date."

Her brown eyes widened. "With the sizzler?"

Jenna and Mai returned from the bathroom with perfect timing. "Oh my God!" Jenna gushed, hands flailing by her side. She took her seat next to Robyn. "You'll never guess who just walked in, sending a million panties crashing to the floor?"

I remembered why these three got on so well, they all had such a way with words.

"Only your hot ass of a boss!" she screeched before either of us could hazard a guess.

Robyn sprung to attention. "Not Blake?"

My eyes swung to Mai as she took her seat. Her excitement confirmed Robyn's guess as accurate. I pulled the drape of my dress across my chest, feeling my heart pounding wildly. This wasn't exactly what I had in mind when I agreed to meet him at the bar.

Nodding her confirmation, Jenna continued, "He's looking *so* good tonight, ladies."

Robyn grabbed her bag and hid behind it, trying discreetly to put on some lipstick. Jenna fussed with her already immaculate hair. I checked my phone. There were no missed calls or texts. Nate wasn't coming in because he'd been unable to reach me.

This was intentional.

"Bet your guy doesn't meet Nate Blake standards," Robyn observed, puckering her lips to check her work.

"Hell, no," Jenna interrupted, giving herself another once over. "Blake is in a league of his own."

"Not gonna be a secret much longer," Mai sang as she leant over, delighting in her full force meddling mode.

"It's not funny," I hissed. I scanned the area, hoping to head him off before he reached us.

"There he is!" Robyn squeaked. Three heads swung, almost in slow motion, in the direction of her gaze. Any lasting thoughts I had over whether I looked nice swiftly went when sultry blue eyes locked onto mine. My stomach lurched.

A smile lifted the corners of his mouth, spreading out lazily until his face lit with happiness.

"Holy hell, that smile," Robyn cooed.

Once again, I was spellbound. Nate came towards me, oblivious of the stir he was causing as he edged through the crowd. Both hands were pushed into black trouser pockets, and a couple of buttons undone at the neck of a long-sleeved slate grey shirt. A shiver chased through my body, desire pooling in my belly, discreetly revealing my unquestionable magnetism to him.

Someone whispered, "He's coming this way!" but I had no idea which excited female it was. I was too busy clinging to the tiny shred of control over my raging hormones before losing it entirely.

Like a hunter circling its prey before going in for the kill, Nate didn't take his eyes off me as he rounded Mai's chair and stopped in front of me. I vaguely heard shocked gasps when he bent down, his hand coming under my chin, and pressed tender lips to mine.

"Kara." His quickened breath feathered over my parted lips.

"Nate," I replied softly. He smiled against my mouth, then drew his head back to glance over my shoulder at the crowd behind me.

"I agree people shouldn't know our business," he said between kisses, "but it's time they know we're together." A rush of heat swamped my body. This was a blatant show of possessiveness, and secretly, I was thrilled he'd done it.

"No fucking way!" Robyn spluttered. Only then did I become alert to three sets of stunned eyes burning into us.

Nate straightened and placed a hand on my shoulder. "Ladies," he smiled, addressing my friends. I faced them, only to see all three—even Mai—gaping. All in shock. All unable to speak.

"This is Robyn and Jenna." I pointed to the girls in turn and watched them evaporate into their seats as Nate reached across the table and shook each of their hands.

"Good to see you again, Mai," he said when he reached my friend next to me, who had come down from cloud nine and was grinning widely.

"Nice work." She gave him the thumbs up, congratulating him on his performance.

"I'm ready to leave," I said, rising from my seat and gathering up my belongings.

"No rush." Nate pressed my upper arm, gently easing me back into the chair. "I'll order more wine."

As he sauntered back inside to the bar, there was a collective rush of released breaths. "Kara!" Robyn squealed excitedly.

"What the fuck?" Jenna joined in. "*He's* the hot date from last week?"

I tried to say something, opening and closing my mouth, but couldn't form any words as my eyes darted between the two of them.

"Early days, girls." Mai rescued me.

"How long have *you* known?" Jenna accused Mai with a pointy finger. "He knew you already."

I wasn't prepared for the onslaught of questions and stood, needing space from the inquisition. "I'll see if he needs a hand." I made my way inside. I found Nate leaning against the bar finishing up a phone call.

He curled an arm around my waist and pulled me close. "It's been too long, Kara."

My hands started on his forearms, then leisurely moved to his biceps. He took my mouth in a soft, lush kiss then moved to my ear. I tilted my neck, letting him work down, not caring where we were or who was watching.

"Do you realise what you've done?" I asked, melting at the deliberately protracted caress. "PA's are notorious gossips. Come Monday, everyone's going to know about us."

He continued as if I hadn't spoken, placing open mouthed kisses in the hollow of my neck and shoulder. When he finally faced me, the mischievous glint in his eyes told me that had been the plan. Nate turned when the bartender approached and ordered more wine to be sent to our table. "I don't give a fuck what anyone else thinks," he said, turning back to me after he'd paid. "Let them be jealous because *I'm* the one you're making love to, *my* bed you're sleeping in." He stroked a finger down my cheek and lifted my chin. "You're my girl, Kara. I'm making damn sure the whole world knows it."

I couldn't wrap my head around him believing men would be jealous of him being with *me*. I knew standing here, locked in his embrace made me the envy of many women. One look around us at the attention he was garnering verified that. There were also three women sat outside who would swap places with me at the drop of a hat. "Think you have that the wrong way around."

"I beg to differ."

I raised a brow and smiled. "You know, I haven't actually slept in your bed yet."

With his own brow arched over gorgeous eyes, he took my hand and led me away from the bar. "Don't count on doing it tonight. You need to know exactly how much I've missed you."

The delicious promise rang in my ears. My body rippled in anticipation of the night ahead. I was dying to be with him again. As we approached the girls, it was plainly obvious we were the hot topic of conversation.

"I'll get another chair," I said, scanning the patio for an empty one.

"No need." Before I knew it, Nate was in my vacated one and tugging me onto his lap. Need and recognition charged through me from this close proximity to him.

"Keep still," he murmured, one hand securing me at the waist. His lips brushed my lobe, his hips flexing underneath me. "I'm desperate to make you come, and your wriggling ass is making me want to do it now."

My eyes shot to his. My skin quickly grew too sensitive, my breasts full and heavy. Nate handed me my glass and settled back into the seat with his own. His lips glistened after he took a sip, and without thinking, I licked along his bottom lip. The mixture of red wine and Nate was potent. But the immense longing in his eyes held the most power over me. In that second, something shifted between us, something so significant I *felt* it leave him and take up residence inside of me.

Nate did, too. I saw it in the flicker of his eyes. He was giving me strength, astutely identifying what I lacked. He broke away from the exchange in our eyés first.

"Should my ears be burning?" he asked quietly, nodding to Robyn and Jenna, who were huddled together chatting. I wasn't sure where Mai was, but knew she wouldn't have left without saying goodbye.

"Probably," I agreed, sipping my wine. "Mine are."Nate nuzzled against my ear, the warmth of his breath tickling my skin as he exhaled from a deep breath. I didn't know if he was being polite in staying for a drink, or if it was all part of his grand plan to ensure everyone knew we were a couple.

There was no mistaking we were. Not by the way he was touching me. Forcing me onto his lap was also a sign for any woman wanting to try her luck that he was taken and to back off. I slotted my fingers into his hand resting next to me on the arm of the seat, appreciating he'd done that for me.

"Are you trying to get me drunk?" I asked with narrowed eyes when he refilled my glass.

"Kara." He breathed my name with the quiet cadence that instantly aroused me. "I don't have to ply you with alcohol to make you want me."

The passion smouldering in his eyes captivated me and bound me to him. He knew me too well. Could expertly read my body. I wrapped an arm around his neck and teased the hair at his nape with my fingertips.

"These past couple of days have felt like forever. I've tasted you in my dreams, felt your hot skin next to mine. The crazy energy that shoots into my soul when you touch me…kiss me." Nate rubbed a thumb along my parted lips. "You're crawling all over me, and I don't want to do a damn thing about it except experience you again."

I licked my lips, my breaths coming faster and growing shallow. I turned into his touch, taking the tip of his thumb between my lips. I sucked, keeping my eyes firmly on his as I grazed my teeth over the soft pad. His eyes grew larger, then darkened to a smoky blue haze.

Oh...wow.

"Jeez, get a room," Mai shouted on her return. My face burnt. "I'm leaving, Mitchell's outside." She made her way around the table, saying goodbye, then disappeared into the throng of people.

"Shall we go, too?" I asked Nate.

"Definitely. I need to get you out of here and out of this dress." He rose quickly, handing me my bag from beneath the table. "Good to meet you both," he spoke to the girls. They gushed goodbyes—to him, not me—and watched us with awe as we left.

Ross weaved the Mercedes through wide lanes of traffic, heading through Beverly Hills and onto Wilshire Blvd. We pulled into a circular driveway of a crescent-shaped high-rise. Nate seized my hand and led me inside. A doorman greeted him by name and nodded indifferently to me as he opened oversized glass entry doors. I wondered how many other women he'd witnessed pass through on the arm of Nathan Blake.

Inside, a spectacular chandelier, all twisted glass and light hung from the ceiling of a double-storey grand lobby that screamed elegance and splendour. As we waited for the lift, the sexual tension was palpable, almost crackling in the air. When the doors glided open, Nate guided me into the empty car with a hand at the small of my back and used a private key to access the twenty-fourth floor.

I don't even think the doors had closed properly before he lunged at me.

Chapter 16

His hips pinned me against the mirrored walls, his lips crashing to mine. Pleasure soared through me from the passion of his kiss and touch of his hands. I could taste the red wine he'd been drinking, berries with a hint of toffee, and the sweet mixture had me craving more.

My bag hit the floor when he spun us until he was against the wall and I was between his parted legs. I held him steady, right where I wanted him, and kissed him back with everything I had.

"God, you feel good," he breathed, sucking the heated flesh on my neck. His hand travelled down the back of my thigh, lifting my leg at the knee. He jerked away when the doors opened, leaving me panting and breathless.

Nate grabbed my bag and dragged me into a private entry foyer, digging into his jacket for keys.

I took advantage of the brief interlude to pull some air into my lungs and straighten the drape of my neckline. He waved a card over a panel on the wall, and double mahogany entry doors automatically swung open and sensor lights came on.

Dragging me in for another kiss, we moved towards a sweeping staircase. "I want you naked," he growled, tugging my bottom lip between his teeth.

"Hmm," I murmured my agreement, already working on loosening the buttons of his shirt as we headed up the stairs.

"You turn me on so much. I've never craved someone as strongly as I do you." Nate pulled the tie of my dress until it fell open. Both hands found their way to my breasts as a low rumble shook his body. I was crying out for his touch, longing for him to make love to me.

I tugged open his shirt and pressed my mouth to the base of his throat, over his collarbone and along his shoulder. He grappled with the cuffs and shrugged out of it. I lost my footing trying to walk backwards up the stairs and slipped, taking Nate with me.

"If you wanted missionary, you only had to ask," he said gruffly, his smile against my mouth. "That had to hurt."

I laughed, taking a minute to breathe. To look at him. To slow the uncontrollable passion down and appreciate being together again. "I'm fine."

Nate sat back on his knees a few steps lower and spread my dress open with both hands, eyes ablaze as they ran over me. "Three days," he muttered, sliding my panties down my legs. "Far too long without your sweet taste."

His mouth was on me, hands pushing my legs wider. He teased my clit with flicks of his tongue, moaning his satisfaction. One hand dived into his hair, the other reaching for support from the iron filigree balustrades beside me. It was a potent image, seeing him feast on me, worshipping me with his mouth the way he did with the words that came out of it.

Hearing the unrestrained groans that told me what I did to him, how much I affected him, I shuddered with the first swell of orgasm. My head dropped back and my eyes closed as the quickening grew and took over. Then his mouth was gone.

"Wait," I panted, "don't stop!"

Nate reared over me, eyes wild with passion. "I want you in my bed," he rasped, freeing me of my dress. With an arm beneath my arse, slipping off my shoes as we went, he carried me the last few stairs to his bedroom.

A small sound, like a whimper, escaped my mouth as my need for him became unbearable. He unclipped my bra and my heavy breasts sprung free as I shrugged it off and let it drop to the floor.

Cool fabric caressed my burning skin as I hit the bed. Nate covered me with his body, still clothed from the waist down and kissed me slow and deep. I arched my back, moaning into his mouth when my nipples brushed his bare chest.

"I've missed you." Nate's hands were in my hair, holding me still, lips moving over my face and neck. He lifted his hips when I reached for his belt, frantic to get him naked. I shoved his trousers over his arse, my hands sliding over it and urging him closer.

Nate rose and stripped by my feet. Gloriously naked, his beauty was breathtaking. My eyes drifted hungrily down to his cock. *Three times*. Three times he'd had his mouth on me, and not once had I enjoyed the same pleasure. I sat, deciding I'd waited long enough to taste him.

I stroked my fingers down his hard length, head to base and back again, watching it stir, feeling him throb in my hands when I curled my fingers around him. I could hear Nate's breathing gradually becoming deeper and rougher. Before I took his cock and placed it right where I wanted to, I allowed my gaze to rise.

Hair that only a short while ago was neatly styled, now fell over his flushed forehead. Unfulfilled need blazed in those smoky eyes, and his sinful mouth was open to accommodate uneven gasps. His immense restraint was wavering with every breath.

"Later," he growled, stepping back. "We both need to come, and I want it to be when I'm buried inside you." Seeing his hands fist his cock, watching him roll the condom he took from his pocket down his thick length so blatantly sexually as his eyes fixed on me made me wet. He had me completely enthralled by the show.

Nate sat on the bed, tugged me onto his lap and sealed his mouth over mine. The slower he kissed me, the more he made my heart soar.

He guided the head of his cock over my opening, using my arousal to slide inside. I lowered, curling my arms around him, and buried my face in the crook of his neck.

"Slow," he breathed into my shoulder. "I want to feel every move you make, every inch as you claim me, taking me in like you can't get enough."

"I can't."

Nate's hands settled around me. I tipped my head back to see his face and began to move at an excruciatingly measured pace. I felt every slide in and out, every time he hit the hidden spot only he had ever reached. And I saw Nate feel it, too.

His eyes were dark, glassy, and expressing a million different emotions so clearly I was overcome.

"Nate." I said his name helplessly. He was already inside my mind. With every caress and deliberate movement we made, he was entering my heart. When we made love, Nate made me feel cherished, wanted, courageous, and a little bit like *me*.

I craved that. I craved this.

"Let it all go," he encouraged. "Let me in. Own me." Nate held my nape, his right hand on my hip. "I'm yours, Kara. All yours…" His lips worked over my shoulder and down to my breasts.

My throat tightened. "So good," I sobbed, eyes closing as an orgasm simmered low in my belly. "You're too much."

The strands of Nate's hair entwined in my fingers were damp with the sweat from my body as I clung to him. Alight with all the sparks and tingles he could induce in me, I was near mindless with the urge to come.

I picked up the pace, hips churning against him. A low groan from Nate in my ear made me shudder, the effect scattering throughout my body. The exquisite feeling of my orgasm reached my groin, gradually spreading through every single cell of my body. I clawed his back, the powerfully lean muscles straining beneath his skin.

"Open your eyes, baby. Show me."

I did. Nate saw me come undone, his wide gaze filling with wonderment. It was made all the more powerful, my thoughts buzzing with the intensity of those hauntingly expressive eyes as they glazed in ecstasy, fluttering briefly when his own release took over.

"Kara." Raw waves of euphoria spread across his face, hips pumping up hard into me. My forehead fell to his. His breath hot and heavy, feathered over my flushed face. "This will never be enough for me."

I tightened my arms and legs, crushing him to me so hard I could barely breathe. The strength of our connection, the way we'd made love, had shaken me once again. All my vulnerabilities came to the forefront of my mind. Sexually we were compatible, still, as much as we both enjoyed it—needed it—there had to be more to us. I wanted to know him, learn all about him as a man.

"You okay?" he asked quietly, tracing my collarbone with his fingertips.

Nodding, I touched his cheek, expressing how much I valued our relationship in that simple touch of adoration. This time, there was none of the apprehension, no worry or uncertainty. Elation and contentment shone brightly in his eyes, his smile was warm and sated. I collapsed onto the bed beside him and stretched my aching limbs.

"I'm gonna lose my mind over you." Nate pressed a kiss above my navel and stood.

All too conscious of my nakedness, I grabbed a rumpled grey cashmere comforter from the upholstered ottoman bench at the foot of the bed and covered up. A slight frown wrinkled his brow. He dismissed his thoughts with a shake of the head. "Are you hungry?"

"Starving," I said, lifting up onto an elbow.

"I'll go wash up, then I'll feed you."

I admired his incredible body, still flushed and carried with immense poise and grace, move across the room and disappear down a small passageway.

Alone, I curled into the luxurious blanket. The bedroom was minimalist, with two traditional light grey suede armchairs facing the bed, and two smoky glass topped bedside tables the only pieces of furniture in the vast room. I scrunched the downy wool to my chest and let out a sigh.

Being with Nate gave me such an intense high, I worried the low would be too devastating for me to handle. I'd been with Stuart for two years and our break-up had ruined me. Two weeks with Nate, and I knew I'd be wrecked if it ended now.

I heard Nate finish in the en-suite and shuffled down the passageway with the blanket still tight around me. I found him in a massive walk-in closet.

"God," I said quietly, using the wall for support. Grey drawstring pyjama bottoms hung low on his hips, drawing my eyes to his pelvis dipping below the waistband. I tucked some hair behind my ear, hot and bothered by the sexy sight in front of me. Nate shoved a drawer shut, eyes twinkling with wry awareness.

"That for me?" I nodded to the navy t-shirt in his hand.

"Um..." Nate pursed his lips, cocking his head in careful deliberation. "Nah, I don't think so. I prefer you naked." He shrugged it on, his smile wicked when the cotton cleared his head.

"Now you tell me." I backed away as he prowled towards me. "And there I was, hoping you were interested in my brain." Even though I tried passing it off, the cautious look Nate gave me said he knew I believed there was an element of truth in his statement.

"I'm interested in *you*," he said when he reached me. He peeled the top back off and handed it over. "Every precious part of you, inside and out."

Nate was straightening the bedcovers, waiting to take me downstairs when I came out from the bathroom. "Do you want to order in or have something from here?" he asked as we headed downstairs. He collected our discarded clothes from the staircase along the way and deposited them in the laundry room.

"You cook?"

He shrugged. "A little."

"Then it would be rude to turn your offer down," I said, following him into a breakfast room. "Maybe you can teach me? I'm terrible."

We ended up in a vast contemporary chef's kitchen. High-end stainless steel appliances were built-in to the chic carpentry of the units, a modern contrast to the period parquet flooring running throughout.

Nate set his phone on the thick white quartz countertop, opened up some wine and told me to get comfy. I settled onto one of the two white leather swivel barstools tucked under the large kitchen island that housed the stove and marvelled as Nate busied himself with preparing dinner.

Nothing sexier than a man who can cook, I told myself. *Especially one doing it half-naked.*

The conversation was easy between us as we ate a delicious warm lamb salad. When my bowl was empty and my belly full, I sighed contentedly, washing the last mouthful down with some wine.

"So," Nate began, "want to discuss what's going on in your head?"

"Pardon?"

He set his fork down and wiped the corners of his mouth with a black linen napkin. "I'm trying to understand how you can switch from being so open, so sure about us when we're making love, yet decidedly uncertain of where we're headed the rest of the time."

I watched his fingers drift along my bare arm as I spun the stem of the crystal goblet.

"I see it in your eyes, Kara. The bareness of your soul when I'm deep inside you makes me crave you all the more. Uncontrollably so. Your vulnerability draws me to you. But when we're like this," he said, gesturing between us, "a shield forms around you to stop me getting close."

The direct, albeit accurate observation, made me uncomfortable. I let go of the glass and clasped my hands in my lap, my whole body tensing.

"Are you happy?" he asked quietly, his left hand settling over mine. I held his curious gaze, way out of my depth.

"Very."

His lips curled. "Good. So talk to me. Help me understand why you're holding back."

My pulse suddenly spiked, starting a frantic rhythm as adrenaline surged through me. How could I tell Nate I was battling to safeguard my heart from being crushed, without letting him know the depth of my growing feelings for him? My legs repeatedly tapped up and down, so I raised our hands onto the island top, hoping Nate hadn't noticed.

"Tell me." His voice was so kind I felt compelled to give him an explanation.

"I'm scared." The enormity of the conversation we were having so soon engulfed my thoughts. With a trembling hand, I picked up my glass, needing a drink.

"What are you scared of?" The tenderness in his tone left a painful ache in my chest. It was dangerous, forcing me onto an edge I was frightened to fall off.

What am I scared of? It was a loaded question. I couldn't give him the honest reply I wanted to. I couldn't say *you* and the million things you make me feel. Of loving you, and having my heart broken when you realise you can't give me what I want, and find yourself in the arms of another woman. "Of looking into those wonderful blue eyes and seeing something I can't have."

His eyes widened. "It's too late for that." His hand came to my face, lovingly brushing my cheek and moving down my jaw. "You already have me. I'll never hurt you again, Kara."

I sucked in a breath and lowered my gaze, not wanting Nate to see how bared I was. "Don't make promises you can't keep."

He lifted my chin. "It would kill me if I did."

I saw truth in his eyes. I swallowed the butterflies that had woken in my belly. All my basic instincts told me to run—*to* him. There was something in this remarkable man beside me I needed.

"You told me you wanted a relationship and I'm trying to give you that." His mouth thinned. "Am I not doing it right?"

I placed a hand over his and leant into the touch, holding him to my face. "You are. More than I expected."

His brow drew in. "Don't let me drive you away. What's preventing you from giving us the commitment we deserve?"

Nate's penetrating eyes could see into my soul—I was certain of that. Why else would he be encouraging me to open up if he didn't know I needed to do it? Needed to free my mind and body of this burden I'd carried for far too long before I could move on. He saw something in me that needed healing.

"You won't drive me away so long as you're honest with me." I slipped off the barstool and stood between his parted legs, settling both hands on his hips.

I wished I could tell him everything but had no idea where to start.

His arms came around me, resting on the curve of my lower back. "I don't have to *try* to feel anything when I'm with you." The rasp of his last word caused my already raging heart to miss a few beats. "Whatever it is, it's just there." The shy smile that banished the last of his concern melted the defences in me he'd so accurately pointed out.

"You give me courage to be myself again," I breathed against his mouth. "I haven't had that in a long time."

When he smiled into my kiss, the butterflies in my stomach took off like a tornado. I gently teased the long silky lengths of his hair through my fingers. "I thought we'd be so different. But we're not. Not where it matters, anyway." I cast my eyes around the designer kitchen. "Materially, we're *very* different," I said dryly, "but none of this is important to me. You are."

I broke away from his adoring gaze, knowing if I didn't, words would be said that were too premature. Too heavy for now.

"I love when you pull my hair," Nate murmured hoarsely. "It reminds me of making you come." He tugged my waist, encouraging me to look at him. "And there you go again."

"What?"

A broad smile touched his lips. "Blushing." I shoved his shoulder. "Come here," he whispered, moving in for a kiss.

It was excruciatingly tender and full of honest affection. His tongue moved in languid exploration, as though we'd never kissed before. Teasing, tempting and quickly making me forget all my fears. My nipples puckered through the t-shirt as they skimmed his bare chest, my body growing lax and compliant as Nate's hands slid over my arse.

The amorous moment was interrupted by the vibration of his mobile as it whirred on the countertop.

"Ignore it," he implored. Curving my hands over broad shoulders, it was easy to obey his order. My head fell back as his mouth slid down my neck. It rang again.

He held me tight against him and reached for the phone. He saw the caller display and glowered, muttering his disdain under his breath.

"Answer it," I told him as it continued ringing in his hand. "They're not giving up."

"Yes," Nate snapped into the phone. He rolled his eyes. "I'm fine, is there a problem?...Where are you?..." His tone was brusk and growing impatient. Then he snickered. "I don't think so."

Reluctantly, he let me slip out of his arms. I sat back down and poured us some more wine. He wasn't pleased with the interruption, nor the direction the conversation was heading. His whole body radiated tension and unease. The carefree, open man slipped away as his face turned grim and pained.

Nate eyed me warily, letting the caller do all the talking. Then he pushed off his stool and tilted my chin up. "A lot can change in a month," he said, his tender gaze never leaving mine. The softness of his voice was at odds with the rigidness of his frame.

I tried to smile, but my jaw clenched tight with anxiety.

"Why are you in LA?" he asked them, moving to the huge windows so his back was to me. One hand reached across his chest to the opposite shoulder. "Look, it's late," he sighed, his voice lowering as he rubbed the back of his neck. "I have to go, I've got company."

Taking my wine with me, I slid off the stool, deciding to give him some privacy. Nate turned, studying me carefully. He moved the phone away from his ear and covered it with his right hand. "Sorry about this, Kara," he said as I headed out the kitchen.

I made a show of it not bothering me as I disappeared back into the breakfast room. At the end of a long hallway, a large dining room flowed into a massive lounge. Dimmed down-lighters and a limestone fireplace added to the warmth of the striking room, furnished entirely with Italian made contemporary pieces in earthy tones.

The door in the middle of the sweeping floor to ceiling windows was unlocked when I tried it. I stepped out onto the huge wraparound balcony. The hum of traffic and nightlife drifted up from below as Los Angeles sprawled beneath me, its grid of lights twinkling as far as the eye could see. The lit skyscrapers of Downtown loomed to my left in the distance.

"Here you are." Nate's arms came around me from behind. He stepped us back from the glass perimeter edge. "What are you doing out here?"

"The city always looks magical from up high."

"I guess so," he said, cautiously peering over my shoulder. "I don't come out here very often."

"Why not?"

"I'm not a fan of heights."

I laughed out loud and spun around. "Why live in the penthouse if you don't like heights?"

"Because it's the best." He smiled unapologetically and shrugged. "If you think this is impressive, wait 'til you see the view in New York."

Hearing him talk about a future together filled me with optimism. My happiness was reflected in his gorgeous face. "You busy next week?" he asked, grinning widely.

My joy was short-lived. "You're going back?"

The smile on his face fell. "On Sunday."

My body sagged as his words sunk in. A knot formed in my stomach. No sooner had we got together, we were going to be parted again.

Nate cradled my head into his shoulder. "New York is great in summertime. Come with me?"

"I have a job." I eased back. "I couldn't drop everything and jet across the country."

Nate was mulling something over in his head, his brow furrowed. "Let's go back inside where it's cooler."

I wondered if his odd mood had anything to do with his earlier phone call. "I need to finalise work for next week," Nate apologised, closing the door behind us. "I want you to make yourself at home."

"Are you always working?" I asked as we strolled back to the staircase. "Even at weekends?"

"Not if I can help it." He gave my shoulder a squeeze. "I'll be as quick as I can."

"Can I have a shower?"

"Sure, I set a few items out for you earlier, but use whatever you need."

I handed him my glass and climbed the stairs, feeling the weight of his gaze on me. At the top, I turned. Nate stood, hand tucked into his pocket and smiled when I met his gaze. Then he sauntered, in that sexy way, out of sight.

I stepped under the huge shower head and let the powerful jets of hot water run over me without wetting my hair. I was the right kind of sore as I carefully washed between my legs. Nate's earthy shower gel brought a smile of remembrance to my mouth and a wild fluttering in my stomach.

I'd always shied away from eye contact when I made love, but with Nate it was different. He was so commanding, so enthralling, I couldn't *not* look. I enjoyed watching him seduce me, get so lost in me, encouraging me to open up with his praise. And it was thrilling to let him watch me.

I finished up in the bathroom and decided to wait for Nate in bed. That was when I discovered his considerate gift, carefully laid out on the ottoman bench—a gorgeous sand coloured satin chemise with contrasting steel blue lace on the bodice and hem.

The bed was magnificent. A huge, custom-sized leather frame in tobacco grey with upholstered cushions to soften the headboard. The crisp white linen, luxurious against my nude skin, smelt freshly laundered. I wasn't surprised by its comfort, likening it to falling asleep on a cloud.

I switched off the table lamp and curled around a pillow. It was a poor substitute for Nate, but would do until he joined me.

THE bed dipped next to me. "Shhh, go back to sleep."

I shifted from my diagonal position to make room, then curled around Nate's warm, naked body when he slipped in beside me. He must've showered because he smelt unbelievably good. "I'm not tired," I mumbled, settling against his chest.

"Then you're a better actress than I'd hoped," he murmured dryly. That made me smile. He moved my hand so it was flat over the beating of his heart. "Sorry I took so long."

I lifted my head. The dimmed hall light illuminated the room sufficiently to see each other, yet provided a cloak of darkness for me to hide behind and shed my inhibitions. Even though we'd made love only a few hours earlier, I had the sudden urge to claim another orgasm from him.

"Is everything okay?" he asked quietly, tugging his pillow higher behind his neck. I nodded, searching for something—anything—to give me an indication he'd be receptive to what I was about to do. His hand slid over my nude skin. "You're not wearing my gift."

"No." I pressed into him. "I like being naked when I'm next to you."

"I like you being naked next to me, too." His playful reply was all the encouragement I required.

"It's later," I purred, lips working over his ear, one hand splaying over his stomach and easing the sheet lower. "You made me a promise."

His muscular frame relaxed beside me. "I did." His hands slid either side of my spine. "You seem to be taking advantage of that."

I grinned against his neck. "You're not the type of man easily exploited. Unless you want to be."

"Hell, sweetheart," he said roughly, "with where your hand's heading, you can manipulate me all you want."

My fingers curled around his quickly hardening cock. "Don't worry," I smiled, raising my head, "That's the plan."

I gave him a long, teasing kiss, humming at the taste of cool minty toothpaste. Nate's hands came to my hair, fingers tangling into the waves. His hold was firm enough to dictate the direction of the kiss but lax enough to allow me to break away and begin my descent of his glorious body.

I took my time, mapping every inch of flesh with my lips and tongue. His growing erection in my hand as I pumped quickened my arousal. I sank my teeth into the dark trail on the flat skin below his navel, my greed and impatience growing too strong.

"Kara, damn it," he hissed, pulling my hair roughly.

I sat back on my heels. Seeing my hand wrapped around his cock made my muscles tense with a sweet yearning as I remembered him sliding deep inside, pleasuring me.

"See something you like?" Nate drawled, both hands tucked behind his head. Watching with stormy eyes, his mouth parted with a sigh as my thumb brushed the head.

Humming my agreement, I lowered my head and licked from base to tip. Nate hissed through gritted teeth when I licked back down and sucked at the base. Fisting him with both hands, I firmed my grip and trailed my tongue to his balls.

"Jesus," he cried hoarsely, hips bucking reactively. The glittering blackness in his eyes told me he desperately wanted his cock in my mouth, banishing away the irrational fear that he wouldn't enjoy it. Gradually, I took him into my mouth. "Ah, Kara."

I was giddy with power, my stomach twisting into knots as electricity surged through my loin. I moved slowly up and down, sliding my tongue over his thick length, applying a little pressure. Never had I enjoyed giving pleasure to a man as much as right now. I was so turned on by taking control I let out a small moan.

"Baby." Nate's voice shook with emotion. "I can't fucking breathe." The uninhibited admission that it was all too much drove me to suck harder. This was what I could do to him. He was as completely mindless as I got when he worked his mouth over me.

"Ah, that's so good." He shuddered as the first drop of pre-cum spilt onto my tongue. He fisted my hair, holding me tight as he started pumping his hips, fucking my mouth. An aphrodisiac of scents consumed me. Shower gel, lust, the unique scent of Nate, all heightened by the increase in body temperature, engrained in my memory. "I'm gonna come so fucking hard."

His warning sent a shiver down my spine. "Yes," I panted, hungry to taste him.

His thighs tensed, the tug of my hair the right side of painful as the unmistakable groan of lost control reverberated in the darkness. Then he was coming. I swallowed repeatedly, drinking him down, licking and sucking until there was nothing left.

Feeling drunk on him, I let him slip out of my mouth with a moan of content. I peeked up at the man I'd taken to his limits and broke.

"Damn." He lifted his head. Even in the dimmed light I could see his flushed face, his hair the disheveled mess I was beginning to love. "I knew those lips would be the death of me."

I smiled my satisfaction, my elation furthered when his mouth curved lazily. He was thoroughly fucked. Because of me.

Nate sat and brushed his lips over mine. Then he buried his face into my chest and held me close. "What are you doing to me?" he murmured, sounding lost.

It was a question I wasn't expected to answer.

Chapter 17

"Are you ever waking up today?"

The voice was vaguely familiar. Half asleep, I kicked away whatever was tickling the sole of my foot. A few seconds later, it happened again. "You're so peaceful when you sleep."

I began to smile when I recognised the low, gravely bedroom voice. "What time is it?" I asked, blinking sleepily.

"Almost nine."

I groaned and snuggled down again. "It's barely dawn."

Nate crawled up from the foot of the bed and lay behind me. "I made you coffee," he said, burying his nose in the crook of my neck and cuddling me against his chest. I shivered and squinted open one eye.

"In a bowl?" I giggled, spotting a vat of steaming caffeine next to me.

"It was the biggest vessel I could come up with. Hope I made it right."

I sat upright, cupping the giant mug with both hands, and took a sip. It was exactly to my liking, strong with a dash of milk. I settled back into the plumped pillows, hoisting the sheet over my breasts. "How did you know?"

"I pay attention."

I was impressed that, although he'd been off his game after our first night together, he's still noticed that little detail.

Nate stretched, and the tiny expanse of exposed golden abdomen between a plain black tee and matching trunks made my toes curl. "You sleep okay? In my bed?" he drawled.

"Eventually." I smiled sweetly. "I was exhausted."

"Can't possibly imagine why." I got the full dazzling effect of his grin when he raised onto one arm and faced me. "I don't usually sleep past five, but when you're beside me…" His brows drew in thoughtfully as he trailed a finger up my arm.

Then he shook his head, sprung off the bed and threw me the chemise. "I'll make us breakfast. I need to refuel."

MY contribution to the feast of omelette, toast and bacon, was another round of coffee. We shared the kitchen like it was the norm, something we'd done a hundred times before. Everything felt…*right.*

I cleared my plate, having worked up a considerable appetite, but the lure of leftover bacon, cooked to my idea of perfection—near cremation—was too much. I glanced discreetly at Nate whilst I snapped a piece off. All sleep-tousled hair, with a smattering of stubble gracing his jaw, I couldn't imagine any woman, even some men, not finding him attractive.

That thought brought me full circle to the brunt of my issues. It was difficult accepting he wanted to be with me, when he could take his pick. I tugged at the hem of the chemise a few inches above my knees, tracing the lace pattern with my fingertip. It such little clothing, I felt more bared and vulnerable than ever.

"Stop it, Kara." The sternness in his voice made me jump. "Stop doubting yourself and second guessing me. It's not a healthy headspace to be in."

His ability to read me was intimidating. I hadn't appreciated I was so transparent, but five minutes with Nate proved how wrong I was. He brought my hand to his lips and grazed the knuckles. With a gentle smile, he sifted a few strands of my hair through his fingers. "I love your hair natural like this."

I forced a smile, glancing towards the window behind me in the breakfast room. It was late morning, and I could already feel the warmth of the day on my back. The last time we spent the night together, Nate had freaked out. This time, I was at his place. There was nowhere for him to run.

He stood and cleared the table. "What do you usually do on weekends?"

"Um, exercise, catch up with friends, the usual," I shrugged, finishing my coffee as I joined him at the sink.

"Any plans for today?"

"Not really." I rinsed the mug and stacked it in the dishwasher. "I'll shower then I can be out of here," I said meekly, retreating to the door.

"What?"

Not wanting to make either of us any more uncomfortable, I tried making light of the situation. "I'm sure you're busy and don't want me hanging around distracting you."

Nate sauntered towards me with that confidence I envied and wrapped his arms around me. "My plans *include* you. You're the best distraction." His gaze was bright and certain as he appraised me. "Spend the weekend with me."

The thrill of his lips on mine joined the excitement swirling in my belly. "That a yes?" he asked hopefully after I'd returned his kiss with much enthusiasm.

I flexed my fingers in his hair, loving the feel of it between my fingers. "I don't have anything here. I'll have to go home and collect some personal belongings."

"I have a better idea." He clasped my hand and led me out the kitchen. "We'll go shopping instead."

"No!" I yanked him so he stopped. "You're not buying me new clothes just for the weekend."

"I can afford it," he shrugged, continuing upstairs.

"That's not the point." I followed him into the en-suite and leant on the marbled vanity, not letting this go without a fight. Nate turned on the shower and took fresh towels from the cupboard by my legs. "I don't expect you to buy me things just because you can," I insisted, my arms crossing in defiance.

There was a suppressed smile on his mouth when he tugged me nearer to the shower. The glass screen was already steaming up with the heat from the water. "You don't *expect* me to," he repeated, "that's why I want to."

My irritation weakened as he undressed me. It was impossible to stay mad when he had that twinkle in his eyes. Stroking a finger across my cheek, he continued the slight touch all the way down my arm to my hand and fit his fingers with mine. Goosebumps showed all over me, my nipples betraying how easily he affected me as they hardened.

"Enjoy your shower." He opened the glass door and ushered me in. "I have to make a call."

WITH yesterday's clothes somewhere in Nate's laundry, I was braless beneath one of his shirts as I made my way downstairs. I found him in an office next to the lounge, talking on the phone.

"Rearrange those meetings." He paced the empty space between an L-shaped executive desk and the windows, his back to the door. He was discussing business, but his tone was kind, suggesting an easy rapport with the caller. I wasn't sure when, or where it had happened, but his hair was damp from a shower and he was dressed casually in long navy shorts, the hem of a grey t-shirt showing beneath a navy jumper.

"See if they'll do Wednesday instead." He turned to check his computer and that's when he noticed me.

It was impossible to maintain a straight face when his jaw dropped. Satisfaction over his floored reaction immediately gave way to something more carnal when heat flamed his stare.

"Let Ross know about the changes" he quickly said into the phone. "Thanks, Riley. Enjoy the weekend."

"Hope you don't mind," I said after he'd hung up, gesturing to my attire.

"Christ, you look incredible." He stepped from behind the desk, his eyes narrowing. "Is there anything beneath it?"

"Of course." I lifted the hem so he saw the edge of his underwear. The phone hit the desk with a clatter as he tossed it aside and lunged for me, lifting me off my bare feet. His mouth was on mine with a desperate passion, so fierce it took my breath away.

"Please say you've changed your mind about needing your clothes."

"I haven't." Smiling, I jabbed his arm. "But I meant what I said. I'm not interested in your money."

"Damn shame," he said with a small shake of his head, lowering me to the ground. "I could get used to you in this."

After getting our things together, we stood in the private foyer waiting for the lift. "We've got until Monday, baby. Let's enjoy the weekend."

"Monday?"

"I've rearranged my trip," Nate said casually, ushering me into the car. "Now I have you for the next forty-eight hours."

I faced his reflection in the mirrored wall. He beamed complacently whilst I grinned stupidly back. I felt like I was free falling down with the lift.

A few hours later we were at the beach house. The wooden deck off the lounge was a real sun trap, so the ocean breeze gently blowing my loose hair around my bare shoulders was a welcome respite to the heat. A bead of condensation trickled down the side of my wine glass on the table to my right, but there were far more interesting sights to admire on my left…

…Like a bare sun-kissed chest. Nate's eyes were shut behind sunglasses, his head back, feet propped up on the footstool. Keeping my hand on his, I hitched the hem of my sundress further up my thighs with the other and swung my bare feet onto his lap.

The edge of his mouth curled up at one corner. He began rubbing the soles with his thumbs. I stretched my legs further, and let my own head fall back, giving in to the bliss from his dexterous hands.

"Let's go out to dinner this evening," he murmured, soaking up the sun.

I laughed. "Half of Whole Foods is currently stashed in your kitchen." The detour on the way was entertaining to say the least. Nate rarely shopped, I had no idea of ingredients required for creating culinary masterpieces, so between us we made quite a pair. To the casual observer we were merely a hand-in-hand couple shopping, a routine event most took for granted. I enjoyed the carefree elation.

"I know." Nate straightened, leaving my feet in his lap, and sipped his wine. "But I want to take you out. On a date."

"Aren't we on one big weekend long date?"

A shy smile crept over his unshaven face. "Hadn't thought of it that way." He settled back and returned his gaze to the ocean. "I'm still taking you out, though."

The serene ambiance was disrupted by the shrill sound of Nate's phone ringing on the arm of his chair. He glanced at it and cursed before lifting it to his ear. "I told you yesterday, I'm not interested."

There was a brief pause whilst he calmly removed his sunglasses. "Listen, I'm not sure what you imagine is happening, but you need to stop calling," he said, rubbing his furrowed brow.

His irritation over the same persistent caller from last night made my skin bristle.

"We both know nothing happened." He glanced at me. "And, *if* it did, it's a mistake I won't be repeating."

When I tried to stand and walk away, Nate gripped my ankles and fixed me with a warning glare. My stomach lurched, unsettled by something that didn't feel right.

"Yes, she's with me now," he said firmly, his mouth thinning. The unconscious clenching of his hands around my ankles told of his irritation. "We'll discuss next week."

He hung up, eyes not leaving mine. The uneasy silence between us enhanced my worries. Nate released my ankles, frowning, and ran both hands through his unkempt hair. "I owe you an explanation."

Bizarrely, the urge to cry swamped me. "You don't have to say anything," I said quietly, lowering my feet to the floor.

"Baby, I do." Nate moved his chair to face me, knees either side of mine, and lifted my fisted hands from my lap. His jaw tensed whilst he searched my face. I stared into his eyes, seeing the same flicker of danger there as the very first time I got trapped in their spell. Except it wasn't danger—it was fear. Or sadness. Whoever had called was a reminder of great sorrow, yet his eyes showed remorse and regret.

"Was it a woman?" My throat burnt with pain. I already knew the answer.

"Yes."

In the blink of an eye, I went from blissfully happy to completely crushed.

"Kara." He tugged me forcefully onto his lap, securing his arms around me so I couldn't leave. "It's in the past," he whispered from the crook of my neck, "she knows I'm not interested. That I'm with you."

"Should I expect frequent interruptions from all your past conquests?"

"No, she—"

"Or maybe she's still current…"

"Fuck, no!" With his fingers on my jaw he aimed my face towards him. His voice sobered. "We were over a long time ago."

I tugged my chin away and faced the ocean. It felt like I was in the middle of nowhere, with no escape. I peeled away his arms and stood, surprised he let me, and wandered inside to the stairs blinking away unshed tears.

"Kara!" I jumped when Nate stopped me on the bottom step, shrugging his t-shirt back on. "Don't get pissed about this."

All my nightmares were coming true. This ridiculously handsome man couldn't be what I needed him to be. He'd tried, but the lure of other women was too tempting to resist. "Let's be real, Nate. It's hardly surprising you've got women calling. Look at you, you're—"

"You don't trust me?" he seethed.

I stared disconsolately at him. Even the anguish contorting his face did nothing to diminish his beauty. Without responding, I hurried up the stairs, needing to put some space between us so I could figure out what sensible action to take. It was no surprise Nate raced quickly behind me.

I was cornered in the master suite. I wrapped my arms around my waist, cold and shivering even though I was standing in streaming sun by the window.

"I told you I don't fuck around. That not good enough for you?"

I could feel the weight of his indignance firing into my back. I glanced over my shoulder. Nate filled the entryway to the room, arms stretched either side on the walls for support. Both his brow and mouth were pressed firmly together. "Don't let this screw up our weekend," he muttered. "She's not worth it."

Without a word, I turned back to the window. My pulse was racing, my stomach churning nauseatingly. I sensed him closing in on me and squeezed my eyes shut when his hands found my hips behind me.

"I've never wanted any woman the way I do you. It's crazy, but I can't function properly without you. Surely you see that?" He lowered his forehead to the back of my head. "Why won't you trust me?" he implored into my hair.

And there they were. Words I'd mulled over time and time again when I'd asked myself whether I could. My heart warmed, the distant notion I *should* trust him flickering in my soul. I turned around.

"I want to." With all my heart I really did. I just couldn't shake the heavy feeling of doubt weighing me down. "I gave my trust freely in the past and had it thrown in my face by two people I believed would never hurt me. So, if I'm not enough—"

"Enough?" A disbelieving laugh followed. "You're everything to me, Kara."

I swallowed hard, touched by his candour, quietly delighted he wanted me as much as I did him. "I'm struggling with this. I hate having all this suspicion inside me, preventing me from giving you what you want, what you deserve. Be patient with me. Please."

"I'm not screwing around," he assured, big blue eyes filled with honesty. "Don't wait for something bad to happen. Take a leap into the unknown. I'll be here to catch you."

My smile was all he needed. He angled his head and covered my mouth with his. It was a slow seduction, no tongues, just lots of open mouthed kisses. Tasting, nibbling, toying with each others lips. It was just enough to send a low hum of desire for more rippling through my veins.

"Let's go shopping," Nate said, smiling against my mouth.

I jerked back. "Not this again."

"Not for you." He shook his head. "I need a new cellphone."

What? I frowned. Was he serious? "You can't just go and get a new phone. It doesn't matter."

"If it makes you happy, that's precisely what I'll do."

Nate had cancelled everything—flights, meetings, rearranged his entire schedule—to spend another day with me. Of course he would get a new phone. It paled into significance compared to that. I giggled. "You're insane."

"I'm beginning to think I might be where you're concerned," he replied with a shrug.

I studied him for a minute, bemused by the sacrifices he was prepared to make. Then, when I remembered how many he'd made already, I took a step closer, lifting his t-shirt so I could touch his warmed skin. "I'm sure there are better things to do around here than shop," I purred suggestively.

Nate's winning smile flashed as he threw me onto the bed and showed me *exactly* how crazy about me he was.

THANKS to the pleasant evening, I wore a navy strapless maxi dress—the only suitable item I'd packed—to dinner. Two orgasms ensured my mood had lifted considerably by the time we were seated at the best table in the house. It was a small cliff top restaurant with magnificent views across the ocean.

Dressed in worn jeans and a short-sleeved casual shirt, with slicked back hair and finely trimmed stubble, the sexual afterglow Nate had made him impossible to resist. I couldn't *not* touch or kiss him, as I fell perilously deeper under his spell with every passing second.

We dined on the finest seafood and wine and told stories of our families and childhoods. I felt a little melancholy, but there was also a lightness in my soul. Reliving happy memories of my mother was cathartic. Nate was charmingly funny, and I loved how he was so relaxed away from the pressures of work and other distractions. I didn't mention it, but I noticed when he intentionally left his phone at home so there were no more unwelcome interruptions.

He was reluctant to talk about much past the age of eighteen, probably to spare me the sordid tales from college and university. Hearing how ordinary his life was made him all the more appealing. There was nothing flash about his upbringing. His later successes were down to hard work and commitment, yet he still managed to stay grounded. I had a suspicion that was due to his family and the people he chose to keep around him. Like Manny, who now lived in New York but had been his best friend since third grade.

I skipped over my own university years, enjoying myself far too much to let those miserable memories tarnish the evening. We talked about my job prior to landing work at RED, a temporary position at one of the big film studios. Nate was a big film buff, and after discovering we shared a common appreciation for the classic films from the fifties and sixties, pencilled in another date when he returned to LA.

We made it home in about fifteen minutes. Nate grabbed us some water whilst I went upstairs. The bathroom was smaller than the condo but equally as impressive. I rounded the huge oval tub set beneath the windows and closed the shutters. All white tiles and chrome fixtures, there was a huge shower head in one corner of the wet room, and two basins in the ceramic vanity. The towels and accessories were the colour of the ocean…and the colour of the eyes I found myself staring into when I emerged from the bathroom.

"Nice shirt," Nate drawled, eying my choice of nightwear—one of his t-shirts—with merriment. I was so mesmerised by the depth of his eyes, I didn't notice he was nude until he'd passed me on his way to the bathroom. *Damn.*

The moonlight cast a silver haze across the rolling ocean. With no sound and nothing to see for miles, I found it extremely serene, yet oddly surreal. This was worlds apart from my usual view. Most nights were seldom quiet, the noises from other residents in the building or outside were a constant.

"Why are you in the dark?" Nate spoke from behind me.

"You can actually see the stars." I sighed wistfully, leaning against the cool glass. "It's an incredible view."

The bedroom light came on, startling me. My surprise was extended when I saw my reflection in the glass as clear as if I were looking into a mirror.

His voice deepened. "Mine is spectacular."

I turned, unable to stop my gaze from wandering over him, head to toe, as he approached. Seeing Nate like this was a view I'd certainly never tire of.

"I want to see your body in all its glory, not hide it in the dark. See it tremble when I cover you with kisses. Watch your face when I make you come." My shaky exhalation was swallowed into his mouth. His tongue slid along mine in a way that made me ache. "You have too many clothes on." His voice was rough. Both hands slipped under the hem of my shirt, taking the fabric with them as they glided back up my body.

Nate edged me backwards to the armchair and lowered us both onto it. He levered over me, one knee on the cushion next to my thigh, and a hand on the back by my head.

"I crave you." His free hand plumped my breast, his lips skimming across my skin. "All of you."

I arched my back as his tongue circled my nipple before being sucked into the heat of his mouth. I lifted my hips so my thigh brushed against his groin and let out a groan when I felt his erection, coinciding with the gentle suck of my other breast.

The longer strands of Nate's hair tickled the flushed skin of my chest as he lowered his gaze down my body to where my legs fell open. He pushed a finger inside me with a low rumble of satisfaction. "You're ready for me." His stroke was firm and exact, confident and the ideal rhythm. He drew out, then slipped two back in.

"I'm always ready for you," I panted, the hand in his hair pulling, the other squeezing the back of his thigh. He blinked up, eyes full of fire and longing, his breathing shallow like mine, all the while his fingers penetrating me. An easy, sensual smile curled his lips.

"Do you have any idea how fucking sexy you are like this? Spread out, gifting yourself to me, letting me pleasure you."

"Please, Nate," I begged, shaking my head.

"Hush, baby." His lips moved over my blazing skin. "Soon." He kicked away the footstool, all the while his fingers pushing in and out without faltering.

Nate knelt on the floor and yanked me to the edge of the seat. He hooked my legs over his shoulders. *God yes, this is what I want.*

"This," he growled, spreading me open with his thumbs, "is beautiful. This is mine."

"Ah, God," I cried out when his tongue speared into me. His hands returned to my breasts, kneading and fondling. I lifted my hips, brazenly riding his tongue. My fingernails dug into the arms of the chair, the heels of my feet pressing into his back.

I bit my lip to stifle a groan, but when Nate gently sucked my clit, the sound came out, a strangled desperate cry of total submission. He was so skilled with his tongue, it drove me wild wherever it touched.

Seeing the dishevelled mop of dark hair bobbing up and down between my thighs was too much. I climaxed with a rush, my body jerking violently as the orgasm rode through me. I was still moaning his name and tugging his hair when Nate moved and I heard the telltale rustling of foil being ripped. He was relentless, his tongue still working over my swollen flesh, keeping me in a constant state of bliss.

My legs dropped from his shoulders, then Nate was up, levering over me, primely masculine, a feral look in his black eyes. He kissed me just as hungrily on my mouth as he had between my legs moments before.

"Turn over," he ordered hoarsely.

I complied and knelt on the seat, arms stretched in front of me for support. In the reflective glass, I could see him gazing at me in wonder as he stood behind me and traced his fingertips the length of my spine. My back bowed under his worshipping touch.

"I'm in awe," he whispered, folding over me. He brushed my hair so it fell over one shoulder, the heat from his nearness making my arms shake as I vibrated with need. He made me wait for it, taking his time, fluttering kisses over my skin, building the anticipation until I started to loose all sense, growing lightheaded from the sensations humming through my body.

I wanted this to last forever. Wanted his adoration, to get lost in him and us. Nothing could touch us when we were like this.

Nate reached my arse and murmured his appreciation. He bit softly, and I clenched, a delirious moan escaping my parted lips. "You like that?" he asked, amused.

"I love everything you do to me…" My thoughts switched from languid lovemaking to a primal need to be fucked when his rigid cock stroked along my slick folds of skin.

"Like when I do this?" He eased into me with a long groan.

"Oh, God…yes." Especially when he did that. I gripped the chair and pushed back into him. Nate held me steady at the hips and eased out. Then he rammed into me again. I knew it was going to be a fast claiming of me as he raced to his own orgasm. Each time he drew back, my muscles tried frantically to grip him and keep him inside. Defenceless and unable to touch him, I widened my legs, needing him to go deeper.

"I'll fuck you hard like this until you accept I don't want to do it with anyone else," he growled, fingers digging into my flesh.

I was riveted to the sight of our joined bodies in the mirrored glass. Mixed with his filthy words ringing in my ear, it was the most erotic scene I'd ever witnessed. A brief second of sensibility over whether we could be seen flashed through my mind. Then it was gone. Because the way Nate was turning me on, making me climb higher and higher as he staked his claim, I didn't care.

"It's too much…" he groaned, "…feels too good." He weighted me, his chest damp and hot as he wrapped an arm around my waist and crushed me back against him.

"I know," I whispered, turning my head to meet his mouth, letting our embrace stifle our ragged breaths. His cock pressed deep inside, stretching me until I couldn't take anymore.

He fucked me to another explosive climax. "That's it," he encouraged, hearing my loud cries. He pressed a flushed cheek to my shoulder. His eyes widened when they met mine in the reflection.

"Fuck." He reared up, hips stilling as he took in the scene. He still didn't break away when I glanced over my shoulder. Sweat dripped off his torso, his lips full and pinked, parted to suck in deep breaths.

I had to look away when he finally did meet my gaze, because his eyes filled with something I couldn't let myself believe to be true…not this soon…

Nate eased out and switched positions, sitting on the chair and encouraging me to straddle him. "Ride me," he ordered hoarsely.

I found him and slid down until his cock was buried in me to the hilt. Using his shoulders for support, I leant back so his cock stroked deeper. Nate turned to the window so he could watch. I could see his reflection, see every move he made, the way he looked as he neared his own release.

I'd seen it before, but what I'd never seen was how *I* looked. The way I moved, the control I had, how sublimely sexual and comfortable I was making love to him. This was how Nate saw me.

Unguarded. *Stripped.* Unable to hide anything and fool nobody.

All self-conscious thought was banished by the slide of his hands all over my body and the pure gratification in his eyes. My insatiable need to come again grew unbearable, spurring me to move faster.

"Baby." His voice was softer now. "I love seeing two of you."

His confirmation took me tumbling over the edge for a third time. I carried Nate with me and we came together, my hands firm on his biceps, his hands tight on my hips, our eyes locked on each other.

"Fuck!" I was physically and mentally shattered as I collapsed into the small space beside him.

Nate's head fell back as he exhaled harshly. "Fuck."

I bit my lip to stifle a laugh but couldn't prevent a giggle from escaping.

A jaw-dropping sated smile crept over his face as he rolled his head sideways and faced me. "That was insane." He brushed my cheek with the backs of his fingers, his eyes glassy and bright. My eyes fluttered closed as I murmured my agreement.

Nate got up and went to the bathroom. When he returned, he found me curled into the chair with the blanket covering me. "You sleeping there tonight?"

"Not sure I can move." I stretched, admiring him as he leant over, caging me with his strong arms.

His eyes softened. "You look phenomenal." Strands of hair fell onto his forehead in that sexy way that made me want to run my fingers through it. So I did.

"Thoroughly well-fucked?" I asked without shame. It was exactly how I felt.

"Best way to be, sweetheart." He moved the footstool back and dimmed the lights. Then he sat beside me, tucking me into his side. I curled around him, covering us both with the blanket, and pressed my cheek to his chest. We fell into a comfortable silence, touching and stroking each other.

"Looking at the sky reminds me of when I was little," I said after a while, staring into the darkness outside. "If I had a nightmare, my father would sit with me on my bed, and draw imaginary shapes with the stars. He'd stay there until I'd forgotten all about it and fallen asleep."

"You were a daddy's girl?" Nate spoke into my hair, pressing a kiss to my crown.

I nodded. "Still am." I hadn't opened up much about my family since moving here. Mai knew the odd detail, but silly sentimental memories like what I'd just shared rarely found time to be revealed. "We've always been close, but after my mother died we—"

Nate sucked in a sharp breath. "Your *mom*?" He stared, eyes full of compassion and empathy. "Kara, I had no idea. I'm so sorry."

I reached for his hand to hold. "You couldn't be expected to know."

"I'm no stranger to grief, but I can't imagine the pain suffered from losing a parent." Something flickered in his eyes, an anguish and remorse over something lost too soon. "When? I mean, how?"

"Four years ago. It should've been a simple operation, but there were complications in surgery. She was far too young…I never got to say goodbye…" I hugged him closer and played with his fingers. "I spent the first year of her death numb with shock. I poured all my energy into taking care of my father and Liam. Being the only girl, I suppose I felt it my responsibility."

"Who took care of you?" Nate asked, his arm tightening around my shoulders. "You needed love and support, too."

"They did." I cleared the tears trapped in my throat. "I made a stupid relationship choice that could've cost me dearly if it wasn't for my family." I wrapped my arm around his waist and hugged, craving his strength. It was given so readily, I managed to pull myself free from the potential gloom I could easily have fallen into.

"Leaving my father was the toughest decision I've ever made," I went on. "He didn't want me to go, but gave his full support because he knew it was right for me."

"Sounds like a wise man."

"He's the best." I used the blanket to dab at my eyes and sniffed.

"You ever consider moving back?" he asked cautiously.

"No. This is where I'm supposed to be."

"Good." He shifted so he could cup my jaw and look into my eyes. "Life isn't meant to be lived in one place. It takes a lot of courage and strength to spread your wings, venture out and do something on your own, for yourself."

"Hmm." If Nate knew the reason why I'd left, perhaps he wouldn't be so complimentary. There was nothing admirable about not staying and facing your problems.

"You know," I said, needing to change subjects, "you should keep your condoms some place handier. Just for future reference."

"Thought I did pretty well, considering I was devouring your sweet pussy."

I looked away, grateful the dark hid my embarrassment. "Then, yes, but not this afternoon." Our spontaneous love-making had taken a momentary hiatus whilst he dashed to the closet to retrieve a condom.

I sensed his smug smile on top of my head. "They were brought from the condo because I didn't have any here."

"Right…" Realising what that implied, I began sliding off him. "I don't need to hear anymore."

"Stop." Two hands came to my shoulders. "Not because I'd used them all. You're the only woman I've ever brought here," he admitted quietly, his finger drawing circles on my back.

I straightened. "Are you serious?"

"Yeah."

I sensed his vulnerability when he tugged the blanket over his chest. "But, why me?"

"This is my home, Kara. When you have all the inspiring natural beauty outside," he murmured, nodding to the windows, "I become the least interesting thing here. I've never met someone who would understand that, who would appreciate it—until you."

I settled back without a word, my brain frantically trying to process everything. Nate brought me here on our second date, barely knowing me, yet he'd opened up and let me in.

"Unfortunately, I meet a lot of superficial women who're only interested in what I have or can give them. You're different." He scooped my hair back off my shoulder and squeezed me closer. "I don't know how, but, sometimes you look at me and I feel like you've known me forever."

God, how could I have got him so wrong? I'd convinced myself he was a playboy, not seeking anything above fucking occasionally—definitely no commitment. Now, he'd blown me away once more.

"Thank you." I pressed a kiss to his chest. "So that wasn't intentional then?"

"What?"

"The mirrored windows? Are you telling me you're not a voyeur? Because you seemed to be enjoying yourself from what I could see."

His head fell back with a hearty laugh. "If I recall it correctly, so were you."

I met his teasing expression with a stupid grin. Nate gazed at me for a minute until all playfulness had gone, replaced with a softer, more reverent expression.

"Kara." Tracing a finger down my cheek, he cupped my jaw. I was never in doubt of his intentions when we kissed, but when he cradled my face like this as our mouths met, I felt cherished, so precious to him.

I knew that, as we cuddled up on the chair, I'd still be smiling when I woke in the morning.

Chapter 18

Daylight filtered in around the edges of the cream blackout blinds darkening the bedroom. I rubbed my eyes and reached to the space beside me in the bed. Empty.

I stretched, making snow angels in the sheets, glorying in how I knew with certainty that no other woman had ever been in this bed before.

With a happy heart I washed and dressed in a skimpy teal bikini—another impulse buy never to see the light of day—and yellow sundress, all courtesy of Nate's mischievous selection when I packed yesterday.

I slid the bedroom windows open and stepped onto the deck, knotting my hair on top of my head. The sun shone interrupted in the clear blue sky, prickling awake my skin. My stomach growled, hungry and needing its morning fix of caffeine.

In the kitchen, a mug waited on the counter and a message was written in chalk on a blackboard wall beside the refrigerator:

Enjoy your coffee. See you on the beach xoxo

Beneath the note was an artistic detailed chalk sketch of a curly haired little girl, and beside it, a stick drawing with Nate's name scrawled above it in childish writing.

After pressing a few buttons on the fancy built-in coffee machine, I sent a quick message to my father, rearranging our fortnightly chat whilst I waited. Nate would be sorely missed this coming week. Too much for someone I hardly knew. Yet, somehow I thought I did know him, more than anyone else really did.

With a small bag of drinks and snacks packed, I took our coffees down to the beach. When I reached the sand, Nate beckoned me over to where he stood in a pair of dark running shorts, damp with sweat and clinging to his thighs. My belly stirred. I dashed across the sand, already hot under my bare feet. "Morning," I said when I reached him, setting the bag and coffees down on a laid out towel.

The smile he gave me was almost as dazzling as the sun. "Hey, beautiful." He was breathless, his chest heaving. Beads of perspiration trickled down his pecs and abs, his torso pumped and shimmering. I wanted to run my hands all over him. Where did he get the stamina from to go running? I was fit, but after the workouts he gave me, it was doubtful I could manage a brisk walk.

"Is this how you usually wake yourself up?"

His eyes wandered lazily over me, his mouth curving. "I prefer other ways, but you were fast asleep."

It took a moment to get his hint, but when I did, I replied shyly, "You could've woken me."

That killer grin flashed across his flushed face. He tugged my hand, nodding to the ocean. "You coming in? I need to cool off."

"No, I'll watch." There was no way on earth he was getting me to strip down to this bikini for everyone to see.

He took a long drink of water, his throat pulsing with each gulp, then tossed the bottle back to the towel. "Don't make me throw you in, 'cause I will." His brow raised in challenge.

"You wouldn't dare." I laughed, shoving his shoulder so he staggered back.

"Sweetheart," he purred, "when will you learn? Never try and second guess me." He locked me firmly against him and kissed me. The feel of his moist skin pressed to mine caused a delicious throb between my legs.

"Oh no," he murmured against my mouth, "now you'll have to get wet. You're just as sweaty as I am."

His roguish charm made me smile. "Okay," I conceded, throwing my sunglasses to the towel. "I'll sit at the edge."

As we neared the water he turned, and without warning, threw me over his shoulder. "Nate!" I shrieked, pummelling his back, kicking my legs wildly in the air. "Put me down!"

He did. He crashed us both into the ocean and under a wave. His arms were still around me when we resurfaced.

"I can't believe you did that!" I spluttered. "I've still got my dress on!"

He shook his hair free of water and grinned. "I said I'd dare."

It wasn't overly cold, but against my warmed skin, the water made me shudder. I wrapped my legs around Nate and clung on.

"See, you're safe with me," he said, his hands coming beneath my arse for support.

And I did feel safe. Those big blue eyes latched onto mine, reflecting the shimmering aqua hues of the ocean. He was beautiful, with the kindest heart and sweetest soul.

The waves bobbed us up and down, the friction between my legs furthering my desire. I ran a hand down his back and pushed between my legs until I found him. A smirk curled the edge of his mouth. "You want to play here?" he asked gruffly.

Intentionally, I bit my lip and nodded. The sensual sound of his groan as our mouths collided made me squeeze my thighs tight around him. We were so caught in the moment, neither of us noticed the huge wave coming until it crashed over us, sending us tumbling to the ocean floor with a thud. In the blink of an eye, he was gone.

"Nate!" I shouted when I resurfaced, choking on a mouthful of ocean. Relief flooded me when his hand came to my shoulder.

"Maybe when it isn't quite so rough we can continue." He led me back to the towels with an arm draped over my shoulder. "That game was fun."

He dried my face with great care and handed me the water. "Drink this." Then he loosened my hair, running his fingers through it like a comb, before taking great pleasure in peeling me out of my soaking dress. My fiery ardour had been put out like a flame as I coughed again, not caring about my appearance as I settled on a towel to dry off.

We demolished the fruit salad and drinks between us. Nate had his camera and occasionally took pictures. He was an accomplished photographer, talking me through what he was doing. To the naked eye the landscape was lovely, but when he showed me how he'd captured it on camera, I was stunned by its beauty.

"Let me put some on your back," Nate said after I'd finished rubbing suncream over my arms and legs. "Your skin is so delicate and fair. I don't want you burning." I handed it over and sat cross-legged on the towel, tucking my hair to one side whilst he positioned himself behind me. I sighed, relaxing into his touch as his hands slid over my skin, massaging with precision.

"I have something to ask you, Kara." The importance in his voice made my head turn. Nate's hand stilled on my lower back. "My parents are having a party in a few weeks for their wedding anniversary. I want you to accompany me."

Excitement swirled in my stomach. It was another clear sign Nate viewed us as more than a fling. "As your date?" I teased, holding back a smile.

"You seem confused. Let me explain." He settled beside me, his body aimed in the opposite direction so we faced each other. "You're my girlfriend. I expect you to be all my dates in the future."

His words hit me with force. All I could do was stare at him, speechless.

"Will you come?" he asked anxiously after a few minutes.

I grinned. "Absolutely."

His lips grazed mine. "M.I.N.E," he spelt between kisses. "What does that spell?"

"Yours," I replied cheekily.

Nate's mouth curled into that sexy half smile that made his cheek dimple. "That's my girl."

"Your turn," I told him, shifting to kneel. I patted the space in front of me and waited for him to move. I ran my hands over his bronzed skin, unabashedly feeling every muscle and sinew before I even got the lotion on him.

"When you're ready," he murmured with amusement. I squirted some into my palms and rubbed them together, then set to work on his skin, all the while thinking how easily I was falling for this smart, good-natured man who appeared to be a little bit taken with me as well. My barriers had been up for so long I wasn't sure anyone would be able to break them down. Nate kept proving time and again that he could, and was more than up for the challenge.

"Tell me about your past," I urged with trepidation. "Relationships," I clarified, when he peered at me strangely over his shoulder.

He shrugged and looked away. "Not much to tell."

"I don't mean *all* your conquests. Only the significant ones." I smoothed my hands over his shoulders and down his arms, purposefully letting my chest brush his back each time I reached down, desperate for his touch any way I could get it.

"There hasn't been that many," he said dryly.

"I doubt that." I'd seen how women reacted to him—knew how I did. And when the subject got raised at the bar, he pretty much confirmed my suspicion that there were any number of women willing to share his bed.

"I'm won't lie and tell you I was a saint." Nate cleared his throat and changed positions, drawing his legs in and resting his arms on his bent knees. "I've had a couple of serious relationships, but lately I've only casually dated. They were never under the illusion it would become anything more."

That was debatable. It was impossible to think women could date him and *not* become infatuated. "You're saying you've never had one-night stands?" I shoved his shoulders gently so he leant forward, enabling me to reach his lower back.

"I didn't say that. Men can separate emotions from sex far easier than women. But—" He turned to me again once I'd finished, his brow knotted. "I haven't slept with every woman I know, or had hundreds of sexual partners. I've always been careful, if that's what's concerning you?"

"All done." I tossed the lotion back in the bag and stretched out on the towel, propping up on my elbows. "Why didn't the serious ones work out?"

"They just didn't." He drank some water and moved closer. He traced a line above the top of my bikini bottoms from one hip to the other, chuckling softly when he saw the way my skin pebbled in reaction to his touch. "What about you? Why hasn't someone so stunning been swept off their feet already?"

Crap. I asked for this.

"I don't know," I admitted timidly, "perhaps I haven't met the right person mentally strong enough to do it." He deserved more, but I wasn't quite ready to relive my shame.

"Here's what I think." He relaxed and stretched his legs in a pose that copied my own. "You need emotional intimacy with a man before you get physically intimate with him. Otherwise, you'd have screwed me sooner than you did."

"Well, of course." I nudged shoulders with him.

The warm, appreciative palm sliding beneath my hair and around my nape made my skin tingle. "I'm glad you made me wait. A man should earn the right to experience the pleasures of this glorious body after experiencing the delights of your mind, not be served it on a plate."

I rested my head on his shoulder, appreciating the reassurance that waiting had been the right thing to do. "And there was obviously a fucking stupid man who let you leave England," he finished. I took my eyes off the horizon and looked into his wise eyes. "Right?" he asked with a raised brow.

I broke eye contact, nodding slowly. "He really messed with my head."

"If I ever meet the fucker, I'll shake his hand," he muttered stiffly.

"Why?" I snickered. "I'd probably punch him. *Hard.*"

"For setting you free so you could enter my world and knock me off my feet."

"God, they taught you well at charm school." I laughed and shook my hair out behind me, tipping my face to the sun.

With a small smile, Nate turned away. A few minutes passed, then, "This would make a great photo."

Tucking my chin into my shoulder, I discovered him holding the camera to his eyes, his wide grin all I could see of his face. "I don't think so." I tried blocking his view with my hand, but he moved back out of reach.

"Let me take one," he begged, "for when I'm away next week."

For someone who usually remained so controlled, Nate could destroy me when his guard slipped and a glimpse of weakness was revealed. I stared down the lens, completely possessed by the brilliant man behind it, and heard the shutter whir.

"Too late," he said, showing me the candid snap. "I've taken it." Then he showed me the others he'd taken whilst I'd sunbathed earlier. I gaped, having no idea he'd been doing it.

"When you look like that," he murmured, acknowledging the silent question in my eyes, "you leave me no choice. You're incredibly photogenic."

Nate lay back, taking me with him, and held the camera in front of us. With his lips to my temple, he took another. This time, the lens was focused on the two of us.

NATE'S dismissive comment to his brother made me laugh. They were chatting on the phone in a way that reminded me how much I missed talking to Liam. We'd had email and text contact, but I hadn't heard his actual voice in a while.

"You're only jealous it wasn't yours," Nate provoked. I continued dragging my fingers through his hair, massaging his head as he lounged with his back to my chest on the sofa. It was difficult deciding which view to look at—the shimmering ocean catching the setting sun, or the half-dressed man currently wrapping my limbs around his waist. "So, I'm bringing my girlfriend to the party next month."

"Your *what*?" I heard his brother's shocked remark through the phone myself.

"You heard."

I ran my nails over his scalp, grinning, and noticed a fine scar cutting through his hairline. The subsequent expletives and laughter that ensued showed the teasing Nate was receiving.

"What about you?" Nate asked him, his hand curving my knee. "No one succumbed to your charm lately?"

I imagined Nate to be very different in male company and was interested to see how he interacted with his family who were clearly important to him.

"Jesus, Will!" Nate cried, startling me. "You're gonna get yourself into some serious shit one of these days." He let out an exasperated sigh and ran a hand through his hair, forgetting mine were there. He caught them and folded my arms across his chest.

Their conversation faded into the background as I daydreamed out the windows.

"Like you wouldn't believe," Nate murmured dreamily, twisting to face me. His eyes and smile were filled with affectionate pride. He laughed and said, "No chance. Kara won't be interested once I tell her the shit I know about you."

Whatever his brother's response, Nate met it with a warm laugh. "I'm off. Go play with your toys."

And he hung up.

"GIVE ME that over an alarm clock any day," I panted, my body still trembling. Nate had woken me this morning with his hands and mouth moving tenderly all over my body, bringing me into consciousness in the most wonderful way. Then, he'd cradled me tight beneath him and made love to me with achingly slow, savouring movements. The orgasms that rolled through me were equally as languid, but nonetheless powerful or intense.

"You said I could wake you." I felt his grin. "I wanted to give you something to remember while I'm away." His hand stroked up and down my bent thigh, his breath warm and shallow against my ear.

"As if I'll forget you." I dragged my fingers through his hair and forced his head back. "And for your information, you gave me two *somethings*."

His mouth curved. "You think I don't know that?" He rolled onto his back and wrapped the condom in some tissue. I followed him across the bed and curled into his side.

The blinds had been raised, the sky outside a faint grey and powder blue, mixing with the pale pink of the rising sun. I couldn't remember the last time I'd been up before sunrise. Seeing this reminded me what I was missing. "It really is a beautiful view."

"It is." His soft alluring tone got my attention. Teasing his fingers through the length of my hair, his eyes were glassy, lips parted in a shy smile. I knew for certain this time he wasn't talking about the view outside.

"I wish we could stay like this," I sighed, brushing my cheek over his chest. It wasn't an option, but it was a sweet dream to have. His arms tightened around me, but he didn't say anything. I ran my fingertips over his abs, circling his navel and continuing down the trail of hair. His cock lay heavily on his lower belly, still semi-erect and glistening with his release. It revved something in me that made me crave him inside me again.

"C'mon." Nate stood. "You shower, I'll make breakfast."

"I'm not hungry." I pulled up the sheet and stretched in the space he'd vacated. My stomach was full of emptiness, leaving no room for food.

"I'll make us something lite," he called from the closet. "You have to eat, keep up your strength. I don't want you sick while I'm away."

I arrived downstairs twenty minutes later and joined Nate in the kitchen. "Here," he said, sliding a tall glass in front of me, "it's a protein shake."

I reluctantly took a sip as he finished off his. It was delicious, flavours of berries and coconut bursting onto my tongue. Nate came around the island, wonderfully naked except for a pair of navy pyjama bottoms. "I'll take a shower, then we'll go."

"I'll make coffee," I called after him as he headed for the stairs.

A melancholy feeling washed over me as I watched him disappear. Saying goodbye was going to be tough, but something I would have to do sooner, rather than later. I sent Mai a text checking she was driving so I could catch a lift home later, then I made our drinks and tidied up to keep my mind occupied.

"You could've left these things here," Nate said upon his return, setting a stylish black leather holdall beside my overnight bag at the foot of the stairs. He draped his jacket over the back of a dining chair and sauntered over to the kitchen.

"I've packed now," I said, handing him his travel mug of coffee. "Besides, I need the toiletries at home." Nate looked thoughtful for a minute as he sipped his drink. "You don't have much for a week away," I noted.

"Most of my clothes are already there." He shrugged. "I just have a few essentials."

I leant into the counter, rolling my mug between my hands. Looking every inch the consummate professional, my core swirled desirously as I devoured Nate with my eyes. Wearing navy with a fine grey pinstripe, white shirt and grey-blue tie, he looked as sexy as the first time we met. His hair was still damp but styled off his now smooth face. "I like you in blue."

Nate's brows shot up. "A compliment? From you?"

His teasing made me shy. I stepped forward and brushed my thumb over the silky fabric of his tie, inhaling deeply when the familiar fresh scent of shower gel washed over me. It somehow gave me a sense of reassurance that we would be all right.

Nate studied me with kind eyes, one hand coming around my waist. "Don't be too sad," he murmured against my temple.

I smiled weakly and pressed my lips to his before uttering words I really didn't want to say. "We should go."

I'D never been more grateful for the heavy rush hour traffic. Crawling along prolonged our time together before having to say goodbye. The mood in the car as Nate drove us to the office was sombre, both of us quiet and reflective. I stared bleakly out the window, seeing nothing, letting the music and lyrics of Anthony Hamilton fill the emptiness inside. As was becoming the norm, he drove one-handed, the other set possessively on my thigh.

Hearing Nate's beautiful voice as he started to quietly sing turned my head. I listened, my mind wandering. He'd caught the sun during the weekend, his skin glowed healthily, the lighter sun-kissed strands of his dark hair noticeable when the sun caught them.

The car slowed in backed up traffic. Nate faced me when we stopped. The longing in his eyes was acutely clear, a certain reflection of the desperate yearning consuming me. I clasped his head and kissed him hard. He knew it was coming and let me take full control, willingly opening his mouth, his hand flexing on my thigh. It was only the honking car horns as the traffic moved that forced us apart.

"Sorry," I said, exhaling harshly as I sunk back into the seat, "but I had to."

"Don't *ever* apologise for doing that," Nate said roughly, swiping a thumb across his flushed lips.

My heart was racing wildly. How was I going to last the next five days without his taste? I squeezed my eyes shut and let my head fall back.

"Tell me your plans for the week," Nate said, taking my hand.

"My friend, Millie, has a gig downtown tomorrow night that should be fun. Other than that," I shrugged, "it'll probably be a quiet one."

"Watch your drinks. And stick together. I'll send the car for you."

"I'm a grown woman. Think I can take care of myself."

He glanced sideways, unamused. "You're also a very attractive one. You're gonna get attention."

His concern and possessiveness was touching. I squeezed his hand. "I promise I'll be careful. Now, what fun awaits you in the Big Apple?"

"Meetings, stuffy business dinners…lonely nights in my bed." His lips twisted ruefully. "No fun."

"Snap—minus the business dinners."

Nate lifted our joined hands to his mouth before pressing a button on the steering wheel and making a handsfree call. A female answered after two rings. "Good morning, Mr Blake."

"Riley, call Andrew, let him know I'm running late."

"Um, okay." Riley sounded surprised. "What time shall I say you'll be there?"

After glancing at the clock, Nate said, "Eleven." As I stared out the window, I thought that wasn't long enough to get to New York.

"Mr Ross and I are already on our way."

Nate cursed quietly. "After he's dropped you, ask him to return to the office. I'm heading there now."

"Something wrong?" Riley asked, sounding a little panicked and a lot curious.

"Nothing wrong," Nate assured her, glancing at me. "Just a slight change in plans."

They finished up and music filled the interior once more. Had he disrupted his schedule for me—again? I reached for his hand. "Thank you."

He squeezed it back. "I'd grind the entire airport to a standstill to spend more time with you, baby."

I took a deep breath, filling my heart with him as a tiny bit of gloom lifted from my spirits. People were waiting on him both sides of the country, yet here he was, taking the time to drive me to the office when he could so easily have someone else do it to free up his time.

"My mom has invited us to lunch on Sunday," he said casually. Meeting the parents was a big step. It would have happened in a few weeks at their anniversary dinner, but by then, we'd be more established as a couple. Now, as profound as our times together were, it was still relatively new. He raised his brows at me. "That okay?"

My nerves grew. "It's been a long time since I've met anyone's parents."

"Been a long time since I've introduced anyone to my parents," he countered with an impish smile.

"Well, then," I muttered, refusing to let him see my own delight, "glad there's no pressure."

ALL too soon we were heading down the ramp, into the dark concrete basement of the underground car park. "Oh, I forgot to check. Did you want dropping a few blocks away?" Nate teased.

"After Friday, I'd be surprised if there's anyone left who doesn't know about us."

He swung into his reserved parking space and switched off the engine, worried as he faced me.

"I'm fine with it," I reassured, placing a hand on his thigh. "It's not what I wanted, but I'm not as bothered as I expected to be."

Nate curled a hand behind my head and urged me close. "Kara," he breathed, his mouth closing over mine.

It was an ardent kiss, full of affection and longing. My heart raced, a tender ache developing in my chest. I tugged him closer by his tie, not wanting to let go, and wrapped my arms around his neck. I wanted to fill my thoughts and senses with him to carry me through until we were united again. And I needed him to know how deep my feelings went without laying myself bare and telling him.

I licked deep into his mouth, loving the way he responded, desperately yet tender. His free hand glided fluidly over the champagne chiffon sleeve of my blouse, his thumb skimming the curve of my breast as he moved down my torso and settled on my waist. An almost agonised groan caught in his throat, the erotically charged sound making me wet.

"I'm going to miss you so much," Nate croaked, eyes closed as we remained nose to nose.

"Me, too," I whispered unsteadily, trying to even out my breaths.

"How much?"

"A lot."

"Not sure that's enough," he murmured. With a final kiss he climbed out. His sudden disappearance didn't distract me from noting yet another level of insecurity he'd revealed.

"See what you do to me," he said gruffly, offering his hand to help me out. I followed the downward flash of his dark eyes to his crotch, now bulging impressively. He pressed me back against the car with the full length of his body and swivelled his hips. "I'll be like this all week—for you."

I ran my hand over his arse and licked my lips. "Can't wait until Friday."

I was triumphant when his gaze dropped to my mouth and narrowed as he growled. "Let's go before I bend you over and fuck you across the hood of the car," he threatened darkly.

That sounded so hot I struggled to refocus my brain and restore my clothing whilst Nate slipped into his jacket and took our bags from the boot.

As we travelled up in the lift, the car filling at Lobby level, sadness descended on me again. The time was fast approaching when we would have to part ways. How could I have grown so attached, get so low and depressed over being separated from someone still so new in my life?

I knew the answer, and knew that meant trouble.

The doors slid open on the Eighth Floor. Nate's hand went to my lower back and he followed me out. "I'll escort you to your desk."

The overwhelming sadness in his eyes mirrored my own. But, if I let this happen, it would officially confirm we were a couple…

Fuck it. I smiled and pushed open the glass doors.

Chapter 19

Mai peered up from the photocopier as we neared, shocked and pleased in equal measure. “Morning guys,” she said, far too chirpily for this depressing Monday morning.

“Morning,” we replied together, causing further glee. Her animal print flared mini-skirt, scarlet vest and black ankle boots lifted my spirits. I loved when she wore this, because it made Michael flip, and not in a good way. He disapproved, so of course, that encouraged her to wear it more often.

I rounded my desk and tucked my handbag away. Nate set our overnight bags by the door and prowled around the office space, hands tucked into his pockets.

“I didn’t appreciate you had your own office,” he murmured suggestively, a devilish smile tugging his mouth.

“Don’t get any ideas.” My lips pursed as I returned to his side. “There’ll be no shenanigans going on in here.”

Nate stopped in front of me. “Shenanigans?”

“You know—entirely inappropriate behaviour for the work environment.”

He cocked his head. “Spoilsport.” Nate touched the bridge of my nose when I laughed softly. “I have to go, baby.” His voice was low and tormented.

“I know.” I gulped my sorrow away, smoothing the lapels of his jacket.

He held me at the nape and pressed his cheek to mine. His chest expanded on a deep breath. “I’ll call when I arrive,” he said, his lips to my temple.

“Take care.” I touched my throat, easing the lump rendering me unable to say more.

Nate nodded briefly and moved to the door. I watched him, eyed his taut arse when he bent down for his bag, his strong shoulders and back when he straightened. "Nate?" I called, stopping him in the doorway. "Being hard all week sounds painful. You might want to do something about it in the interim. Still thinking of me, of course."

His eyes took on that addictive sparkle, his lips curving in that sexy, lazy way that made my heart thump. "Oh, I will," he replied smoothly. "You can count on it. I expect you to have the same dirty thoughts about me, too."

And with that, he was gone.

I leant back on the desk, mortified and aroused as hell. What on earth possessed me to suggest that to him? It felt good saying it, and I was certain he enjoyed hearing it, but still…

Nate stopped and spoke to Mai. She nodded, said something back, then came into my office. "That man is too handsome for his own good."

"Hmm," I acknowledged vaguely.

"So it's all official now?"

I straightened, dragging my thoughts back to the present. "I wasn't left with a choice after his performance on Friday, was I?" I moved my overnighter away from the door, then flopped into my chair, heaving a huge sigh.

"Well, I'm glad."

"I could tell you were impressed."

"You need it, Kara." Mai shut the door, meaning she wanted a long chat. "Someone to take control. Leave it up to you, no one would ever know." She was so insistent, so sure of what she said, because she knew *I knew* she was right. "That's why I told him to do it."

"What?" I spluttered, rocking back in my chair.

"At the party. You think you're not good enough, but he's crazy about you."

I knew she'd been meddling, but had no idea she was giving Nate a sisterly talking to. After retrieving my phone from my bag I set it back under the desk. "What's that?" I asked, pointing to the manila folder clasped in her hand.

Mai eagerly sprung to attention. "Before I show you," she said, wandering over, "did you know your boyfriend has four private homes, owns numerous investment properties, the three companies under NTB Group, plus dabbles in a squillion other business ventures? Not to mention the dollars he's made playing the stock market and—"

"Stop!" I held my hand up to cut her off. "Is that what it is? His business portfolio?" My head spun. Obviously I knew about NTB, but the rest? That was irrelevant. It wasn't my concern.

"Oh no," she smirked, "this is *way* more interesting."

Dread filled my stomach. "What have you done?"

"It's nothing bad," Mai insisted, flipping open the folder. "See this woman?" She jabbed a finger to a photo of a woman, likely of Middle Eastern descent and probably a few years older than me. Brunette, petite, all curvy and so pretty it was unreal. "Yasmina Sadek," she went on, spreading the remaining papers across my desk. There were many pictures, but she wasn't alone in the rest. Nate was with her.

"Who is she?" I choked, coughing to remove the jealousy trapped in my throat.

"Ex-girlfriend maybe? These photos were from social events, parties and so on. The most recent was last month." Mai sifted through them and pulled out an article dated June. "I've tried, but I can't find any pictures of them doing normal shit together in private."

I contemplated the evidence in front of me. It was bad enough I'd recently parted with Nate whilst he flew off to New York to get up to God knows what, with God knows who. Now, I was being confronted with images I honestly wished I hadn't seen. "Thanks Mai," I moaned, shoving them away. "Now I feel more inadequate than ever."

"Why show me these?" I asked accusingly, miffed that my so-called friend would do such a thing. She knew I was paranoid about my body, mindful of my trust issues.

"Hey," she said, a protective arm coming around my shoulder. "I didn't mean to upset you. You asked me about his other women, but I knew you wouldn't do anything about getting any answers."

"So you did?"

She nodded and squeezed harder. "I was hoping for a fugly chick, but it's no surprise she isn't. One look at you says Blake only pulls the gorgeous women."

"Not helping," I grumbled.

She hastily bundled the stash away. "You're missing the point. There's no evidence of him falling out of nightclubs with hundreds of different women. I've gone back two years—there's nothing. Even with this one," she said, waving the folder in the air, "it's all business. He isn't the playboy you think he is." Mai walked purposefully to the shredder in the corner. "Either that or he's hidden it well. But, you've been together, what, two weeks? There's already pictures popping up everywhere on the internet."

I watched her send all evidence of Nate's past into tiny pieces of paper confetti.

"I'll get you a cappuccino," she said, edging to the door with her head down, "then we'll plan tomorrow night."

Deep down, her intentions had come from the heart. But all she'd managed to achieve was make me curious as to whom this mysterious Yasmina was, and how significant she'd been to Nate.

JUST before eleven I received a text: **ABOUT TO TAKE OFF. WISH U WERE COMING WITH ME X**

Now, more than before, I wished I was, too. Because my doubts over trust, combined with the uncertainty of not knowing what he was doing, all blurred with the images I'd seen of him posing with this attractive brunette on his arm, as a catalogue of the last two years of his life flashed before me. And to think it only ended last month…Was I his rebound?

Because I was distracted, it took about five minutes before noticing an unknown number had come up and not Nate's name. Curious, I replied: **HAVE U GOT A NEW PHONE?**

A few moments later, I got the answer I secretly hoped for: **YES X**

"THESE smell divine, Kara." Mai was busy arranging twelve roses in a vase she'd found in the kitchen cupboards. I'd received twenty-four exquisite English roses in milky creams and blush pinks from Nate with a handwritten note that still had me smiling:

The dirtier the better…Nx

I was under strict instruction from Mai to keep half here, and take the other half home to remind me of Nate wherever I was. Not that I needed it. Thoughts of him hadn't left me since he had this morning. I leant forward for a sniff and discovered she was right.

"How was lunch with your parents yesterday?" I asked her, stroking a flower head fondly.

"Oh, you know." Distractedly, she pushed the final stem into the water. "Ate far too much, as usual."

I'd experienced a few Harvey family dinners and could sympathise. Her mother was a chef, so the food was always fantastic. That's where Mai had honed her skills. "Talking of family," I said, placing the lid back on the box of remaining roses I was taking home. "Nate's invited me to his parents' anniversary dinner in a few weeks."

"You're kidding?" Mai immediately stopped tidying up and gaped at me. I shook my head, smiling proudly. "And you still think he's not serious about you?"

"I'm beginning to accept he might be." *You're my girlfriend*…those words had floated around my head since Nate said them. I collected the box and nodded to her to carry the vase. "Before then, I'm going to lunch on Sunday to meet them."

"Holy crap!" We'd only taken a few steps when she stopped. "Meeting the parents. Twice! I haven't met Mitch's more than that in two years."

I laughed. "Maybe because they live in Florida?"

"Geography is no excuse." She dismissed my observation with a wave of her hand. "So, you and Nate—it's going well?"

"Yeah," I replied distantly as we entered my office. I set the box on the filing cabinet and made space on my desk for the vase, brushing aside the sandwich I couldn't face eating at lunch. "It's all so fast though. It's scary."

"Love is a funny thing. Happens when you least expect it and there's nothing you can do to stop it."

Did Mai really think this was love? Much as I tried, there wasn't another word I'd come up with to accurately describe my feelings. "I don't know why, but when we're together, everything makes sense. I spent so long freaking out about being used for sex, but he wants this entirely as much as I do."

"Well, duh. I got that much the minute you floated in the office with the brightest smile on your face last Monday. You wouldn't have given him that second chance if you didn't think he was worth it."

I checked my phone for missed calls or messages. "The party is black tie. I'll need something fabulous to wear."

"Ooh," Mai clapped excitedly. "Love a good shopping spree. Especially when I'm spending someone else's money."

"Get back to work." I shooed her out of my office with a smile. "Your vicarious break is over."

I sank into my chair with only my thoughts for company. It would be hard, but I had to be mentally strong and believe that whilst we were separated we wouldn't fall apart. The connection we shared was unlike anything ever experienced before. The sex, without question, was the best I'd ever had, but we weren't just fucking. At least I wasn't.

Realisation hit me like a blow to the chest. I spun the notecard from the flowers between my fingers. I was more than ready to take that leap of faith.

I'd already jumped.

DAMN ALARM.

With tired eyes staying firmly shut, I found the culprit that had brought an early end to my delightful dream. Only when I couldn't silence it did I appreciate my phone was actually ringing.

Excitement shot through me as I pressed the camera button on and waited. "Hello," I answered, rubbing my eyes awake. After what seemed like forever, the image of Nate's beaming face filled the small screen.

"Morning, sleepyhead. Did I wake you?" Nate asked with a hint of humour.

"Yeah," I murmured, snuggling into the duvet, content spreading through me from seeing him and hearing his voice. "I was having a great dream."

"Of me, I hope." His eyes twinkled, his gorgeous face backlit with the daylight from the huge loft windows behind him.

I grinned. It was almost like he was laying beside me. Almost. "You might've made an appearance." He'd done more than that. My vivid dream had been so real, I'm sure I actually climaxed in my sleep. My heart was still thundering in my chest.

"Well, it sounds like it was a good one. Need a minute to catch your breath?"

I flushed. The man could still embarrass me from over two thousand miles away. God, that sounded a long way. Too far.

"Where were we?" Nate asked. The rasp in his voice sent a tingle across my already stimulated skin.

"A deserted beach."

"No audience?" he lilted.

I thought back to our erotic performance in front of the beach house windows, remembering how turned on I was seeing us making love. "No audience, Mr Extrovert."

His warm laughter brought a whole new sense of loneliness to mind. Nate had only been gone a day, yet I felt like I hadn't seen him in weeks.

"Well, I can't wait to make your dream a reality," he purred, settling back. He was lounging on a bed set against the wall, with Manhattan as a picture-postcard backdrop.

"Good luck locating a deserted beach in LA."

His smile widened. "I know one in Hawaii."

My cheeks ached from my own grin. Stranded on a remote beach with Nate as my only distraction sounded idyllic. I stretched, not wanting to leave the comfort of my bed, as we discussed our plans for the day. Nate's first appointment was in forty minutes, still he was in no rush to end the call. It pleased me to hear he wasn't cramming a week's worth of meetings into five days, having missed most of yesterday travelling.

"I've just had a great workout," Nate said. "I thought of you while I showered."

A very real image of him in the shower came to mind. Shimmering wet, tanned skin, droplets of water clinging to the ridges of his muscles…

My stomach fluttered, the pressure in my groin forcing me to squeeze my thighs together for some relief. Even though he had on a white t-shirt, I couldn't stop myself from asking, "Are you still wet?"

"Are you?" he countered with a raised brow, his voice deep and perceptive.

I sucked in a shaky breath. The sensation of my phone vibrating in my hand as the alarm went off made me laugh. "You're incorrigible."

"What can I say? My hands aren't nearly as good as yours anymore."

I gave myself a self-congratulatory hug. "And I miss you, too."

That made him smirk. "Have a great day, Kara, I'll call later."

I forced myself out of bed and drew open the curtains. "I'm out tonight," I reminded him, resting my forehead on the cool windowpane. "I'm taking Mai to cheer her up."

"She missing me, too?" Nate drawled.

"Yeah, like every other woman in the building," I shot back.

"It's all a façade, Kara," he sneered, slightly irritated.

"An incredibly beautiful one, though."

There was a moment of silence before eventually Nate said, "They might be missing me, but you're the only one I'm lost without."

I blew out a breath, unable to respond. His voice was sad and dejected, like he'd rather be anywhere but the place he was. That, and the loneliness in his eyes, made me yearn to hold him in my arms even more. I wandered through the lounge towards the kitchen.

"You call me then," he insisted, "let me know you're home safe. I'll be awake." I reached for my mug and started preparing my first caffeine hit of the day. "Now, go get your coffee."

AT 10 a.m.. I received a text: **I MISS YOUR HANDS**

I tapped a quick reply discreetly beneath the table, as I sat in a particularly boring meeting with Michael and some other accountants: **I MISS YOURS TOO**

When Nate's immediate reply came back, it earned me a disapproving glare from my boss. I silenced my phone, resisting the temptation to read it until I got back to my office… **I MISS YOUR MOUTH**

That made me giddy and hot. **MY BODY MISSES YOUR BODY** I sent back.

I heard nothing for fifty minutes until… **I'M HARD**

It was a mistake reading that as I sipped my water because I ended up snorting it instead. My phone vibrated again: **YOU, YOUR MOUTH, FRANKLY ALL AREAS OF YOUR ANATOMY, HAVE KEPT ME THOROUGHLY DISTRACTED THROUGH MY MEETING**

I looked up and saw Mai heading my way. **YOU FREQUENTLY DISTRACT ME MR BLAKE** I text back, followed by: **GET BACK TO WORK X**

Nate didn't take heed of my suggestion as my phone went off again with another message: **I MISS THE WAY YOU PULL MY HAIR THE MOST…**

"Ready for lunch?" Mai called from the threshold of the office.

"Give me a second." I couldn't leave him hanging, so I sent another as I grabbed my bag, determined it would be my last: **DO SOME WORK!**

"Sexting the stud again?" Mai linked an arm through mine as we left my office.

"Hmm," I replied, distracted by Nate's fast response: **CONSIDER ME TOLD. GOING FOR A COLD SHOWER X**

I could've spent the rest of the day flirting, but my body couldn't cope with the torment. I was drowning in Nate Blake. And that frightened me.

"Enjoy it while it lasts." Mai peered up at me from beneath thickly mascaraed lashes, her wiser than her years observations sensing I was out of my depth. "Let's get sticky ribs and wings, washed down with margaritas. I'm starving."

WE arrived at my place a little after six. The plan was to change, then have something to eat at The Mint before Millie hit the stage around 10 p.m.

"Who's the perv in the car?" Mai nodded at the unkempt man sitting in the driver's seat of an old Lexus parked a few cars from mine. Even with us both looking, he made no attempt to hide the fact he was staring.

"Not sure," I said, locking the car. "He was there the other night, too."

"He's still staring." Mai hovered by the front doors after I'd let us in, glaring daggers at the mystery man. "Think he's a paparazzo?"

I collected the handful of junk mail from my mailbox, tossing it straight into the recycling tub. Thoughts of my safety flashed through my mind. "Did he take pictures?"

"Not that I saw." Whoever he was, Mai rewarded his persistence with a flip of her middle finger.

"Forget about him." I dismissed his relevance as unimportant as we headed upstairs. But truthfully, I found his presence disturbing. Was he watching me regularly?

I GOT my answer the next morning.

I'd been buzzing after a great night out. Millie had rocked the club, convincing me and the few hundred revellers that she was going to be a huge star. When I called Nate at almost 4 a.m. his time, I'd indulged him in a little flirtatious phone sex, aided by the fuzz of alcohol for courage. I didn't go all the way, still shy and diffident when it came to my body. It wasn't for lack of yearning to bring myself to orgasm, which I did once I'd hung up.

I was keeping busy at work and succeeding in occupying my thoughts with things other than Nate, when I found myself the subject of yet another salacious story online. I stared at the blog page Mai had so kindly loaded onto my computer.

"Look on the bright side, K," Mai urged, draping her arm around my shoulders. "They got your age wrong. Says you're only twenty-one. Take it as a compliment." Only Mai could find something positive in a trashy, misreported piece of journalism—and I used the phrase lightly.

The only accurate wording accompanying the photo of us embracing outside my apartment was the suggestion it happened before we spent the night together. And my name, clear as day in bold print underneath. The rest was a lame attempt to create problems, with references to how unstable our *'long-distance'* relationship was, and suggestions neither of us was taking it seriously. That pissed me off the most and triggered yet another round of self-doubt.

"Someone who knows me has gone behind my back and divulged this information," I seethed. They evidently knew where I lived, too.

"It wasn't me," she shot back.

"I know." I patted her hand reassuringly as she squeezed my shoulder.

"The world is full of jealous bitches," Mai said. "Get used to it, though. If you two are serious, there's gonna be a lot more where this came from. Nate's gonna take you out, show you off."

I fell back into my seat, exhausted and mentally drained. I'd never dated someone in the public eye, and Nate was, no matter how reluctant he was to be in it. I had to toughen up and embrace the new direction my life was taking.

ROBYN joined us for lunch at a new sushi bar two blocks away. Enjoying some girlie time was a great distraction from the revelation that my anonymity had gone. I was returning to the girls after a bathroom visit when my phone rang from the depths of my bag.

I answered with a soft, "Hello." The surge of ineffable emotion I got upon hearing the achingly tender, "Kara," from Nate's lips almost knocked me off my feet.

"How's New York?" I asked, my grip tightening on the counter for support as I slid back onto the stool beside Mai. They both rolled their eyes and resumed their conversation.

"Too damn far from you," he breathed. "This distance is killing me."

The pressure in my chest grew. I turned my back to the girls for privacy. "And me." The extent of how deep my ever-growing feelings were both terrified and calmed me. Before I became a sentimental mess, I changed topics. "What have you done today?"

Someone tapped me on my shoulder. I twisted and found Mai and Robyn ready to leave. I followed them out whilst Nate talked. I hated thinking of him working all night, having no respite from the demands of his job, so I was pleased to hear he'd had a reasonably quiet day and achieved a lot. I balked when he asked about my plans, coming to a standstill on the pavement.

"You don't want to know what Mai has planned for me tonight," I told him, cringing.

"Well, now I'm intrigued," he murmured, his voice raspy and so incredibly sexy.

Even though he couldn't see me, I covered my face to hide my shame. "She's taking me to a pole-dancing exercise class," I rushed out.

"Damn." Nate exhaled. "Can—"

"No," I cut him short, "you won't be getting a private performance." It might've only been a few weeks, but I'd learnt a lot about Nate, too. When he cursed under his breath, I knew it was with humour. "Need another cold shower?" I asked coyly.

"I've got five minutes to get myself together before I have to face the ten executives waiting in the boardroom." I heard the creak of leather, followed by sounds of him moving. "Christ, you know how to push my buttons."

The two friends who'd been marching ahead of me stopped and turned, finally noticing I wasn't with them. My smile was filled with gratitude for the tiny brunette hurrying me up with an exaggerated roll of her eyes. Even though I'd kicked myself when she told me this morning, with great satisfaction, that I'd agreed to this crazy class last night, I appreciated her thoughtfulness in keeping me occupied.

After agreeing to talk again later, we said a long goodbye like a pair of young lovers, neither of whom wanted to hang up first. I jogged to catch them up after finally ending the call.

"Nate?" Mai asked.

"How is the sex god these days?" Robyn added, running her eyes over me with a gleeful smile. "Giving you a good time by the looks of it."

"He's missing K like crazy." Mai relinked arms to cross the busy junction. "I've lost count of the number of phone calls. Blake's fallen for our girl *big* time."

"Tell me about it," Robyn said with a rueful sigh. "Those kisses last Friday sizzled with sexual attraction. Talk about warning everyone else to back the fuck off."

"See, K?" Mai nudged me. "Everyone sees it."

"Gah, wish some would rub off on me. It's been forever since I've had a guy so hot for me." Robyn was gorgeous and got a lot of attention, but she was picky about who shared her bed.

"I know, right?" Mai continued, the two of them gossiping as though I wasn't there. "Mitch is great in bed—when I get him there—but romance is on vacation at our place. A permanent one." She tried making light of it, but the reality of how big the void was growing between them had started to sink in.

"It won't last," I pointed out. My eyes travelled up to the top floor of the building we all worked in, and my stomach dropped, knowing Nate wasn't up there.

"*Whatever.*" Their unified statement made us all laugh.

"I wouldn't give a shit for romance if I had that hot-ass in my bed every night." Mai stepped into the revolving door, followed by Robyn.

I still hadn't decided whether to be offended or proud that my girlfriends lusted so openly after my boyfriend. What I did note? I didn't feel the immediate flicker of jealousy and doubt I once might have.

"I'd happily pick his dirty designer suits off the floor," Mai went on, barely pausing for breath as she swiped through the security turnstiles. "Hell, I wouldn't even complain about the toilet seat being left up, so long as he had me screaming his name out every night."

"Mai, you have a remarkable knack of turning every conversation into something smutty," I scolded quietly, hoping the few colleagues waiting for the lifts didn't overhear.

"One of my many talents." She blew on her knuckles then buffed them on her chest, smiling proudly.

I shook my head as we crowded into the car, answering the gentleman next to the panel when he asked what floor.

"What?" Mai's innocent tone was entirely at odds with her lewd topic of conversation. "I expect to be old, like in my thirties, before my sex life dies. At my age, I should be coming like an express train."

The greying man beside her who'd been listening with much interest received the full-on flirt, when Mai winked and rubbed his arm suggestively.

That girl was going to be slapped with a sexual harassment case one of these days. I could see it coming.

THURSDAY MORNING, I was still laughing. I'd died of shame at having to swing around a pole in front of ten strangers, but the degradation had been worth it, just to see Mai showing off. She'd convinced herself a backup career in the clubs was hers for the taking, should the need ever arise.

"You gonna show Blake some of these moves?" Mai had asked in the middle of a particularly acrobatic move.

“God, no,” was my hasty reply. But maybe one day, in the distant future, it might be fun…

I could barely contain my excitement, knowing that tomorrow Nate would be back. My eyes sparkled back at me as I grinned stupidly at my reflection in the bathroom mirror. I finished up and headed back to my office, but got sidelined by the enormous bouquet of vibrant sunflowers taking pride of place on Mai’s workstation. “Wow, these are gorgeous.”

“Gorgeous flowers from a gorgeous man,” Mai cooed.

“Mitch finally got his act together and realised how lucky he is?”

“Nah-ah.” She beamed from ear to ear. “These are from Nate.”

“What?” My attention snapped to her expectant face. She held up the card so I could read the typed note:

THANKS FOR TAKING CARE OF KARA. NATE.

The unfounded jealousy trying to rear its ugly head gradually abated.

“Can’t wait to get them home.” Mai tucked the card in her desk drawer. “Like you said, Mitch needs his ass kicking into gear. Another guy digging on me might make him rethink his attitude.”

I tilted my head, my lips pursed ruefully. Mai was as straight up as they came, not one to play petty games. Watching her head down that path reminded me how lucky I was being with Nate. “I’m sorry, Mai.”

“No biggie.” She shrugged.

“How about a blowout at Tram? Maybe a sneaky cocktail whilst we’re there?” I suggested for lunch, hoping to lift her spirits.

Mai straightened and grinned. “Now you’re talking.”

Chapter 20

My hopes of a relaxing evening were thwarted the second I stepped out of my car and got accosted by two men. One bombarded me with questions about my relationship with Nate—how long had we been dating, where did we meet, and so on. The most bizarre question he asked was the one troubling me the most—did I know who he was with on the East Coast? As if it was any of *his* business.

The second pursued me across the lawn to the front doors of my building taking photographs. They didn't let up until I was out of sight. I struggled into my apartment and collapsed on the sofa, panicked and breathless.

"I'm so sorry." Nate let out an exasperated sigh. I hadn't planned on mentioning it to him, but he knew something was bothering me and eventually prised it out of me.

"I should toughen up," I said quietly, heading into the bathroom. Maybe a long, hot soak would calm my nerves. "Dating a tabloids dream means I should get used to it."

"You shouldn't have to," he snapped out. "I've never been hassled to that extent before. As much as they're annoying, the press is usually courteous with me. There are laws they have to adhere to. Did you catch who they worked for?"

"No." I perched on the edge of the tub, picking at the hem of my robe as the water ran.

"This is all I fucking need after the day I've had."

My skin prickled at the severity in his tone. He hadn't greeted me in the usual loving way, which I'd put down to him being in company. Now, I sensed there was more to it. "They didn't get anything from me," I reassured him. "I was too frightened to speak."

Nate murmured some kind of vague response. He sounded distracted.

"Is everything all right?" I asked warily. His silence doubled my anxiety. I heard him talk to someone in the background, his voice muffled. He usually managed to separate me from his work so I received all his attention. "Nate?" I prompted again.

"You're staying at the condo tonight. I'll arrange for Ross to come collect you."

"Nate, I'm fine. I've locked all the doors." I didn't tell him I'd wedged a chair under the front door handle, like that was going to prevent someone from breaking in.

"Why the fuck did this happen now? When I'm not there to protect you?" His annoyance and frustration was rising. "Get your things together. I'll call you back."

The line went dead before I could object.

I turned off the running tap, then paced in my bedroom, confused and edgy. My mobile spun repeatedly in my hands as I waited, growing more and more agitated with every passing second. I hadn't dared peek out the window to see if the men were still there. When my phone finally rang again a few minutes later, I was so wound up I cried out at the intrusion into the strained silence.

"Ross is on his way." Nate's voice had lost its edge of belligerence, the knowledge I was being taken care of appeasing him.

"It really isn't necessary."

"The hell it isn't! Don't fight me on this, Kara," he warned. "I'm not in the fucking mood."

"Fine," I snapped. For tonight, at least, I'd let him have his way. Nate's condo had state of the art security and private entry, making it virtually impossible for outsiders to get into the building. It would give us both peace of mind, but I was mindful it couldn't happen indefinitely.

Nate's tone was much calmer and warmer when he spoke again. "Baby, I want to protect you."

I drew a deep breath through my nose. He could get to me so easily. As I exhaled, the tension left me in a rush, all irritation forgotten.

"Get settled in, open some wine, take the bath you were running," he said quietly. "I'll be back before you know it."

I did everything he asked. I packed an overnight bag to see me through until Monday, on the assumption we'd be spending the weekend together. Ross was pressing the intercom barely twenty minutes after I'd hung up from Nate.

"Why aren't you with Nate?" I asked him from the backseat as he drove us to the condo.

"Mr Blake doesn't like to take me away from my wife," he offered, full of admiration and respect for his boss. "Our first baby is due in a couple months."

"Congratulations."

His teeth flashed white, a genuine smile filled with expectant father pride. As much as he was ruthless in business, Nate was a considerate boss; another layer of him I found utterly endearing. I pulled the sleeves of my sweatshirt over my hands, having pulled on leggings and the nearest top in a rush to dress, and snuggled into the leather seat.

Ross parked up in the underground garage between the Bentley and a BMW SUV, and took me upstairs, ushering me into Nate's home. With an assurance that he wasn't far, should I require help, he left me to settle in for the night. I headed to the master suite that spanned the entire upper level of the condo. Swathed in the golden glow of the setting sun, it was warm, calming… safe. I stood on the threshold for a minute, staring at the sparkling city through the windows, but my gaze eventually snagged on the sumptuous bed.

The last time I'd seen it, it was a delicious mess of sex-crumpled sheets. Now, it was pristinely made…and a large white gift box sat at an angle on one corner. I edged towards it, my stomach quivering with nerves and a little excitement. Should I open it? *No,* I shook my head. I'm not even supposed to be here.

I went to the closet to unpack. I was carrying my toiletry bag into the en-suite when I heard my text alert chime from inside my bag in the bedroom. It had to wait because what I found in the cupboards and drawers of the vanity literally knocked the air from my lungs. They'd been fully stocked with all of my usual products—everything I could possibly need for overnight stays.

God. I leant into the vanity, my legs shaking. In fact, my whole body trembled. But I wasn't freaked out. His generosity was profoundly touching. He'd taken notice, been interested in getting to know me and what I liked. It was an intimate demonstration that he genuinely cared, and of his hopes for a future together.

My phone beeped again, reminding me of the text: **YOU CAN OPEN THE BOX**

So I did.

A strapless corseted satin bodice in the palest pink, with detailed beading, accented with a small bow at the waist, gave way to a chiffon overlaid floor length skirt. My hands were shaking, because intuitively I knew, as I searched inside to locate the label, this wasn't simply any old dress. It was vintage Christian Dior, finished with year and identification number. It would have cost a fortune.

I sat on the bed and did the only thing I could think of. I called Mai.

"Wow," she muttered, adding a whistle for effect after I'd told her everything.

"It's far too much," I said soberly. "The toiletries I can deal with, but not this." I ran an awed hand over the gown as it lay beside me on the bed.

"It's a gift," Mai scolded me. "You can't give it back. You'll kill his feelings."

That was the last thing I wanted to do. I'd offended him enough already with my inherent insecurities that prevented me from fully committing to our relationship. Nate knew I had my reasons, and I knew this was his way of letting me know how important I was to him. "God." I wiped away a tear as it trickled down my cheek. "I sound like such an ungrateful bitch."

"You sound like someone scared to fall in love," Mai said gently. "You are, aren't you? Falling in love?"

"I didn't think I could do that again," I sniffed. But this week had been hell. I yearned for Nate so badly it physically hurt. I longed to see his face, touch his skin. See the look in his eyes when he gazed at me. Wake up and have the first thing I see be his smile. "It's only been a couple of weeks. I sound ridiculous."

"I think he loves you, too," Mai offered sagely.

"Because he's lavishing me with expensive gifts?" I mumbled, slipping off the bed to get a tissue from the vanity. "Any man can do that. Doesn't mean he loves me."

"There aren't many who go out of their way to find one that means something to the woman receiving it. A guy who only wants to fuck around, even a rich one, wouldn't spend the time and effort personalising the gifts like he has. No matter how awesome the woman is in bed."

My laugh was a garbled mix of crying and genuine happiness. Mai always made me see how stupid I was being. I said goodbye to my omniscient friend, reminding her I wouldn't need a lift in the morning.

I took the dress to the closet. The rich smell of polished wood and leather warmed my bones. Comforting and welcoming, as I hung it up, the stress of the past few hours began to abate.

"THEY were supposed to be a surprise for you tomorrow." Nate had called back about an hour later to check I'd settled in okay. There wasn't the sound of music, laughter and chatter that had been in the background when we spoke earlier. Instead, it was eerily quiet, with only muffled sounds of his movements. I suspected he'd left the dinner early—if you called sometime after 11 p.m. his time early—and gone home.

"The dress is gorgeous. Thank you. I can't wait to wear it to the dinner in a couple of weeks."

Nate exhaled quickly, sounding relieved. He cleared his throat and lowered his voice. "It's fast, isn't it? What's happening between us…"

My heart started thundering, my stomach churning. "Yes," I answered quietly, afraid to say more. I pulled myself up using the edge of the bathtub and reached for my wine, sending a slosh of water over the rim and onto the tiled floor.

"Where are you?"

I laughed. "In the bath, doing as I'm told, drinking a rather nice glass of vintage Chardonnay and reading a book on European Architecture and Design."

Nate's breath hitched. "God, I wish I was there with you."

"Me, too," I breathed, rubbing the twinge in my chest. "Tomorrow?"

He laughed quietly, and I knew he was wearing that naughty smile I adored. "It's a date, baby."

I relaxed, happy he sounded better than when we first spoke. Putting it down to tiredness, I figured it best to let him go. "You should get some sleep."

"I should, but I don't want to," he murmured. "I treasure our conversations."

My eyes closed. With few words, Nate could touch my soul. Before I blurted out things I shouldn't, I said, "You'll be no good to me if you're tired."

"Oh?" His voice grew husky. "Planning on doing those naughty things you've been dreaming about to me all night?"

"If you're lucky." My flirtatious response didn't surprise me. I was beyond that, having accepted the effect Nate had on me a while ago. "So the sooner we sleep, the sooner you'll be back."

"Kara." He said my name with that hint of a whisper that frequently made me ache for his touch. "I…" He paused as if about to say something important. Something that set my pulse soaring with expectation. "Don't worry, you're safe now."

"I won't. See you soon."

"You will."

THE pulse in my neck throbbed wildly, an unsteady rhythm, missing a few beats as the speed increased. My eyes flared open as I struggled for air. Everything was strange…this wasn't my room, wasn't my bed. For a minute, I was disoriented. I clung to the pillow I was wrapped around, hugging it closer. Gradually, the sleep-induced haze began to recede, my fogged brain clearing as the beloved clean, fresh scent reminded me of my whereabouts.

The bedroom was dark. I was on Nate's side of the bed closest to the door. It was ajar, allowing a narrow strip of light from the hallway in. I frowned, unsure whether I'd left it that way when I finally collapsed into bed around midnight.

With a deep sigh, I rolled over to face the windows and closed my eyes again. The unease faded, but a hum of recognition tingled my skin. "It's because you're in his bed," I mumbled, rationalising why I sensed Nate's presence.

But it didn't go away. It grew stronger. When I heard movement from the corner of the room, I bolted upright, clinging the sheet to my chest.

"Hey, beautiful." A distinctly familiar voice came from the darkness. The shadow in one of the armchairs moved, edging forward. Gradually, his face filled the strip of light shining through the door.

"*Nate.*" My shoulders dropped with relief.

He unfolded from the chair and came over, settling beside me on the edge of the bed. "It's okay," he whispered, stroking my hair reassuringly behind my ear. "I didn't mean to frighten you."

I leant into his hand, reaching for his face in a similar embrace. It was rough with a dusting of overnight growth. "What time is it?"

"A little after five," he murmured, his thumb brushing my cheekbone. He was still shrouded in shadow, but his eyes glittered in the dark.

"What are you doing here?"

"Try keeping me away." He shifted, drawing one knee up onto the bed, keeping his hand on my face. "It made no sense being there, when the only place I wanted to be was here, with you."

I climbed into his lap and wrapped my body around him, covering his mouth with mine. It was a languid, romantic kiss, the culmination of days of pent up desires, the violent passion we shared simmering beneath the surface. Love flurried around my stomach, every cell in my body revving with arousal and the physical desperation to be with him as he licked into my mouth the way I adored.

"I thought I had to wait another day to see you," I whispered, holding his face in both hands and covering it with relieved kisses.

"Surprise," he whispered back. And it was. He must've gotten on a plane not long after we spoke, and now, here he was. I wondered how long he'd sat in the chair before I woke. He tipped me back and stared at me without a word. I could barely see him, but there was something about his silence that niggled me…a feeling that all wasn't as it seemed.

His thick cock pressed through his trousers, hard against my naked sex. The urge to make love grew, my muscles reflexing in hungry anticipation of having him inside me. My hips rocked of their own accord as I pulled him closer by the nape and grazed my teeth down his tensed jaw.

"Go back to sleep," he murmured, his breath welcome on my face. "I'm gonna grab a shower." He lifted me off him and stood, moving away towards the closet.

I recoiled into the pillow, his rejection like a physical blow. Why didn't he want me as much as I did him? When the light came on as he moved down the passageway, I got to see the man I'd missed terribly…the man who was saying one thing but doing another.

"What's wrong?" I managed to choke out.

"Nothing," he said calmly, reappearing. It looked like Nate, but something was different. He was detached, growing more withdrawn and subdued with every passing second. The unbelievable beauty of his face was marred with worry, his brow drawn in, his jaw rigid. But it was the haunted look in his tired eyes as he studied me while unbuttoning his shirt that sent a chill across my skin.

He pulled the belt from his trousers and moved out of sight. I scrambled forward on the bed, craning my neck to see down the passageway. "Something's wrong. Talk to me," I pressed, even though I was dreading his response. I hoped absence had made his heart grow fonder, not make it forget.

"There's nothing wrong, Kara," he scoffed. "You're tired. Go back to sleep."

His outright lie infuriated me. "Don't patronise me," I snapped. "I'm not a fucking child."

He reappeared, barefoot, and stood in the hallway, his powerful frame illuminated like a halo surrounding him. He exhaled harshly and ran a hand through his already messy hair. "It's been a strange week, that's all. My mind's fucked."

It didn't sound like Nate talking. My heart beat furiously as I sat back on my heels, my palms damp as they rested on my thighs. The way he was closing off, shutting me out, took me back to the morning in my apartment and the rejection I'd felt. I drew a deep breath of courage, and cautiously asked, "Do you still want me?"

He moved fluidly across the room until he was kneeling in front of me on the bench. He tilted up my chin and gazed into my eyes. No words. *Nothing.* His eyes smouldered dark and fervent, unable to conceal his true feelings no matter what his actions suggested. "More than I've ever wanted anything in my entire life."

I blinked and jerked my chin away to get a better look at him. I ran my hands down his bare chest, the connection between us charging through my fingertips. It was still there. That energy, only stronger, more concentrated, a damn near tangible force crackling with sexual tension. I angled my head so my lips brushed his. "Then prove it."

His hands dived into my hair, the force of his mouth crashing to mine almost knocking me backwards. I basked in his hunger for me, loving how he kissed me, firm and possessive, all-consuming. Any doubts I had absolved as I gave myself to him, my body telling him he owned me.

I broke free and shuffled backward to create some space between us. Using the fire in his eyes for courage, I reached for the hem of my chemise. With deliberate, exaggerated movements, I eased it over my head until I was kneeling nude in front of him, my hair tumbling down my back.

He sucked in a shaky breath, his hands flexing restlessly by his side. Nate could make me feel wanton and sexy with just one look. At that moment, when his deep blue eyes met mine, I could do anything—*would* do anything—he wanted me to. No inhibitions. No self-criticism.

Just be me.

I ran my hands over my hips, inching further up my body, all the while fixing on his eyes, drawing on them for strength. My breasts were heavy, aching and straining towards Nate, like an invisible current was there. I moaned quietly as I cupped them, the tiny bit of relief not nearly enough to satisfy me.

"Christ," Nate hissed, "you're more exquisite than I remembered."

Nate told me he needed the connection of making love to fully understand me, so I had to give him that now, to bring him back to me.

I reached for his hands and placed them on my breasts, encouraging him to touch me. The bewilderment in his eyes was barely perceptible in the dark. But it was there. He palmed them, tentatively, his thumbs brushing the puckered nipples. The small growl in his throat hardened them to a painful point.

"Forget the shower," I murmured. "I want you now." My nerves were given away by my tremulous voice as I reclined back on the bed, my whole body a tangle of nervous energy as I waited with baited breaths for him to join me.

He moved fast, stripping off the last of his clothes before weighting me with his deliciously firm body. He captured my mouth, coaxing it open with gentle licks along my lower lip. His tongue slid inside and explored my mouth, making me physically long for it in other places.

"I've been starved of you, Kara. I want under your skin, want to crawl inside your head. To possess you completely, as you have me," he rasped against my throat, teasing the pulse point with the tip of his tongue.

"You are…" I gasped, the combination of his mouth and hands on my burning flesh too strong to ignore, "…you're everywhere."

I arched my back, urging the hand cupping my breast to give me more. He circled the nipple, softly moaning, before sucking it into his mouth. Heat washed over me as I strained upward, desperate for the warmth of his body touching mine. His tongue, hot and slick, drove me out of my mind. I shifted my legs, wet and needy for him.

"Touch me," I begged, clinging to his biceps.

"Where?" His voice was gruff against my breast as he teased the other, lavishing it with as much attention.

"You know where." I was panting, writhing beneath him. The urge to come was so acute I was more than willing to do it myself if he didn't get me off soon.

"Tell me," he purred, darkly. "I wanna hear you say it."

I moved his hand from my breast and placed it between my parted legs. "Here." I pressed his middle finger into my damp, tender folds. A low groan resonated against my neck, his chest vibrating against mine.

I held him there, writhing with pleasure as his tongue invaded my mouth and he fucked me with his finger. He pushed in another, stroking the wall inside me, turning me on like never before. My hips moved, my clit rubbing his palm. I moaned loudly when he hit a particularly sweet spot. I threw my hands above my head, surrendering to his command.

"I'm so fucking turned on, watching you, seeing what I do to you." Nate's voice, husky and rough, drifted through my senses.

"Nate." I climaxed without warning, shamelessly riding his fingers as my orgasm pulsed through me, my body convulsing beneath his.

"God, I've missed that sound." Nate's thumb found my clit. He kept up the pressure, prolonging the climax, making it roll through me over and over. The needy surge for him inside me took over. I hooked my leg around his and coaxed him on top of me. He reared above me, eyes wild, full of lascivious thoughts. I reached between us, finding his thick cock, swollen and hot, and positioned the crown against my slick opening.

"I need you, Kara." He pushed gently, barely an inch inside me. My skin misted with a wash of heat.

"It's okay." I hooked both legs around his waist and tilted my hips in encouragement. He filled me, then stilled at my gasp. I could feel every inch of him, his heat, his hardness…all of him, inside me skin-to-skin. Nate's face was raw with emotion, wonder and admiration flickering in his eyes. I'd never seen him so unravelled, so unguarded. I'd never seen him more beautiful.

"Kara." The tremble in his quiet voice was excruciatingly revealing of his feelings. The sound slid, like a warm, comforting drink, through my body and seeped into my blood. He brushed his lips over mine. "Baby, you feel…"—he shook his head—"it's unbelievable."

"You are," I whispered, consumed with him. I stroked his hair back from his eyes so I could see them. "Make love to me, Nate."

His mouth covered mine, drugging me with love, lust and a million other highs I never wanted to come down from. With unhurried, deliberate rolls of his hips, he gave me what I wanted.

"I've waited all week for this," he whispered against my mouth. "I won't be without you again for that long."

Tears welled in my eyes. I couldn't imagine my life without him either. "I'm scared you're going to break my heart," I blurted out of nowhere.

"I can't break it, baby. It's already broken." His forearms framed my head, his hands coming to brush the hair from my face as he moved inside me, his breaths coming heavier and deeper. "I'm going to fix it back together again. I promise you that."

In that moment, he owned me. He understood everything about me without having to hear it.

"No man will ever touch you like this again," he muttered roughly, sinking into me with a deep roll. I shook my head. I didn't want another man's touch again. My hands cupped around his shoulders as I blinked away my emotions. The pressure was building again, his cock stimulating inside and out, the base rubbing the bundle of nerves in my clit. My neck arched as the tensing grew.

"Mine." Nate groaned, sinking into me again with unhurried, tantalising movements. "You belong to me."

"Yes." Dawn was breaking, blanketing the room in a romantic light. I hugged him, our bodies grinding against each other, our lips moving over any skin they came into contact with. He was on me, in me, he was everywhere. It was heaven.

"Come, Kara. I have to feel it."

His apparent wish for me was my undoing. I came on command, tensing around him. I dug my nails into his shoulders, clawing frantically to hold on and not fall away. Nate groaned against my neck, an almost agonised sound, as he filled me over and over, relentlessly thrusting into me. He came so brutally I felt every pulse of his cock. He stayed there for a long time, coming deep inside me, nuzzling into my neck, not allowing me to see he was as stripped as I was.

WHEN I woke and checked the time, it was nearing midday. I snuggled back into the position we'd fallen asleep in, on our sides facing each other, legs scissored and holding hands with the sheet bunched at our waists. Nate was fast asleep, any traces of stress gone from his precisely symmetrical face. Thick, long lashes curled over his captivating eyes, a straight nose, and underneath, the most delicious mouth, capable of giving such pleasure.

I drew a deep breath when I remembered what had happened a few hours earlier. Nate had made love to me again without pausing for breath. It was a strange, but very welcome, sensation to feel him growing harder and lengthening inside me. We'd rolled around the bed as the sun came up, not stopping until we were both exhausted. Only then did we fall into a satisfied slumber, neither of us willing to let go of each other.

Nate stirred and blinked open his eyes. "Hey."

My stomach quivered purely from the way he looked at me, with unequivocal devotion. "Hi," I said shyly.

The arm resting beneath my head flexed as his fingers sifted my hair, massaging softly. Worry flickered over his face. "Condoms."

"Pardon?"

"We didn't use condoms."

I stretched my legs, sore in the most wonderful way. There was something sublimely primitive about the flagrant stickiness between my thighs. I felt branded. He'd claimed me. The affected pride in his eyes made me shiver. I'd done something with him that I'd never shared with another man, not even Stuart. I could tell he knew that.

"It's okay," I finally confirmed, releasing his hand so I could touch his chest. "I'm on the pill."

He pushed up onto one elbow, his eyes flaring. "You are?"

I nodded, chewing my bottom lip. "I've always taken them as back up. I wanted to be sure about you before saying anything."

"About *me*?" Nate didn't conceal his shock, nor his widening smile. "I told you I've never been promiscuous."

Nate laid back down and held me to him, his hands soothing me, calming his own mind too, as we quietly adjusted to the change in direction of our relationship. In our desperation to be with each other, neither of us had thought about safety. It was a clear demonstration of how much he trusted me.

Of how much I trusted him.

Chapter 21

His weight crushed me into the mattress, taking my breath away with a long roll of his hips. Nate unclasped my hands from his nape and stretched them above my head until my fingertips brushed the cushions of the bed head. I'd woken after another nap with him sliding into me again.

I moaned, slotting my fingers with his, and squeezed. I was immobile, the movement of my hips working with his all I could do. His face was flushed, the dark silky strands of his hair clinging to his sweat-damp temples.

"You're the most decadent indulgence," he murmured against my mouth. "Let me worship you—love you."

His words spun in my head. My grip tightened. This extraordinary man, his eyes so large and full of devotion, rotated his hips and sunk deeper than I was certain he'd even been.

I whimpered as he took my pleasure to another level. The fire burning in my chest spread to my stomach…and lower still, until I couldn't hold it back any longer.

His mouth slammed into mine, silencing me as another orgasm coursed through my body in a tender wave. It was unforgiving, obliterating all thought, never-ending. Nate groaned, drawing our entwined hands down by my head, securing me to him, sheltering me as I rode it out.

With a firm hand under my arse, he rolled us over until my weak limbs straddled his hips. He gazed up at me, the shadows of whatever had been troubling him long gone from those engaging eyes. One hand came to my face, cupping my cheek. "Make love to me," he urged with the gentlest voice. "Show me what you're still afraid to say."

The way I kissed and caressed him, loved him as I moved on top of him, guaranteed he knew *exactly* how I felt by the time we were done.

"I can't believe you told Michael I had to spend the day in bed," I said a while later. By now, it was dusk. We'd spent the whole day sleeping, talking and making love.

"Riley's good at stretching the truth when necessary." Nate was draped over me, his lips on my neck where they'd been teasing and tempting for a good half hour whilst I played with his hair. "I told her to give the message to Mai."

"Why?"

He raised his head, grinning. "Because Mai's even better."

I laughed. His perceptive brain clearly extended to understanding the inner workings of my friend. Mai could be *very* persuading when she had to be.

"Shall we take that bath you promised me?" he asked.

"Hmm, sounds good." I could feel his eyes following me as I went into the bathroom. I caught sight of my naked, thoroughly well-worked body in the mirror as I loitered in there, stretching whilst I waited for the tub to fill. Then I saw Nate watching me from the doorframe.

Self-consciously, I turned away to swill the water. The room filled with the scent of cedar oil with a sweet orange hint, a calming aroma intended to soothe and relax. I was anything but, when Nate grabbed me from behind, my inner muscles clenching instinctively when his cock pressed into me.

He was hard.

"You're a machine," I laughed, facing him.

"Your fault." He moved in, pressing tiny kisses all over my face that made me melt. But I needed a rest.

I backed up, careful not to fall, and climbed into the bath, humming as I lowered into the water. Nate gathered some fresh towels from the cupboard and hung them on the heated rail. I was still awed by his faultless conditioned frame and sighed inwardly when I recalled how masterful he'd been during the course of our marathon sex-fest.

"Sit here," I told him, pointing in front of me. He obliged, sinking gracefully into the water so it barely rippled.

"This feels good." His hands curved around my legs, wrapping them tight around his waist as he leant back into me. "It's been a tough week."

"Was it productive?" I asked, massaging his temples.

He murmured vaguely as his eyes closed. "It was challenging. And tiring. I didn't catch much sleep." His voice turned cold, distant, much like in the early hours of this morning. "I ran into an old acquaintance who might be cause for concern. I've returned with a whole other set of issues."

A chill moved through me again. "Want to talk about them?"

"No," he answered hastily. "I have to deal with this on my own." How could he slip away from me so quickly? After what we'd shared today?

"Well, I'm here if you need me." I pressed my head to his, breathing him in, glad he was back in my arms.

He tugged my arm across his chest, the sweet kiss on my knuckles his quiet acknowledgement of appreciation for not trying to probe for more. "I asked my security team to investigate what happened last night," he offered soberly.

I didn't say anything. I'd have been more shocked if he *hadn't* done it. I was also mentally exhausted and not willing to rock the boat. But the sense of ill-ease crept further over my skin.

We stayed in the bath until the sky turned black with nightfall. The quiet times were interjected with details of our respective weeks, but otherwise, we just enjoyed each other's company. When the water was cooling, Nate climbed out. He quickly rubbed his taut body down, then helped me out and started on me.

"We have to make sure you're dry everywhere," he murmured, a smile teasing his mouth as he parted my legs.

"Thought you preferred me wet down there?" I bit my lip to stifle a groan elicited by the slight pressure he was exerting.

His smile turned salacious. *"Always."* With a brief kiss, he led me into the bedroom. "It's late, we should eat. Are you hungry?"

"Not for food," I admitted quietly.

Nate cocked his head, bemused eyes scanning my face. "That," he murmured, backing me up to the bed, "is an invitation to dinner I'll never refuse. Now I know how good you feel, I want more."

"Now?" I grinned as he settled on top of me, his touch revving my need for him. I didn't doubt for a second he could go again.

"Right now." Soft lips moved down the curve of my neck to my collarbone. "We've got a lot of catching up to do."

SATURDAY MORNING started out much the same as Friday night ended. Trying to count the number of orgasms I'd had in the past twenty-four hours made my head hurt.

Nate's edginess had gone, his whole demeanour brighter as we shared breakfast in bed. After a good night's rest he was back to his old self. It was impossible to fake the searing intensity in his eyes when we'd made love, the strength of his feelings so powerful I *felt* them in his touch. I only hoped being back here, in the cold light of day, had afforded him some clarity and the opportunity to put his worries aside. For a while, at least.

I lazed in bed and finished my coffee. Nate was in the shower, singing a Bruno Mars song so loudly I could hear him, even though he was in the master suites' second bathroom I didn't even know existed.

"You sound happy," I noted when he entered the bedroom. His body dazzled me, his chest shimmering with remnants of water. I set my mug on the tray and moved it to one side.

"I feel superb." He rolled his shoulders and stretched, gifting me a breathtaking smile. The tiny white towel wrapped around his hips slipped lower down his groin.

I crawled over the bed and slipped out to stand in front of him, pulling on a robe to cover up. "I'm so glad you're here, Nate."

His hands curved my throat, his forehead lowering to mine. "My moonshine," he whispered, eyes closing.

"Moonshine? Isn't that a potent concoction, so strong, one taste and your world will never be the same again?"

He pierced me with a deadly serious stare. *"Exactly."*

I pushed back, expecting more, but Nate looked like he'd said too much already. Not wanting to dwell on it any longer I pressed a swift kiss to his mouth, then headed towards the en-suite. "Can we go shopping today? I want something new for lunch tomorrow, and I'd like your opinion."

"Out to impress?" he called.

"This is a big deal," I said in a break between brushing my teeth. "I don't want to embarrass you."

"That could never happen." Nate leant into the doorframe, studying me intently. "But I'm not about to pass up the opportunity of a private striptease."

My brow raised, my mouth curving. He loosened his towel and placed it in a concealed laundry chute. My eyes wandered over his magnificent body, recalling how good it felt against mine. Nate eyed me in a similar fashion. He smiled, that sexy half-smile capable of doing strange things to me. "Maybe I can treat you?" he asked.

"You've spent far too much already."

"I want you to know how important you are to me." Uncertainty flickered across his face. From what I'd learnt of his past, I thought he was keen to avoid shallow women at all costs. I wasn't sure why he considered it an appropriate way to express his feelings to me.

"I don't need gifts to know," I insisted. "You're doing fine without all that. Honestly."

"I am?"

It broke my heart seeing such a self-assured man lack confidence where it mattered. I finished rinsing and dried my mouth. "You are."

"I can put it in a fancy gift box if it makes a difference?" he drawled. Ignoring him, I took my new toiletries over to the shower. "If I didn't have money, would you still have difficulty accepting my offer?"

I stopped untying my robe. "No."

He frowned. "Why not?"

"Nate, it's because you *do* have money that makes it an issue. I'd hate for you to think I was taking advantage."

"I know you're not." He shook his head, his mouth set in a thin line. "I have far too much for one person. Where's the good in having it, if I can't share it with people I care about?"

I shrugged, unable to give him a reason. His wealth did bother me, but I had to accept it if I wanted a future with him. I came from a middle-class background. Liam and I were fortunate to have had a private education, but our parents had worked tirelessly for everything they had. *I'd* worked hard. I caught his eyes as he moved towards me.

He'd worked hard for it, too.

"Okay," I conceded. "Thank you."

"My pleasure." Nate kissed my forehead. "I'll call ahead, get everything arranged."

UNDER the pretence of combing my wet hair, I faced the closet opposite and followed Nate as he moved gracefully around it as he dressed. I'd missed that body. Missed admiring it, caressing it…succumbing to it and all the pleasures it gave me. As much as I didn't want us to be all about the sex, the past day had taught me I coveted the connection as much as Nate.

"I know that look." Leaning into the doorframe, jeans his only item of clothing, Nate crossed one ankle over the other and ran a hand casually through his hair. He cocked his head to the side, mouth twisting into a smirk.

My cheeks reddened at being busted ogling him. *Again.* "What look?" I asked, turning back to the mirror.

"The one on your gorgeous face." He came in and cuddled me from behind. "I can assure you, the feeling is entirely mutual." His lips brushing my lobe made me weak. I watched him move along my shoulder, his arms closing harder around me over the towel. "But we have an appointment shortly with a personal shopper."

I was about to protest about how unnecessary that was but thought better of it. Besides, what girl doesn't enjoy being treated like a princess once in a while? I followed him into the closet to dress when he released me.

"Do you have enough room for your clothes?" Nate asked as he slipped a blue and white gingham shirt from a hanger.

"Plenty. It's only my stuff for the next couple of days."

"Leave them here. I'll move my belongings into the second closet." He straightened the hem and moved over to his accessories.

"I only need a drawer or something." I shrugged, brushing him aside so I could retrieve my underwear from the drawer.

His mouth curved. "An entire closet is too much?"

"A little," I said, laughing at his grand gesture. "Thank you anyway."

Nate came to me, clear eyes studying me, both appreciatively and warily. I nestled into his hand when he cupped my face. "I don't think you understand what you mean to me, Kara," he said quietly.

"I do." At least, I was beginning to.

"I'm not sure." He curled a damp strand of hair around his finger. "I want to give you the world."

"I've already got it," I said, tugging him closer by his shirt. "I've got you."

With leisurely licks of my tongue, I explored his mouth as if it had been weeks, not hours since I'd last tasted him. Toying with him, seeking out the spots that made him moan, I'd come to learn I could knock him off centre just as easily as he did me.

AUDREY, the efficient blonde personal shopper at Nordstrom, had selected five outfits for me, complete with co-ordinating shoes and bags. All my style, but more vibrant in colour than my choices of late. I tried the first one, a Michael Kors one-shouldered dress in cerulean blue. It was exquisite, but Nate insisted I try them all before deciding. Each one became my new favourite until I had no idea which to choose. That all changed when I put on a printed orange Roberto Cavalli dress.

"This one?" I mouthed whilst Audrey fussed around me.

From where he lounged in his armchair in the huge dressing room, Nate's adoring eyes met mine. The way his mouth half-curved from behind his hand gave me my answer. I knew I'd found the one.

En-route back to Nate's after lunch, we stopped at a luxury boutique that stocked couture lingerie. For some inexplicable reason, the sight of him browsing racks of luxurious intimate apparel made me blush furiously. I tried persuading him not to buy them—he had, after all, spent a fortune on my outfit—but he didn't listen.

He selected numerous co-ordinated sets—underwear and nightwear—and bought them all. "Not sure what I'm gonna enjoy more. Seeing these *on* you or taking them *off* you," he purred in my ear when he thought the shop assistant couldn't hear. Her smirk, as she packaged them up, told me she had. Nate's grin confirmed he'd actually intended her to.

WE took advantage of the late afternoon sun by hiking up into Runyon Canyon Park. It was only a short distance from iconic landmarks and the hustle and bustle of the colourful city, yet I always felt a million miles away from it up in the hills.

"You've quite a pace on you." Nate stood, hands on hips, watching me as I stretched using the back of a bench for support. My skin was damp with sweat, making me wish I'd worn a crop top and shorts rather than the hot pink tank and black Capri leggings.

"Go hard or go home." I shrugged and swapped legs, clasping my ankle behind me.

"Excellent attitude," he purred in that sexy whisper and took a leisurely swig of water from the bottle. His windblown hair was wet, his brow and temples dotted with perspiration. Dressed all in black, his muscles pumped so the thick veins coursing through his body were pronounced under his skin, strength and sex emanated from him in waves. Lust knotted my stomach.

"Fancy a race?" I took the bottle from him and gratefully gulped the still chilled water. His brows rose above the rim of his sunglasses. "How about we run to the end?" I challenged.

"Such confidence, Miss Collins."

"I'm fast, baby."

A predatory smile crept across his face. He removed his Aviators and placed them next to the water bottle on the bench. "So let's make it interesting." Lifting the edge of his t-shirt, he wiped the sweat from his face.

I stepped forward, placing my palms flat on his torso, brazenly touching the compact slab of muscle. "How?" I didn't stop, even after Nate dropped his t-shirt and rested both arms on my shoulders.

"If I win, I get to be inside you *whenever* I want, *wherever* I want."

"Seriously? And that's different to any other day, how?"

He gave me a wolfish smile. "I'm not always with you when I want you."

Oh. The sensual growl of his voice reawakened my libido. "You want me to be at your beck and call? Use my body for your own sexual gratification?" I'd accused Nate of wanting me purely for sexual reasons, but being with him that way, experiencing that intimacy was something I was beginning to crave as much.

"I wouldn't put it quite like that. Hopefully, you'd enjoy me equally as much."

A thrill ran through me. Part of me wanted to tell him he'd won already, and to claim his prize there and then, on the bench overlooking the sprawling smog hazed city of Los Angeles. "And me?" I asked, lips brushing his. "What do I get if I win?"

"Me," he said simply with a shrug, "to do with as you wish."

"Sounds like a similar prize to me."

"That's for you to decide." He smiled and stepped back, promptly ending my enjoyment. "I'll give you a head start."

I considered his wager as I pulled his Lakers cap back on and pulled my ponytail through the back. Whoever won, we would both be winners. "You'll do anything?"

"Anything."

I smiled sweetly. "You're on!" I was already sprinting away up the dusty track, laughing, before Nate had slipped his sunglasses back on.

For a good ten minutes Nate stayed behind me. His pace was steady, more of a jog than a sprint, whilst I was going flat out, determined to beat him. I was plotting all the different things I could get him to do in my head. It was those ideas that spurred me on and helped me push through the pain barrier.

As I approached the end of the trail, Nate was gaining on me. When he came alongside me, I acknowledged his cunning smile with one of my own and surged ahead, marginally beating him to the finish. I bent over, hands on my knees, and dragged some much-needed oxygen into my lungs.

"Looks like I'm your sex slave this evening," Nate murmured, lifting my shoulders and straightening me up. I eyed him with amusement, suspecting he'd allowed me to win. He could've easily beaten me if he tried.

"Only tonight?" I pouted, curling my hands around his neck. "That's not fair. Your prize had an indefinite timeframe."

Nate smiled and pressed his lips to mine. My already pounding pulse sped as he teased his tongue along the seam and slid his tongue into my hot mouth when I willingly opened.

"You know you have me anytime you want me," he breathed emphatically against my lips. "Always."

HOT jets of water pummelled my tired muscles. I twisted and turned, groaning as I rolled my head back and let the water cascade over me. I'd gone ahead and showered once we arrived back at the condo whilst Nate took a call.

"Enjoying yourself?" Nate's gruff voice startled me. I wiped the steamed up glass door, clearing a gap so I could see out. I ran my eyes the length of him as he leant against the wall, stopping when I reached the impressive bulge in his shorts.

"Not nearly as much as you it would seem." I pushed open the glass door. For a long minute we stared, riveted to our respective views. "You coming in?"

My invitation was met with surprise. He shoved off the wall, lips twitching with a smile and prowled over. He stripped until he was wonderfully naked and joined me. He caught my chin between his thumb and finger and tipped up my face, brushing his lips over mine as he reached behind me. "Hold this."

I took the shampoo he offered and poured some into his cupped hands. Was he going to give me a floor show? Let me watch him as he washed? I couldn't think of anything better.

"You won the bet," he breathed, moving behind me. "Let me take care of you."

With dextrous fingers, Nate washed and conditioned my hair. The touch of his hands massaging my scalp was bliss. After rinsing, he set to work on my body, using his shower gel to cleanse me. He took his time, branding me with the scent I cherished so much. My body went lax as his hands slid over my hyper-sensitive skin.

When he finally cupped my breasts, I moaned with relief. Passion flamed in his eyes, his hunger matching my burning desire for him. "My turn now," he whispered into my ear. He dropped his hands and stepped back.

He'd washed everywhere except between my legs, and one look at the curl of his lips said leaving me bereft of the ultimate climax had been deliberate. My breaths were fast, my heart beating furiously. I licked my lips and reached for my shower gel.

I stood behind him, enjoying the strength of his shoulders and back as I lathered up his body, branding him in a similar way.

"I love your hands on me," he murmured. His skin broke out in goosebumps, even though the water was hot. I kissed them away, over his shoulders and down his back. I snaked my arms around his waist, running my soapy hands over his stomach, and shuddered as my body came into contact with his.

Nate braced his hands on the tiles, leant forward and parted his legs for balance. I ran my hands over his arse, letting out a small laugh when his cheeks clenched under my caress. "You know what you're doing to me," he muttered, tugging me in front of him. He backed me up to the wall. "Tease."

Before he could make the contact of mouth to mouth, I grinned and slid down the tiles until I crouched in front of him.

"What are you doing?" he asked gruffly, staring down at me. I blinked up at him looming over me, not moving so his frame shielded me from the water.

"This." I swirled my tongue around the tip of his rigid cock. His stomach clenched.

"Baby, you won, remember?" His voice was uneven.

"I do." I teased him with soft flicks up and down his shaft, getting a thrill from him watching me seduce him. "This is how I want to claim my prize."

A small smile curved his sinful mouth. His gaze was hot, his frame growing bigger.

"Just enjoy it," I told him. I circled the swollen head of his cock with the tip of my tongue then took him to the back of my throat.

"Fuck, Kara," he groaned, steadying his legs. The longer I sucked, the louder and rawer his moans became. I hollowed my cheeks and slowed down, wanting to prolong his pleasure.

"Baby." His fingers curled around my jaw. "Your mouth is too fucking good."

Desperate to taste him, I pressed my tongue to the underside of his thick cock, feeling the veins pulsing beneath the silkiness of his skin. My clit swelled with unreleased tension, as turned on as he was.

"Kara." He jerked my face up. His eyes were wide and daring. "Make yourself come. Show me—*ah, Christ*." He bit his lower lip when I grazed the tip with my teeth.

I'd never masturbated in front of a man before, but it felt so natural I did without hesitation. I cupped his balls with one hand, the fingers of my right slipping and sliding over my clit, moving in the same rhythm as my mouth.

"That's it," he encouraged. He still had hold of my head, restraining me as he burst into my mouth so fiercely I almost choked.

My orgasm screamed through my body, leaving me a trembling heap on the tiled floor. Nate hauled me to my feet and crushed his mouth to mine.

"I love how you fuck me with your mouth," he growled. "So greedy." The water fell like rainfall, splashing across his shoulders. Nate shoved me to the wall, curved a hand under each thigh to lift my legs around his hips and drove into me so hard I cried out at the sudden intrusion. "And you love how I fuck you with my cock."

"Yes," I panted. I loved when he got cocky and dirty with his mouth. Raw and uncensored when we fucked, sweet and tender when we made love, his words always matched the mood. I shuddered with pleasure, my mind filling with remembrance of how good it was having Nate inside me. "I love it."

His pace was unrelenting, fast and urgent, like it had been days since we'd made love.

"I've wanted you in here for so long," he murmured, brushing damp hair off my face. "Soft and wet. Our bodies slipping and sliding against each other." He grasped my chin, the tips of his fingers digging in as he held me and savagely ate at my mouth.

I was still recovering as the wave of another orgasm began rolling through me. I groaned, hands sliding over him. It was physically impossible to get any closer, yet it was never close enough. I wanted him like an addiction, yearning to feel him in my bloodstream and flowing through my body. "I'm coming…"

"I know." Nate shifted and changed angles, tilting my pelvis with a firm grip of my arse. The rubbing of my clit pushed me into a second orgasm.

"God, you squeeze me so fucking tight when you come." His hips stilled as I milked him, drawing his release out with the force of my own. He pumped into me, crying my name. I cupped his face as water dripped from the tips of his hair, catching in his eyelashes and running over his chiselled face.

I was falling further and further under his spell.

Chapter 22

I dropped my knife and fork onto my empty plate and set it on the floor beside me. Nate and I had chosen to eat Thai takeout in the media room watching a baseball game. I had no idea of the rules, but Nate had kept me thoroughly entertained. He was so animated, calling out encouragement to the players and cursing the decisions made by the referee.

I stroked his hair as he lounged on the floor, leaning back against the sofa. I was wearing one of the sets purchased earlier, a silver-grey silk chemise and matching robe. Nate wore casual black lounge pants and t-shirt. Of course, he looked casually handsome as always.

"This is nice, baby." He took a swig of beer from his bottle and twisted, resting his arm on my curled up legs. "You and I relaxing, no expectations or false pretences. It's better than I imagined."

I smiled. "You say it like it's a novelty."

He shrugged. "It is."

"I doubt you spent many Saturday nights alone." I trailed my fingers along his arm. Nate didn't reply, but his body tensed. He reached for the remote and switched off the giant TV. "You can admit it," I said when he'd settled back again. "You're a good-looking man, Nate. I know I wasn't your first."

"I've told you already. There's nothing else to say."

"Why are you being so secretive? We all have pasts," I offered quietly, setting my glasses on the square end table beside me. "I guarantee yours is nowhere near as screwed up as mine."

"Christ, Kara! It's not fucking important." Nate shoved to his feet and headed to the kitchen, taking our plates with him. I gathered our drinks and rushed after him. I wasn't sure what just happened, but I was determined to find out.

When I joined him, he was leaning against the sink staring at the wall, his features twisted in annoyance. "It's important to me," I encouraged, setting his empty bottle on the counter beside him. I pressed a hand to his shoulder. "I want to know all about you like you do me."

"Yeah," he scoffed, shrugging me off, "except you won't let me in either." The ferocity of him tossing the plates into the sink with a crash panicked me. My ears began to ring with the sound of my heart thudding in my chest. Nate glanced sideways, his face set. "You're keeping secrets, too."

I winced at the harsh truth of his words. What right did I have, asking him to open up when I couldn't do it myself?

"Kara." His fingertips drifted over my cheekbone. I jumped, taken aback by the veneration in his touch and the gentleness of his voice. "I don't want to argue, to spoil an idyllic couple of days."

I hated seeing him like this, so lost and bewildered, out of control. It went against so much of what I treasured about him. Yet it gave me comfort to know he wasn't just an ideal high on a pedestal, completely out of reach. Nate was human, and he was here, with me.

I stepped closer and rubbed his arm. His eyes were mesmerising, the pupils almost fully dilated. My breath caught when I saw the depth of his feelings swimming in them as he stared back at me. The tiny tick of his jaw pulsed as he gritted his teeth. "I'm trying to do right by you. Trying my utmost to shelter you."

My body tensed. "From what?"

Nate caressed my face, seeking and finding strength the way I did from him. His eyes were fretful and undecided. God, what had happened to make him behave so out of character?

I wrapped my arms around him and pressed my cheek to his chest. His heart pounded frantically. His shower gel still lingered on me, and mine on his skin. The two scents, woody and almond merged together, giving me an inevitable sense of calm and assurance. "What happened in New York?" I asked, quiet and wary.

The fortitude I got from his arms as they enveloped me lasted a few short seconds until he reluctantly admitted, "I met an old girlfriend."

I shoved away. "You *cheated* on me?" I couldn't believe it was happening again. All the lies and deceit polluting my life, infesting my mind and poisoning my heart.

"*Jesus no!*" He urged me back into his embrace, his grip so tight I couldn't move. "I'd never hurt you like that. Forget it. I don't want you going crazy over someone that isn't worth the effort."

"*I* decide what is or isn't worth it. Not you!" I pressed my forearms to his chest, battling to resist him. My fighting only made him hold harder until I could barely breathe. I gave up. "You don't have the right to say what's best for me," I muttered in defeat.

"The hell I don't," he snapped. "My job is to take care of you. Cherish you and keep you safe." He relaxed his grip but still held me in his arms. "I'll do whatever it takes to make that possible."

Tears welled in my eyes. One escaped when I blinked, and rolled over my cheek.

Nate swiped it away with his thumb. "Don't." He pressed his lips to mine in the sweetest, most impassioned embrace. I always got the truth in his kiss. The fact he could convey such strong emotions that way blew my mind.

"I'll talk," he finally murmured into my hair. He moved away and leant back on the counter, his head bowed, fingers tapping restlessly on the lip of the quartz surface as he composed himself. "A couple years ago, I got screwed over. Completely humiliated. Everyone important to me, some business associates too, they all knew about it. She almost ruined my business." I watched him scrub over his face with both hands as he relived his shame. "I thought I knew Ash, believed I could trust her, but she…" He shook his head, his voice muffled by his hands. "I didn't see it coming because I let my own guilt cloud my judgement."

I frowned. "Guilt over what?"

Avoiding eye contact, Nate went over to the wall of windows. Both hands came up for support as he leant into them and dropped his head. He cut a lonely figure standing there in the shadows, burdened with the jagged edge of painful memories. "I'm the reason for her twisted behaviour all those years ago."

His shoulders lifted with a small, resigned shrug. "After that, I decided all women were the same, they all had ulterior motives. I built an emotional wall so fucking big no-one could get in, then I used them before they used me."

"Not anymore though, right?" The idea we were over, that he'd used me, or worse, been unfaithful because it was ingrained deep in his core that emotionless sex was all he was capable of made me nauseous.

Nate glanced back over his shoulder. "Not anymore," he assured gently, shaking his head. "I could've used drink or drugs—which would've been quite ironic—to make me forget. Instead, I chose the worst vice of all—*women*."

I stroked my throat, trying to push the bile back down. Nate wasn't a saint, I knew that, but the unanswered question over precisely how many women he'd slept with crept into my mind again. I could count my sexual partners on one hand. The way Nate was talking made me think he'd need both hands and feet and still wouldn't have enough digits.

"Hey," he murmured, approaching cautiously. "It isn't as sordid as it sounds. A select few women who shared a mutual need for pleasure without commitment, that's all." He circled me and went to the refrigerator. When he offered me a bottle of water, I shook my head, waiting uneasily for him to continue.

"My whole outlook shifted the second I met you." He unscrewed the lid and took a swig. "I wanted more than that emotional distance from you. When we made love the first time in your bed, the way you looked at me…" He shook his head slowly. "You scaled that wall, then you took a sledgehammer to it and sent the whole fucking thing crashing down in one go."

The surge of love I had for Nate was so strong I was light-headed. His finger stroked my jaw affectionately. He looked exactly how I felt. Clueless to how this had all happened between us, but so very grateful it had.

"I'm obsessed with you," he went on. "Everywhere I look, I see you. Everything I do, I think of you. You're constantly on my mind no matter where I am. But you can't, or *won't* let me in, and I'm going crazy trying to figure you out." His hand fell from my face. "If you keep cutting me off emotionally, pushing me away, it's gonna break us. And I can't let that happen. I'm in too deep."

Stunned by his impassioned honesty, I stepped forward and wrapped my arms around his neck. I had to give something back. "I haven't been on a single date in over a year," I started quietly. "You're the only man I've considered having a relationship with in that time, and I'm scared shitless by the speed and intensity it's all happening with. I lack confidence, have serious self-esteem issues, and a massive hang-up on trust." I took a deep breath. I was trembling like a leaf.

Nate stared at me with wide, compassionate eyes. "You're the complete opposite of me," I continued shakily. "Your self-assurance and contentment are two of the most attractive qualities about you. Being pursued by you, and the almost arrogant way you did it, was and still is, a massive turn-on. So, for someone normally so open with me, when you refuse to talk, it makes me suspicious."

His brows drew in momentarily, then, "She wants me back and—"

"*What?*" I shoved him so hard he lost his footing and fell back against the counter. "Why on *earth* would you assume I didn't need to know this?"

"You don't." Nate lunged for me but I was faster this time. I dodged his hand and darted to the other side of the kitchen island. Everything I'd fought against had come to fruition. I was in love and I was going to get hurt.

"Nothing happened," he said sternly, his hands visibly shaking as they raked through his hair. "I don't want her."

"Explain why you're so shaken if the meeting was innocent. I'm trying desperately not to jump to conclusions, but you're making it difficult not to by refusing to tell me the whole story."

Nate clasped his nape with both hands. "It brought back memories. Memories I've tried forgetting. I recalled how gullible I was, how trusting I'd been, how guilty I *still…*" The words trapped in his throat as his voice trailed off.

My heart ached for the shattered soul standing in front of me. The harrowing recollection of my own trust issues flooded back. Hearing he'd been screwed over perversely gave me hope he wouldn't do the same to me. He'd suffered, too. He knew how bad it was to have the one person you'd given your heart to, break it into a thousand pieces and not care.

I had to respect him not wanting to go into details. God knows I hated to. I was left depressed for days if I dredged all that crap up and dwelled on the what ifs. There was no chance of running into ex-boyfriends when I lived in a different country. Nate wasn't as lucky. He had a past, one I had to accept if we were going to move forward from this.

"Talk to me!" Nate's yell snapped me out of my thoughts. "Tell me what you're thinking!" He slammed the bottle down on the counter.

"This isn't about me!" I cried, astounded he'd deflected it back on me. "I wanted *you* to talk."

"You don't get it, do you?" he seethed, ridding his hand of spilt water and cursing at the spillage on the counter. "You have no idea."

"No, I don't!" The thud of my heart grew louder in my ears.

His eyes were large as they fixed on me. "Kara, I'm—" He didn't finish. Just shook his head and sighed as he picked up the bottle. "I don't deserve you," he murmured soberly. "I'm going to work in my office. I need to clear my head."

"That's it?" I bit out. "You're going to walk away after that self-depreciating comment?"

He studied me. A shield had formed across his face, his eyes cool and lifeless, concealing all emotion. "Go to bed. I'll join you later."

A chill chased down my spine. He'd given up. He brushed past me, heading to the doorway.

"How about I go home instead?" I said to his retreating back.

Nate stilled. But he didn't look back. "You're already there," he said softly. Then, without another word, he disappeared.

I stood for a minute, dazed and confused. He was pushing me away in one breath, then complaining I won't let him close in another. What was that about?

I trudged upstairs to pack my clothes. All hope had gone as I filled the overnight bag. I left the dress Nate had gifted me. Tomorrow, he could face his parents alone and explain why I wasn't with him.

Only when I reached the bathroom and saw all my toiletries did I understand walking away wasn't the answer. This broken man cared about me and had gone out of his way to make me comfortable so I would open up to him.

It was nearing midnight by the time I'd unpacked, and Nate hadn't made an appearance. I collapsed into bed, mentally and physically exhausted. Laying on my side, I stared numbly out the windows. The only sound was the climate-controlled air conditioning whirring quietly in the background.

I'd never been so alone and a million miles from home. This was our first fight, and I hated going to bed with unresolved tension between us. Hot, irritable and restless, I yanked the chemise over my head and tossed it to the ottoman bench.

Since Nate's return from New York, we'd taken two steps forward then moved three back. He didn't strike me as the moody type, too even-tempered and calm to get riled easily.

Unless it was me. It seemed I could provoke a reaction without even trying.

Deciding I wouldn't sleep until we'd made up, I shrugged on the chemise again and padded downstairs to his office. Nate sat at his desk, illuminated by the angled desk lamp to his right and the glow from the computer on his left. He glanced up briefly, his troubled eyes scanning me as I stood in the doorway. "I'm still here," I said quietly, nervously twisting the lacy hem between my fingers.

"So it would seem," he said soberly. He took his focus from the papers clenched in his hand when I moved closer. I wished I could banish the grief tarnishing his captivating face. He watched me warily as I rounded his desk and spun his chair to face me.

I stepped between his parted legs and cupped his face. "I'm sorry for pushing you."

Nate's eyes filled with warmth. His gentle hands were like an electric shock to my flesh when they curved my bare thighs. "I'm the one who should apologise," he murmured, pressing his cheek to my belly. "I'm taking my grievances out on the wrong person."

"It doesn't matter." I cradled his head, playing with the hair around his ear.

"It *does* matter." He shoved to his feet and stroked my upper arms with gentle, reassuring hands. "Being apart affected me more than I thought possible. I knew I'd miss you, but exactly how much completely floored me. I'm struggling to adjust to all this."

"We both have issues, Nate. Let's resolve them together."

His brow knitted. "When the time is right I'll explain everything. Promise you won't draw your own conclusions without hearing me out first?"

"Okay," I whispered hesitantly. It was a big ask, but not unreasonable. The way I saw it, it was another step closer to learning to trust again. It wouldn't be easy, but I was willing to try.

"Let's go to bed." Nate smiled softly and twirled my hair in his fingers. "Think we could both do with the rest."

As we climbed the stairs together, I put all crazy assumptions, wild guesses and wrongdoings to the back of my mind, making a conscious decision to live in the present and not the past.

THREE hours later, I woke weighted with uncertainties. Nate was sound asleep beside me with an arm draped possessively across my chest, his back gently rising and falling with each steady breath.

What was so tragic he still carried the burden of guilt with him to this day?

It must've been bad to make his ex-girlfriend seek revenge years later. And now she was back, under what circumstances I wasn't sure. I had to decide how much I was prepared to fight for Nate, but without knowing the full story, it was difficult to plan my approach. Would I be strong enough to win? Was *I* enough?

Fed up with asking questions I couldn't answer, I shifted onto my side and faced the window. Nate stirred, his arm moving to my waist as he curled into my back. My body stirred to the nearness of his naked flesh. We hadn't made love when we came to bed. All I needed then was to feel his arms around me, hold him in mine, and enjoy the tender kisses that reaffirmed we were both where we should be. Now, I was drawn to him, craving his touch in other ways.

Nate fidgeted again. I carefully peeled him off me and crawled out of bed. He needed to sleep, get some perspective on events of the past week, not have me disturbing him because I was horny.

Dressed in his t-shirt, I took my phone and wandered downstairs. After getting some water from the kitchen, I stretched out on the comfortable sofa in the lounge. Half an hour of yoga meditation later, and I'd barely touched the surface of my agitation. I meandered around the condo, stumbling upon undiscovered rooms of the sprawling penthouse.

I ended up in Nate's office. The angled desk lamp was the only light in the room. Without disturbing the papers littering his desk, I sat in the leather swivel chair and rolled it in. Something I hadn't noticed earlier now seemed glaringly obvious.

Directly in front of me, impossible to ignore, was a framed black and white photograph. I lifted it with trembling hands and brought it closer. With an elongated stretch of my body, head tipped back so my wavy beach hair touched the towel beneath me, my eyes were shut and lips parted. It looked photoshopped, but it wasn't. It was all natural—and it was all me.

God. He'd said he wanted me with him when he took the intimate, candid picture last weekend. Here I was, in an image practically sizzling from the frame. It was incredibly sexy, a woman captured in a moment unawares by the photographer. It was like seeing myself through Nate's eyes. He saw this, not a girl filled with inadequacies and imperfections.

Tears filled my tired eyes. I didn't know if they were happy or sad ones. Now, more than ever, I wanted comforting, needed some security to bring me peace—necessities Nate satisfied when he wrapped his arms around me. Without them, I settled for a familiar voice.

"Is everything all right?" My father's concern brought a welcome smile to my face. "It's the middle of the night isn't it? What's wrong, darling?"

"It's nothing. I just can't sleep."

"You sound a little low…?" I remembered why I never called my father when I was on one of my downers. He could detect my depression from five thousand miles away.

"Heard from Liam lately?" I asked, steering him away from further delving. I sat back, hugging my knees, and listened whilst he told me about my brother's travels.

"I haven't spoken to him in a while," I mumbled. "I'll try and catch him this week." I traced around the intricately carved wooden frame holding the image I couldn't stop examining as it nestled in my lap.

"Kara?" he said cautiously. "Have you met someone?"

My eyes darted to the gap at the door, thinking of Nate not too far away. How could he tell? I took a deep breath and confessed, "Yes."

"Why didn't you say? You can tell me anything, you know that." His admonishment was mild, his words encouraging.

"I don't know." I sighed. I hadn't told him because I didn't want him worrying about me getting hurt all over again. I could manage that perfectly well on my own. "Dad, I really like him."

"And he undoubtedly is utterly taken by you," he stated with parental certainty. "Is he treating you well?" I knew by this point, he'd made himself comfortable in the Chesterfield armchair positioned next to the phone in the lounge, hoping for a long chat.

"Like I'm someone really special."

"Because you are, darling. Is he handsome? Your mother repeatedly told me my suave good looks were her downfall." His fake immodesty made me laugh.

"Unbelievably so. His heart is pure gold." My stomach fluttered merely talking about Nate. I was drawn back to the photo. "He makes me feel alive, gives me strength…I feel like I'm finally content with who I am, and it's because of Nate."

"You sound like you're in love," he offered cautiously.

"It's too soon for that. Listen, I'm going to try and sleep." I faked a yawn and rolled my shoulders, guilty over not being entirely truthful. I didn't know what to say, how to explain. How could I make him understand when I didn't myself?

We said goodbye, and I was pleased he let me go without more questions or probing. I put the photo back on the desk and inadvertently knocked the remote mouse, waking the computer…

Another image of me at the beach filled the screen. I was laughing and my hand was reaching for the camera. I sat for a few minutes and straightened my thoughts, massaging my temples and combing my fingers through my hair, trying to ease my mind. I really needed some sleep before meeting Nate's parents for lunch.

I left the office and slammed into Nate. "Shit!" I yelped. "You scared the life out of me!"

Large, warm hands came to my shoulders to steady me. "It's after four in the morning." The gravelly, just-woken-up sound of his voice stirred something low in my belly. "Why are you up?"

His hair was messy, the way I liked it, his eyes heavy with sleep. I couldn't stop my arms from going around his neck. "I couldn't sleep. I came downstairs so I didn't disturb you."

His brow drew in. He glanced over my shoulder to the room I'd vacated, then back to me, but he didn't question what I'd been doing in there. "What's on your mind?"

I don't know how it happened, but he had me up against the wall and was pressing his weight into me. His face was temptingly close to mine, the sliver of light from the open office door beside me glinting in his eyes.

"Stuff." I shrugged.

Nate drew his head back an inch so I could see his raised brow. "Stuff," he repeated, testing the word.

"Meeting your parents…you," I admitted, blinking away from his penetrating gaze.

Nate stiffened. "Me?" Then his head dipped in realisation. "Ah, because I fucked up again."

I didn't want him feeling like he was constantly screwing up because he wasn't, but he had to understand I required total honesty. My silence was met with a resigned sigh. Both his hands curled around my head, holding me against his shoulder.

"I watched you sleep for hours." His lips brushed my temple. "I can't have been asleep long before you woke."

Contentment filled me from learning he'd taken consolation in me in such an intimate way. Feeling brave, I stupidly asked, "Want to talk?"

Doubt flickered in his eyes. Nate stared at me for a long minute. I felt like he was sussing me out, deciding if I was ready for his confession. "No," he said with blunt finality. My gut twisted, eyes widening at his outright refusal to talk. "Not while you're still worked up."

He massaged my tense shoulders, his able fingers exerting the ideal amount of pressure to both relax and entice. I decided to let it go. Arguing with such a headstrong man was too draining, too exhausting.

"C'mon." Nate seized my hand and led me towards the stairs. "Fuck stress. Let's work it off together in bed." The salacious smile gracing his full lips when he glanced over his shoulder suggested I wouldn't be getting the sleep I promised my father anytime soon.

Chapter 23

"Shave or no shave?" Nate scrubbed a hand over his chin as he faced the mirror in the en-suite.

"No shave." I washed the remnants of serum from my hands, grateful my hair hadn't taken too much taming this morning. I dried them and turned towards him. "I like this." My fingers drifted over the smattering of stubble on his cheek and ran along his jaw. Whilst I loved the clean shaven look Nate sported for work, I enjoyed the more rugged one equally as much. It suggested he was happy, relaxed and untroubled—something I wanted for him after the last couple of days.

"Okay, then." He shrugged, then stripped out of his underwear, giving me a treat he knew I enjoyed. "I'll grab a shower," he called out, disappearing into the second bathroom. Most people got a shelf in the vanity cupboard; I'd been handed an entire bathroom. It was an over-the-top gesture, but one I was beginning to expect from Nate.

I finished up and went to dress. My stomach growled, twisting into knots of anxiety and nerves. I hadn't managed breakfast, too on edge about meeting Nate's parents, my apprehension increased when he told me his sister and her family were joining us, too.

I was sitting on the bench in the bedroom buckling up my heeled sandals when I sensed Nate approaching. "Do I look okay?" I called out, glancing up when I was done. My breath hitched as I ran my eyes over him. Yesterday, he'd willingly allowed me to pick something for him but refused to let me pay for it. He didn't even try it on, but I knew the pale periwinkle shirt would emphasise the piercing blueness of his eyes.

It did, to a dramatically striking effect.

"You look breathtaking." He helped me stand and turned me around. His hands splaying over my back before he zipped me up set my soul on fire and my pulse soaring.

I cleared my throat and faced him. "You're not so bad yourself."

"This?" Shoving his hands into the pockets of his dark jeans, he smiled shyly and rocked back on his heels. I gave him a wry smile—I'd never seen him look *bad* in anything. Wanting to have my fingers in his hair I moved closer and began styling the damp strands. I loved how his hair could be smooth and elegant one minute, then all sexy bedroom hair the next.

Today, it was definitely the latter.

"You're getting that look again." Nate's rasp that could seduce me with just one whispered word ramped up my desire. "Begging me to take you to bed." He took a step closer until our bodies met, his hands coming to my ribcage.

I shook my head and laughed softly. If I had a look, surely it was permanently there when we were together.

"And as much as I want to," he purred, running both hands over my arse and squeezing, "we really don't have time." Challenging me with a raise of his brow, his lips curved against mine. "Unless you want to explain to my mom why we're late?"

"No," I stuttered. Sex-mussed and flushed wasn't the ideal first impression to make.

Nate's smile flashed. "Didn't think so. So let's go while I still have a shred of self-control left."

ALMOST an hour later we arrived at his parents' house. A sweeping gravel driveway led to a sprawling Spanish-style villa, painted pale yellow with wrought iron window guards. Nate parked the Bentley and faced me after he'd silenced the engine. I wasn't sure if he was nervous, but knew I sure as hell was.

"Be yourself," he assured me, "they're gonna love you." He grinned, then something caught his attention over my shoulder. "Showtime."

Nate climbed out, giving me a stolen opportunity to check my appearance for the millionth time in the rearview mirror. Taking a deep breath, I smiled at him and took his hand as I stepped out.

"Mom," he acknowledged the woman waiting for us on the doorstep, arms outstretched to welcome him.

"Nate." His mother beamed as Nate stooped to her level, giving her a one-armed hug because the other wasn't letting me go, and kissed her cheek.

"Kara, this is my mom, Sadie." He tugged me closer. "Mom, this is Kara."

"It's so wonderful to finally meet you," she gushed, extending her hand. Flawlessly made up, she wore an elegant lilac belted shift dress with sheer sleeves. A beautiful amethyst pendant sparkled around her neck and matching earrings dangled through the hair around her ears. Kind, hazel eyes smiled at me. With lowlights in shades not dissimilar to my own running through shoulder-length hair, she could easily pass for an age ten years younger than I'd calculated her to be, given the thirty-five year wedding anniversary she was about to celebrate.

"And you, Mrs. Blake."

"Please, call me Sadie." She stepped inside and called over her shoulder, "Everyone's out back."

Nate placed a hand at the small of my back and followed me through the arched doorway, framed with vibrant red hibiscus, and into the cool interior of the house. "See?" he whispered into my ear. "Nothing to fear."

The smell of home cooking wafting throughout the house caused my mouth to water. Memories of Sunday lunches at home sprung to mind, making me homesick and missing my mother.

"Nat! Nat! Nat!" The excited calls of a child echoed through the tastefully decorated family room. A mass of blonde curls sped towards us as the child launched herself into Nate's arms.

"Betsy!" He caught her in a big bear hug, tickling simultaneously until she was shrieking with laughter. In the blink of an eye, Betsy was joined by a boy, no more than two years old, equally as loud until he found his spot in Nate's other arm. "Hey, Charlie bear!"

My heart swelled as I observed Nate's ease around the children. They adored him, and the feeling was obviously mutual. He was grinning from ear to ear. Nate introduced me to two of his sister's children, then jostled them until they were both in one arm so he had a free hand to take mine again.

Sadie led us through open French doors to a flagstone patio whilst the children chatted exuberantly to Nate. Shaded by a purple bougainvillaea strewn pergola, a long table to seat ten was set in a cream theme with a bouquet of wildflowers in the centre. Rolling lush lawns, edged by palms and ornamental grasses, were broken by a large in-ground pool sparkling in the sunlight.

Nate set the children down when two men and another small boy made their way over. The elder one, presumably Nate's father, was tossing an American football from side to side whilst the other dragged the small boy, who was clinging shyly to his leg, with him.

"Good to see you again, son." The man with salt-and-pepper hair, golden tan, and brilliant blue eyes greeted Nate with a hug and typically male back-slapping. He was tall and distinguished, dressed in beige trousers and a white shirt.

"Dad, this is Kara," Nate said, stepping back to my side.

The older gentleman tossed the ball to Nate and turned his attention to me. He took my hand and lifted it to his mouth. "A pleasure," he smiled, kissing my knuckles, "call me Thomas."

The old-fashioned gesture made me giggle. After being introduced to his brother-in-law Simon and the small child Tommy, Nate took me over to a woman sat beneath a sun umbrella.

"Mel." Nate kissed the top of her head.

"Little brother," Mel replied, shooting him a wry smile.

"I want you to meet my girlfriend, Kara." Nate snaked an arm around my waist. It didn't escape my notice that Mel was the only one he introduced me to as his girlfriend, almost as if stressing the point to her. He brushed my hair aside and pressed his lips to my nape.

"Hi." I offered her a friendly smile.

"Hey." She eyed me curiously and waved a greeting, not standing up as she cradled a tiny bundle in her lap. With mousey hair and the same intelligent eyes as her mother, Mel was pretty, with a fantastic figure for someone who'd had four kids—the last only a couple months ago judging by the tiny infant suckling her breast.

Sadie poured us all a refreshing champagne cocktail as we joined Mel in the shade and watched the boys resume their game of football. It wasn't long before Betsy attached herself to Nate, perching on his knee and getting him involved in brushing her doll's hair, which he did without hesitation.

"So, you two haven't been together all that long?" Mel asked with an accusatory lilt. Her attempt to set me on edge worked. I pretended I hadn't heard and carried on watching the game.

"Long enough to know Kara isn't mentally unstable." Nate's hand settled over mine. What on earth was that supposed to mean? Did he previously date nut cases?

I glanced at Mel. She fixed a courteous smile on her lips before turning her attention back to the baby. "You know Will has a new girlfriend?"

"Not sure she qualifies for that status. Unless you mean someone else's girlfriend," Nate deadpanned.

"Seriously?" Mel shot him a look of disgust, which he shrugged off. After a minute, she sagged back into her seat. "God, what is wrong with my brothers?"

"Hey! Don't include me in your disparaging assumptions. Will's the one fu—"

"Nate!" I nodded my head to Betsy, reminding him kids were present. He grinned and turned back to Mel.

"Will is the one who's *friendly* with her, not me." He lifted his drink to his mouth. "He's big enough to handle himself."

"I'm looking out for my brother, Nate. He needs to be careful." Mel shot Nate a discerning look like there was an unspoken understanding between them. I remembered him saying Mel was overprotective and smiled as I bent to pick up the doll Betsy dropped onto the floor. Liam was eighteen when our mother died, a vulnerable age. I took it upon myself to watch over and guide him, so I understood where Mel was coming from.

She was pleasant enough, but after that exchange, I wondered if she was appraising me, sussing out if I was good enough for Nate. He laced his fingers with mine and smiled a reassurance. I didn't want anything from Nate, only him, and if that's all Mel was concerned about, I had nothing to fear.

LUNCH was filled with easy conversation and laughter. I loved seeing Nate interact with his family. To them, he was just a caring son, brother and doting uncle. I soon felt like one of the family, for which I was grateful, as it eased some of the disapproval I obviously had from Mel.

Sadie made a sumptuous meal of spicy roast chicken, homemade gravy and roasted vegetables. Having finally relaxed, my acceptance of a second helping was met with much gusto from Thomas.

"No need to make the joke again, Nathan," Sadie scolded. I flushed and pursed my lips at his impish smile.

"I've always been partial to breast," he'd admitted earlier when Thomas asked which cut of meat he wanted. "Now, it's legs *all* the way." His lewd comments even raised a smile from Mel, much to Sadie's chagrin.

Nate doted on Betsy, sharing his lunch with her as she sat on his knee throughout the entire meal. He even pretended to feed her well-loved toy Dalmatian puppy when Betsy declared him hungry.

"Does your father have grandchildren, Kara?" Sadie asked, catching me watching Nate.

"No." I shook my head and wiped the corners of my mouth with the napkin. "I'm the eldest, and my brother is only twenty-two. He won't be getting them anytime soon."

"But, you do want children, don't you?" She sat forward, eyes darting between Nate and me.

"You'll scare Kara off, mom," Mel chipped in, "all this talk of kids."

"It's okay." I smiled at Mel and turned to Sadie. "I'd love to have them, with the right person."

Sadie gave me a warm, meaningful smile that gave me a strange buzz inside. Nate stroked my shoulder affectionately, his arm draped over the back of my chair. He leant closer so no one else would hear and whispered, "Home run, baby."

THE grandfather clock chimed four in the family room we'd retired to after lunch. The traditionally decorated space was a dedication to the Blake family achievements. There were awards in glass display cabinets from school and business, framed degree and masters graduation certificates, all testament to how proud Thomas and Sadie were of their three high achieving children.

The men had taken the three older children outside to burn off some energy, leaving the ladies inside to talk. I was getting on well with Sadie, in a lot of ways she reminded me of my own mother. Nate had obviously given her the heads-up regarding my bereavement, and I appreciated that. It meant I didn't have to be put in any awkward situations of having to explain. Suddenly, the shrieks of laughter from the garden were broken by a wail of tears.

"I'll go," Sadie said. She stood, Aimee asleep in her arms, and stepped into the garden.

Mel sat beside me on the large tan leather sofa. "So," she began, sipping her water casually, "how are things between you and Nate?" Her tone was even, her expression impassive, giving no clue as to her mood or where she might be heading with her line of conversation.

"Fine." I fussed with my dress, careful not to spill my peppermint tea as I balanced it in one hand.

"Just fine?" Getting up, Mel wandered to the doors to check on the children outside. "I've noticed how he's been looking at you. I think Nate would answer very differently."

My pulse began to race. "We're good. I really care about him." *Actually, I might love him…*

"Nate has lots going for him. He's seen as a great catch by some women. Looks, wealth, incredible successes." She glanced over her shoulder, arms crossed. "Wouldn't you agree?"

I set my china teacup down in the saucer and crossed my legs, not liking her confrontational attitude towards me. For some reason, Mel disliked me, and the thought saddened me. Never having had a sister, I hoped when I met someone I'd be close to their family as well.

"Only by the shallow ones," I said. "I can't change any of those characteristics, but they're not why he's special to me. Yes, he's gorgeous, yes he's successful. I admire his ambition, but I'm not interested in his money. I have my own career and can take care of myself."

Mel came closer, arms still folded as she stayed the other side of the coffee table. Her eyes were sharp and assessing, like she wasn't sure whether to believe me. "My brother is a virtuous man. I don't want to see him taken advantage of again."

I smiled inwardly at her forthright manner—a trait that must run in the family—and thought how much it suited her profession as a straight-talking divorce lawyer. "I have morals, too. I can assure you my intentions are entirely honourable."

Mel's lips twitched with a smile, her eyes widening with interest. "I don't expect anything from Nate except his honesty," I continued as she lowered onto the seat beside me. "He knows that."

"He's been hurt before," Mel said softly as she set her drink beside mine. "It wrecked him." My thoughts wandered back to last night and all Nate had revealed about the stress his previous girlfriend caused, not only for him but also his family. "Call me an interfering big sister, but I need to ensure it won't happen again."

"You're an interfering big sister." Nate's hands came around my shoulders with a reassuring squeeze as he spoke behind me. I wasn't sure where he'd come from, or how much he'd overheard, but his stern caution to Mel said it had been enough.

"It's fine, Nate." I placed a hand over his but kept my eyes on Mel. "Be thankful you have people who care enough to speak their mind."

Mel's eyes softened as she nodded a small approval.

Nate kissed the top of my head as everyone started coming back inside. "We should go."

WE gathered in the airy hallway to say goodbye. My eyes snagged on a collection of family photographs arranged on a Queen Anne table against the wall. They were mostly of Nate and his siblings and pictures of the grandchildren. One stood out from the others. Nate was probably late teens, with disorderly lengths of hair framing bright eyes, and a killer smile telling of boyish cockiness. God, I bet he was a real heartbreaker through college.

Nate's arm came around my waist. I grinned when he offered me a recreation of that roguish charm when he realised where I was looking. My whole body shivered, attraction pulsing through me. He still had the ability to break a thousand hearts with a smile. I only hoped mine wasn't the next casualty.

"Kara, you coming Betsy party?" a tiny voice asked. I felt a tug on my dress and looked down to see Tommy staring back up with the biggest, innocent brown eyes. Everyone stopped talking, stunned by the boy who hadn't uttered a word the entire time we'd been here.

I crouched to his level and gently asked, "When is Betsy's party?"

"'Vember," Betsy cut in. "I gonna be five." She proudly held five fingers up and placed a protective arm around Tommy which he dutifully shrugged out of with a grimace.

"November," I repeated uncertainly. I had no idea where Nate and I would be in a few months.

"Want come with me?" Tommy continued with a shy smile.

Nate crouched beside me. "That's real kind of you, buddy. But, you're not quite big enough to drive yet, so how about I bring Kara to you? She can meet you there."

"You be like Ross?" Tommy asked, his head tipped curiously to one side.

"Yeah," Nate laughed and ruffled Tommy's hair, "like Ross."

"Okay." With a shrug, Tommy disappeared back behind Simon's legs.

We both rose together and faced each other. Nate tipped my chin to meet his mouth. It was only a small kiss, but the fact he did it without consideration, knowing everyone was watching, caused the claim he had of my heart to strengthen.

"It really was lovely to meet you, Kara." Sadie took both my hands and beamed.

"And you." I squeezed her hands. "Thank you for lunch. I miss good old-fashioned home cooking."

"Then you must come again, soon. That's an order."

I smiled. "See you in a few weeks."

"I'm looking forward to it." Pulling me down into a full embrace, Sadie kissed either side of my face, giving her blessing.

NATE drove the car away from the house with an ease I admired. We waved goodbye to everyone stood on the doorstep, and as we pulled onto the road, I was satisfied I'd made a good impression on them. Well, most of them.

"So? What do you think?" Nate turned the volume down until John Legend sang quietly in the background.

"That lunch was delicious, and the lemon tart was to die for." I flipped down the sun visor and checked my appearance in the mirror. My cheeks were flush from the couple of glasses of white I'd enjoyed with lunch.

"You looked like you enjoyed it."

"You saying I ate too much?" I grinned, patting my belly, pretending to be offended.

Nate snorted a laugh. "Nothing worse than a woman who picks through her meals. You gotta love a woman with a healthy appetite."

I rummaged in my tote for my sunglasses. The sun was still bright as it set in the western sky, leading us back to the city. "I get a ferocious appetite around my period. I've been known to devour obscene amounts of chocolate without pausing for breath," I stated, slipping them on.

"Your period's due?"

"Started this morning," I replied, embarrassed enough not to look at him. After what we'd shared sexually, I had no idea how he could still make me feel like an inexperienced young girl.

"Didn't time my trip very well, did I?" he ruminated, stroking his chin.

"You didn't." I finally faced him and saw he was smirking. "Remind me to give Riley my monthly cycle so she can add it to your schedule."

"Think we can leave that one between us, baby." Nate patted my knee, lips pursed wryly. I was lucky, I only suffered for a few days a month, but hadn't had to consider anyone else in a while. Knowing Nate wouldn't be agreeing to a few days apart, I figured he'd have to put up with it. If we were having a relationship, there'd be plenty more of these times to come.

"What do you think of my family?" he asked, settling our joined hands on the centre armrest.

"Mel thinks I'm a gold-digger."

Nate snickered. "She doesn't."

"My entire outfit, including underwear, was bought by you. Maybe I am," I joked.

"I know you're not," he stressed. "That's *why* I happily bought them for you."

I wondered how he could be so sure about me after his confession regarding women wanting to exploit him. Being a smart businessman usually meant having to be a good judge of character, able to run with situations based on gut instinct. The fact he'd let his guard slip in the past and been taken for a ride was clearly still an issue that bothered him. I squeezed his hand harder.

"Okay, she was a little off," he conceded. "I'll talk to her, she'll come round. Sometimes she takes the role of vigilant sister a bit too far."

"Because of your past?"

"Hmm," he agreed vaguely, removing his hand from under mine and running it through his hair.

"And Will's? Sounds like he's behaving badly."

"Mel thinks Will is heading down the same path I trod." He glanced nervously across at me. "Don't worry, Mel liked you." Pushing my hair behind my shoulder, he gave my nape a small rub. He didn't elaborate, so I didn't push him anymore.

"Betsy has you wrapped around her little finger." I thought back to the gorgeous little girl who hadn't left my man's side all afternoon.

"Guilty." He grinned and held both hands up in surrender.

"You're brilliant with them. They adore you."

Nate smiled shyly. "Think I've got competition with Tommy. He's painfully shy, yet you scored a date with him."

I threw my head back and laughed. "What can I say?" I shrugged. "No man is immune to my charms."

"I'm definitely not," he murmured.

I settled into the seat for the ride home with a contented smile. As far as meeting the parents go, today was an overall success.

LATER that evening, Nate's fingertips stroked indulgently up and down my spine as we cuddled in bed. I lay atop him, nuzzling into his neck, fingers tracing the contours of his wickedly sensual mouth. He snapped at my finger, making me jump.

"Hey," I giggled, lifting my head. With a playful smile, he kissed the tip better before placing my hand over his heart. I couldn't wipe the smile off my face as I returned to the comfort of his neck.

"I need to give you something important," Nate said, adjusting the pillow supporting his back.

"Oh?"

He eased me off him and stood, stretching as he disappeared towards the closet. I sighed inwardly at the magnificent sight, more so when he returned and I got a good full frontal view. I shifted across the bed to make room when Nate climbed back in and looked at what was clasped in his hand.

"It will give you access to everywhere—the garage, elevators, the doors."

"R-really?" I stuttered, my voice quivering with a million emotions. Apprehension, excitement, elation…*love?*

Nate pressed it into my palm. "You shouldn't feel like a visitor. Treat this place like it's your home." His eyes were full of certainty and truth. "Because it is, Kara."

I spun the card that looked more like my security pass for work than a key between my fingers. "Is this because of what happened last Thursday?"

Nate shifted and tugged me on top of him again so my chest was pressed against his navel. I propped my elbows either side of his hips so I could raise up and look at him. "I was planning on giving it to you anyway," he said. "The way I see it, Thursday's incident justifies my actions."

"Are you sure?" I blinked up, searching for any signs of trepidation. There were none. Only the look of a man who was fully committed and ready to take the next step.

He clasped his hands over mine, covering them so the card was pressed securely between them. "One hundred percent."

He swept a strand of hair away from my eyes. That simple touch of adoration had me closing my eyes and taking a deep breath to swallow the surge of love I had for Nate in that moment of unguarded commitment.

"I can't tell you now," he whispered, his voice choked with emotion, "but one day, you'll know precisely what you mean to me. How special you are, and how you've enriched my life, simply by being you."

I crawled up him and flung my arms around his shoulders, hugging him so fiercely it hurt. Even though everything was happening at break-neck speed between us, it all seemed to align and fall into place. Nate's gesture seemed like the most natural thing in the world. "I don't know what to say," I whispered into his ear.

"Say you'll leave your clothes in the closet, and bring some more belongings over so you don't have to keep returning to your place every few days." His hands worked in long, massaging strokes up and down my back.

"I don't need more, you've already got me well supplied with lingerie and toiletries." I pushed up on my hands, hovering over him, and traced his lobe with the tip of my tongue. He shuddered beneath me. I worked down his jaw to his chin with a smile.

"I thought women never had enough clothes?" Nate parted his legs so I slipped between them, then he hooked his ankles over my legs, trapping me against him.

"True," I conceded lightly, working my way down the other side to his other ear, "but I'm not like most women."

The shy smile and sparkle of adoration in his eyes ripped through me when I met his gaze. He moved closer, his hands coming from my spine up to clasp the back of my head, and murmured, "Never has a truer word been spoken."

Chapter 24

Feeling presentable and cool in a midnight navy sheath dress and nude heeled slingbacks, I made my way downstairs to the kitchen.

"Buenos días, Kara."

I stopped outside the laundry room. A short, black haired woman, mid-forties smiled at me. "Er, morning," I replied uncertainly, recalling my basic Spanish. Who was this woman?

"These ready when you go." She unloaded what looked very much like my workout gear from the washing machine and loaded the dryer. "Señor Blake say you want later?"

I smiled and nodded, offering my thanks, then continued on to the kitchen. Nate was sitting at the breakfast table reading a newspaper, but turned intuitively towards me.

"Morning, baby." He smiled softly. The look got me every time and made me want to throw myself at him. One hand came to my hip when I neared, his mouth lifting willingly to meet mine.

"Did you know there's a strange woman rifling through your laundry?" I sat beside him, gratefully taking the mug of steaming coffee handed to me.

"Maria, my housekeeper," he said, grinning. "I'll introduce you properly before we leave."

"This looks delicious," I said between careful sips, tipping my head to the colourful fruit salad and juice waiting for me.

"Thank Maria," Nate said, emptying the last of his own hit of caffeine.

"I just did for doing my laundry. She didn't have to do that."

"It's her job."

"To look after you," I said, feeding him a strawberry, which he accepted with a shy smile, "not me."

Nate folded the paper and set it beside his empty plate. "When you're here, she'll take care of you, too."

I shrugged, conceding it was no big deal. It wasn't like Maria was handling my underwear or anything… "Oh, God."

Nate jerked his head back. "What's wrong?"

"I'm embarrassed thinking of a complete stranger handling my delicates."

His eyes twinkled mischievously. He gave my knee a gentle squeeze then rose from his chair, fighting a smile. "Surely washing some is better than none? We don't want everyone knowing about your penchant for going *sans* underwear, do we?"

"Once," I corrected, chewing my lip to stop my own smile from spreading. "And that was only because *someone* decided to rip them off."

Nate carried his mug over to the built-in coffee machine in the kitchen for a refill. "Feel free to do it again," he taunted with his back to me. His choice of business attire was giving my favourite navy a run for its money. A crisp white shirt, blue-grey trousers with black accessories to coordinate with his tie said sharp and elegant, sophisticated and on-trend.

And they hugged his arse exquisitely.

Smirking, I keenly dug into breakfast, buttering some toast to satisfy the perpetual carb craving I experienced during my period. "I thought I'd be missing yoga tonight. There's no way I'd have got home and back to the Valley before six."

"That's what I thought. I may have to work a bit later tonight, so we'll meet here when you're done. I'll have Maria make something that can be kept warm until we're home."

I brought the condensation-covered tumbler of grapefruit juice closer to my mouth, my eyes narrowing warily, watching Nate over the rim as he returned. "I was planning on going home tonight."

"Okay." He shrugged. "I'll come to you."

"I meant alone."

"And you think I'm letting you out of my sight?" he snickered, swapping mugs and taking mine for a refill. "After what you went through last week?"

"I over-reacted."

"I won't consciously put you at risk," he snapped, "so don't ask me to." The unsaid threat behind his words was only appeased by the knowledge he was only behaving so crazily because he cared and wanted to protect me. From what, I wasn't sure.

"You can't keep me by your side twenty-four-seven. As much as I'd enjoy being there," I added, hoping to lighten the suddenly tense atmosphere.

Nate glanced over his shoulder, the glare in his eyes sending a chill down my spine. "It isn't up for discussion."

I set my tumbler back down and resumed eating. The stressful weekend had left me drained and I wasn't in the mood for another argument. "I thought it might be good to spend the night apart. After Saturday," I shrugged, hoping that explained how much his mood swings had affected me. With my own hormones running riot, there was the increased possibility of us arguing again if we spent too much time together.

"I thought we'd cleared that up?" Nate settled beside me again, blowing the top of his coffee then taking a measured sip, his brow slightly creased as he processed my words.

I'd learnt a bit, but the circumstances surrounding his ex in New York were still muddy and vague. "It's not like we can do anything."

"You mean make love?" Nate asked. I nodded. "And you *still* think that's all I'm interested in?" The offence in his voice cut me like a knife. He set his mug down and shoved his plate away so he could rest his arm on the glass table.

"Nate, I don't." I was cross with myself. Nate had gone out of his way to prove he wanted a relationship, and now I sounded like I hadn't noticed or appreciated his efforts.

Taking his hand in mine, I tried blocking out the offence raging in his eyes. "I love being with you. And I know you want more. I'm hormonal and testy, likely to throw out random insults without thinking. I didn't think it fair you suffer with me."

"But I *want—*"

I pressed a finger to his lips so I could finish. "The weekend was as difficult as it was wonderful, for us both. Clearly something is troubling you." I squeezed his hand further, my heart constricting with love from the way his eyes were warming again. "A night apart might be good for you, give you some space to clear your head."

Nate stood and cupped my face, his thumbs pushing under my chin so I looked up at him. "I've had a whole goddamn week of space, Kara. Give me more, I won't know what to do with it. You calm me. You give me clarity. When you're not around, I struggle to make sense of anything."

That pleased me. Nate was becoming my anchor, someone to steer me and help me focus on what was important in life. But I couldn't become reliant on him to be there for me all the time. Once more, I found myself in the position of having to choose between my friends and the man who had become extremely important to me. "With no family here, my friendships are all I have. I don't—"

"You have me," Nate said, pressing a kiss to my forehead. I hated the fact that the question of whether I actually *did* popped into my head.

"I don't want to be one of those girls who drop their friends at the first signs of romance. I can't risk losing them." My decision was beginning to feel like a bad one as his lips moved down my neck, bared as a result of my hair being tied back in a low ponytail. My legs fell open to let him step closer.

"Real friends won't bail on you for wanting to spend time with your boyfriend," he murmured roughly into the hollow of my neck. "Especially after spending a week away from him."

"I know." I sucked in a breath when Nate sucked gently. "And I know they won't," I continued shakily, my knees tightening around his legs. "Because it's you, they actually encourage it, in the hopes of obtaining some juicy gossip."

Nate's delicate, seductive touch ceased, his eyes growing dark and assessing as they drew over my face. He took a step back, leaving me empty. "I don't tell them anything," I reassured him, reaching for my coffee because the air had grown decidedly chilly again. "Not sure they'd cope with the hotness."

The corner of his mouth lifted into my favourite sexy half smile. After a long silence, he relented. "I enjoy spending time with you. There's nothing I'd rather do. Spending all day without you, knowing you're so close but I'm unable to see you doesn't bear thinking about." He took the mug and set it down so he could hold my hands. "I want our day's to begin and end together. But—" he silenced the protest I was about to make with a brief kiss, "I understand your friendships are important. So, enjoy your time with them, so long as you're thinking about me while you do."

I cocked my head, trying to figure him out. There was no way he'd just backed down and agreed to me spending the night at my place. I wasn't about to argue, though. I clasped the knot of his tie and urged his mouth down to mine. "I always am."

WE finished breakfast then made our way to the lobby, stopping to collect my workout gear from the laundry room. Nate said something to Maria in Spanish, and presuming it was an introduction, I extended my hand.

"Hello."

Maria stopped ironing and, wiping her hands on a towel, made her way towards us. Her eyes were like black onyx and shone with kindness, her olive skin barely aged. She patted my hand approvingly and conversed with Nate in fluent Spanish. He had such a distinctive, sexy voice, but hearing him talk in a foreign language sent it to a whole other level.

"She said you're beautiful," he told me, smiling proudly as he picked up a sports bag packed with my yoga clothes. "Ready?"

"Yep." I turned to Maria. "Gracias, Maria."

Maria offered her goodbyes, shooing us out so she could finish her household duties.

"Since when do you speak Spanish?" I asked him, collecting my tote from the foot of the stairs as we passed.

"Since I grew up with a Mexican housekeeper. She taught me a few words."

A few words? He shrugged it off and followed me into the lift. "A man with many talents."

"Sweetheart," he purred arrogantly, backing me into the corner with a smug smile, "you know I am."

AFTER settling into the back of the Mercedes, Ross drove us both to work.

"Manny's coming in on the red-eye Thursday from New York," Nate said, his thumb brushing my knuckles. "I'm seeing him Friday, then meeting up with a few of the guys for drinks in the evening."

"Sounds like fun. I have my girls night out to keep me entertained."

"Thought we could meet Saturday for lunch. I want him to meet you."

Glad he wanted to introduce me to yet another important person in his life, I shifted sideways and leant back into his side, folding his arm around me. "Can't wait."

"Good, I'll let him know." Nate's phone vibrated against my back where it was tucked inside his jacket. "Clark," he answered shortly, "what have you found?" He straightened, removing his arm from my shoulder. "They're not associated with any agencies?" He glanced briefly at me then switched his attention to the scenery passing by his window.

I found my own phone and settled into the seat, deciding to message my father and Liam. Ignoring the late night phone chat, I'd missed our fortnightly catch up. His mind would be working overtime after my revelation, so I felt obliged to reach out and let him know I was okay.

"They can't just vanish. There must be something you've missed, go back and check again." Nate spoke calmly, but there was an underlying menace in his words as he conducted his business. I finished my message then shut my eyes and let his conversation wash over me. I wondered how such a sensitive, loving man could hold such immense power that had people withering into nervous wrecks from a perfectly executed sentence or pointed stare.

It was only when I heard him say, "Security," that I paid attention again. I opened one eye. Nate was staring at me intently, his beautiful face set with worry and the driving necessity for answers as he continued questioning whoever was on the other end of the call. "In the meantime, I want additional men to watch Kara. Immediately."

I shook my head fiercely, mouthing "no". Security protection was so unnecessary. Nate remained impassive as he turned away again. "Until I say otherwise," he stated, then with a curt "Thank you," ended the call.

Without giving me a chance to speak, he tucked the phone back in his jacket and said, "Pout those alluring lips at me all you want, but I told you I'd keep you safe at all costs. I won't change my mind about this."

Nate was a man on a mission, and my stubbornness earlier had likely prompted this outburst of over-the-top craziness. As far as he was concerned, he was ensuring my safety, for his peace of mind as much as my own. If that meant pissing me off, so be it.

"You also agreed to explain fully what happened in New York and you haven't," I grumbled.

Nate turned sharply, the muscles in his jaw tensing. "I've told you already, nothing happened. What I haven't explained are the circumstances for her return, and why I have a problem with her being anywhere near you. Near us." He glanced at his stunning Patek Philippe watch, one of many in his collection of timepieces. "Eight-fifty a.m. on the way to work isn't the time."

"You're making it worse not telling me, leaving me to second guess you." I crossed my legs and angled my body away from him, tapping my phone on my knee. I wasn't sure any time would be the right time to hear what he had to say.

"You promised you wouldn't," he said sadly. His hand covered mine, halting the anxious tapping. "I don't want to get into it now, then you rush off to your office with inevitable questions I'm unable to answer because I'm not there." He prised the phone from my hand and kissed my knuckles. "Just trust me."

My breath caught, then released in one long slow exhalation. I still wasn't sure if I was capable of doing the one thing Nate repeatedly kept asking me to do. Yet I knew what it was like to have secrets. Deciding not to force it, I edged closer and wrapped my arm around his waist, settling my cheek on his shoulder and appreciating the comforting arm that came around mine. "Okay."

MAI wanted all the details from my weekend as she made coffee in the kitchen. Her exhilaration over the key made me laugh.

"Moving in together!" she shrieked, spilling half the milk over the worktop.

"I'm *not* moving in with him. It's only been a few weeks," I reminded her. "Far too soon to make that type of commitment." I wasn't paying attention as I wiped down the counter. Cohabiting was a major milestone, one that after three weeks together, we absolutely weren't ready for. So how was it possible to feel a tiny bit of disappointment that he *hadn't* asked me to move in? I shook my head.

"Kara," Mai muttered disapprovingly. I scrunched up my face, preparing for a telling off from the know-it-all standing behind me in a vivid orange A-line skirt and patterned blouse. "It might be too soon, but Nate's giving you everything you wanted. Don't question his sincerity. Has he done anything to make you wonder if he can be trusted?"

I outlined what I'd discovered about events whilst he was away. Mai listened carefully as we strolled back with our coffees, waiting until I'd finished before offering her opinion. "You've done the right thing in giving him some space. Let him tell you in his own time. There's a reason why people are *ex*-girlfriends or boyfriends."

"You don't think I'm being naive?" We reached Mai's workstation and she sat, careful not to crease her skirt.

She shook her head. "Innocent until proven guilty."

"Why are you convinced Nate won't break my heart?" I asked, lowering my voice so the three other women on the adjoining workstations didn't hear.

"No idea. But you've changed and I like the new you." She shrugged and scanned my bare arms and legs. "You're flashing the skin a bit more, taking risks, got a certain sparkle that comes from having great sex." I opened my mouth to reprimand her but she continued before I could. "You're getting stronger, and I suspect he has something to do with that."

If my friends were noticing the changes in me, I wondered what Nate thought. He was the one making it possible, and I was curious to know if he knew it. I sipped my cappuccino and checked my watch, seeing it was nearing ten.

"Relationships are never certain, Kara. Look at me, I've agreed to spend forever with Mitch. Right now, that's the last thing I wanna do." She wafted her left hand in front of me.

"Your ring!" I gasped. The tiny diamond ring was noticeably absent. "What have you done?"

Mai slipped her headset over her shiny black hair with poise and grace, the picture of coolness, entirely unaffected by the bombshell she'd dropped. "Mitch pissed me off so bad last night. I dropped the ring in the glass of water by our bed when I left this morning. Hope he chokes on the fucker."

"Mai, you don't mean that."

"No," she said with a grin, raising her hand to be high-fived, "but it was hella good to say it." I pursed my lips, convinced she wasn't telling me the full story. Finally, when I didn't return her display of female solidarity and left her hanging, she relented. "Okay, I emptied the water out over his head, *then* dropped it in. Happy now?"

I snickered. Sometimes, I felt a tiny bit sorry for Mitchell. *Sometimes.* "What did he think of the flowers?"

She rolled her eyes and pursed her lips. "Said they were nice. *Nice!* Can you friggin believe it? Didn't ask who sent them or anything. I was pissed off all weekend. I tweeted the shit out of it so everyone knows what a dirtbag he is." That meant at least five thousand random people had read her dirty laundry. She didn't know that many people, but subscribed to those programs where you spent dollars and earned followers. Her fingers started thumping her keyboard as she tapped away, scowling at her screen. "Fucker," she seethed again.

"Do I need to take you out for lunch?" I asked with a smile, giving her arm a gentle rub. Mai's gloom always lifted with some cocktails at noon.

She grinned. "Yeah, baby."

Laughing, I started off back to my office. "Oh, Mai," I said, turning back to her, "get this. His sister thinks I'm a gold-digger."

Mai snorted. "It's not what's in his wallet you want. You need what's in his pants more."

Once more, my dear friend had lowered the tone of the conversation.

MICHAEL cancelled our weekly meeting, so I decided to tackle some work I'd been delaying starting. After spending two hours going stir crazy trying to reconcile figures for a project, I understood why I'd been putting it off. I pulled off my glasses, squeezing my eyes shut and rubbed my temples to ease the headache threatening to erupt.

When I opened them, I caught sight of Nate striding through the banks of workstations towards me. All sophisticated and refined, he looked as hot as I remembered when I watched him dress this morning from the comfort of his bed. He managed to be elegantly classy, yet incredibly sexy at the same time. Not many men pulled that off. Adrenaline surged through me. What was he doing down here?

He spoke briefly to Mai, then continued to my office. One hand was tucked behind his back as he stopped the other side of my desk.

"Can I help you, Mr Blake?" I asked coyly.

His head was bowed, but his eyes lifted to meet mine, the corner of his mouth curving into a half-smile. I visibly squirmed in my seat as my body heated.

"I have something for you," he said, his voice low and quietly composed.

"Now that sounds intriguing." My eyes dropped briefly to where his hand still remained behind his back. The dimple in his cheek deepened.

He placed three giant bars of Teuscher Swiss Chocolate, all tied together with a cream bow, on the desk and pushed them in front of me with his forefinger. "You mentioned enjoying chocolate. I thought these might help satisfy you while I'm unable to." His eyes were hazy with need. I imagined my own looking the same as I reached for the sweet treat. All I craved right now was him, and not being able to indulge in him was the sweetest torture.

"Poor substitute for you," I breathed, unravelling the bow.

Nate's eyes flashed with the briefest glimmer of surprise. In slow, practised strides, he made his way around the desk, unbuttoning his jacket. In the next breath, I found myself caged into my chair by a brooding, sexy as hell man. "Right answer," he purred, lowering his face to mine.

I sucked in a shaky breath and began unwrapping a bar, all the while holding his gaze. "How are you going to get your kicks the next couple of days?"

He declined when I offered him the first chunk. My taste buds burst into life when I ate a piece. It was so good I let out a small murmur of appreciation as it dissolved in my mouth.

"For a well-educated woman, not to mention an English one, you have an extraordinary turn of phrase. I'm confident I'll find a way, though," he murmured, the pad of his thumb swiping over my lips. "These still work, don't they?"

My tongue darted out to wet my lips as I nodded. Seeing him suck the chocolate he'd collected from my mouth off his thumb made all the muscles low in my stomach tense. I knew I was blushing as a wash of heat crept up my neck to my cheeks.

"Then I shouldn't have too many problems getting my kicks, as you so eloquently put it. You know how much I crave your sweet mouth." I gasped into his kiss, shocked by the intimate gesture in such an open environment. Anyone could be watching.

My hands went around his neck because I didn't care if they were. My whole body vibrated from his strong, imposing presence. "Hmm," he murmured darkly, "chocolate and you. What a wicked combination."

I felt weak from the look in those smoky eyes as they lingered on mine.

"Unfortunately, I can't stay and indulge in some more. I have to leave for a meeting." Nate straightened and adjusted his trousers. My smirk over his predicament was met with a raised brow of amusement.

"Where is it?" I asked, fighting to claim my breath.

"Downtown. Ross is waiting in the car."

I snatched my security pass off the desk. "I'll walk you out, I could do with a break."

I ignored Mai's joy at seeing us together as we passed hand-in-hand, too busy struggling to keep up with Nate as we strode briskly to the lifts. The playful boyfriend had disappeared. In his place, the poised, driven businessman with an aura surrounding him that gave off an unattainable, slightly intimidating persona.

The lift doors slid open and Michael stepped out. "Ah, Kara," he said, glancing between the two of us. "I was coming to check up on you. How's the stomach? Gastro's a bad thing, I had it once when—"

"Kara's busy right now," Nate cut in, raising our joined hands. I grimaced at the shock and disapproval on Michael's face.

"I'll be back in ten minutes," I apologised as Nate led me into the empty lift, "and my stomach's much better now, thanks for asking."

"Right, okay…glad to hear—" The doors slid closed on Michael's bemused face.

"Don't think he was expecting that." Nate grinned and tucked me closer.

"Not sure I was either." I only hoped Michael didn't hold our relationship against me, or treat me differently now he knew I was with Nate.

My lover. Our boss.

ON the way home, I toyed with the idea of asking Mai to drive me over to Nate's. During dinner with the girls, my inadequacies had decided to make an unwelcome appearance. If I wasn't able to physically connect with Nate, not give him the self-proclaimed connection he craved from me, would he be forced to look elsewhere to satisfy his insatiable needs? After all, no relationship for two years meant he hadn't had to deal with the inconvenience of periods. In the past, if he wanted a fuck, he just went out and got one.

Despite my nagging doubts, I went home. I was about to head indoors when one of two burly men approached me. "Don't be alarmed, Miss Collins. We're your security detail. I'm Carl," he said, introducing himself, "that's Joe."

Joe was sweeping his eyes up and down the road, his back to me, but turned and nodded his head. I looked at them both, unsure how they'd managed to fit inside their sedan car. They were massive. "We'll be out here all night," Carl, the bigger of the two said. "Any concerns, call this number." He handed me a business card with the name and number of a private security firm on it. "We'll be with you right away."

He had the type of eyes that inspired trust, even though the size of him was menacing, and not someone I'd want to meet in a dark alley. "Thanks."

Thinking they were in for an uneventful night, I headed inside.

Chapter 25

"Good morning, Kara."

Ross nodded his head and opened the rear door of the Mercedes waiting for me. At least I'd been given some forewarning that I'd be driven into work. Nate had called half an hour ago and informed me he'd prefer that over driving myself, even with Carl and Joe acting as escort. I hadn't argued. I was learning to pick my battles with Mr Blake wisely. "Morning."

I waited until Ross climbed in before handing him a travel mug of coffee and some sachets of sugar through the front seats. "A gift."

"You shouldn't have." He looked uncomfortable as he took it and cautiously sipped it. "But, it tastes great. Thanks."

"Your boss has you running all over town for me. It's the least I could do."

Ross smiled widely and placed it in his drink holder. "Have a peaceful night?"

"Are you asking, or your overprotective boss?" I buckled up and caught his friendly smile, suggesting it was a little of both. "Well, you can tell him I'm still intact," I confirmed, wrapping both hands around my cup.

"Mr Blake cares a lot for you, Miss Collins."

It was a small reassurance without overstepping the mark and betraying Nate's trust, and it was much appreciated. Their relationship was more than employer/employee—they were friends, too. Nate valued Ross' loyalty and discretion, he was a trusted confidante. "Why is he obsessed with my safety?"

"I'm not in a position to say." That made me more suspicious. Celebrities had paps, crazed stalkers and much worse, yet most of them didn't have armed guards. Having one made me *more* nervous, not less. Ross eyed me warily through the rearview mirror.

"You're right, I'm sorry. I shouldn't have asked."

Ross smiled apologetically and started the engine. I barely heard my mobile phone ringing from the depths of my handbag over the advert on the radio.

"Are you with Ross?"

I rolled my eyes at Nate's concern, then grinned when Ross caught me doing it as he quietened the volume. "Yes, you at work?"

"Been here a couple of hours." I don't know how he survived on the few hours' sleep he got. Whilst I was an evening person, Nate was definitely a morning one. My mouth twisted wryly. Actually, he was a morning, noon and night man. "Without you keeping me warm, what's the point in staying in bed?"

"I can keep you warm tonight. Do you still have that dinner?" My breathing space from each other had lasted all of a day before I was missing him.

"Unfortunately," he mumbled dismissively.

Being with a group of businessmen while they hashed out the finer points of the Star deal wasn't my idea of fun, and the last thing I wanted to do. Putting my needs aside, I asked, "Need a date?"

"Really?" he said, surprised by my offer.

"Yes." I was a big step, one I was ready to take.

He cleared his throat and muttered, "I appreciate it, but it'll be all business."

"All right then." I watched gated driveways and tall hedges pass my window in a blur. "I'll miss you."

"I'll miss you more," he murmured, his voice achingly tender. "Remember that."

AFTER a long day at work, I opted for a run over the gym. I set a gruelling pace, pushing myself to the limit. My body was coiled tight with sexual frustration and a hollow feeling in the pit of my stomach.

I let myself into my apartment and snatched my ringing phone off the kitchen counter. Taking a deep breath, I was still breathless when I answered.

"Um, think I have the wrong number," Nate joked. "Didn't realise I'd called a sex chatline."

"You shouldn't have those numbers anymore," I panted, walking into the en-suite. I turned on the taps to run a bath then made my way back into the bedroom.

"Talk dirty to me, baby."

I saw my already flushed face turn redder, but played along. "I'm all sticky... *very* sweaty...in need of a strong pair of male hands to give me a good rub down..." The catch of his breath spurred me on. "But, I'm alone, so it looks like I'm gonna have to do it *all...by...myself...*"

"Ah, Kara." His voice turned raspy and ached with need. "Walk me through that, step-by-step."

I laughed softly, catching sight of the time. "Wouldn't want to make you late for dinner. Another time, maybe."

His groan of agony sounded so sexual I had to sit on my bed. "I'll be with you around eleven," he murmured, "midnight at the latest."

"Oh?" I said, toeing off my trainers.

"That too late?"

"Not at all, it's just...I assumed we weren't seeing each other. I was planning an early night." Even with the two men keeping watch, I wasn't comfortable about going to bed and leaving my door on the latch so Nate could let himself in.

"I wasn't thinking. Lock up and get some sleep."

Relief mixed with disappointment flooded me. I loved how Nate knew my thoughts without needing an explanation, but was still saddened not to see him. "Thank you."

"Anything happen tonight?"

"Nothing. I even managed a run with my two new best friends," I told him, referring to Carl and Joe who'd trailed me in their car. I balanced the phone on my shoulder and peeled off my leggings. "Can you call them off now? I'm sure you can determine better use of their time."

"They're doing their job. What better use could there be?" he replied smugly.

Exasperated, I shook my head and returned to the en-suite to turn off the taps. "If someone was out to get me, surely they could reach me at work?"

"Don't count on it."

I figured I was probably being watched there, too. "But," he continued, "if tonight is uneventful, I'll consider giving them a couple days off."

I wiped the mist from the mirrored cabinet to see my face. Then I rolled my eyes at myself, but it was aimed at Nate. From tomorrow, we'd be together anyway so they wouldn't be necessary. "Hope your dinner meeting is a success, Nate."

"See you in my dreams, baby."

HAVING RECENTLY got Nate back from a week of absence I was desperate to spend time with him. Alone. He'd given me remote access to his calendar, so mid-morning Wednesday I decided to use that privilege. I booked an hour out at 2 p.m., the only time he had free in a packed day. Then I text him: **FANCY A LUNCH DATE?**

I'LL CLEAR MY SCHEDULE

ALREADY DONE X I returned with a smile: **MEET U UP THERE AT 2. I'M BUYING**

Shortly before I was due upstairs, I ducked out and bought a couple of wraps and smoothies from the local deli, then made my way to my man.

"Hey, Kara." Ramón greeted me like I was an old friend when he stepped out of Nate's office. "He's waiting for you in there. You saved me a job today," he grinned, nodding to the lunch. Then he winked, "I owe you."

A little embarrassed, I told him it wasn't necessary, then scurried inside.

"Kara." Nate prowled towards me. *Those eyes.* Even from a distance they were luminous, sparkling with expectation. His index finger lifted my chin as he planted a kiss on my lips. "I wasn't sure what devious plan you had for lunch," he said, taking everything from me and walking towards the windows behind his desk, "so I did this."

Outside, on a small shaded terrace, a small round iron table had been set with cutlery and folded white napkins. In the centre was a single white lily stolen from the display in Reception.

I linked my arm through his and bumped shoulders. "You're a bit of a romantic, really, aren't you?"

"It's all for you." We stepped outside, and after taking a moment to properly say hello, we ate an undisturbed lunch. It was a precious time, one I realised I'd had so many of already but hoped for many more.

"Are we going home together tonight?" Nate asked, finishing off his turkey and grilled vegetable wrap.

I smiled, loving how he thought of his place as our home. "Sounds good."

"I'll be done by five so we'll leave whenever you're ready." He wiped the corners of his mouth with a napkin. I chewed my bottom lip and scooped up a piece of avocado that had fallen onto the wrapper from my wrap. "We'll get dinner out, or eat at home. Your choice."

His gaze was hot, the smile now teasing his lips carnal. I shifted in my seat to alter the pressure on my wanting clit. "You look like you want me for dessert," I murmured, sucking my finger clean.

"You taste sweeter than any dessert." He lifted my hand to his mouth. Again, he had me transfixed as he sucked each finger in turn, using his tongue the same way he did on other areas of my anatomy. Pressing his lips to my palm, he returned my hand to my lap and without preamble, asked, "Do you still have your period?"

"Yes."

"Well, then," he said, the backs of his fingers brushing my hot cheek, "you'll have to have me for dessert instead."

"We can't spend all our time in bed," I laughed.

"Why not?" I knew it wasn't a serious question from the playful tilt of his head and dancing eyes. "You love being in my bed."

His confident air caused a tight knot in my stomach. *How could he do that?* I'm certain I didn't have the same effect on him, I don't even think I could if I tried. Taking a sip of my banana ginger smoothie, I sought to halt the simmering need for Nate and restore some sense to my brain. "A meaningful relationship requires more than just sizzling sex."

He flinched. "We have more." He shoved his chair back so the iron legs scraped across the concrete and headed inside, throwing his rubbish in the bin before going into the bathroom.

"We do," I called out from the threshold of the outer door. The running tap stopped and Nate reappeared, drying his hands on a towel.

"Go home after work."

I approached cautiously, conscious I'd offended him. "I wasn't brushing you off."

"I know. I'll pick you up at seven."

"We can leave together. It's not a problem anymore."

"Go home and change. I'm taking you out—on a date." Nate threw the towel into the bathroom and took my hands, his eyes warm and affectionate. "We haven't had many. It's time to change that."

A broad smile crept over my face. "Does this mean I get to lose my shadows?"

"When I'm not with you, they are. Get used to it." He went to his desk and removed a file from the drawer.

I joined him and picked up the photo proudly displayed on his desk. It was taken at the beach, a headshot of us both with Nate pressing his lips to my temple.

"Do you recall what either of the men who harassed you looked like?" he asked.

"Not really, it happened so fast. Why?"

He opened the file and pointed to a security camera still. "This man was caught outside here a couple of weeks ago."

I examined the image, but it was difficult to see his face beneath the baseball cap pulled low over his brow. "And you think it's the same person?"

"Possibly." Nate drew a deep breath and closed the file. "My security team are investigating. Whoever he is, he's pretty smart at hiding."

I clung to the photo pressed to my chest, resting my hip to the desk, and gulped back a frightened sob. "They're after me?"

Nate moved fast, coming to me and prising the photo from my white knuckles. "I suspect you're being targeted only as a means of reaching me," he assured, gathering me protectively in his arms. "That's why I need my team with you a while longer while we figure this out. I can't let anything happen to you."

It was further affirmation of his deepening feelings for me, and the kiss that followed was equally as loving. A no-holds-barred, uninhibited kiss, with no concern about where we were or who might see. "You can ditch the shadows later though," he murmured against my mouth. "You're coming home with me tonight. I need to feed you your dessert."

NATE picked me up at seven prompt looking seriously hot in dark denim, a white shirt and unruly tousled hair. It was a warm evening, but I'd slipped on a short-sleeved black blazer over a red lace camisole with panties to match, black skinny jeans and the red heels I'd worn to the bar.

We'd passed the condo on our way, pulling up in Westwood Village before strolling to a small art deco cinema screening classic Audrey Hepburn, one of my favourite actresses. At the gilded ticket booth, the woman serving us fawned all over Nate, ignorant of my presence as she purred and flirted her way through the transaction.

He took no notice. He was more interested in the side of my face, watching me glare at the woman old enough to be his mother.

"She's gorgeous isn't she?" Nate said to her, the arm around my shoulder pulling me closer. "I can't keep my eyes off her."

When I faced him, eyes wide with shock, he planted a sensuous kiss on my lips. The woman blushed so badly I actually felt sorry for her. "Yeah," she spluttered, handing me the tickets with a harried smile.

"What did you do that for?" I asked quietly as we moved away.

"She was making you uncomfortable. It was disrespectful, so I called her out on it." He spun me in his arms, taking me in an impulsive embrace, oblivious to the throng of people milling around us.

We snuggled on the back row, feeding popcorn to each other, enjoying the normality of our date. After a lite bite at a grill around the corner, we went home to the condo.

"LET me make you come," Nate pleaded, sliding his hand between my legs. He cupped me, then applied more pressure with his middle finger so it felt like the lace material was non-existent. "You want my touch."

I moaned and pulled him closer, keen to taste his mouth again. Side by side on the bed, we were a writhing tangle of wanting limbs, our connection forbidden by mother nature. The circling of his fingertip over my clit, his thumb grazing the flat of my stomach along the edge of my underwear was doing crazy things to me, and he knew it.

"Yes," I panted into his mouth, devouring him with long, languid kisses. A warm, talented hand slid beneath the lace, followed by a groan so deep it shook his chest. I dragged my nails over his back down to his bare arse and gripped hard.

The rhythm of his hand, in perfect sync with decadent licks of his tongue, was making me climb higher to the edge of orgasm. I hooked a leg around his hip, opening wider for him. "Oh, God."

"You're close," he breathed, lowering to pull a hardened nipple into his mouth. "I won't last much longer. Give it to me."

"Now…right there…" I bit my lip, clutching him against me as I fell apart, crying his name over and over into his neck.

"Yes, baby. Let me hear you." His voice shook, his control slipping away with as much speed as mine.

He'd got me off so easily. Being with Nate had opened my eyes to a whole new sexual awareness of my body. The way I looked, how I moved. *What I wanted.* And I was starting to love it.

Nate rolled me on top of him and caressed my jaw. "Take me in that sweet fucking mouth of yours. Make me come."

Those words held so much power and changed the dynamics entirely. I was the one in control now, not him. I wriggled quickly down his body, keen to give him the same pleasure he had me. "Hmm," I murmured, taking his cock all the way to the back of my throat.

"Fuuuck." He wrapped my hair around his wrist and fisted his hand.

I sucked enthusiastically, alternating sensation between tongue and teeth, hearing his muttered profanities and praise as my head bobbed up and down. He swelled in my mouth and his hands dived into my hair the exact second he exploded. "Sweet fucking Christ, you're too good," he panted, holding me captive. Days of pent up tension flooded my mouth that I eagerly lapped up.

I stayed there, nuzzling his groin whilst we both regained control of our bodies. "I feel like a horny teenager," I admitted. I'd barely come down from my own high before giving Nate his, so only now could I fully absorb how quickly we'd both come undone.

"Tell me about it," he muttered, his breathing resuming its normal rhythm. I crawled over him and collapsed onto my back beside him. "You could make me come just from making out. Doubt many teenagers would orgasm that way."

"And you couldn't make me? Nate, you make love with your mouth."

When he didn't respond, I turned fractionally to see if he'd fallen asleep. The grin on his face caused my heart to stop briefly from its gorgeousness. "I like that." The tip of his finger feathered along my lips. "So do you," he paused to kiss me, "in more ways than one."

With a playful dig in the ribs with my elbow, I turned to the window, hooking my right leg outside the sheets. Nate switched off the table lamp and spooned behind me, wrapping an arm around my waist and nuzzling into my hair. It had been frantic and passionate, but the pleasure I took from driving Nate to the brink and seeing him fall apart when he was in my mouth, sometimes with such ferocity it shocked me, filled me with confidence and pride.

And it was one of the most liberating moments of my life.

Chapter 26

"Where the hell did you find that?"

I stared, wide-eyed at the picture of two lovers embracing on the pavement amid a throng of curious onlookers. Within hours, the clinch worthy of an epic romance Nate and I had shared was receiving numerous hits on an internet blog.

"Well, um," Mai stammered, looking extremely sheepish. "I kinda set up Google Alert."

"For Nate?"

"For you." She winced at the thunderous look I gave her. "Don't be pissed with me. It's exciting. My BFF is famous!"

I snorted. "I am *not* famous." I yanked my bag onto my lap and dug out my tin of lip balm. "I feel like I'm being stalked," I whined, slathering on the strawberry balm. Add in all of Nate's obsessions with safety and I was becoming a little more than freaked out.

"People wanna know what Nate-sexy-as-fuck-Blake is doing," Mai said, swiping the pad of her index finger over the waxy balm and dabbing her own lips. "You're newsworthy by association. This blog gets all the scoops on you two. It was the first to break your relationship, now this. There's a fashionista one that's loving your style, and—"

"Stop." I held up a weary hand. "Please stop." Scrubbing both hands over my face, I sighed. "If you want to keep reading this garbage, go ahead. Only do me a favour?"

"Sure thing, sweet cheeks," she smiled, her eyes dancing with fevered excitement.

"Don't tell me about them anymore. I don't want to hear about any of it."

Mai returned to her desk, subdued and sorry for herself. I didn't have time to worry or feel guilty. I was in the right, entitled to defend my privacy any way I could. I would have to become more vigilant and alert to my surroundings, that's all.

A little after seven, Nate arrived at my apartment with a small overnighter and laptop bag to work on later. Whilst he showered, I ordered dinner from the organic cafe I regularly used. We ate cross-legged on the sofa and watched repeat episodes of Friends. Afterwards, Nate propped his feet on the small round ottoman stool and the laptop on his lap.

I curled up and enjoyed watching him work, fascinated by how fast his mind worked to resolve issues, and how easily he manifested ideas and suggestions for strategies and plans. He remained focused, even when he joked I was distracting him. When Indecent Proposal came on TV, I soon became engrossed in the film, even though I'd seen it many times before.

"Are you seriously crying?" Nate laughed, catching me wiping my eyes with a tissue.

"What?" I shrugged, taking another from beneath the coffee table. "He let his wife sleep with someone else, now he's devastated."

"More fool him," he murmured. "If you were mine, I wouldn't share you with anyone."

I grinned, realising he'd been watching as he repeated one of Robert Redford's lines. "Thought I was yours?"

"Ergo, my point is proved."

Shifting to the other end of the sofa, I propped my bare feet in the gap between his stomach and the laptop. "You're a gazillionaire, have you ever made an indecent proposal?"

"I want to," he purred provocatively, eyes darkening as they raked the length of my body, "to you."

I turned back to the TV. "I slept with you for free."

"Poor negotiations on your part, baby."

"Don't think so." Nate had given me guidance to discover myself again. That alone was worth far more than any amount of money. "Besides, I wanted to be romanced first. You had to prove you were worth the risk." I shrugged, stifling a smile and faced him again. "Girls are suckers for all that."

"Hmm." Keeping one hand wrapped around my feet, the other stroked his chin thoughtfully. "You want to be wined and dined?"

"Wined, dined, then taken to bed for some exceptionally good sex," I admitted shyly.

Nate's mouth curved lazily, whilst his eyes flared with unfulfilled desire. It was the same way he always looked at me. Like he could never have enough. He lowered his feet to the floor, snapping the laptop shut and setting it down beside them, deliberately taking his time with measured movements. Then he tugged my ankles, pulling me flat on my back.

He crawled over my body and straddled me, the brunt of his weight taken by his thighs. "I can wine and dine…seduce you." The intimacy of his quiet voice stabbed at my chest and squeezed all the muscles in my groin tight. His talented hands found their way beneath my tank and cupped my bare breasts.

"Copping a feel isn't seductive."

"No?" he teased, head tilting as his smile widened to his eyes. His thumbs skimmed my nipples. I shook my head, unable to speak for fear of a groan escaping my mouth instead. He lowered to graze the hard point with his teeth over the fabric. "I can tell you like it, though," he murmured, blinking up through thickly lashed eyes.

I let out a long breath, squirming beneath him. Nate removed his hands and pinned mine above my head so they dangled over the arm of the sofa. "Allow me to try again." His mouth swept over mine and started nibbling along my jaw. "This better?"

"Better," I whimpered, filling my lungs with the fresh, clean scent of his washed hair and skin, "but keep going. I need to be sure."

I felt him smile. "See?" One hand trailed down my arm, caressing my torso, and slid beneath my arse. "I told you I could do it."

"You're pretty good at it, too." I pushed my breasts into his chest, desperate for contact.

"Yeah?" Nate sat back, releasing my hands. His eyes shone triumphantly from having his sexual prowess confirmed. I spread my fingers over his thighs, appreciating the thick slabs of muscle beneath his black sweatpants. "Are you still bleeding?"

I nodded, embarrassed, as an ache swirled its way through my core. "A little bit."

"Damn." Nate dropped his head, but I could see the playful smile creeping over his face. "I was kinda hoping you'd keep those glasses on, make all my wet dreams come true."

THE NEXT morning I woke with a driving urge to make love. I was aroused, merely laying beside Nate, the knowledge he was near seeping into my psyche, making me wet between my legs. He was propped up with pillows—his customary sleeping position—his breathing even and rhythmic. His right arm curled around my shoulders as he slept with me tucked safely against his chest.

Tentatively, I tiptoed fingertips over sculpted pecs and down, not stopping until I found him beneath the sheet. Nate's upper body rolled, like a wave moving through him. Fearful of him waking and me losing my nerve, I circled a hand around his morning erection and began masturbating him.

Nate hummed his enjoyment, a rough gravelly sound from deep in his chest, quickly followed by a sleepily breathed, "Fuck, yeah," that had all my senses tingling with feminine supremacy.

Sliding on top of him, I held him steady and took him inside me with a quiet gasp.

I caught the flutter of his opening eyes just as I lowered to kiss him. He took a second to respond, not fully alert. Then he opened up and let me in, his tongue joining mine in a lazy, wake up embrace.

Nate's hands finally found me, gliding up from my waist. He gathered my hair and held it away from my face in a makeshift ponytail.

The look in his hazy blueish-grey eyes was unlike anything I'd witnessed before. The unquenchable thirst he constantly had for me was present, but something else lingered behind it. It was almost a sense of pride, of accomplishment. Nate cocked his head, his cheek beginning to dimple as he waited for my next move.

I started to rock, my palms pressed to his ribs for balance. An orgasm was brewing, purely from him being inside me, stretching me, throbbing and swelling. He was magnificent, full of sexual masculinity as he sat back for the ride, his eyes twinkling in the early morning light. Occasionally, he licked and suckled my breasts as they bounced mere inches from his face, but mostly he quietly watched me, focusing on my face…and losing control with every ragged breath he took.

Sweat dotted his upper lip as he bit down on the lower one. I saw the spark in his eyes, the brief fluttering shut of his eyelids, the second he fell over the edge. *"Kara."*

Nate stilled my hips with both hands, pumping into me ferociously as he came.

"Ah, God!" I was right there with him. The shudders of my orgasm spurred through me, every single nerve ending alight with sensation. I collapsed onto his chest, hot and flushed, the sounds of our heavy breathing and racing hearts in my ears.

"Jesus, where did that come from?" Nate panted, his fingers winding into my hair. When all he got was a small shake of my head in response, he gave a long contended sigh and pinned me to him, working a hand up and down my spine.

Mmm, I could get used to this. Abstaining for a few days whilst I had a period didn't feel like so much of a hardship if playing catch up was this much fun. When my limbs felt like they belonged to me again, I sat astride him. Damp, messy hair and beautifully pinked cheeks, my breath caught as I gazed into his bright sparkling eyes.

I was becoming addicted to Nate, to this, and the way I felt when we were together. My shyness was abating, and I was becoming more comfortable in my own skin. A few short weeks ago, I wouldn't have dared make the first move as brazenly as I had. I basically jumped him the minute I woke. No talking. Nothing.

"Good morning," I said softly, brushing my hand through his hair.

"Waking up with my dick inside you makes it a *fantastic* morning." Nate's magnificent smile flashed as he squeezed my arse. I grinned and rolled off, scissoring one leg with his and settled into his side. "You're frisky this morning, baby. What's gotten into you?"

"Waking next to a sex-god can do that to a girl."

He snorted. "A sex-god?"

I giggled and tugged him closer. "Sorry, did I say that out loud?"

Nate tipped up my chin. "You did." His glorious face was so bright with happiness, I had to touch him, almost to check he was real. I stroked his jaw from ear to chin and swept my lips over his neck, tasting the saltiness of his still slightly damp skin. Then I buried my face in the crook of his neck so he wouldn't see how deeply I was falling for him.

"What time are you meeting Manny for golf?" I asked, outlining his pecs with my finger.

"Ten."

"I never had you down for a golfer."

"It's a businessman's sport. A time to make deals, gather contacts. It's an easy way to spend the day catching up." Nate reached across and checked my phone for the time. "I'll go home after we've dropped you at work." He curved my thigh, urging my leg further around him like he was settling in for a while, and began drawing circular patterns on my flesh.

"Ross is coming here?"

"Yeah," he said, his hand moving to my bare arse.

"When?"

"In about thirty minutes." He laughed when he saw my panic.

"I better get ready," I said, trying to free myself.

"No," he breathed into my hair, "I want to lose myself in you a little longer before facing my day."

"I can't stay late tonight to make up time. Mai has us meeting the girls straight from work."

"Fine," he sighed, his grip relaxing. "Don't drink too much tonight. And stick together as a group."

Smiling, I sat and swung my legs off the side of the bed. "All day, when you're out on the golf course, *playing with your balls*, think of me," I suggested casually, staring him right in the eye.

Nate gave me a wicked smile. "I'd rather *you* played with them."

"I know," I murmured. "And now I've guaranteed, every time you take one out, every time you tee up, you're going to be reminded of me and how badly you want me."

I moved so fast he had no time to catch me when he lunged forward. Instead, I left him sprawled naked and so goddamned sexy across my bed in a groaning heap of sexual frustration. I bumped the en-suite door closed with my hip and went to the shower with a swagger and a smile I'd never experienced before.

AFTER the great start to my Friday, the workday was relaxed and relatively uneventful. My co-workers were chilled and everyone was winding down for the weekend. Except for Michael.

At ten minutes to five, when a lot of staff were leaving, he'd called me with a last minute request. Now, I was scrambling to piece together a high-level financial presentation for him to review over the weekend.

"Why didn't he ask for it earlier?" Mai whined from the visitor's chair where she'd been waiting impatiently since five.

"Don't know." I kept my focus on the computer screen, concentrating on my accuracy.

"It's Friday night for fuck's sake!" Scowling, Mai collected the papers spewing from the printer. "Doesn't he get we have lives?"

"Apparently not." We were due to meet Robyn and Jenna at Estrella at six—twenty minutes ago. Mai dumped the papers on my desk and slumped back into the seat. "You should help with this," I suggested. "Brush up on your analytical skills."

"Bullcrap. My analytical skills will be finely tuned tonight, when I check out the finest men this city has to offer."

I snorted a laugh. "Are you ready?"

"Just have to re-do my make-up." Mai was gorgeous as she was. Her hair was shiny and sleek, face flawless and subtly made-up, and her tiny frame poured into a thigh-skimming LBD, with obligatory four-inch black heels. Fortunately, I'd managed to change and get ready before Michael threw our plans into disarray.

"Do that whilst I pull this together and hand deliver it to Michael. We'll leave when I return." I shoved my seat back and stood, gathering the presentation pages together.

"You best put your jacket on before you see him. Those tata's look fan-frickin-tastic in that jumpsuit."

"Go!" I covered my chest with one hand and pointed to the door with the other. Mai didn't argue and skipped off to the bathroom.

"I've emailed a copy and printed one out," I told Michael, who was at his desk playing Solitaire on his computer. That put my back up. "Here." I thrust the papers under his nose and stepped back to the doorway.

After fifteen minutes of silence whilst he read through, and then re-read it again, I was itching to leave and audibly sighing. Unprofessional, but I was getting annoyed and suspected he was doing it deliberately. I checked my watch for the umpteenth time, hoping my subtle hints would tell him I had to be somewhere else.

"Good work, Kara. I'll enjoy reading it more thoroughly later," Michael finally offered. *More* thoroughly? He tucked it into his briefcase and leant back in his chair, his rounded belly making one button on his shirt pop. "How's everything going? Settling in well?"

I'd worked here for almost two months, yet only now did he deem it necessary to ask how I was. "Everything's great, thanks. I'm really enjoying it."

"Hmm, I'm sure," he muttered, brown eyes assessing me. "You look nice. Who's the lucky guy?"

"Um..." I crossed, then uncrossed my arms, uncomfortable with his perusal. "No guy. I'm meeting friends for drinks."

"Oh well," he suddenly said cheerfully, "have a good weekend."

"You, too," I called, already halfway back to my office. Mai sprung from her chair the second she saw me, collecting my bag from her workstation.

"No need to go in there," she said, gesturing to my office. "I've shut everything down and locked up." She stripped my jacket off me and shoved my black envelope clutch into my chest. "Let's get outta here."

AFTER wine and tapas in Estrella, we all hopped in a taxi and continued our night at a bar in West Hollywood. By 11 p.m., much alcohol had been consumed, and plenty of laughs had been had. To escape the sticky heat and heaving throng of people inside, I joined Mai outside whilst she had a cigarette.

"Where's Nate drinking?" Mai asked on a long drag.

"Not far from here," I said. "Manny's at the Mondrian."

She perked up, her pretty face taking on that mischievous appearance. "We should go say hi."

My brows lifted. "No, we shouldn't."

"C'mon, it'll be fun."

"It's getting too crowded in there," Jenna announced as she and Robyn joined us. "Let's go someplace else. Any suggestions?"

I closed my eyes because I knew what was coming before Mai even opened her mouth. "I know just the place!" I heard her exclaim.

The queue outside the Skybar wasn't all that long, and eventually the doormen allowed us past after some sweet-talking from Mai and proof of age. She strutted through the discreet white door at the side of the hotel. I followed, yanking up my top and fussing over my appearance, hot and flustered.

The bar was modern but comfy, and with a distinctly more refined clientele. Gorgeous men and women adorned cushioned stools in earthy tones scattered around low-level tables. Steps led down to an outdoor terrace, where more patrons enjoyed a party-like atmosphere with uninterrupted views of the LA skyline.

"Drinks," Mai announced, zoning in on the bar. She ordered four apple Martini's, conveniently forgetting she'd recently sworn off them. After being served, she gave a coquettish flick of her hair as thanks to the bartender. "Now, where's that fine man of yours?"

"Not sure." The four of us moved away from the crowded bar. I wasn't sure how Nate would react to me being here. I edged us towards the stairs when I heard a rich, throaty laugh that was all too familiar..."You *have* to be kidding me."

"Kara!" Mai cried, slamming into my back and almost sending us crashing down the steps. "What the fuck?" She followed my eyes and saw what had caused me to freeze.

Walking around the pool edge, his head lowered close in deep conversation, was Nate and a petite brunette. His hand was lightly grazing her lower back—skin to skin—and hers was around his waist.

"It might be nothing." Mai tried reassuring me, but my pulse was racing and heart thundering at an alarming speed. I couldn't move.

"Yasmina Sadek," I muttered through gritted teeth, gaping at the beauty wearing a short silver cocktail dress that shimmered as she moved like a second skin.

Mai dragged her eyes from me back to them. "Shit, you're right."

They reached their group of friends—two men and two women—and sat. Close. The group didn't blink at the couple's shared intimacy, nor when the dusky beauty pawed at Nate's chest over the white cotton of his shirt.

Warning bells started ringing in my head. I downed my drink in one go, ignoring how violently my hand was trembling.

"I'm sure it's nothing," Mai repeated, her eyes large and fearful. I could see the doubt creeping into her thoughts the more she stared at me. Nate chose that exact moment to plant a flirty kiss on the corner of Yasmina's mouth as her fingers twirled in the hair at his nape.

"Still convinced?" I sneered cynically.

"Girls!" Jenna called. Her and Robyn had found space at a table and were busily making room for us to join them. They'd also managed to order shots whilst I'd been watching my world fall apart before my very eyes.

My feet carried me over, but my mind was lost in other thoughts. I sat, sliding the olive off the stick with my teeth, and contemplated how all my hopes and dreams had been destroyed so quickly. He'd been found out. Blatantly flirting, basking in the reciprocal attention, was making me sick. I knocked back a shot. Then I knocked back Mai's.

"Getting pissed isn't the answer, K."

I dismissed her scorn with a wave of my hand. Obliterating my pain with alcohol sounded like the ideal solution to me. A heavy, thumping bass tune was pumping out from the DJ on the decks. My head was beginning to feel the numbing effects of alcohol, but mixed with the noise and a fog of deceit, it really started pounding.

Nothing made sense anymore.

Through the blur, it hit me. He wanted to prove a point, one I'd known all along. That he could have who he wanted and would quickly replace me when I'd served my purpose. Little did I know it would be with a woman who'd been a constant in his life for years.

"I'm sure there's a reasonable explanation," Mai offered cautiously. "He said he was meeting friends. Don't torture yourself with something you don't know for sure is happening."

"Why do you always stick up for him? If you think he's so great, go ahead, be my guest. Looks like he's fair game tonight." I dropped my head, staring into the next full shot glass lined up in front of me. "It'll be history repeating itself all over again."

I tipped my head and swallowed down the tequila, wincing at the taste but not sucking on the lime. Mai stared, crestfallen and wounded by my vengeful comments.

"Sorry," I sighed.

"I'd never do that to you. I'm always Team Kara." She reached for my hands. "Let's go down," she said, standing. "If he is fucking you around, he'll have me to answer to." With large, determined eyes, I knew she meant business.

I wobbled when I stood too quickly. I would never get past the unknown, past the constant questioning of a man's intentions unless I confronted him instead of running away.

With shaky legs, I headed to the stairs.

Chapter 27

Nate was too enraptured with his other girlfriend to notice Mai and I approach their table. I tapped him on the shoulder.

"Kara!" He pushed to his feet, the most beautiful smile lighting up his face, and pulled me into his arms. "You came."

I stiffened and jerked back when he tried to kiss me. Holding me at arm's length, he gave me the once over with confused eyes. I wondered whether he knew I was falling apart when his glorious eyes flinched and a line began to form on his brow.

"Been here a while, actually," Mai warned. I was too enraged to speak.

Nate blinked slowly, from me to Mai and back again, sensing something was off.

The music was louder outside, with lights bouncing off the pool surface in time to the pulsing dance beat. His male friends were baying behind him, heckling him for an introduction. "You look stunning," he breathed, unable to stop his eyes from raking me in their usual way.

Pain lanced through me, threatening to weaken my resolve, until one of the blondes asked, "Who the hell's this?" sneering contemptibly down her probably plastic nose. *Catty bitch.*

Deciding I could be one too, I draped an arm around Nate's shoulder, marking my territory, and eyed her with loathing. Yasmina sat, smiling sweetly at us, saying nothing. Spotting a full tumbler on the table, I briefly considered throwing it over her but concluded it would be a waste of alcohol. Instead, I swallowed it in one, scrunching my face in distaste when the amber liquid hit the back of my throat and scorched its way down.

"Take it easy!" Nate snatched the glass from my hand, muttering apologies to his startled friend as he placed it on the table.

"Fuck you."

His expression was thunderous when he faced me. "What the hell's wrong with you?" he seethed, his voice low so no-one else heard.

The bitterness made me gulp back the knot of terror in my throat. "We should talk."

I headed back to the stairs with Nate hot on my heels. When there was enough distance between us and his friends, I stopped and faced him.

"You've proven your point. You're pissed off." Nate's words were clipped, his eyes fierce. "Tell me why."

I gazed despondently at the man who knew me so well, who always got me, and wondered how he could have misread the situation so badly. He genuinely had no idea what had upset me. I could see it in the deep pools of his eyes.

"Kiss me like you mean it," I dared, brushing my lips against his.

He pulled back slightly, his brow drawn in. "You want an audience to watch us fuck with our mouths?"

My free hand curled at his nape, urging him closer so I could trace my tongue along his bottom lip before sliding it into his hot mouth. All my grief and anger poured out as our mouths clashed and teeth bumped with fervour. I wanted the touch of his mouth engrained in my memory, our last kiss breaking me as I said goodbye. I yanked his hair, knowing how much he enjoyed it but wanting it to hurt, not turn him on.

It was frenzied, desperate and hungry, but Nate still managed to be tender, a skill I would forever admire. One hand cupped my face, the other gripping my waist, as he held me to him, cherishing me the same way I thought he did when he was buried deep inside me.

I yanked away, steadying my breath, and from somewhere fixed a smile on my face.

"That meaningful enough?" Nate asked roughly, still holding me firm, eyes big and dreamy as he caught his breath.

I nodded. "I've meant every one, too." And I had. I might not have verbalised my feelings, but he'd got it from my kiss. Right from the first time our lips touched, sealing our fate, the strength of emotion that passed between us had been there. Deep. Profound. Unquestionable.

"Now," I whispered into his ear, my voice vibrating with rage and unshed tears, "I'm leaving. Enjoy the rest of your evening."

"You're what?" Nate gripped my wrist and stopped me walking away.

"Get off me!" I hissed. The flick of my wrist was so quick I managed to free my arm and flee. I dodged people hanging by the pool, desperate to make my escape and not cause a scene.

"Kara!" He caught me. This time his grip was firm and unrelenting.

"Let go!" I tried throwing him off.

"Explain yourself," he snapped. His eyes were wild, his chest heaving as he stared at me with icy coolness.

"Explain *my* self?" Blood pumped through me, the sound of my heart drowning out the music. The effects of alcohol had burnt off, now I was buzzing with adrenaline. "I saw you."

"Saw me *what*?"

"I've seen pictures of the two of you. I know who she is, Nate." My fingers curled around my clutch.

"Is that so?" he sneered.

"You kissed her." My voice wavered, recalling the unpleasant image of another woman wrapped in my man. I wasn't sure how much longer I could hold back the tears.

"No. I kissed *you*."

My frustration increased. "Stop talking your way out of this."

His eyes flared angrily. "Stop fucking around and ask the question you actually need to." He released me and raked a hand through his hair. "To *yourself*."

Trust. Women who were vastly more attractive than me could easily entice him away with fewer demands and expectations than I had, but if I trusted him that shouldn't matter. My head was swimming with jealous thoughts, the feeling of deceit surpassing everything else. There was no way of making any sense of the situation anymore. I was beyond being reasonable.

Nate took a deep breath to calm down. "Have you checked your cellphone lately?"

I shook my head. He threw his head back and laughed in disbelief, pissing me off even more. There was nothing funny about this. "Why are you laughing?"

"Because I can't believe how fucking immature you're being," he snapped. "It's laughable."

"Immature is not having the balls to tell me when it's over. *Immature* is going behind my back and fucking someone else whilst feeding me a pack of lies, telling me how much I mean to you, when the reality is, I mean fuck all!" I stabbed at my chest, a pointless attempt to remind him who I was.

"You're still on this absurd crusade I'm gonna fuck you over?" he muttered, the aggressive bite to his tone sending me cold. To the casual observer, Nate was the picture of calm, unwilling to draw attention to our spat by remaining cool and unaffected in his demeanour. Inside, however, the taut coil of fury was winding tighter and tighter, the stony glint in his eyes revealing just how furious he was.

"You're all the same…" I mumbled despondently. I cast my eyes over the cityscape behind him, not liking the way he looked at me.

"Fuck that, Kara! Don't judge me against every other asshole you've had in your life." He shook his head, hands coming around his nape and rubbing. "I've *never* given you reason not to trust me."

I hugged my tote to my chest. "There's no point carrying this on if I don't." Except, I thought I might. On the verge of breaking down, and sensing the unwanted attention we were beginning to draw from curious onlookers, I tried to leave.

"Kara." I was jerked around and my tote dropped to the ground, falling open on impact and scattering the contents across the patio.

"Shit!" I crouched to gather the lipstick and purse at our feet. Nate lowered until we were the same height, and tried helping. Mortified with the spectacular performance we were putting on, I slapped his hand away.

Face to face, his eyes searched mine. "I know you don't mean it," he said, his voice agonisingly accurate. "It's in your eyes. In the golden flecks that dance when you look at me."

A tear fell onto my cheek. The only other man ever to notice the dappled sun effect of my eyes was my father. "I'd started to believe I could trust you," I sobbed. "You fooled me."

Nate sucked in a shaky breath. The long fingers of his left hand curled around the keycard to his place. The sign of commitment I'd carried with me like a prized possession. He tried giving it back.

"Keep it," I muttered, pushing to my feet. Nate rose with me. "Give it to the next woman who falls at your feet." My eye line snagged on the blonde bitch giggling to Yasmina—who wasn't laughing—as she revelled in us arguing. "Give it to your Arabian beauty," I sneered. Jealousy and hurt spiked in me again. "Actually, forget that. She probably has one already."

He glanced briefly over his shoulder at his table of friends. "This is ridiculous," he sighed, slotting his fingers with mine. "I've got you. There's no-one else for me."

"You had me," I corrected, freeing my hand, "not anymore."

"Don't say that."

"Be honest with yourself. We had nothing really, did we?"

He let out a frustrated sigh. "Every time I see you, I fall for you all over again. You consume me, you've given me the impossible. Everything I thought I couldn't have, didn't deserve. I can't let you throw that away on a whim, over some stupid misunderstanding."

"We had great sex." I took a step back and shrugged. "It's all you ever wanted from me anyway." I wanted to antagonise, provoke him. Make him suffer an ounce of the pain I was. Yet, as the spiteful words fell from my lips I knew I'd gone too far. My heart broke for us both.

"The hell we did! You know it's more than that. You *know* it is," he implored. If I wasn't being such a bitch, I'd have stopped right there and dragged him home for some make-up sex. But I was on a roll.

I laughed spitefully. "You're right. It was amazing. Best I've *ever* had," I declared, my voice rising. "That what your ego needs to hear?" Every bone in my body hurt, certain I'd never experience his loving touch again. Never feel so liberated as when his eyes met mine as we made love.

Nate's tongue darted out and wet his tempting lips. His gaze dropped to my mouth, and for a second, I thought he might kiss me. He turned away with the ghost of a smile gracing them. "It *is* amazing, but I'm not fucking you like someone who doesn't give a shit about you." I gulped when our eyes locked and I saw his despair. "It's obvious how I feel, Kara."

"Not to me. Not when you do this." He'd told me so openly, his heart endlessly worn on his sleeve. More than anything, I needed to hear it right now. Wanted him to make me feel like I was his world. Needed words never shared between us before.

"I'm not doing this. Not here," he muttered roughly. His hand slid into his jeans pocket for something but came out empty.

"Fine by me." I spun on my heels and took a step before he had my arm in a vice-like grip.

"I'm not done. We'll discuss this at home." He radiated confidence, fully convinced I was leaving with him.

"It's over," I whimpered. "There's nothing to discuss. You know how important trust is to me, yet you couldn't help yourself."

"I've told you the truth, Kara. I'm not justifying my actions further, but I won't let you leave without telling me what's really going on."

I hated how he knew me so well, could see when I was hiding something away. "I'm not staying."

His chest deflated, shoulders sagging in defeat. Large, captivating blue eyes stared at me. "You're mad at me, I get it." He released me and pointed up the stairs. "But if you walk out on me now, don't expect me to chase after you. I won't play that game."

My shattered heart screamed not to leave, but I had to be strong. I wasn't going to be second best again. I gulped back tears as the finality of the situation hit me like a blow to the chest. My vision was blurring with tears and I was shivering. I swiped at a falling tear and whispered, "I don't want you to chase me."

I squeezed my eyes shut to block out the pain scarring his face when he sucked in a breath.

"Wait here," he snapped. "I've left my cellphone on the table and need to call Ross. This is far from over." With powerful strides, he started towards his friends who were still watching this whole sorry saga unfold.

I was up the stairs without a backward glance, not daring to look back, frightened by what I might see if I did. Miraculously, a taxi pulled up outside the hotel and four young men climbed out. I scurried, head down towards it. "Hey, you okay?"

"I'm fine," I lied through tears to whoever had spoken to me. I dived into the back seat, letting one of them close the door, and slouched low. I wasn't sure who I was expecting to see me, because the one man I hoped would, was nowhere in sight.

I gave the driver my address then pulled out my phone. There it was—the unread text from Nate: **MISSING YOU BABY. COME JOIN US X**

I gulped back a sob as the reality of what I'd just done hit me hard. Mai called within a minute. "Whatever you said, you got to him."

"Is he okay?" I sniffed.

"He's acting cool as. Offered to take me home," Mai said. I could barely hear her above the background noise of music.

"Oh." I closed my window, earning a scowl from the cabbie. It was warm, but I had goosebumps chasing all over my skin. "Nice to know he gave me five minutes before moving on."

"Kara," Mai gently reprimanded. "He's saving face. Underneath, I can see he's a lot mad, a little humiliated, in shock, but above anything, he's…"

My skin prickled, this time not from grief but with hope. "He's what?"

The phone muffled, suggesting she was trying to be discreet. "Lost. Hurt. Shattered. Destroyed."

The tears started again. "I'll call if I need anything, Mai," I choked out, desperate to hang up. "I'm going to sleep, get a clearer perspective in the morning."

"I doubt you'll do any of that. If you wanna talk, want alcohol, ice cream, chocolate, whatever, you know where I am. I'll even make your favourite tiramisu if you want."

I fumbled with the clasp of my tote, hoping to find a tissue in there. "Mai, you're the best."

"Be strong. I'll let him know you're okay."

I ended the call and switched off my phone, filled with a harrowing pain over my loss.

THE cloud of depression had settled firmly around me by the time I flopped onto my bed. My mind was empty, my body numb. The tears that had racked my body the entire journey home had subsided. I had no more to cry. Now, my head thumped with a vengeance, whilst my stomach churned. Alcohol and anguish mixed together until I couldn't last any longer. I scrambled off the bed, scarcely making it to the toilet before I vomited.

I collapsed on the floor, hugging the bowl and heaving until there was nothing left inside of me. I was spiralling into a familiar dark tunnel, self-pity and regret suffocating my brain. How could I have been so stupid? Allowing another man to screw over my life *again*? Cursing my weakness, I hauled my sorry arse up to the basin.

The hollow face blinking back at me in the mirror, all blotchy red, pale skin and swollen unfocused eyes, wasn't me. It was the *old* me. The woman who had been here before and sworn never to let this happen again.

Yet as I glared at myself, I saw something new. There was a spark of fight in my eyes that hadn't been there the last time I was heartbroken. All it had taken to free my spirit was one special person, a man who had forced me to confront what was really going on inside my head. I was still clinging onto my hatred for Stuart and had vented all my pent up animosity and resentment onto Nate. My past had found its way to my present—because I allowed it to.

I brushed my teeth and staggered to bed, kicking off my heels in spectacular fashion. They flew across the room and landed with a thud—one by the door, the other targeting the chandelier before dropping onto the bed. Not caring, I dragged the cover over my fully clothed body and curled into a ball.

The pain crippled me. My whole body pined for Nate. The man who'd made me believe in possibilities, who'd dared me to dream again, given life to my fractured soul. He had single-handedly broken down all of my barriers and made me feel.

I hated how I'd humiliated myself. How I'd let Stuart and those bitches at Nate's table win. I'd never been so possessive of a man as I was Nate, and seeing him with Yasmina had wound me up, made me launch accusations that deep down I knew were completely untrue.

And that was the difference. This time, I knew I'd made a terrible assumption and drawn stupid conclusions. Nate would never intentionally deceive me.

"I won't chase you…" His warning echoed in my inebriated head. I hugged the sheet to my chest.

"No going back," I mumbled sleepily, the haze of slumber beckoning. "You've lost him…you walked…"

Chapter 28

The irritating sound of the intercom being repeatedly pressed roused me from a tortured sleep. Groaning, I dragged the pillow over my head, praying to be left alone. When peace had been restored, I lifted my head, blinking in the emerging daylight seeping through the crack in the curtains. *God, I felt rough.*

I closed my eyes, desperate for more solace from sleep. Anything to avoid the reminder of last night from eating into my thoughts. The intercom went again. "It's six-thirty!" I moaned aloud after checking the time. There was only one person this persistent. I swung my legs out of bed, taking a minute to let the room stop spinning before standing.

"Thought I asked you to leave me alone, Mai?" I mumbled into the handset.

"Kara." Nate's hesitant rasp made the hair on my nape stand on end. "Let me in."

Okay, maybe there were *two* headstrong people in my life. I leant my forehead on the wall and closed my eyes, my whole body sagging with resignation. I pressed the buzzer and wandered to the door to wait.

Steady footsteps grew louder. I leant into the open door, desperate to regain some physical and mental strength. My breath caught, my heart thumped wildly in my chest when Nate rounded the stairwell and paused. Anxious eyes met mine, holding me captive for a split second. Then, his whole demeanour altered. He grew taller, climbing the last few stairs with renewed purpose.

"Christ, you look terrible," he muttered.

"You don't look so hot yourself." Except he did. He was wearing long navy shorts and a simple white t-shirt. It was obvious he hadn't slept much, yet the fact he was mad, brooding and serious somehow made his face more austerely stunning. Mix that with how good he smelt, all fresh and outdoorsy, and I was done for.

"Hope you didn't drive over," I muttered, "you've been drinking whiskey all night."

Nate's eyes narrowed. He shoved the door wider and barged past. "If you'd taken a second to check instead of coming over all guns blazing, you'd know my drink of choice was the beer. I don't touch spirits, Kara," he growled. "Neither do I condone drinking and driving."

He set the basket of groceries tucked under his left arm on the kitchen counter and headed to the bedroom. Having no idea what was happening, I hurried after him. In the private sanctuary of my room, awareness of him and all that we'd shared rushed through my bloodstream, spreading a yearning for a connection lost until every bone in my fragile body hurt. Nate kept his back to me, grabbing my treasured vintage Givenchy overnight bag from the closet and carelessly tossing it on the bed. If I wasn't so upset over everything else, I might've cried.

"You can't steamroll your way in here, acting like nothing's happened!" I yanked open the curtains and blinds, wincing at the sharp intrusion of daylight to my hungover brain.

"Oh, I disagree," he said calmly. He went to my underwear drawer and grabbed a handful. "When you strut into the bar acting completely irrationally, behaving so out of fucking character, I can do whatever the hell I want." Stuffing the delicates into the bag, he returned to the closet to grab some clothes. "I'm furious with you."

"Me? I'm not the one fucking around with someone else!" I moved to the bed, pulling the lingerie from the bag and attempted to pair up the sets.

"You don't truly believe that." It wasn't a question. Nate stopped his mindless browsing of my clothes and turned, crossing his arms.

And honestly, I didn't. I collapsed onto the edge of the bed, lace and organza scrunched in my hands. "I don't strut."

"No. You don't," he muttered, "because you have no fucking idea how brilliant you are, how incredibly beautiful your fractured soul is. That you have absolutely no reason to fear *any* other woman in my life." He came over and lifted my chin with a finger. He was still mad, but those magnificent eyes warmed as they looked directly into mine. "You're the only one, Kara. The only one who matters."

"What do you want, Nate?" I asked wearily.

"You." He left me reeling in the bedroom and returned to the kitchen, choosing not to acknowledge me when I finally recovered from his declaration and joined him a few minutes later.

"You don't chase women," I pointed out, hiding my delight that he was here as I slid onto a stool. Watching him make coffee with such familiarity of my home caused a sob to bubble and catch in my throat.

"I don't," he said curtly, taking the milk from the fridge. He shook the carton and peered inside, checking the tiny amount left. With a muttered obscenity, he tossed it in the bin and started unpacking the basket. He added a dash of fresh milk to my coffee and handed it over. "You have me doing all shitloads of crazy things I've never done before. The fact I *am* here should tell you a hell of a lot about the magnitude of my feelings for you."

It spoke volumes. When Nate said something, he meant it and stuck by it, and no-one could persuade him otherwise once his mind was made up. No-one it seemed, except for me. Because here he was. Feigning indifference, I sipped my coffee.

"Or maybe not," he mocked, glowering at me with steely blue eyes, "because you already have this preconceived opinion of what I'm about. Of the type of man I am." He started opening and closing cupboards with force. "Who gives a fuck I could possibly be different to what you expected, huh?"

From the beginning, I'd branded Nate as a player, someone who would break my heart. I'd tried reading every bad motivation imaginable into his actions, when ultimately, there was nothing sinister in them at all. Over time, he'd shown me not all men were the same—that he wasn't anything like Stuart—and I hadn't given him credit.

"Goddamn it!" Nate slammed another cupboard shut.

"What are you looking for?" I cried.

"Advil, Tylenol, whatever you have." Giving up, he slouched back against the bench top, wrapping a hand around his mug.

I breezed past him and retrieved the painkillers from the only place he hadn't looked. Needing to reach the glass from the shelf behind his head, I approached. He annoyed me by not moving so I had to stand on tiptoe and reach over his shoulder, which meant having to lean into him at an unbearable close proximity. Only when I smelt his freshly washed hair did I consider how terrible I must have looked. I hadn't taken any make-up off or brushed my hair, and my clothes were crumpled from sleep.

Nate's hand came to my hip, steadying me as I lowered back onto my feet. "I missed you last night," he whispered into my ear. "I don't like sleeping alone."

The forcefield of energy sparked and ignited between us, trapping me so I couldn't move away. All I wanted was to throw my arms around his neck and have him hold me. I forced myself not to look at him, knowing it would be my downfall. I managed to step away, going to the fridge for some water.

"Here," I said, handing him the glass and packet.

"I don't need them," he said quietly. "They're for you."

Of course his concern was for me. I blew out a breath and knocked two back, not stopping until I'd emptied the glass. We stood, either side of the kitchen, both leaning against the bench tops, both stubborn and incensed.

"Go and shower." Nate nodded to the bedroom behind me. "I'll have fresh coffee and breakfast ready when you're done."

How was it possible one person could break me with their betrayal, then again with their kindness? When I didn't budge, Nate took two steps forward until he was in front of me. He spun me around and began lowering the zip on my jumpsuit. "This wasn't quite how I envisioned taking this incredibly sexy outfit off you," he murmured. His lips were warm and cautious as they worked over my shoulder. And very welcome.

My hand clutched my top, preventing it from falling down, while the other sought balance from the bench top. My neck rolled to the side, yielding to Nate far too easily than I wanted to. But I couldn't stop myself. His touch was magical, a hypnotic caress that always consumed me, made me willing and compliant.

"Let's get out of here," Nate said gently. "We have lots to discuss."

"Where are we going?" I sucked in a breath and nuzzled the side of his head with mine.

"Somewhere we can both think straight, with no distractions." His hands ran over my waist and hips. "Well, *fewer* distractions."

I saw the curl of his lips as I hurried off to shower.

I dressed to get his attention, slipping on a white tank and denim miniskirt that had been in hibernation at the back of my closet for far too long. All without underwear. I'd even taken my time slathering body lotion on in the bedroom rather than bathroom, putting my self-conscious thoughts aside, all in a vague attempt to get a reaction. That's why I was annoyed when I got nothing. Not even a lusty smirk of recognition or a simmering gaze.

Within the hour, we were heading to the beach house. The bright start to the day had given way to darker skies as we neared the coast. The air was still frosty between us, neither of us talking much, but it was gradually thawing. My mobile rang about twenty minutes into the journey.

"What the heck were you thinking last night?" Mai scolded me. "Nate was so pissed off with you when you left."

"He still is," I mumbled, turning away for privacy.

"You're with him now?" I could feel her excitement buzzing down the line.

"He's kidnapped me." I glanced at Nate and saw his mouth twitch. I couldn't see his eyes behind his sunglasses, but knew they were laughing. "If I'm not in Monday, tell the police I'm with him."

"A little overdramatic, don't you think?"

"Says the queen of drama." It felt good to laugh. A brief respite to the tension, but I knew it couldn't last. During my shower, I'd mulled over the events of the past twelve or so hours. He wasn't that much of a bastard to take me to the beach house then dump me.

If we were to move on, conversations neither of us might want to hear needed to happen.

WHEN we reached the beach house, Nate took my bag upstairs whilst I went to the lounge, mentally preparing the conversation. I was edgy and frightened, but ready to let him in. I was sitting on the sofa when he finally joined me. He carried a steaming mug of something in each hand and gave one to me. "I made you tea."

It was strange he'd opted for tea over coffee, considering I'd never drunk it in front of him before. The gesture was profoundly touching. My father always made me tea when he sensed I needed to get something off my chest. "Isn't that what I should be doing? Being English and all that?"

Nate cracked a strained smile and strolled to the windows barefoot. I followed his gaze to the trees swaying in the wind outside, and the rough swell of the ocean, dark blue with white foamy wave breaks. I cradled my tea, grateful for its warmth.

After a few sips whilst he worried something over in his mind, Nate glanced over his shoulder. "Mai explained what happened with Stuart."

"*What?*" I shot him an indignant look.

"No one deserves to be cheated on, made to feel worthless. No man is good enough for you."

"Even you?" I sniped.

"Even me," he agreed flatly.

I set my mug on the coffee table and drew my shoulders back. "I made a promise to myself to never let a man do that to me again."

"And I haven't." Nate let out a long sigh. "I don't want to fight your past anymore, Kara."

"She shouldn't have told you." Mai had no right to stick her nose into my business. It was up to me when I told Nate, not her.

"Someone had to," he scoffed. "You never would."

"I might have." I swallowed, turning my attention to an imaginary spot on the wall above the fireplace. "One day."

"And that's what pisses me off the most." He started pacing, stopping only to set his mug beside mine. "You've driven home the point about needing total honesty, yet you couldn't afford me the same decency. Can you see how hypocritical that is?"

I nodded, my agreement caught in my throat. Nate shook his head, disappointed, and let out an exasperated sigh as he moved in front of the TV. Right in my line of sight. "You've never given me reason not to trust you, so I do, with all my heart. Implicitly," he stated, placing a hand on his chest. "But, you haven't always been honest."

"I've *always* told you the truth," I spat, offended by his accusations.

"There'd been a constant memory holding you back. Except when we made love." His voice lost its irritated edge and grew softer. "That's when I finally get the real you. The wildly sensual woman who comes alive in my arms. Whose touch and kiss conveys far more to me than words ever could." Nate skirted the table and dropped to his knees in front of me, clasping my fisted hands in his. "You believe in yourself enough to give not just your body, but your mind, your soul. You trust me. I want that all the time, not just in bed."

"Someone to dominate?" I asked disbelievingly. "Because I won't be told what to do, or when to do it, by anyone. Not again."

"That's unfair. We're equals. Sexually, you're becoming as much of an instigator, and I treasure that element of surprise when you take control."

Nate was right. I loved him possessing me, but I enjoyed taking charge, too.

"To a certain extent you're right," he continued, thumbs brushing the backs of my hands. "When you surrender to me, completely let go of whatever demons you're fighting in your head, nothing can come between us. *That's* the submission I want."

"Nate." I touched his jaw, rigid and tight beneath his clean shaved skin. The big, beautiful eyes, full of admiration as they stared at me, surely mirrored my own. Then, they narrowed.

"Then last night happens and it's like you're determined to sabotage our relationship. Don't make me question whether I should've left you alone when you told me to, instead of finding myself unable to breathe if I'm not with you." His hand came to my face. "M.I.N.E. What does it spell?"

I wanted to give him the response he was expecting. Only I was still hurting. "It spells *mine*, Nate."

His eyes flared.

"M.I.N.E," I repeated, jabbing a finger into his chest with each letter. "It works both ways." Standing, I had to escape the vortex that was Nate Blake. I was being sucked in by his heartfelt words and needed space to gain clarity. "Do you know how sick I felt seeing you with her? With your hands on her?"

"Not at the time." He twisted and sat in the spot I'd vacated, legs spread, one arm draped over the back. He appeared so calm and unaffected, yet the cool gaze that followed me as I edged away revealed his lingering anguish and shock over my pronouncement.

"Women fall in love with you too easily. You're gorgeous, emotionally intelligent, sensitive and so generous with your affection. Whatever you think, Yasmina wants you back." My arms folded over my chest. "Acting like you're open for that to happen doesn't work for me."

"Jesus Christ, Kara!" Nate pushed to his feet with an arrogant shove and marched towards me. "Yasmina is Manny's sister."

"Who you dated for two years."

"What? No!" He stopped abruptly. His hands went to his hair, his usual reflex when he was frustrated. "I didn't want to build a reputation for having a different woman on my arm every time I went out, so when I attended functions where I'd be in the public eye, she accompanied me."

"Did she accompany you to bed?"

"Never." He scrubbed his face with both hands. "None of this matters. I know who I belong to, which woman has captured my heart."

I scrunched my face, drawing a deep breath as I massaged my brow. My head throbbed, overloaded with new insight and confusing confessions. Nate cocked his head to the side, examining me with eyes that had lost their sparkle. He was drained, worn out from all the misunderstandings, tired of the confrontation. When he spoke, his voice was agonisingly gentle, his words vehement.

"You have nothing to envy. You own me. All of me," he vowed. "There's nothing left for anyone else. The whole world could be falling apart around me and I wouldn't notice, I'm that caught up in you. You're all I see when we're together."

"What about when I'm *not* there? Do you still think about me then?"

"All the fucking time." His expression hardened. His eyes raked me, from messy ponytail to pink painted toenails. I was visibly shaking, partly because I was cold, but mostly because I was a fragile mess of emotions. "Be all possessive, I get it, I *want* it. I feel exactly the same way about you." Nate bypassed me and went to the fireplace.

"How would you feel if another man touched me like that?"

"I'd ensure he never touched anything else again," he muttered, crouching to stack chopped wood into the hearth. "But I'd trust *you* enough to know you'd never act on it. You need to reciprocate that, otherwise…"

He didn't have to finish. Everything he said was right. I grabbed my tea from the table. It was cold, but I still drank it. "You know," I started wearily, leaning my shoulder to the cold window, "since you came into my life, my head is so screwed up I can't think straight. I don't know how to handle the feelings you've stirred up in me."

Nate turned fractionally, his side profile revealing a man wary of my next words. He'd done everything in his power to prove he was worth the risk, yet I still wasn't sure I would ever fully trust a man again. The need to protect myself from being used or hurt still clung to me. I was scared to love. Scared to trust.

"If I can't get over this," I mumbled shakily, tears welling in my eyes, "what does it say about our future?"

"Is it a possibility? That you won't?" I could hear the fear in his voice. And those expressive eyes couldn't meet mine, so I knew he was reeling as much from this as I was and didn't want me to see it.

I set my empty mug down. "I feel like I'm running through a maze and can't find the way out."

Nate straightened and faced me. The most painful expression of lost hope and veneration tainted his eyes. The veins in his hand popped as he clenched a block of wood. "You want out?" he asked, eerily calm.

"Yes!" I cried in exasperation. Then, "No…God…I don't know anything anymore…"

"Christ, you're so fucking frustrating!" He dropped everything and rushed to my side, folding me into the embrace that sheltered me from the world and reassured me more than words ever would. "You have to be the most stubborn, infuriating woman I've ever known."

Helpless in his arms, I felt so fragile I worried his strength might break me, physically and mentally. He smoothed my hair off my face, stroking it repeatedly behind my ear.

"Don't you see?" Nate's lips brushed my forehead. "There's never a moment we're apart because you're here, with me." He took my palm and placed it flat on his chest. "Feel it. You're the beat in my heart."

It was racing, like my own. A frantic pulse against my hand. A lone tear trickled down my cheek. "Don't," Nate whispered, bending to kiss it away. "You tears are killing me."

I nuzzled against him, sliding my palms beneath his t-shirt so I could feel his warmth. We stood, quiet except for the occasional sniff as tears freely flowed, soaking a patch on his shoulder. "I'm so stupid," I sobbed. "I thought you two were—"

"I know what you thought. But this has to stop. You need to talk to me when something is bothering you, not bottle it all up." Nate led me to the sofa and settled me on his lap. He peeled away a few soggy strands of hair stuck to my cheek. Then, using the hem of his t-shirt, carefully dried my face. "Why is it so difficult to accept that I love you?"

My eyes widened, and I'm certain the world stopped spinning. "Wh-what…" I stuttered between sobs, swallowed and cleared my throat, "…what are you saying?"

"You know," he said, quiet but certain. Running weary eyes over his serene face, I swiped at the new tears forming in my eyes with the heels of my palm. "I could say the words, Kara, but they're nowhere near enough to convey what I feel for you. It's gripped me so strongly, I'd die if I lost you."

My breath was coming short and fast. I smoothed a hand down his chest. The connection I felt proved I wasn't imagining this. Nate cupped my face and raised my gaze back up to meet his. “You know,” he implored, those glorious eyes like liquid. Clear, shiny and free from any doubt.

“Say them anyway,” I urged quietly, needing the validation of his words before allowing myself to truly believe it.

He blinked a couple of times, thumbs gently stroking my cheekbones. Then he gave me the killer blow of his sexy half-smile. “I’ve fallen in love with you.”

I sucked in a sharp, shaky disbelieving breath. The sound of blood rushing through my body towards my heart filled my ears. “You’re…in *love* with me?”

He tipped his head back and laughed softly. “Is it really so unbelievable? Outside my office that first time, you gave me few words, simply a shy smile. Then you reached in and stole my heart. You’ve been holding onto it ever since.”

“Nate—”

His lips swept over mine. “Don’t say anything.” He tugged me into the safety of his arms, holding me like he was never letting go. And he wasn’t. I felt like I could burst with happiness.

The love radiating from Nate seeped into my mind and soul. Every slide of his palm on my back, every delicate touch of his fingertips in my hair, each murmured, “I love you,” whispered into my ear, cemented his commitment and strengthened our bond.

I didn’t think it possible, but as the beat of his heart lulled me into sleep, I actually started believing there was a future for us out there, just waiting to be grabbed.

THE next time I opened my eyes, I was curled up on the sofa with a blanket covering me. The fire was blazing, the spit and crackle from the flames accompanying the wind outside. I rolled onto my back and found Nate sitting by my feet, one arm over my ankles.

“Hi.” I don’t know why, but I suddenly felt really shy. With the one foot hanging outside the blanket, I wriggled my toes against his thigh, like a cat preparing its bed to sleep. He returned my small smile with one of his own.

“Feeling better?”

“In so many ways.” I pushed off the cover and sat, hugging my knees. “What have you been doing?”

“Watching you sleep.” The backs of his fingers brushed my warm cheek, and instinctively I turned into his caress, covering his hand with mine.

“Some might find that slightly creepy,” I teased.

"Do you?"

I shook my head. "I love it."

Nate's smile reached his eyes, a telltale sign he was really happy. I caught sight of his camera on the coffee table and my gaze narrowed when it returned to him. "What have you been photographing?"

"Nothing," he said, far too innocently. He glanced outside. "Up for some fresh air?"

I turned. "In this?" Large storm clouds were gathering on the horizon, gulls and hawks circling above monstrous waves pounding the shore below.

"C'mon," Nate said, patting my legs and standing, "you need to change." He handled me like a delicate flower, dressing me in clothes he'd brought down from the closet, having already changed himself whilst I slept. After pulling grey leggings under my denim skirt, he knelt in front of me and tied up my white Converse. "I presume this skimpy outfit was chosen for my benefit?"

I nodded, pleased he *had* noticed.

"It's cold out," he said, pointing at my chest and grabbing a sweatshirt. "The braless look works for me, but I don't want anyone else getting to enjoy your lush tits." Happy I was wrapped up enough, he grabbed his camera and led me to the doors.

A bitter, salty wind whipped my face and hair when I stepped onto the deck. "Only crazy people would go out in this," I shouted as we jogged down the steps and across the lawn, both laughing freely.

Nate pulled me to his side and pressed his lips to mine. "Then we're fucking insane!"

Chapter 29

We made homemade pizza for dinner, both relishing the simple routine as we chopped vegetables and drank bottles of beer. At one point, Nate took me in his arms and spun me in the kitchen, dancing in time to James Morrison who sang about not letting go. When the song finished, he dipped me back and rewarded me with a luscious kiss.

After dinner, I stood alone on the deck and watched the sheet lightning flashing through the clouds, illuminating the swell of surf. Nate's hands settled either side of mine on the glass perimeter, caging me in when he joined me. "Think the storm's heading back out," he said, nuzzling my ear.

"Hmm. What have you been doing?" I asked, my hands settling over his.

"Arranging your surprise."

"Ooh, I like surprises." Grinning, I turned to face him.

"C'mon then." Nate ushered me back inside and secured the doors before leading me upstairs. Excitement rushed through me, eager to discover what he'd been up to all the time he'd been gone.

When we reached the closet, Nate shrugged off his sweatshirt. "Get naked," he instructed with a challenging raise of his brow.

I smiled and obeyed, removing my sweatshirt and leggings. "I love this kind of surprise."

Nate cocked his head and smirked, his brow still raised, no longer in challenge but with wry amusement. I reached for the waistband of his sweatpants. "Nah-ah," he said, backing out of reach, "not me, only you."

Now I was really confused. I hurried out of my clothes and handed them over. Large eyes turned hot as they travelled up and down, his lips parting to accommodate increased breaths. My spine straightened proudly, thrusting my breasts forward. I *wanted* him to look at me. Feel his desire prickle every inch of naked flesh as he drank me in.

"Kara, you're incredibly beautiful," he growled, reaching for my face as his mouth hovered over mine. "I want you so fucking badly right now."

"Take me." I stepped forward, straddling his thigh as he nudged between my legs, and slid my hands into his hair. "I need to be fucked."

His head snapped back. "Jesus! What happened to the shy woman too afraid to tell me what she wanted?"

I took his hands and moved them to my arse. He didn't take much persuading, his palms sliding over me, cupping and squeezing. "Think your earlier confession sent her packing."

His neck rolled, giving more of his flesh to my mouth. "If I'd known that was all it would take to set the siren free, I'd have told you a hell of a lot sooner."

I stilled. When had Nate realised he loved me?

"I've known for a while," he said, leading me into the bathroom.

My eyes widened when I took in the scene. The bath was full, bubbles almost spilling over the rim. Ylang-ylang and vanilla scented the room from the many lit candles, and towels were warming on the heated rail. "You did this? For me?"

"It didn't start out as quite the romantic weekend I had planned." He turned to me. "I'm hoping it will finish that way."

"What's the occasion?"

He looked taken aback. "You don't know?"

I shook my head as I took his hand and stepped into the bath. All my worries and stresses literally washed away as I sunk into the warm water.

"You're really not joining me?" I asked when he crouched beside the tub.

"This is all for you. Let me take care of you."

I scooped up a handful of bubbles and playfully dotted some on the tip of his nose. Nate blew them off with a grin. "Lay back."

I obliged, drawing a deep breath of heavenly scented air. Using gentle pressure, he began massaging my shoulders. "When you sat in my kitchen and admitted how frightened you were, the enormity of how deep my feelings ran suddenly became apparent. You made me reassess all my priorities. I knew I had to put my own fears and desires aside, and be strong for you. How easily I could do that confirmed the truth of my feelings."

My mind drifted, lost in wonderful dreams of this loving man attending to me. A man who'd placed more importance on what I needed from him and given us a chance. I'm not sure how much time passed before Nate spoke.

"It isn't all about sex for me," he murmured, "not with you."

My spine stiffened. My vicious accusations were still eating away at him. "I know."

"But I love making love with you. You're so tight and warm, I can't help myself. When I slide inside you…"—he pressed his lips to my shoulder—"it's like nothing I've ever experienced. It's so right, the perfect fit. We were made for each other."

Nodding, I remained quiet, leaving it open for him to talk some more. "I can't be sorry for wanting you," he said, "and I refuse to refrain from touching you every goddamn chance I get."

"I don't want you to," I breathed, my pulse quickening. His fingers were moving deftly over my décolletage, and my nipples were erect and occasionally peeping through the bubbles, begging to be caressed. "I shouldn't have said that. I apologise."

"Forget it." Nate waved a wet hand in the air, dismissing its importance. "I know you were upset and angry. The same way I know you've been flying under the radar for far too long, hoping no one would notice you. *But I did.* I noticed you, Kara."

I stilled his hands and twisted to face him. His eyes were focused, so blue, radiating pure love and commitment. It pushed words and thoughts I never believed possible to have again to the forefront of my mind.

I tried saying them, but they refused to come out of my mouth. My heart had been armoured against attack for too long, fearful of being hurt, of loving again. I cupped his nape, urging his mouth to mine, desperate to show him another way. The kiss started gently, but like a wave approaching the shore, it gradually built, gaining strength with each passing second. *God.* My heart swelled so much I had to pull away to catch a breath.

"That's for making me realise that I'm not the woman I thought."

"Kara." Nate hugged me close, showing no concern for how wet he got. "Don't you see? The sweet-natured, smart, funny, gorgeous woman you are has always been there. Your star has always shone so brightly." He shifted to kneel beside the tub, arms still around me. "A broken heart and mistrust blindsided you. I simply encouraged you to open your eyes and use that inner light to sear through the darkness."

Never had I felt as alive and free as I did right now. This bath was a cleansing of the soul, a ritual to wash away all the bitter memories and start over. I pulled back and clasped his hands tight. "Can I tell you something?"

"Anything, baby, you know that."

I chewed my lip and took a deep breath. "Stuart hated blow jobs. At least, from me anyway."

Nate's brows lifted. "O-kay, that was so *not* what I expected you to say."

I chuckled. "I want no more secrets. Let me explain what happened."

"No need. As I said, Mai told me."

"She doesn't know the half of it," I admitted. Mai was only aware that I'd been cheated on. No dirty details. "We met at university. Stuart was a bit of a bad boy, used to smoke and drink. I watched him work his way through dozens of women before he targeted me in our final year. During the summer he underwent an entire transformation, cleaned himself up. Dating me was all part of his game-plan to get ahead. I was just being used."

"Which is why you had trouble accepting I was being genuine," Nate murmured, using his thumbs to work over my palm.

"Hmm," I agreed. "Six months in, he started telling me how to dress, who I should be friends with, where I could go. We would argue, and sometimes…" My mind drifted to a dark place, where images of his fury flashed like lightning in my mind. "He wanted me a certain way so no other man would be interested."

"*His* insecurity," Nate muttered gruffly, "not yours."

"I see that now."

"Anyone who got to know you would see how enchanting you are, regardless of your outer beauty. That's all a bonus."

"People rarely got the chance. I've always been a little socially awkward, so it was easy to stop going out. When I did, he was with me."

Nate frowned. "Your family must've noticed you were becoming so introverted?"

"I didn't live at home so it wasn't always apparent, but they did. Liam especially. He told me to leave numerous times, said it wasn't healthy."

"He was right," Nate snapped. "Why didn't you?"

I lifted a shoulder. I'd asked myself the same question many times before, and never found an answer. Until now. Staring into the piercing translucent eyes of a man who worshipped me unconditionally, I finally confronted it.

"Stuart didn't care about me. I latched onto the nearest person, trying to fill the void my mother had left, hoping to find the love I'd lost and missed. It was all completely for the wrong reasons, but I was drowning in grief. He took advantage of my weakness."

"*Bastard.*" Nate moved around the tub, massaging my other arm with a touch more aggression than before.

"I agree." I drew my knees up and rolled my neck. Reliving my past was making me tense, even with Nate trying his hardest to relax me. "Fast forward to last year. We both worked for Morgan Sanders. We were at a hotel with colleagues, celebrating our exam successes. My best friend was there, the third wheel in the house we shared—"

"You *lived* together?" Nate's hand stilled, his grip on my upper arm squeezing hard.

"More by circumstance than by choice." I covered his hand with mine, encouraging him to release me. When he did, it took a second for the colour to return to my skin. "I've never lived with a man, not properly," I assured him. His shoulders relaxed, his attention returning to my fingers, careful not to let the ruby band slip off.

"We had a room booked for the night." I tipped my head back, my brow furrowing. "It was odd he'd left me alone. When I couldn't locate him I went upstairs, thinking he'd got drunk and passed out. I stumbled into our room looking for him…" I laughed bitterly. "Boy, did I find him. Standing, trousers bunched around his ankles and his dick in her mouth."

Nate winced. "There's really no need for this," he said, cradling my face and pressing a kiss to my lips. "I wish you hadn't been fucked over, but I don't care about the rest. Hearing it only makes me appreciate you more."

"Please let me finish. I want closure. Let me get everything off my chest so I never have to talk about it again."

His eyes held mine for a long time. Eventually, he sighed. "Okay," he murmured, "if it's what you need." Then he completely stunned me by stripping off and slipping into the bath at the other end.

Finding the strength I always did from the deep pools of love gazing back at me, I continued. "I didn't see the busty brunette's face because she didn't have the decency to stop. But I knew it was her. I'd seen that dolphin tattoo on her arse enough times to know it was my best friend."

"Jesus," Nate muttered harshly, placing my right foot on his chest so he could massage my calf.

"Sometimes, I still see his face. The lazy drunken smile curling lipstick smeared lips when he invited me to join them in a threesome…the wild eyes when he attacked me a few weeks later."

"The fucker did *what*?" My foot landed with a splash back into the water as he straightened.

"You don't get to decide when this ends," I mimicked Stuart's snarl. "I'm the one who controls this relationship." I stroked my neck with both hands. "Just as his fingers pinched hard around my throat and his fist made contact with my cheek, Liam barged in."

"He hit you?" Nate bit out.

"Once," I confirmed quietly. "He got really mad."

His fingers were rigid, almost pulling his hair as he pushed them through the glossy chocolate strands. With my hands either side of the tub, I pulled myself upright and caught his forearms, lacing my fingers with his. "There were other times he came close but never did."

Nate took a deep breath, trying to calm down. Anger wasn't the right way to deal with this. My beautiful lover always knew what to do or say in any given situation. "Did you report him?"

I shook my head. "I just wanted to forget everything."

His lips thinned in disapproval. "Physical abuse, verbal and mental abuse, it's fucking abuse whichever way you look at it."

Hearing Nate say it didn't make it any easier to acknowledge. "The rest is a blur. Yelling. Struggling. Liam dragged me out whilst Stuart nursed a bloodied broken nose on the floor."

"Liam should've fucking killed him." I'd never seen the harsh gleam of vengeance in Nate's shimmering, almost navy eyes, darker against the paling of his skin. A chill chased up my spine.

"Stuart decided he was the injured party and took his revenge by spreading malicious rumours at the office, calling me a slut behind my back, rubbishing my work. He sent me threatening text messages, saying if I didn't go back to him he'd kill himself and I'd be to blame."

"Jesus fucking Christ. The man was one fucked up son of a bitch." He pulled me forward, sending a wave of foamy lukewarm water spilling onto the tiled floor, and cradled me in his lap.

"He threatened Liam with assault, that's why I didn't go to the police. I couldn't put it on my dad."

It felt like an age before Nate spoke again. "No one will ever touch you like that again. Never make you feel that way. I'm making that promise to you now," he vowed, his voice choked with hard-edged emotion.

"I knew he wouldn't do it. The bastard was too selfish."

I waited a while before continuing, a little shaken by the rage still coiled in his tense frame. In a much quieter voice, I said, "They'd been at it behind my back almost the entire two years we were together. Our relationship was built on lie upon dirty lie. None of it was real. I hate how I allowed myself to get trapped in that situation and not be strong enough to get out."

"Ah, God." His head fell back to rest on the lip of the oval tub. "Fucked over by two people you'd invested your trust in. It all makes sense."

I nodded. Finally, he understood why I'd been closing myself off, the reasons for my overreactions and jealous behaviour.

Staring at the ceiling, he quietly said, "At least now I know your resistance to opening up wasn't because of me."

God. For a man sure of himself in so many other ways, when it came to us, he was just as at risk and scared of being broken. Until now, I'd never appreciated that I held as much power over him as he did me. "It's never been you," I reassured, kissing his chest where his heart beat rapidly beneath.

I gave him time to digest everything. I'd done a lot of talking, but there was a lot of unspoken explanations for Nate to absorb that were equally as important. At the most inappropriate time, I began to laugh. "You know what the stupid thing was? The only thought I had when I saw them together was, why did he never let me give him one?"

Nate lifted his head and held my gaze. The one eyebrow he had drawn in with bemusement straightened. Then the corners of his delicious mouth lifted. "I can't answer that," he murmured, smudging a thumb over my mouth. "Having these bee-stung lips wrapped around my cock is something I'd happily allow all fucking day long."

I splashed his chest, laughing. "Oral sex is such an intimate act. I often felt we were missing out, not having that connection. He never went down on me, either. Having that intimacy with you is something I cherish."

Nate's mouth closed over mine. I revelled in the purity of his lips, the tender way they caressed mine, the unqualified expression of devotion they conveyed as he set the fireworks off in my belly. "Listen," Nate murmured, arms wrapped around me, one hand stroking my hair, "about what happened in New York."

"Let's not talk about it." I knew there were things he hadn't opened up about. Still secrets behind his smile. Whatever happened in New York was only a small chink in a bigger story. Now wasn't the right time to hear it. There'd been enough confessions already for one night, and I truly believed when the time was right, I'd learn more.

"To be honest, I don't think I require an explanation." He gave me an uncertain look, like he wasn't sure where I was going with this. "You love me. You told me it wasn't important and I accept that. Right now," I said, linking my fingers with his, "all I want to do is curl up in bed, lay my head on your chest like this, and fall asleep with your hands in my hair."

And that's exactly what I did, safe in the knowledge I was exactly where I should be. In the right frame of mind, and definitely with the right person.

MY FEET wouldn't budge when I tried moving them. I was well and truly riveted to the spot. Nate had his back to me, pummelling a punch bag swinging from the ceiling in the centre of the home gym in the basement.

After waking without him beside me, I'd followed the sound of music playing throughout the house and found this treasure at the end. *Wow.*

The muscles of his bare back rippled, taut skin glistening with sweat, the veins in his arms and neck throbbing from exertion. His concentration was so focused, he had no idea I was there as I leant into the doorjamb.

Watching his lower body move, hearing the sounds he made, I fidgeted with a restless desire for him. He bounced lightly on his feet in perfect time to the R&B beat. I imagined dancing with him in a hot, sweaty nightclub, grinding against me, moving with me. He was the type of man that would get women flocking to the dance floor to be near him. Not just because of his looks, but because you'd know he'd be great in bed from the confident way he moved.

I could've stayed and watched this performance all day, but I had an idea and dashed upstairs to dress.

"You sound like you've been having fun down there," I called out when I heard Nate coming up the stairs forty minutes later. I stopped chopping fruit and glanced over my shoulder, catching sight of him wiping his face with the towel slung around his neck. All sweaty, out of breath and flushed skin. "Thought I was your favourite way to wake up?"

He grinned wickedly. “You are.” He kissed the back of my head when I turned to chop some mango. “I wanted you to rest, so it was either a workout or a cold shower and my left hand.”

I bit my lip and kept my eyes on the knife slicing close to my fingertips. Nate stole a slice and popped it in his mouth. “I’ve made you blush again,” he murmured teasingly, the backs of his fingers brushing my cheek.

“Go take that cold shower.” I nudged him with my hips. “Brunch is almost ready.”

My timing was perfect. Carrying our coffee to the dining table, I cast an appreciative eye over Nate as he stood perusing the display. Fresh from the shower, smelling so good my mouth watered, sexy as anything in jeans and a t-shirt, his usual state, I concluded.

“You’ve been busy.” He pulled out the chair at the head of the table for me.

“Toast and fruit I can manage. That bakery in town has a great selection of pastries,” I offered casually, stifling a smile.

“You walked into town?” Nate sat and handed me the plate piled high with warm baked goods.

With an innocent expression, I took a chocolate croissant and said, “The Bentley drives like a dream.”

“You took my car?” His brows rose as he tried and failed to hide his delight.

Nonchalantly, I lifted a shoulder and blew the steam from my coffee before taking a sip. I’d terrorised myself to death driving his car, the powerful engine much stronger than I was used to in my own. I thanked God when I pulled into the small car park and found it almost empty. “That okay?”

His amusement increased. “What’s mine is yours.”

We ate brunch, sharing the sort of comfort and easiness that came from years of being a couple, but with the sparkle and excitement of a new relationship. I thought about how far we’d come in such a short space of time. “That first night, outside the wine bar, why didn’t you kiss me?”

Nate sat back in his chair. “I wanted to. Desperately.” One side of his mouth started to curl up. “I thought I’d ruined my chances.”

“By not kissing me?”

He shook his head. “Nothing went as planned.”

“Because you didn’t get me into bed?”

“No.” The blue of his eyes gave way to the growing black as he raked the length of my body, much like they had back then. “I think I knew before then I wouldn't be taking you home."

"Liar." I stood to fetch some more juice from the refrigerator. "Don't think I didn't notice the eye-fuck."

Nate threw his head back and laughed. "God, I love when you curse. That accent gets me every time."

"That's another thing," I said, making my way back. "Why the English obsession?"

"It's a Kara obsession," he corrected. "The rest? Merely a country dear to my heart. England was my haven when I needed to get away from here. I have a lot of fond memories from my time there."

"You moved there seeking solace, I came here." I topped up our tumblers. "Do you think we were drawn to each other without realising?"

"You mean like fate? Destiny?" He grabbed my hip and stopped me from returning to the kitchen.

I shrugged. "I believe everything happens for a reason, even the bad stuff. At the time, we might not understand why things are as they are. But, I believe eventually a lesson will be learnt."

Nate nodded in agreement, eyes sparkling, his lips curving. "Wanna know a lesson I learned the first time you spoke to me?" His hand slid under the hem of my t-shirt, around to my lower back, skin on skin. My legs went weak from that simple, innocent caress. "That hearing the simplest of words from your mouth is the craziest turn on. Watching those luscious lips shape vowels is incredibly erotic. Makes me instantly hard."

Smirking, I set the carton on the table then nudged his legs apart with my knee. I settled onto his lap, hands at his nape for balance. "Let me think about this for a second." I looked over his shoulder at the kitchen counter, covered with the mess I'd made. "How about…yoghurt?"

"It's working."

I moved my mouth closer to his. "Oral."

"Ooh, good one." His grin flashed against my mouth, but I saw it in his sparkling eyes.

I angled my head and kissed him with everything I had. He returned it with as much enthusiasm, absorbing me into his kiss so expertly, knowing precisely how firm I needed it. The strength of his hands sliding up and down my spine and rocking me so my clit rubbed against the seam of his jeans made me moan.

"I adore you," he breathed, "you're my world. I can be everything you need." Nate grazed down my neck, the gentle bite into my shoulder making me shudder.

"Talking is great foreplay," I breathed, "but how about some visuals?" My t-shirt flew in the air as I tossed it over his shoulder. He hummed his appreciation as my breast filled his hand, my nipple pebbling against the white lace of my bra.

"This surge of confidence you seem to have developed is sexy as fuck," he muttered gruffly. Dextrously, he snapped the catch and launched it in the same direction. He licked at my breasts, sucking and kissing, cupping and caressing. Desire shot through me, muscles twisting and tensing, contracting, a silent call from my body to his.

"I want you, Nate," I whispered.

A lazy, sensuous smile crept across his face. With his thumb, he freed my bottom lip from between my teeth, then kissed me hard. His tongue invaded my mouth, sliding forcefully against mine, bruising my lips until they felt swollen.

He stood me quickly and peeled my yoga pants down my legs. "Special occasion?" he rasped, his nose burying into my panties, his breath hot on me.

"What?" I lifted his chin, unsure what he was referring to.

He grinned. "You're wearing underwear."

I loved when he got playful. "May I suggest you take them off? *Quickly.*"

He obliged, eagerly stripping me until I stood nude before him. Hiding my body—the body that demonstrated how deep my feelings ran for him, that had been concealed behind real and emotional barriers long enough—was pointless. Nate knew me from the inside out.

Lounging back in the chair, his tongue darted out over parted lips, his breath heavy. Need consumed me. I yearned to experience the hotness of his skin against mine, the thickness of his cock inside me.

Bending forward, knowing I was giving him an eyeful, I loosened his belt and lowered the zip on his jeans. I grinned when I freed his cock, stiff and ready with such little stimulation, and lifted my gaze to meet his.

A wicked smile spread across his flushed face. "You want me, you got me."

I straddled his thighs until we were merely inches apart. Instinctively, he reached down, running both hands the length of my legs from ankle to thigh. He straightened, inhaling as he brushed his cheek over the small strip of my pubic hair. Dizzy, my head fell back, eyes closing as my hands found their way into his hair. Struggling to decide what I wanted more, the urge to make love outweighed the craving for his mouth on me. I shoved him back, tipping his chin up to look at me.

"Your mouth between my legs is so good," I murmured, dragging his full lower lip between my teeth. "But right now? I need this." I lowered until I'd taken the entire length of him inside me.

"Christ, Kara!" His fingers dug sharply into my arse. My muscles clenched, flexing and drawing his cock deeper, stretching me to the hilt. He hadn't prepared me for the sheer size of him, so I'd anticipated the sting. "That's it, baby. Take it all in."

I moaned and rose again, sliding back down easier than before. I'd missed this connection. The desire, hunger, and the fact Nate could satisfy me in every possible way.

He lured me into a deep kiss as both hands cupped my breasts, fingers working the nipples until the urge to taste me became too strong for him to resist. I arched my back, moving my hands behind me to the table for support. The heat of his mouth as he covered a nipple sparked the familiar tightening low in my stomach.

I dropped forward until I looked him in the eye once more. My chest constricted with love. I stroked a finger down his cheek and ran it over his lips. Everything I felt for him choked in my throat.

"I love this," I murmured, brushing my lips over his. "Promise you'll never stop making me feel this good."

His hands came to my hair, holding me against his mouth. "You're mine," he growled, his hand diving between my legs. "I promise I'll never let you forget that again." Finding my clit with his thumb, he circled me.

Once, twice, then I was gone.

"HOW did you know I was different to all the others?" I asked Nate as we got ready for bed after our lazy day. He continued brushing his teeth, white Armani briefs his only item of clothing.

"What's with all the questions today?"

"I don't know." I took off my bra and tossed it into the concealed laundry bin in the closet. I was fully nude and didn't care. "I suppose I'm still adjusting to the enormous change in our circumstances. Just gathering all the pieces of the jigsaw."

"Well," he said, drying his face, "other women tended to take whatever they got offered, no questions asked. You were completely upfront in letting me know you wouldn't settle for anything less than you deserved. I admired your inner strength and fearlessness."

"I'm not strong," I snickered, exiting the closet and rounding the corner into the bedroom.

"You are. At the time you didn't know, but you held all the power. Everything between us happened on your terms. I was so certain you were right for me… you made me break all my rules."

"What rules?" I tugged back the bedcovers and slipped between the luxurious high thread count sheets.

"Never mix business with pleasure. Never let my guard down. *Definitely* never set myself up for a second knock back," he said lightly, "or fourth, in your case." He settled beside me. "The list is endless. I sacrificed it all."

From the beginning, both of us had recklessly broken rules that had served us well in the past. The immense magnetism between us was too strong to ignore. I tugged his arm around my shoulder and raised his hand in front of me. His fingers laced with mine, playing and stroking.

Nate cleared his throat, his voice deepening. "After spending the night with you, then fucking it all up, you were unbelievably strong enough to give me a second chance. I have immense respect for you, more so after learning of your past." He shrugged and adjusted the pillow behind his back. "You made me work harder than I've ever had to before."

"Was I a challenge?"

"Sort of." Nate had the grace to look embarrassed by his admission. "I admit, I thrived on the chase, but I respected you for not just laying down and opening your legs. Immediately, I knew you saw past the face and hefty bank balance."

"It's never been about the money, Nate." I twisted towards him. "And as for this face," I said, palm pressed to his cheek, "I hate to burst your bubble, but you're really not that attractive. I've definitely seen better."

A lie and he knew it. His eyes flared, a wide smile quickly chasing across his face when he caught my playful grin. He pinned my arms above my head, throwing one leg over mine. "Why, Miss Collins, if I didn't know any better, I'd say you enjoy playing games with me."

"Me?" I grinned. "Never."

"I'm not sure you deserve the gift I have for you now."

"Gift?" I wanted my fingers in his hair and flexed them in his grip. When he released me, he sprung off the bed so fast I didn't get a chance to do it.

"Close your eyes and hold out both hands," he ordered, walking away. A minute later, he reappeared, one hand tucked behind his back. His eyes sparkled impishly as he waited by the closet. "I said close them." My heart beat a little faster as I complied, nervous but excited. I pushed up the bed, grinning from ear to ear.

The bed dipped beside me, then a small box dropped into my upturned palms. "Open them."

A duck egg blue box tied with white ribbon in a perfect bow sat in my hands. I blinked from it up to Nate. "Something from Tiffany's?"

"Take a look inside."

A delicate chain threaded through a platinum starfish pendant studded with diamonds slipped from the pouch into my hand. Its simplicity was breathtaking. "It's a starfish," he pointed out.

"I can see that." I giggled, meeting his bright eyes.

"Do you like it?"

"It's gorgeous." I caressed the charm with my thumb. "I'll treasure this. Thank you."

"Here," he said, taking it from me. "Let me put it on." I lifted my hair so he could reach around my neck. His breath next to my ear, and the small kiss that followed sent a shiver across my skin. "Happy Anniversary," he whispered.

"I'm sorry?"

"One month ago, we shared what I hope was our last first dates in the wine bar. This is to mark that momentous occasion."

Whoa. I was astounded he'd remembered the date, and chosen to commemorate the milestone with such a romantic gesture. But I didn't get why the starfish.

"Estrella de Mar—star of the sea." Nate fingered the delicate pendant against my chest. "A mysterious creature of delicate beauty. A symbol of healing, regeneration, longevity, but above all, infinite love."

I thought my chest might explode. I crawled into his lap and curled my arms around his neck. The clarity and devotion in his eyes brought a lump to my throat. Nate had a heart of pure gold. "I'm longing to give you the words you deserve to hear. It's just…I—"

The breath he'd been holding released. "I've heard I love you many times," he pointed out with quiet resignation. "They should've said I love your car, I love your condo. Words mean nothing if they're not substantiated by actions. You show it. I *feel* it."

The stubble on his jaw tickled my fingertips as I trailed them along the cut line and across his lips before I pressed mine to them. "You're incredible, Nate. My heart is so full of you. You know that, don't you?"

"I know, baby." He shifted us both beneath the covers and switched off the light. Shrouded in darkness, only the faraway sounds of the surf and wind outside penetrated the gentle whispers of our combined breaths as we drifted into sleep.

Chapter 30

"You can't be mad at me." Mai pouted indignantly, eyes never leaving her mobile phone screen. "You should've told him, not leave me to deal with your shit."

"I know." I took my credit card back from the shop assistant who'd generously relieved me of one hundred and fifty dollars for a pair of baby pink lace knickers. An expensive purchase, but one Nate would enjoy when I wore them this weekend. "Sorry."

"Nate had a right to know what he'd been up against," she said, finishing her tweeting and tucking her phone back in the bag almost the same size as her. God knows what she had in it. "You wouldn't like it if you were fighting ghosts from his past, would you?"

"I sort of feel like I am." I smiled my thanks and took the bag from the cashier, waiting until we were walking away before continuing. "That's why I overreacted so badly. Well, that and my own history with troublesome exes. The unwelcome return of Nate's ex is bothering him. I can't put my finger on it, but something's not right."

"He won't tell you?" Mr Mai steered me back into the jewellery store we'd visited earlier so I could collect my other impulsive purchase presently being engraved.

"He tried a couple of times. I told him it wasn't necessary." I left her trying on jewellery and went to collect Nate's gift. When she returned to my side, I elaborated. "I'm trying not to make assumptions. If I want us to have a future, I have to learn to trust him."

"And do you?"

Without a second thought, I nodded. "I trust him to deal with her, and trust his reasons for not wanting me involved. We cleared the air. Nate knows everything."

Keeping her attention on the ring she'd slipped on, she raised her hand in the air and admired the coloured stones. "And for being a jealous girlfriend you got a diamond necklace?"

My right hand went to the pendant around my neck. Nate's gesture of love still had me reeling. Mai turned, her teasing smile giving away her delight. "If you're not buying anything, can we get some lunch?" I said, rubbing my stomach. "I'm starving."

Mai picked her bag off the counter and linked her arm through mine. "He's gonna go cray-cray for two weeks while you're on vacation visiting your dad."

I cringed. "When I said he knows *everything…*"

Never one to hide her displeasure, she made a tsking sound. I didn't have to look to know I was in trouble. "You haven't told him?"

"Not yet," I mumbled, shaking my head. "I will. Tonight."

"Learn your lesson, K. Tell him before he finds out another way."

I arrived at Nate's condo not long after 10 p.m., using the key he'd returned to me on the drive into work this morning to let myself in. I'd struggled to get into yoga, and even dinner and drinks with the girls couldn't relax me. Psyching myself up to break it to Nate that I was going away was stressing me out.

I dropped my bags by the stairs, slipped off my heels and padded along the dimly lit hallway, knowing exactly where I'd find him. He was looking at the open door of his office, anticipating my arrival.

"Hello." I paused, taking a minute to admire him. The businessman slipped away, his eyes growing lucid and welcoming, but shadowed with tiredness. His easy smile lifted my own exhaustion. Then it stopped, just short of making his cheeks dimple.

"You okay?" He spun his chair, inviting me to fill the empty space in his lap. I did, grateful to have his arms around me.

"I'm fine."

He murmured with content, kissing my temple then my mouth. "Good night?"

"Hmm." He smelt deliciously fresh and clean. I snuggled into him, my head resting on his shoulder, and summarised the events of my evening. "What have you been doing?"

"Working." Nate hugged me closer, sighing into my hair.

I glanced at the computer screen, noting at least six file tabs open. "Have you stopped at all for a break today?"

"I've been to the gym." He shrugged. "And ate dinner."

I'd fully intended to tell him about my trip, but when I teased my fingers through his unruly hair and his eyes closed and didn't open, I knew it wasn't the right time. "C'mon," I said, slipping off his lap, "you're exhausted. Time for bed."

There was no argument. He willingly followed, leaving his workspace in organised chaos, and let me lead him upstairs. We were both asleep within minutes of hitting the sheets.

IT WAS nearing 6 p.m. when we entered the condo Tuesday evening. Maria had gone, leaving us a delicious Spanish chicken stew warming in the oven. I'd planned on trying out the private gym in the complex with Nate, but after being cooped up all day in the office, wanted to get outside instead. After much coaxing, I'd managed to get Nate out for an early evening stroll to stretch our legs and grab some dessert for later.

"Who was trying to reach you at three a.m.?" Nate asked, steering me around the small crowd piling into the already crammed bus that had just stopped. Wilshire Blvd was bumper to bumper with people heading home, the steady flow of traffic often slower than our walking pace. We were in the minority. Nobody walked in LA.

"I didn't hear my phone ring." In the rush to leave for work this morning, I'd forgotten to pick it up from the bedside table and hadn't checked it all day. I slid my hand into the back pocket of his jeans, lingering there a while before retrieving my phone. I'd tucked it there for safekeeping because I had no pockets in my tank or yoga pants.

"Don't think it was a call," he offered, noticing me checking the missed call log. "Why leave that on when you're with me at night?"

"In case of emergency."

"Baby," he snickered, swinging an arm around my shoulder, "a magnitude ten could shake this city and it wouldn't wake you."

I bumped hips as we walked, laughing because he was right. There had been two minor tremors since I arrived here, neither of which I'd experienced. If it hadn't been for Mai telling me, I'd still be none the wiser. I practically skipped a few steps when I saw my brother's name and excitedly opened the message. "Liam's coming to LA! Look."

Nate took the phone I was thrusting in his face, and with a wide smile, read the text aloud. "Hey, Bambi…" I waved off the puzzled look he gave me and urged him to finish. "Get your ass ready to party. I'm coming to visit. Hope your Cali friends are hot, haven't had a shag in weeks. Text you the deets later. See you on 8th Oct. Luv ya."

I clapped my hands gleefully. I'd never gone this long without seeing Liam and missed him dreadfully. Having him here was going to be fun.

"Okay," Nate said slowly, tucking the phone back in his pocket. "Explain Bambi."

"Hello?" I motioned to my lower half. "Legs?"

"Ah," he murmured darkly, "don't remind me." Nate wrapped me in a one-armed hug and kissed my forehead. In trainers, I was a few inches shorter, making it easy for him to do. "You even have a few freckles, too," he teased, tapping the end of my nose with his finger.

"Shut up!" I warned with a smile, swatting his hand away. We resumed walking in the twilight hours, my favourite time. When the sky was darkening and lights were coming on, it gave a magic to the city I loved.

"His timing is perfect. I'll have a couple of weeks after I get back to get everything sorted." I came to an abrupt halt on the pavement, cringing. Preferring not to chance a look at Nate, I turned to the closest shop window display.

"Back from where, exactly?" I could feel his eyes burning into the side of my head, even though I knew they would be cool, absent of their usual devotion.

"England," I confessed, timidly.

"England?"

I nodded, noticing I'd stopped outside an upmarket jeweller. The smartly dressed assistant in the red brick fronted store holding my attention removed a tray of glittering diamonds from the window, giving us both a knowing smile as he did. "It's my first trip back. My father's really looking forward to seeing me."

Guilty, I walked away, leaving Nate to process my bombshell. After a minute he caught me up. "When do you leave?" he murmured calmly, though I knew he was less than impressed this was the first he'd heard about it.

I cringed again. "Next Friday." I kept my gaze lowered, watching the concrete disappear under my feet as I walked.

"Next fucking Friday?" He pulled me to a stop again, his hand gripping my forearm. "Were you just gonna get on a plane and hope I didn't notice your absence? Because, honestly? I'd notice. I *always* notice."

"It's only for two weeks." *Only*—like that made everything sound better. In truth, I was dreading being apart from Nate. I'd barely managed five days when he was on the East Coast. So much had happened since then, so many more feelings had developed between us, I wasn't sure I could survive without him.

"I hate the idea of being apart for that long, too." I manoeuvred his hand until I'd linked an arm through his and resumed walking. "I've considered cancelling more than once."

"Do it. I won't be separated again, I told you that."

I sighed and angled my head to rest on his shoulder. "I have to see my father. This is always a tough time for him."

"Give him a holiday. Bring him here to visit you instead. I'd like to meet him."

"The tenth is mum's birthday…I promised I'd be there." I appreciated the tender kiss Nate placed on my crown, his silent demonstration that he understood my reasons for having to go back. He smacked the button when we reached the crossing, shifting restlessly, both hands in his pockets. He might've understood, but he hadn't forgiven the unintentional omission. I rocked on my heels as we stood, silent, waiting for the lights to change.

"Who are you flying with?" Compassion now smoothed his previously irritated edge.

"Would you believe it if I said Star?"

An unexplainable emotion flickered in his eyes as he regarded me cautiously. "Take the jet."

"No!" I snickered.

"Take it," he snapped, leading me briskly across the street. "Leave when you want, come back sooner."

"I'm not taking the private company jet, Nate."

"It's mine," he stated. "Like you."

I shook my head. "I'm not an asset, unlike the jet, which is." We stopped outside a coffee shop that was still open. I wasn't sure if the offer was serious, but when I caught the determination in his eyes, I knew he meant every word.

And he was expecting me to take him up on it.

"Seriously," I insisted, curling windswept tendrils of hair behind my ears, "you arrange that, I won't be impressed. Let me travel commercial."

Even with his disapproval, Nate still looked so damned hot. I could never stay mad at him because each time I saw him, I melted. The light breeze had blown his hair into that bedroom style I loved waking up to, and his skin had a healthy outdoor glow. His white Henley top hugged his shoulders and biceps, and the jeans showcased lean legs and that seriously fine arse.

I stepped closer, linking my arms through his and wrapped them around his waist. "I'm sorry I didn't tell you sooner," I said, kissing the hollow of his throat. "I was going to, but the longer I left it, the harder it became to broach the subject."

"I'm pissed off, Kara."

With my lips to his neck, I worked slowly up to his mouth. I'd let both of us down and it made me feel shitty. "How can I make it up to you?"

I felt the tension leave him as our bodies pressed together. Succumbing to my blatant attempt at distraction, he snaked his arms around my shoulders and let his forehead fall to mine. "I'm trying to stay mad at you," he murmured.

"Two weeks, Nate. Then I'm back. No more trips," I assured unequivocally. There was no need, but I stood on tip-toe and kissed his nose.

"You'll miss the annual gala dinner I'm hosting."

"I meant to ask you about that." My calendar had gradually been filling up with social functions, presumably by Nate's assistants, and this one had caught my eye. It was obviously important, so I hadn't wanted to raise it with him until he knew I wouldn't be going. "What's it for?"

"A fundraiser for families affected by alcohol related accidents." He rushed the words out, glossing over them and their significance. My brow furrowed, not understanding the relevance of such a charity to Nate.

His shoulders dropped as he stepped back out of our embrace. As he blew out a breath, those eyes turned grey, filling with sorrow. "Too many people I've loved have lost their lives because of alcohol." Turning, he began walking to the door.

"Hey," I whispered, pulling him back. The questions over what he *hadn't* said hung heavier than the words he had. I rubbed his arm, urging him to open up more.

Nate's jaw tensed. The fact his gaze was on my mouth worried me. Why couldn't he look me in the eye? "A friend…" he started quietly, then choked up. He shook his head and spoke again, this time more firmly. "My grandparents were killed by a drunk driver. I set up a charity in their honour."

My chest cramped with his pain, his grief mixing with my own. Suddenly, his obsession with my safety made sense. Losing loved ones in such tragic circumstances had made him the overprotective man he was today. "I'm sorry," I whispered.

Nate's hands curled around my nape. "Let's go home. Our time together is limited. I don't want to waste another second out here."

Respecting his privacy, I didn't push him to elaborate. Clearly he wanted to erase his sad memories in other, more physical ways. "Patience," I breathed, my pulse quickening at our close proximity. With one last kiss, I pulled him into the coffee shop. "All good things come to those who wait," I assured him, eyeing up the massive slab of tiramisu behind the glass counter.

With a swift playful smack on my backside, Nate ordered. And just like that, I was forgiven.

Chapter 31

For nine in the evening, my apartment block was unusually quiet. Nate wouldn't be with me for at least another hour, so I'd decided to take a long soak in the bath.

My day had been hectic. Deadlines were looming and plans needed putting in place to cover my upcoming absence. I was still racked with guilt over not being entirely honest with Nate sooner about my trip away. Nate had been edgy on the drive into work. I thought he was still annoyed with me, he blamed it on having to attend the dinner meeting he was currently at. I'd opted to spend the night at my place. I needed to start thinking about our trip away this weekend.

My eyes flew open at the sound of the intercom. It was too early for Nate, so thinking it was one of the neighbour's visitors, I ignored it, hoping they'd ring the correct one sooner rather than later. A few minutes later my phone vibrated behind my head: **ARE U HOME?**

YES I replied to Nate: **IS THAT YOU DOWNSTAIRS?**

OPEN UR DOOR

I shot upright, sloshing water everywhere. "Crap," I muttered, stepping out. I mopped the mess with a towel then wrapped it around me as I hurried to the door. Footsteps dashed up the stairs and a few seconds later, Nate appeared.

"Hey." Happiness danced in his eyes.

"I should probably give you a key to this place." Letting him in with a wide smile, I locked the door behind him.

"You sure?" He started to grin. "That means we're getting serious."

"It would have saved me getting out the bath," I said, adjusting the towel. "I wasn't expecting you this early."

"Try keeping me away," he murmured, eyes running the length of my body. Pulling the edge of my towel until I fell into him, he tilted my chin and touched his sweet lips to mine.

"I'm soaking wet."

His eyes narrowed, his smile both sexually arrogant and challenging. "Is that an invitation?"

One finger trailed down my neck, across my chest, lower over my belly until he reached the apex of my thighs. I swallowed hard. Something trickled down my inner thigh, and honestly, I had no idea if it was water or something else. I was incredibly turned on from the slightest of touches.

Nate spread open the towel with his fingers and cupped me. "Jesus," he muttered harshly, taking a deep breath, "you weren't lying." Held captive by his darkening eyes, I couldn't move or break the spell. His middle finger circled my opening, drawing the wetness from inside me up over my clit and down again. The slow, deliberate lick of his lips caused a tight pull low in my stomach.

"I brought dessert, but it's gonna have to wait." He left me a trembling mess of need and stashed the take-out box in the refrigerator. "You look far tastier." He grabbed my hand and took me to the bedroom, pausing briefly to look at the bed before continuing into the en-suite.

"How come you're so early?" I asked, watching him survey the romantic candlelit space. It was warm, steamy and humid, the air sweetly fragranced with almond oil.

"My prospective clients would leave early, too if this magnificent sight awaited them at home." Turning, Nate curled a hand around my face, his fingers sliding into the roots of my tied-up hair. "Is the water still warm?"

"Hmm," I nodded. My anticipation notched up another gear.

"Get back in," he urged, peeling off my towel. His eyes widened, his chest inflating as he sucked in a deep breath. Tossing it onto the vanity, he sauntered into the bedroom and shrugged off his white dress shirt. His grey trousers quickly followed.

It was a tight squeeze as Nate slid behind me, legs straightening either side of mine. I laughed. "Don't think my bath was designed for two tall people."

With a contented murmur, Nate pulled me back against his chest and wrapped one arm around me. I watched his throat work down a sip of wine before he placed the cold glass against my lips and tipped it up.

"How was dinner?" I asked, my voice breathless and aroused all at once.

Nate smiled knowingly, twisting to set the glass behind him. "Let's not talk about that right now." He kissed my neck, massaging my nape and shoulders. The slickness of the oily water aided his firm, yet sensual movements.

Sighing, I pushed back against his chest, needing his hands elsewhere. My breasts were heavy, yearning for his caress, so when he took my cue and cupped them, I let out a small moan of relief. "Seems you and I are getting married," he murmured into my hair, brushing my erect nipples with both thumbs.

"Apparently so." My head rolled back against his shoulder. Mai had suggested the very same this morning when she confronted me with that annoying online blog again. There was a picture of us outside the jewellers—allegedly shopping for rings. "How do they know exactly where to find us? It's like we're being followed…"

"I have my suspicions we are," he said tightly.

"We are?" I craned my neck to look at him. "Who by?"

"Let me take care of it." Nate sensed my fear and slid his arms around me, holding me tight whilst pressing reassuring kisses to my shoulder. "First, I have to take care of you."

With his fingers gripping my jaw he took my mouth. Tasting me with gentle licks, expertly teasing my tongue with his, it quickly turned into a more urgent embrace.

His left hand followed the curve of my breast, running down over my stomach and pressing between my legs. I could barely open them in the confined space, but I was so greedy for his touch that I brazenly lifted one leg and settled it on the rim of the tub.

All my inner muscles tensed around his middle finger as he pushed inside me, gliding in and out, rubbing the inner wall, sending waves of ecstasy throughout my body. Thoughts of inaccurate reporting went out the window. I wanted the hard cock pressing against my spine inside me.

I reached behind me but before I could touch him, Nate lifted me, straightening his legs and forcing mine to bend and come down either side of his. My heart was racing. This was going to be a fucking and I wanted it desperately.

"Yes," Nate hissed as he drove into me. I wobbled and cried out, my entire body tensing. "Take it," he muttered roughly.

I knew he'd never harm me, and because I had that knowledge I was safe, I relaxed. Leaning forward, I started to move, my hands on the bottom of the tub working with his hands at my waist to gain a quick rhythm and keep me supported.

"Kara," Nate moaned, his grip tightening on my flesh. He started thrusting his hips, meeting me as I sank down. This position gave me an entirely new sensation, different to the other times he'd taken me from behind. I was in control of this one, I could dictate where I wanted him.

And I needed that. Needed to regain some of the confidence that had slipped away after not giving him the honesty I held in such high regard from him.

His wet hands slid up my spine to my shoulders and urged me to lean back into him. One hand cupped my breast, the other lowering to rub my swollen clit. My orgasm was building fast, so quick I struggled for breath. I arched my back, hands on the sides of the tub for leverage.

"So good," I whimpered, my head falling back next to his. I spiralled out of consciousness as the powerful orgasm took over and crashed through me. I screamed out, not caring who heard.

"Keep going," Nate growled into my shoulder, "make it last. I want you still screaming my name when I come." His finger circling my sensitive clit ensured it did, wringing every last drop of strength I had out of me.

Water sloshed around us as I brought Nate to his own ferocious climax. With a final thrust he stilled, his cock jerking as he emptied into me. His groan of release echoed around the tiled walls as his teeth sunk into my shoulder.

I sagged into him, arms folding over his. The raging beat of his heart thundered against my back, his ragged breath hot against my neck. After a minute, I twisted and kissed his jaw. "I'm glad you stopped by."

He laughed softly. "So am I."

We stayed that way, temples nuzzling, hands caressing. "Fuck," Nate muttered when he pulled back. "I've marked you."

I lifted my shoulder to see the spot his thumb was stroking. Teeth marks had broken my skin, but only just, and a small bruise was forming. It didn't hurt, and I certainly hadn't felt pain at the time. Knowing how hard I made him come, that I'd driven him so wild and abandoned, was a crazy turn-on.

Not wanting him to worry, I lifted his chin so his regretful eyes met mine. "You left your mark on me a long, long time ago, Nate." He blinked slowly, the corners of his mouth lifting as I kissed him. "Now, I hate to ruin the moment, but my legs are killing me."

"DO YOU ever have any food in here?" Nate leant on the open refrigerator door, inspecting the sparse contents of the shelves.

"Not really," I said, arriving in the kitchen. I sipped my coffee. Nate straightened and shut the door. Even in yesterday's clothes he still looked impossibly handsome.

"What do you eat? Besides yoghurt and grapefruit."

"I get by with the bare necessities. Coffee, bread, fruit." I tipped my head, lips pursed as I stifled a smile at his displeasure. "I told you, I'm a lousy cook so I get food as and when I need it. Here," I said, tossing him an apple from the bowl. His reflexes were fast and he caught it easily.

"You need to look after yourself, Kara." Nate shoved off the counter where he'd been leaning finishing his own coffee, and prowled towards me. "You'll have to stay with me more often," he purred, "so I can ensure you're well-fed."

My stomach flipped and my heart missed a beat. I'd heard that smoky, implacable tone many times before. Nate wasn't only talking about eating actual food. It was a direct reference to my newly found sexual appetite for him.

"Well," I stammered, "you certainly never leave me hungry."

He tipped up my chin. Longing swirled through my body when I glimpsed the sensual curve of his mouth as it neared mine. *Would I ever grow immune to that smile?* His lips lingered on my own, teasing, waiting for more.

Obviously, going down on him first thing had done little to curb his desire for more. And honestly, the orgasm he gave me in return had only succeeded in making me crave him further. But, with the time approaching 8.30 a.m., we had little time for round two. With that in mind, I smiled sweetly and freed myself from the sexual force field surrounding him, and edged towards the door.

NATE insisted Ross stop en-route so he could get breakfast for us both. I promised to eat at my desk and tucked the yoghurt and granola pot into my bag. We shared the apple and discussed plans for tomorrow and the weekend. Getting away together would be perfect and I wished Friday would hurry up and get here.

I stood beside Nate on the pavement outside work and waited whilst they arranged their day. My hair was tied back, and I wore a simple camel fitted dress with nude heels. The warmth of the sun prickled my bare arms and legs.

"Have a great day, Miss Collins, Mr Blake." Ross addressed me, then Nate.

I slipped my hand into Nate's as we approached the revolving doors. He glanced sideways at me, the side of his mouth curling up. "You sure about this?" he asked, lifting our joined hands in the air.

"Oh, yes." I smiled. "Everyone needs to know you're off the market."

"Sweetheart, that happened weeks ago." With a reassuring squeeze of my hand, he steered us towards the stationery doors and breezed through without breaking contact.

We attracted more than one interested glance. With a smug smile, I could only imagine their thoughts. This wasn't the first time we'd been seen together, but it was the first time we'd made a conscious statement confirming our relationship. The fact Nate was so underdressed for business was adding to the heightened level of curiosity.

"Has no one ever seen you like this before?" I whispered, nudging him as we approached the security turnstiles.

"Not here, no."

"Imagine their faces if they knew you were commando underneath?"

Nate beamed from ear to ear, knocking me off my feet as only his smile ever could. I still couldn't believe we were a couple sometimes. He steered me away from the turnstiles and through the brushed metal gate one of the guards held open. "Perks of dating the boss," he teased, nudging me back playfully. He knew I still hated thinking of him like that.

When the lift arrived, we stepped in last after the few late starters. My hand was still tightly clasped in his as he waved his card over the panel and pressed our respective levels. This time, nobody offered polite greetings. Instead, there was an expectant silence filling the air.

Nate released my hand and snaked an arm around my waist. A couple of women behind me gasped, not too discreetly. I wanted to giggle but managed to muffle my amusement with my hand. He was playing games with them. So I decided to join in. The car slowed at level eight.

"Have a fantastic day." I touched my hand to his cheek, loving the tickle from his overnight growth, and brought his mouth to meet mine. It was a simple kiss, but it spoke volumes to him, to me, and to the few who witnessed it.

The breathtaking smile he gave me stayed with me for the rest of the day.

IN a day that had been long and busy, I'd managed to run a few errands and pick up some lunch for myself, Nate and Mai whilst out. When I popped upstairs to deliver it, Nate was on a conference call so I had to leave it on his desk. Other than a brief phone conversation to inform me he had a rescheduled meeting at five, we'd barely talked all day.

I travelled to the condo with Ross, preferring the company of my own thoughts to polite conversation. It was nearing six when I exited into the private lobby and ran into Maria.

"Buenos tardes," she greeted me, black eyes searching behind me. "No Señor Blake?"

"He's still at the office." She nodded, though I wasn't sure she understood. "Hasta mañana," I called after her as she pushed open the door leading to the service lift.

With a warm appreciative smile, she said, "Buenos noches," and left.

I washed away the working day in the luxurious shower. After drying my hair, I opted for a gorgeous claret red silk floral slip that skimmed my thighs, finishing the look with a matching robe. Then I moved all of Nate's toiletries from the second bathroom back into the one given to me, stealing a quick sniff of his Tom Ford cologne before placing it on the marbled vanity. Even that brief inhalation fanned the flames of desire flickering in the pit of my stomach.

I appreciated his thoughtfulness but wanted to share this space, be able to take a shower whilst he shaved, and not be separated by walls. Silly, but that's what Nate did to me. I didn't want to miss a second of his life anymore.

With everything back in their rightful place, I went to the closet and dug the purchases I'd made on my shopping trips from my cream tote. As I passed the centre island, the scent of coral peonies sitting on the top wafted into the air. Nate had added them to give the sumptuous room a less masculine feel; another example of how considerate he was.

I sat, cross-legged on the bed, worrying the black trinket box with my thumbs. This was a huge step for me, for us. Our relationship had intensified quickly, and whilst that might have frightened the old me, I wasn't the least bit scared. Giving this to Nate, letting him know what he meant to me, and subsequently how much I was willing to let him in and trust him, felt so right it didn't get a second thought.

I set the box on his bedside table where it would be seen just as my phone lit up on my own side of the bed. Crawling over to grab it, I was already smiling before I saw Nate's name: **ON MY WAY X**

Thinking I had about thirty minutes, I went to finish up in the bathroom. I was moving my Dior gown to hang beside Nate's tux so it wasn't forgotten when Ross collected our bags tomorrow, when…"Hey, beautiful."

I jumped, spinning around. Nate leant against the arched entrance, watching me keenly. "Hey, yourself." I moved towards him, licking my lips because he looked so damn good.

His hair was slightly messy, how it tended to be by the end of the day. Nate's way of winding down on the ride home usually entailed the loosening of his tie, though not fully removing it—which I found incredibly sexy—and running a hand through his hair a few times as the public persona disappeared, and the private man took his place.

But what really did me in and hit all my buttons was the navy Lanvin two-piece. I swear Nate Blake grew more attractive with each passing day.

"Sorry I missed you today." He reached out, welcoming me into his space. "Thank you for lunch."

"You're welcome."

"What's this?"

I looked at the trinket box in his other hand. From nowhere, my heart started pounding with nerves. "It's nothing…silly, really."

"It looks like something of the utmost importance to me." After brushing his lips over mine in a sweet hello, he led me back down the hallway into the bedroom. Settling on the edge of the bed, Nate parted his legs and pulled me between them and onto his thigh. With his left arm around me, he held the box in both hands and opened it. He sucked in a breath. "Is this what I think it is?"

I nodded, chewing my lip. We both stared at the silver key attached to the keyring of an entry fob. The longer the silence stretched, the more I started regretting my decision. Nate obviously thought I'd been joking about having a key to my place. I covered his hands with mine and snapped the lid shut.

"Kara?"

"It doesn't matter." I pushed off his lap and went to his bedside table. "Keep it here for another time," I told him quietly, nudging the drawer shut with my knee.

"Baby." I squeezed my eyes shut, the softness of his voice bringing a lump to my throat. Reaching around my legs, he pulled open the drawer and retrieved the matte leather box. "This," he said, rising to his feet behind me, "is the most precious gift I've ever been given."

I turned to face him. "I'll only accept it on one condition," he said gently, sliding his hand over my jaw so his thumb reached my cheekbone, brushing tenderly in a familiar act of reassurance.

"Which is?"

"That you promise me it's only temporary." Only the mischievous twinkle in his eyes prevented a full on panic over what he meant. "That we'll share our respective homes until we have one we can call *ours*."

I threw my arms around his neck and hugged hard, breathing him in and becoming intoxicated by his uniquely masculine scent. If I had any doubt over the enormity of my feelings for Nate, they disappeared in the blink of an eye. He had my heart, locked away safely in the vacated space his own had left behind when it took up residence inside my chest.

My lips moved from the loosened collar of his shirt, up his neck to below his ear where his pulse throbbed. I undid the single button of his jacket and placed both hands flat on his stomach, loving the way his body tensed with anticipation. Slowly, I glided them up to his shoulders, listening for the change in his breathing as I relieved him of his jacket.

I wanted to show Nate how much he'd changed my life, needed him to feel my gratitude and ultimately, my love.

Chapter 32

I took a deep breath and sighed happily. God, I loved the smell of freshly brewed coffee.

When the built-in machine had finished, I carried the two mugs over to the fridge and added milk to mine. The golden early morning sun warmed the kitchen, casting light into the airy space through the one-way tinted glass as it burnt off the smoggy haze of the city at my feet. There was a stillness in the air—an absolute contrast to the riotous emotions dancing in my body. I'd been awake half an hour, too excited to sleep longer. From midday today, Nate was going to be all mine for approximately seventy hours—not that I was counting.

I crept back upstairs to the bedroom. Nate was still fast asleep, stretched across the rumpled sheets, head turned to one side. I set both cups down on the table next to his head, unable to take my eyes off him. I folded my arms over my chest and cocked my head for a better look. Standing to admire him without fear of being caught, I fell for him all over again.

He was serene in repose, his upper body raised slightly by the pillows at his back, the longer strands of his hair falling haphazardly onto the pillow. All that gave away our lengthy crazed lovemaking the night before were the dislodged comforter barely clinging to one corner of the bed, and our clothes strewn across the thick pile carpet.

I was wearing his shirt and pulled the collar up to my nose so I could smell his addictive scent. Nate shifted, his lips parting to let out a small murmur not dissimilar to the gentle sighs he breathed into my ear when I was pinned beneath him. The innocence of his mouth hid the fact he'd given me two orgasms with it last night.

As I wandered down the narrow hallway, passing the closet on my way to the bathroom, I was more than a little impatient to see my man in his tux tomorrow night. Undoubtedly, he would scrub up well.

Nate's lazy smile greeted me when I returned to the bedroom. From the threshold of the room, I studied the glorious sight of him lying there, still half asleep, with the sheet pushed just below his navel. Without a word he straightened, and with a curl of his index finger and a sexy smile, beckoned me over, patting the vacant spot in his lap.

I crawled up from the foot of the bed until I was straddling him. Warm hands slid up my thighs and beneath the tails of his shirt, settling on my bare arse with a squeeze.

"Why are you awake?" he asked, angling his head in invitation to his mouth.

I obliged with a sweet kiss, running my hands over his chest, down to his waist. Grinning, I replied, "Too excited."

"You must be very excited to wake before me." Continuing to work his lips over my face, he murmured, "I'm excited, too."

"You're *always* excited in the morning." The impressive tenting of the sheet at the apex of my spread thighs proved me right.

"Good point." He smiled widely. "I'm loving your choice of outfit." Without breaking eye contact, he began to pop the few buttons I'd fastened.

"And yet you're so keen to relieve me of it." The quiver of my voice gave away how easily Nate turned me on. My hips shifted forward, seeking the ridges of his cock.

"Because I've been privy to the beauty hiding underneath." With the tips of his fingers, he trailed over my collarbone, then down between my breasts to my navel.

"You don't have time for this," I murmured, quite unwilling to put up any sort of real fight. Nate pushed aside his shirt, his feather soft touch setting off all the nerve endings in my body until it felt like an electric current was being passed under my skin.

"I *always* have time for you." His tone was intimate and raspy, commanding my full attention. I buried my nose in his hair as he cupped both breasts, circling the nipple of one with his tongue before sucking the hard point into his hot, wet mouth.

"What about your breakfast meeting?" I reminded him, my breathing laboured. The last of my coherent thoughts scattered when he eased a finger into me, causing another instinctive rock of my hips.

"Breakfast?" He fixed me with smouldering glazed eyes. After a few languid strokes of his finger, he brought it to his mouth and sucked.

Fuck.

Nate pulled my head down and sealed his mouth over mine. It was tender, loving yet wildly erotic. After luring me into a state of delirium with his lush kiss, he flipped me onto my back and was over me before I figured out what was happening. "Well, it is the most important meal of the day."

His hips circled, his cock rubbing against the delicate folds of my damp flesh, using me to masturbate. He'd barely touched me, yet in a few short minutes I was aroused and soaking wet.

Nate was down my body in a flash, the overnight growth tickling my breasts as he paid them brief attention before sliding between my legs. Those bright eyes glanced up through heavy lids, alive and dancing with hunger. "And you, are definitely the most exquisite delicacy I've ever had the pleasure of tasting."

I cried out as the tip of his tongue circled my clit. He licked down, and when he reached my opening, hummed his enjoyment. The sheet twisted in my grip, my legs draped over his shoulders, heels digging into his back. He started slow, building my anticipation, focusing entirely on my own needs.

Suddenly, he froze.

"Please…keep doing that," I begged, my brain too focused on preparing for the onslaught of orgasmic pleasure to think of anything else.

"Shhh," he warned, raising his head.

My mind raced back to full cognisance as the sound of a woman's voice intruded into my impure thoughts.

"Fuck!" Nate jerked back, his eyes wide with shock.

I still didn't comprehend what was happening. He called out in Spanish, and after a reply came back, he relaxed with a smirk. "Maria."

"Shit!" I scrambled out of his hold and shuffled up, dragging whatever I could grab of the sheet with me. "Why is she so early?"

"She probably thought we'd left already. I'm usually downstairs by now." Nate slipped off the bed and leisurely strolled, butt naked and with an impressive erection, over to close the door. I darted off the bed and sprinted down the passageway. He shouted one more thing to Maria before I heard the bedroom door close.

"Kara," he called. A tap on the now shut en-suite door followed. "Let me in."

"Nothing like an unwelcome visitor to kill the mood." The flushed face of a woman in a state of high arousal stared back at me as I braced my hands on the vanity.

"But I haven't got you off," he moaned through the door.

"And that is *definitely* not happening now."

JUST after 1 p.m., I stepped into the luxurious cabin of Nate's private jet. Tastefully decorated in neutral tones with fern green accents, it was deceptively bigger than the outside had led me to believe. Four cream leather seats around a walnut table were to my right, behind them a matching sofa in the lounge area, complete with television. On my left was a workstation, decked out with the latest technology for the business savvy entrepreneur gripping my hand as he followed me in.

"Welcome aboard again, Sir."

I turned towards the suited young man holding two flutes of champagne aloft on a silver tray behind us. "Miss Collins," he said, nodding and smiling.

Nate waved me into one of the four seats, then joined me. At some point between dropping me home, attending—late—his breakfast meeting, and going into the office, he'd changed into jeans and a navy polo shirt. "Thanks, Anthony," he said to the man placing the bubbles in front of us.

"You're welcome. Lunch will be served as soon as we reach altitude. Anything else you need?"

"I have everything I need right here," Nate said, giving my hand a squeeze. Of course, I blushed. With his lips twisted in humour, Anthony disappeared towards the back of the jet and shut the partition door, giving us absolute privacy.

Andrew, the pilot I'd been introduced to in the private lounge before boarding, made an announcement through the overhead speaker. Then I felt a small jolt as we slowly started moving. I buckled up and relaxed into the soft leather, placing my hand over Nate's.

"To the weekend," he toasted. I raised my flute to his, giving an excited murmur of approval as I took a sip. I felt like a child the night before Christmas, so eager to spend our first trip away together.

Leaning into his shoulder, I kissed his cheek. "Thanks for showing a girl a good time."

"We haven't been yet." He smiled widely. "You might hate it."

"I'm with you. I'm going to love it."

WE followed the coast north. Anthony served a delicious poached chicken salad and strawberry tart for dessert. Nate declined his own but happily shared a bite or two of mine as we moved to the sofa and got comfortable for the rest of the short journey. I hadn't forgotten our earlier failed attempt to make love, and couldn't wait until we arrived at the hotel to finish what we'd started with no more interruptions. In the meantime, a little foreplay at thirty-thousand feet couldn't hurt.

I removed his hand from my legs and pulled myself onto his lap, mentally congratulating my last minute decision to wear a black printed ruffle miniskirt with my white tank. Nate's head fell back, the sparkle in his eyes telling of the impurities running through his mind.

"I've never joined the mile-high club before." With a smile of intent, I hitched my skirt up just short of revealing my underwear.

His eyes dropped immediately, lips parting with a sigh. As always, his hands came to my thighs, as though he could never resist touching me. He swallowed. Then made a point of dragging his eyes ever so slowly back up to meet mine. "You want to take this to the bedroom?"

"Here works for me."

The astonishment in his eyes was clouded with desire, his cheeks pinked, his smile wide and daring. Accepting his challenge, I ran both hands down his chest, skimming erect nipples, until I reached his belt.

Nate lifted the satellite phone from behind his head to his ear. "How much longer Andrew?"

The one hand gripping my thigh tensed as I rubbed against his crotch and let out an intentional moan low into his ear. When I sat back, his gaze was fixed on me. He nodded then hung up. "We have ten minutes."

"Okay." I shrugged, slipping the end of his belt through the loop on his jeans and tugging it through the buckle. "Sometimes, quick is good."

A single brow rose, before a wicked smile touched his lips. I popped open the button of his jeans and slid my hand inside. Over the cotton of his briefs I started masturbating him. There was little need. He was hard as stone, pulsing in my hand.

I felt brave and wanted to maintain eye contact whilst touching him, but

Nate had other ideas. His eyes closed as his head rolled back. A groan of content escaped his mouth as, with the tip of my tongue I traced along first his upper, then lower lip. Before I could move my head back to tease him, Nate grabbed my face and slammed his mouth to mine, sucking my tongue into his mouth.

The jet jolted as we hit turbulence and shook before dropping. The sensation in my stomach was exactly the same as when we kissed.

"Fuck," Nate bit out, firing scorching hot eyes at me. "This is going to have to wait. We're about to land."

"EXCUSE the cliché." Nate nodded to the shiny red two-seater convertible Ferrari waiting on the tarmac. "Will's idea of class."

I laughed. "It's not that bad."

"Think yourself lucky, wearing that skirt," Nate said, opening the passenger door. "He could've sent the Harley."

It wasn't long before we were driving through a landscape covered in grapevines. Nate handled the car with precision, but the cut of impatience had me wondering if he was experiencing the same level of sexual frustration I was. The music playing on Nate's phone through Bluetooth only added to the flames of desire licking my insides.

"This music is very sexy," I purred, stroking Nate's thigh from knee to crotch. Slowly.

"Sexy?"

I nodded. "Very."

Without another word, he curved his fingers around my knee and unhurriedly ran his palm up my thigh, under the hem of my skirt. I didn't care in the slightest that the wind blew my skirt up, flashing my underwear. Craving his fingers, I pushed my hips forward and shoulders back.

"Open your legs," he ordered roughly.

I glanced sideways. His sight was firmly fixed on the road ahead, but his mind was clearly on a different track. Without shame, I did as he'd asked. I made an embarrassing mewing sound when his middle finger pushed against the silk of my panties in a slow, torturous circle.

Nate blew out a breath and shifted a little closer. Pushing them aside, his fingers settled against my slick folds of skin. "Christ, you're soaking wet."

"Do it!" I urged, unable to withstand the wait. Given the foreplay that had been going on since this morning, I had no idea why he was shocked. Because of the awkward angle, he only just penetrated me with the tip of his finger, but it was enough.

Nate looked cool as anything. I looked closer, noticing the throbbing vein in his neck and the beads of sweat dotting his upper lip. His knuckles were white around the steering wheel. When my eyes reached his groin, his erection pressed into the crotch of his jeans.

I wanted to lean over and return the favour. But I couldn't move. His touch was too masterful, too good to let him stop.

I pushed my ankle boots to the floor and rocked my hips, riding his finger, hungrily seeking more. I tossed my arms freely over my head, feeling the wind catch through my fingers.

Nate was finger-fucking me in a convertible car, where anyone could see as we drove along, and I couldn't care less. That's how carefree and abandoned he made me feel. That's why I adored him so desperately.

I was only aware we'd stopped when Nate awkwardly reached across and shifted the gearstick into park, his right hand still occupied with pleasuring me. He silenced the engine but left Maxwell singing his sexy song.

"We're here?" I panted out—on the verge of coming like crazy— and sucked in some air, straightening to look around.

"You need an orgasm," Nate growled. He removed his hand from between my legs and took off his sunglasses.

"I would have had one, too if you hadn't stopped." My heart thundered in my chest, the whir of traffic rushing past on the main strip behind us mixing with my heavy breathing. We were on a small side road, nowhere near civilisation, with the sun beating down.

Nate unclipped both our seat belts, then pushed his chair back as far as it went. "Climb onto me."

"What? We can't have sex…here?"

"You've been tempting and toying with me since I woke and found you half-dressed in my shirt."

"I have not!" I spluttered. Nate cocked his head, brow raised. "Okay, maybe a little bit."

"You want me to fuck you. I know it—you know it. Get your sassy little ass over here so I can." With a tug of my arm he pulled me out of my seat. I was about to wedge my knees either side of his hips when he stopped me. With a twirl of his finger he ordered, "Other way."

Ungracefully, I turned in the tiny space and faced the windscreen. Catching the string of my panties, I giggled as I fidgeted to take them off. Nate was equally as frantic in freeing his cock.

"You're such a fucking turn-on." Nate pushed me forward and shoved up my skirt. He quickly found me, grabbing my hips and slamming me down onto his cock.

I cried out, relief as much as pleasure hitting me. Bracing my hands on the steering wheel, I leant forward, trying to ease the feeling of being so damn full of him and lifted again.

Nate pulled me onto him again, fingers digging into my hips as he thrust up to meet me. His hands travelled over my ribs and cupped my breasts. "Sometimes, quick is good," he reminded me, his tone laced with predatory sensuality.

"God, yes." I shut my eyes and started to move, chasing the orgasm that had been so elusive all day. The exhilaration of knowing we could be caught spurred me on. Yet as much as I wanted quick and dirty, my pace settled into the rhythm of the music.

"Faster," he snapped. "Harder. This needs to be quick."

Holding my hips firm, he began lifting me up and pulling me down, impaling me onto his cock. A flash of perspiration broke out over my skin. My orgasm was imminent, everything pulsing and contracting inside. Beneath me, Nate's thighs tensed. One hand pushed beneath my skirt and found my clit. "You need to come," he growled. "Now."

The tiniest amount of pressure broke me. I came with one of the fastest, most shattering orgasms I'd ever experienced. "Nate," I cried. My forehead hit the steering wheel, all control of my trembling body gone.

Nate crushed his chest to my back as he came with a muttered curse. For long minutes, he pumped into me, his cock swelling as he released everything into me. Finally, he crashed back into his seat, taking me with him.

"Oh my God!" Stunned, I dropped my head back to his shoulder. Then I started laughing.

"Well, I've never had that reaction before." I felt Nate smile against my damp neck and tried to stifle my amusement. "Not quite the mile-high club, huh?"

"Definitely more thrilling."

"I'll say. You've undoubtedly brightened many a fellow driver's day."

"You certainly brightened mine." I curled a hand around his neck and shut my eyes. It didn't take long before the reality of what we'd just done seeped into my thoughts.

As both hands wrapped around my ribcage, Nate rolled his head back and let out a long sigh. "God, Kara. You're my Achilles heel. I lose focus when I'm with you. I get reckless."

He sounded like he wished our hot encounter hadn't happened. I twisted to look at him. "Didn't you enjoy it?"

"Baby." He titled my chin and brushed his lips tenderly over mine. "I loved it. Always do. But the idea of that being splashed over the latest gossip blogs is something I *don't* enjoy. Anything that tarnishes our lovemaking doesn't sit right with me."

I curled his windswept hair between my fingers. Picturing anyone I knew seeing those images brought home the reality of the situation. It was a spur of the moment thing, but our carelessness could cost us both dearly.

"Having said that," Nate continued, freeing me from worry, "I definitely plan on letting you take advantage of me again very, very soon."

"That wasn't me," I chided him with a playful smile.

"You started it, I finished it."

With a swift kiss on his cheek, I clambered back into my seat and attempted to straighten out my clothes.

"Check the glove compartment. Hopefully there's tissues," he said, hoisting his jeans back up. I found them and handed some over. Then I cleaned myself up, and thoroughly embarrassed, stuffed the used ones into my bag to dispose of privately.

"Put these back on." Nate retrieved my panties from his footwell and handed them over. "Don't like the idea of your ass being bare when Will meets you." He zipped up his fly and started on his belt, adding, "Don't think we'll tell him you fucked me in his car."

"Oh my God!" I cried again, burying my face in my palms. My embarrassment gave way to an uncontrollable fit of the giggles. It wasn't long before Nate joined in as we headed towards our destination.

"WELL, well, well. If it isn't America's sexiest bachelor," the mellow voice of a man lilted behind us as we checked in. Nate took our room key from the immaculately coiffed receptionist, smiling as he turned around.

"Cut the crap, Will." The two men greeted each other with a handshake that turned into an affectionate hug. "And you can keep your bachelor title. I'm very happily taken," he stated, tugging me to his side.

"Ah, yes." Will turned to me. "The woman who's finally tamed my big brother." He spread his muscular arms wide. "Do I get a hug or what?"

Will pulled me into his solid frame with a force that unbalanced me. He was tall, with playful aquamarine eyes, naturally tanned, and curly coffee-brown hair. Whilst Nate had more of a refined, sculpted face, Will's features were fuller and more rugged, his body buff from using weights to bulk up.

With a genuine smile, he held me by the shoulders and scanned me up and down with mischievous eyes. "What's a pretty girl like you doing with a guy like him? Nate is shooting way above his mark this time."

"Then she's definitely out of your league, so get your dirty hands off her." It was a playful warning from brother to brother, but Nate still pulled me back to him, staking his claim.

"Woman," Will said, "you are frickin' hot! Let's cut to the chase—when are we getting hitched?"

"Show some respect," Nate snapped. His disdain only amused Will further.

"I see the full-on charm offensive is a pre-requisite in your family." I grinned at Will.

"Didn't think his silver tongue worked on you, Kara? You made him work his ass off." Will folded his arms and rocked back on his heels. "Well played."

Had I missed the introduction bit? I glanced at Nate. His earlier displeasure had gone. Now he was shy over being outed. I hugged his arm. Nate was so *not* a bashful person.

"Don't look so surprised," Will went on. "I've heard all about you. Guys talk too, ya know." Turning to address Nate, he said, "You're right, bro. She's gorgeous."

With a congratulatory pat on Nate's shoulder, Will turned us towards the lounge. "C'mon, drinks are lined up at the bar. I was expecting you earlier. My car still in one piece?"

"The compensation for your cock is fine," Nate assured him. I giggled. All distinguished gentleman constraints had gone. Nate was a guy as much as the rest of them. Yes, he spoke dirty to me when the mood dictated it, but listening to the sibling banter showed me another layer of his personality. "We had a great ride in."

I nudged his side, getting his double-meaning even if Will had no idea what it meant.

"Traffic hold you up?" Will asked over his shoulder as he walked away.

"No." Nate grinned at me. "We took the scenic route."

A bellhop arrived and whisked away the trolley stacked with our luggage and garment bags. "I have to freshen up," I reminded Nate quietly.

His smile widened. "Will," Nate called, "meet you there in ten. Just need to go upstairs."

"Man, you've lost your touch. Give the girl more than that." And with a wink at me, Will strolled into the lobby bar.

OVER a meal eaten sitting at the bar, Will held centre court, keenly regaling us with stories about Nate. It was heartwarming to watch their interactions, listen to them trade insults, and watch Nate laugh, relaxed in our company. Will's good nature and wicked sense of humour reminded me of Liam and raised memories of the teasing my own little brother often gave me.

Will's large hand covered the slender fingers of the female bartender when she replenished their empty beer bottles with full ones. It lingered discreetly whilst they shared a heated stare. "Thanks, Nicole," Will murmured, his tone a few levels lower than normal.

Sandwiched between the two of them, I finished my third glass of the vineyard's finest Merlot as tiredness hit. Stretching, I stifled a yawn. "More wine, Kara?" Will asked, preparing to summon Nicole back.

"God, no. I'm stuffed."

"Well, I didn't like to say, but damn, you can put away some food. That burger didn't stand a chance of getting cold. Where'd you put it all?" Gleaming eyes raked me up and down again.

I glanced at Nate, took a breath, then boldly said, "Having lots of sex with your brother helps keep the weight off."

Nate dropped his head and burst out laughing, his fingers rubbing his brow as he shook his head. The pink hue colouring his cheeks made me proud. Finally, after all this time, I'd made him blush.

"Jesus!" Will cried, throwing his napkin down on the bar. "A little more information than I asked for!"

"And on that note," I said, slipping off the barstool, "I'm going upstairs." I pushed the metal stool in, amused when they both politely stood.

"Everything okay?" Nate asked.

"Yes, just tired. You should stay, though."

"Kara." Will stepped away from the bar. "Things were about to get interesting. We'd reached the teenage years. You don't want to miss them."

"Tell me tomorrow. I'll look forward to it."

"Guess it buys me time to think of some real hideously shameful stories." He gave me a full-on kiss on the lips, more than surprising me. His daring grin suggested he'd done it on purpose to annoy the shit out of Nate, and from the scowl on my boyfriend's face, it had worked.

"If he wants to keep use of his legs," Nate murmured, clasping my elbow and leading me to the exit, "he won't ever do that again."

"He's playing you. It meant nothing."

"Yeah, well, he might be my brother but that won't stop me kicking his ass." When we reached the bottom of the grand staircase leading to the second floor, he turned me to face him, both hands on my shoulders. "You sure you don't want me to come up?"

"No, I'm going to make use of the huge bathtub then crash." I placed my palms on his chest and leant in for a kiss. "Spend some time with Will. Come up when you're ready."

"In that case, I'll be there in five." He squeezed my shoulders and watched me climb the stairs, eyes not leaving me until I'd disappeared out of sight.

Chapter 33

The farmhouse adjoining the Lonely Oak vineyard had been extended and converted into a luxury twenty-five bedroom boutique hotel with spa. The vibe was French Provincial with authentic vintage furniture imported from the Loire Valley. Impeccable and elegant, but warm and inviting, decorated in nude tones with pale gold accents.

The bedroom alone was bigger than most hotel rooms, with a huge open fireplace and seating area. A wrought iron chandelier dripping with cut-glass beads hung from the exposed wooden beams—frankly, I wanted to take it home. It was gorgeous. The pièce de résistance, however, lay the other side of arched windows—lush hills covered with grapevines, miles upon miles in every direction you looked, interspersed with the last violets of lavender.

Even after our morning bedroom workout, Nate still had enough energy to drag me on a run in stifling heat. It was a great way to explore the impressive surrounding landscape belonging to the family. And with Will joining us, I was the luckiest woman alive, running alongside two seriously fit men working up a sweat.

"What are you opting for?" Nate asked, strolling into the lounge after his shower. For the past fifteen minutes my head had been stuck in the Spa Menu, deciding on a treatment.

"I'm spoilt for choice."

"Have whatever you want." He lifted my bare outstretched legs and joined me on the country style sofa. "My treat."

He smelled deliciously clean and was dressed in a fitted navy collared shirt and graphite grey trousers. “Do you really have to work? I feel guilty being pampered while you’re in the office.”

“It shouldn’t take long. Will needs me to cast an eye over some business contracts.” He opened up the calendar function on his mobile phone. “We also need to ensure everything is sorted for tonight.”

“Anything I can do?”

“No.” He patted my knee. “I might join you if we’re done in time.”

I returned the menu to the table and took a few grapes from the fruit platter. “Not sure how I feel about another woman’s hands all over your body,” I noted, popping one into his mouth.

He chewed and swallowed, smirking. “Not sure how I feel about one touching you either. Can I watch?”

Laughing, I stood to collect my essentials from the bedroom. “How can you still be so horny after this morning?” I called out, shoving my purse into a white crocheted summer bag.

I jumped when Nate’s hands found my ribs, a brief stop on the way down to my backside. “For you,” he murmured into my ear, “I’m horny all the time. Your ass is looking particularly pert in these tiny white shorts.”

“That’s what you said first thing, right before you sank your teeth into it.” I turned in his embrace, halting his enjoyment. “Hate to think how sexually frustrated you’d be if I wasn’t here.”

“You better believe it.” And with a killer of a smile, he kissed me.

THE outdoor swimming pool was a relief to the intense heat of the midday sun. I sat on the edge and dangled my legs in the sparkling water, awash with a happiness and contentment that had eluded me for a long time. A few middle-aged couples, shaded by cream sun umbrellas, lounged on cushioned sun loungers sipping drinks served by two sprightly young girls in conservative knee-length shorts and white polo shirts.

One woman stopped briefly to chat as she passed to collect a towel from the cabana, asking if I was Will’s guest. Her shock upon hearing I was with Nate tickled and pleased me. It backed up Nate’s admission there had been no one serious in a while who had earned an invitation here.

With my appointment in ten minutes, I stood. Sadie and Mel were strolling towards me. “Kara.” Sadie’s arms spread open as she approached. “Nate told us we’d find you out here.”

"Lovely to see you both again." I returned her warm embrace.

"Mom," Mel said as she finished draping towels over two beds, "you take the lounger next to Kara. I can't lay beside her with a body like this." She wore large, dark sunglasses, but I could tell she was giving me the once over. *Here we go again.*

"That sarong is pretty." My compliment was a cautious one. We hadn't spoken since the lunch date, and I wasn't sure where we stood.

Then with a genuine smile, she kissed both my cheeks. "Thanks. I won't be taking it off for sure."

"Are you kidding me?" I scoffed as the three of us moved back to the loungers. "If I look anything like you post-babies, I'll be delighted. You have a fantastic figure."

"You should see her dress for this evening," Sadie gushed, clasping Mel's hand. "She looks wonderful."

Dressed in a pale blue cover-up and large floppy sunhat to shield her ageless skin from the sun, Sadie looked terrific herself.

"Shit!" Mel exclaimed as she flopped onto a bed. "I forgot my hat and I've just gotten comfy."

"Here." I tossed her the straw hat off my head. "Use this. I'm about to visit the spa."

"Excuse me, I must say hello to Angela and David." Sadie gave a hesitant wave to one of the couples.

"You didn't invite their daughter did you?" Mel sat and peered over her sunglasses.

"Don't be ridiculous, Melanie." Flustered and awkward, Sadie gave me a tight smile and hurried away. The air around us had thickened with tension.

When Sadie was at a safe distance, Mel muttered, "If I see that bitch a day before I die it'll be too soon." She picked up the drinks menu and studied it. "It's a shame you're heading off. Hoped we could bond over a cocktail or three."

"I would've liked that." And I meant it. Her opinion of me had clearly shifted and it genuinely made me happy. "Let's do it tonight."

"Sounds perfect. In the meantime," she said, tipping her face up to the sun, "I'm gonna kick back and make the most of my kid-free time."

With a wave, I left her soaking up the sun and headed to the spa for a spot of pampering.

ALMOST five hours later I floated into the suite. My plan for a basic massage was thwarted when I arrived at the spa and discovered Nate had booked me an array of treatments. For starters, I was scrubbed head-to-toe with sea-salt, then massaged into a state of bliss with a cashmere lotion mixed with real twenty-four carat gold leaf, leaving my skin with a satiny sheen and silky softness. I was served lunch and champagne, then had deluxe manicures and pedicures, before being whisked away to another room where my hair was washed and styled in cascading waves, channelling Old-Hollywood glamour.

I entered the bedroom just as Nate's shirt cleared his head and landed on the chaise. "I've just spent the entire afternoon in heaven," I announced, approaching him. He turned, hands sliding into his trouser pockets. Placing my palms on his bare chest I swept my lips over his. "Looks like I might still be there."

"You certainly look like heaven," he murmured.

"My skin feels like it, too."

"Can I check?" He tugged the sash of my robe until it fell open. Laughing, I batted his roaming hands away. "Your laugh sounds like heaven." He cupped my throat and ran his nose under my jawline. "And you smell like it. That only leaves one more sense to check out."

I offered my mouth for him to taste. Instead, Nate angled my face away and sucked on my neck, moving until he found the sensitive spot below my ear that made me shiver. "I already know how good you taste…how good this tastes," he muttered, fingers pushing between my legs.

I squeezed my thighs together. If he succeeded in getting into my panties, I wouldn't be able to say no.

"Shower with me," he asked, dragging his teeth along my jaw.

"I'm afraid you'll have to settle for a kiss. This perfection," I pointed to myself as I stepped back and retied my robe, "has taken hours of effort and a *lot* of your money. There's no chance you're mussing me up."

He stood there, his semi-erect cock straining against his fly and watched me with narrowed, amused eyes as I flopped onto the bed. That look was in his eyes, where I just knew he wanted to devour me. If it hadn't been for the doorbell ringing, the entire afternoon would have been a waste of time. "Expecting company?"

"Room service." Nate went to answer the door. A few minutes later, he returned carrying an ice bucket and two flutes.

"Nothing can surpass the French for true Champagne." Draping a white napkin over his forearm with flair, he showed me the bottle—Moët and Chandon Dom Pérignon 2003 Rosé Champagne. "Can I pour you a glass, Mademoiselle?"

Laughing, I pushed off the bed. "Have a shower—*a cold one*—then we'll drink it together." I set about removing his clothing and ushered him into the bathroom.

Being able to watch Nate dress behind me as I added the finishing touches to my makeup in the dressing room mirror was a treat. When he eased his legs into black tuxedo trousers without underwear, I smirked. "You're going commando tonight?"

"Hell, yeah." His grin was cocky as he pulled on his white shirt. "Adds a bit of spice to these black tie events. I've always done it."

My core contracted at the idea of spending all night with him, knowing that beneath the suave exterior of his Tom Ford tuxedo was a deliciously naughty man. I went into the closet to retrieve my gift. "I bought you a present."

He looked up as he finished fastening his watch strap. "You did?"

Nodding, I offered him the black box. "Hope you like them."

Nate took it and sauntered to the bed, sitting down before he opened the lid. My heart raced as I waited with bated breath. He fingered the contents, then after inspecting more closely, lifted his head. His expression was my most favourite of all. The look of love.

Completely disarming me with his smile, eyes spoke to me the way only his ever could. He didn't have to say it. I knew.

"Help me put them on?" he asked, walking towards me.

"Sure." With a relieved smile, I took out a platinum cufflink, engraved with our entwined initials, and fixed them one at a time to his French cuffs.

"I'm such a lucky bastard," Nate said, clasping my face and kissing my forehead.

"You are." I took a minute to appreciate him, then asked, "Can you help me into my dress?"

"That just sounds so wrong."

I fetched the gown and handed it over. His breath hitched as I stripped off, eyes devouring me as he crouched by my feet. Using his shoulders for balance, I stepped into it and turned so he could fasten me up. His lips pressed softly up my spine as he fastened the bodice, trapping his kisses against my skin.

We both stared in silence at our reflection in the full-length mirror. When I caught his gaze, there was a dark, salacious glint in his eyes. I swallowed and asked, "What do you think?"

Nate shook his head, hands resting on my hips. "I have no words."

"Is that good?"

"You've stolen my breath away," he murmured, clasping my hands and entwining our fingers. "Absolutely enchanting."

I felt exactly the same. Nate hadn't got his jacket on, and his hair was a disorderly wet mess from his shower, yet he still looked utterly gorgeous. "Tell me what you see," he urged.

"In you?"

He laughed softly. "No, in you. Do you see what I do when you look at yourself?"

I studied the person staring back at me quietly. I did look pretty, but that had more to do with the exquisite couture dress I wore and the hours of attention I'd received at the spa.

"Well?" Nate asked.

"I see a shy woman, still a little self-conscious, all too mindful of her misgivings, but hiding it well with a pretty dress."

His mouth thinned, his head shaking, saddened and disappointed as he turned me to face him. "Know what I see?"

I shrugged.

With the tips of his fingers brushing my cheekbones, he implored me to believe his next words. "A truly remarkable woman, whose inner strength and beauty has no bounds. A woman finally free from the constraints of her past, who knows who she is and is ready to embrace that person. Someone who lights up my world brighter than the stars in the night sky, offering me the chance of a future I never thought I could have."

The words he spoke radiated bright like a light from those captivating eyes. I let out a soft sigh of sheer happiness. Raising my knuckles to his lips, he kissed them before planting a sweet kiss on the underside of my right wrist. "And someone who's wrist is a little too bare."

"Pardon?" I followed him with tear-filled eyes as he removed something from the in-room safe.

"You're not the only one who came bearing gifts." A long red jewellery box was between slender fingers when he returned.

"Nate, you've given me more than enough already."

He popped the lid and waited. When I saw the contents, my hands flew to my mouth, stifling my gasp. "This is far too much."

"Nothing will ever be *enough* for you, Kara." Nate carefully slipped the delicate bracelet out and draped it around my shaking arm. Pink and white pavé diamonds glittered on my wrist.

I sucked in a breath to steady my speeding heart, and tried to halt the sob bubbling inside. It was no use. Staring at the bracelet—at Nate—in outright shock, a tear I desperately didn't want to fall tracked over my cheek.

"See this, right here," Nate said softly, brushing the lone drop away, "is *exactly* why I adore you. When you let down that guard and let all your raw emotion out without apology. Things matter to you. I just want to wrap you up, nurture you, cherish you forever."

"I don't want to cry." Disappointed, I swiped at my tears. "My makeup is ruined."

"At least I'm ruining it for the right reason. Mai will be pleased." He removed his white pocket square and started dabbing at my eyes.

"What's she got to do with it?" I sniffed.

"I was issued a stern warning. Smudge your lipstick, not your mascara."

I snickered. "One of her insightful gems."

"If I did," he went on, "said she'd bust my kneecaps, total my car, and force Riley to poison my coffee. She's fierce. I was pretty intimidated."

I sniggered. Inside that tiny frame of hers lived a massive heart. For the first time, I actually considered Mai as a best friend—a sister I never had. "And you took a threat, from that tiny thing?"

Nate shrugged with a smile. "I indulged her, allowed her to think she'd bothered me. There's a difference."

"Thank you. I love it." And to show how much, I hauled him close and pressed my lips to his. The kiss quickly deepened. I relished the devotion in his touch, the profound love that made my stomach flutter. I was completely lost to him. A life without him didn't bear thinking about.

He was the last man I would ever fall for again.

I drank in the finished product, rooted to the spot. The bespoke tuxedo formed Nate's lean frame immaculately, accentuating his trim physique. Nothing, however, could detract from the savage beauty of the man wearing it. With the cut lines of his closely shaved jawline, lightly tanned skin glowed with an inner peace, and his eyes shone the brightest blue. Flawlessly well-groomed, his hair had been smoothed back, much like the night of the Acacia party. I literally thought I might have to pick my jaw up off the floor.

"You look so..." I tried regaining some sense. Finally, I managed a feeble, "Handsome."

Nate's lips curved as he straightened his sleeves, pulling so the cufflinks were exposed.

"But something's missing." I hitched up my dress and removed my lacy panties. His mind quickly caught up. This was going to drive him wild, possibly over the edge.

"There." I arranged them neatly in his pocket so their identity was concealed and gave it a pat. "Perfectly co-ordinated."

"Jesus, Kara!" His growl rumbled through my alert body, the hand grabbing my bottom sending spurs of heat over my already flush skin. "Knowing this fantastic ass is bare and I'm wearing the offending garment like an accessory is too much. Fuck," he rasped, lowering his head, "I can smell you on me."

I ran a hand over his chest, down to his groin, cupping and fondling his cock. "And to think there's nothing beneath this?" I bit my lip, glancing up. "You really know how to tease me."

"That makes two of us." Our bodies pressed together, my hands trapped between us. Fiery lust was replaced with a tender intimacy. "How do you grow more beautiful every time I look at you?"

My gaze lowered to his shoulder. His adoration and genuine heart still confounded me. A man who could have any woman he wanted had chosen me. I was who he'd fallen in love with.

"Now, if your hand stays where it is, we won't make it to this party." His voice had that gruff rasp that got me hot and feeling wanton and sexy, because there wasn't the uncertainty over exactly how good his promises of fantastic sex were anymore. I knew. And, I knew what made him even crazier for me was when I came out of my shell and unleashed the seductive temptress inside. All I could think was fuck the party, let me drag you back in there and do all sorts of naughty things to you.

"Those thoughts making you blush," Nate murmured, clasping my hand and heading to the door, "keep having them. Every time I glance at you, I'll enjoy knowing you're thinking of me and how hard you're gonna make me come."

Flushed with embarrassment yet full of feminine empowerment, I followed him into the hallway.

The lounge bar was full of family and friends, all resplendent in their finery. Nate never let me out of his sight, proudly introducing me to the other guests as his girlfriend. One hand was constantly on me, either around my waist, gently caressing my shoulder or firmly linked in my own. His touch calmed me in what would otherwise have been a nerve-wracking experience.

"Mel, you look fantastic," I told her when she arrived. Wearing a floor length black one-shouldered gown, her light brown hair was styled high on her head to highlight a swanlike neck.

"Spanx" she confided with a wink.

"Oh, yes," I laughed. "Me, too."

"That's exactly what I should be giving you for being such a naughty girl," Nate growled into my ear. I'd never been into that kind of thing, but had to admit, with him in charge I couldn't fail to get excited by the suggestion. He smirked and fondled his newly acquired pocket square.

I was relieved when we were asked to take our seats for dinner.

"YOU and Will organised all of this?" I asked Nate quietly as we finished our vichyssoise, one of my favourite soups.

"Why are you surprised? You told me I had the whole wining and dining seduction mastered to perfection."

The dinner setting was one of the most romantic I'd seen. Fairy lights twinkled on clipped miniature hedges and topiaries lining a rectangular stone terrace. Seven round tables draped in fresh white linen had been set for eight, all with individual heaters to ward off the night chill. The table centrepieces were large pillar candles in glass bowls, decorated with lavender and herbs that fragranced the air.

"Hope you've brought that appetite of yours." Will, sitting on my right, patted my shoulder and winked as the main course was placed in front of us—a Provençal style sea bass with steamed vegetables. "I've definitely worked up a hunger."

"Have you been in the gym?" I asked, sipping my champagne.

"Kara." With a lewd grin, Will shot me a narrow-eyed glance. "Her name's *Bethany*, not Jim. Male on male shit—not my thing."

I promptly choked on my bubbles which made him howl with laughter. Even Nate grinned. Luckily, the rest of the table didn't hear. Thomas, Sadie, Mel and David were in deep conversation. According to Nate, Bethany was a nice, well-behaved girl, and Will's go-to-date for special occasions such as this. One you share with the family and not the boys—his words, not mine. I'd been speechless when he confirmed it had actually happened before. The pouty brunette seemed a little put out by the fact I was sat between easily the two most attractive men in the room and not her.

By the time dinner was over, the corset of my dress was definitely snugger. I'd been drinking since early afternoon in the spa and the warm fuzz of alcohol was also threading through my veins.

"Once again you haven't let me down." Will nodded an acknowledgement to my empty plate.

"Hell would have to freeze over before I left any of that Clafoutis. So bad for me, but so good." I wiped the corners of my mouth with the napkin and set it beside my plate.

Nate's arm immediately came back around my shoulders when I sagged into the back of my chair. He leant closer, turning his head away so no one could hear, and murmured, "You look so damn beautiful. I can't take my eyes off you."

It was true. Even during the times he couldn't physically look at me, he was connecting through touch, as though his fingers could convey what he was so desperate to see with his eyes. Had it been anyone else I'd have found it suffocating. But I loved knowing Nate needed me that much. I felt exactly the same.

"I noticed," I whispered back, "and I like it." Shy, I bit my lip when I caught Mel observing us. "Even if you are just protecting your investment," I pointed out, jangling the bracelet so the precision cut gems sent shards of light bouncing across the table.

Nate drew his head back. "You are far more precious to me than any piece of jewellery." He pressed warm lips to my wrist, then worked his way back up to my ear. "Don't think I've forgotten you're gloriously naked beneath this dress."

Everything deep inside clenched at the husky tone and implication of his words. "Nor I you," I replied, stroking his thigh.

His fingers were blindly toying with the bracelet. "I need to fuck you so badly."

"Shhh." I placed a finger to his lips, hoping he wasn't heard. I doubt he'd have cared if his broad grin was anything to go by. I stroked his face, following the strong, smooth jawline with my fingers. Then I leant in and kissed him. I wanted more but was conscious of the eyes watching us.

"Put her down, man." Will pushed out his chair and stood. "Mom wants us up front."

A large sandstone sculpture framed with an iron arbour separated the dining area from the dancing section. Behind that, a stage for the band waiting to play. Nate, his parents and siblings, stood centre stage in front of us all. As the eldest son, Nate gave the speech.

The consummate professional was present, but his demeanour and words were relaxed, full of respect and admiration for his parents. "You inspire me. Give me hope that everyone has a soulmate, and to never take it for granted if you're fortunate enough to find them in this life," Nate continued, bringing what had been a humorous, lighthearted speech to a close on a more serious note.

He turned to his parents, both teary-eyed to his left. "Dad, if I make my future wife half as happy as you've made mom, I'll be doing my job as her husband."

Thomas acknowledged Nate's sincerity with a pat on his shoulder. Nate cleared his throat, then the entire focus of his speech altered. He glanced up, intense blue eyes locking me firmly in their sight. The air thickened, like the calm before an impending thunderstorm. The crackle of chemistry was instant, like someone had flicked on a switch.

"Dad always told me, when you find the one who resides in your head—the one you can't go a second without thinking about, the one you'd lay down your life for—never let her go. Because she is the one who will forever live in your heart."

Enraptured, love bloomed inside my chest. Bethany offered a dreamy sigh of awe, but I was too caught up in the man of my dreams to respond. Suddenly, the world shifted, righted itself, then started spinning again, smoother and more purposeful than before.

He talked to *me*, heat firing from his eyes. Mere seconds passed, yet it felt like time stood still. Will shuffled closer and spoke into Nate's ear. Nate took a minute to compose himself, then straightened, turning to his parents. "You are each other's forever. I love you both." He raised his glass high in the air, voice breaking with emotion. "Happy Anniversary."

I scrambled for my champagne and stood on shaky legs, toasting Thomas and Sadie. Everyone gave a rousing round of applause as they stepped onto the dance floor while the family returned to the table. "That was beautiful," I said to Nate when he joined me again.

"That last bit was for you."

I waited for him to lower the champagne flute from his mouth before kissing him. "I know." Resting my head to his, we watched his parents dance in a contented silence, arm-in-arm. The way they moved across the black tiled floor so easily, and in perfect synchronisation, reminded me of being a young girl and watching my own parents dance.

I felt Nate tense before he muttered under his breath. "Christ." The couple I'd seen at the pool earlier were making their way over. His mouth thinned as he greeted them stiffly. "Angela. David."

"Nate, so lovely to see you again." The woman's smile was tinged with shame. Mel watched with caution whilst Will looked like he was ready to jump in at any moment. Their concern baffled me.

"Yes, it's been a while." Nate brought me into the conversation. "This is my girlfriend, Kara." Then he turned to me. "Angela and David are old family friends."

I reached out a hand to each of them. "Hello."

"My, she's a pretty one," David said, clasping both sweaty hands around mine. Nate's vice-like grip on my waist tightened possessively. The tension between the three of them was strained, the atmosphere decidedly cold. The older couple fidgeted awkwardly as an uncomfortable silence descended upon us.

"So, we've heard a lot about you again lately," Angela started cautiously, almost afraid. I would be too if I was on the receiving end of the withering glare Nate gave her. "Will we see more of you, too?"

"Highly unlikely," Nate replied stiffly.

Angela recoiled, but quickly regained her demure composure. "Thank you for giving her another chance."

Nate snorted. "Like I had a choice." He glanced over his shoulder, ignoring Angela's genuine gratitude. "Please excuse us," he addressed them both. "I'd like to dance with the love of my life." With a diplomatic goodbye, he ushered us onto the dance floor to join the other guests.

"Why the frosty atmosphere?" I asked, nodding to the couple as I settled into his hold.

"No reason." We began to sway in time to Van Morrison. There was no mistaking the way Nate held me so close demonstrated his familiarity with my body. The slow, almost indecent movement of his hips pressing his groin to mine. The one hand resting on the curve of my backside, the other stroking the exposed skin on my back. Our synergy was perfect, like we'd been dancing together for years—the way we were in bed together. The longer we danced, the more the strain eased from his highly strung frame. Nate leant his head to mine and began to sing.

"I love when you sing to me," I murmured, closing my eyes.

I felt his smile. "You've noticed?"

"Every time." I took a long inhalation, his heady scent making me sway as much as he did, leading me in the slow dance. As the song finished, he dipped me in one last extravagant move that had the crowd clapping. With anyone else I'd have been thoroughly embarrassed, but in Nate's arms I was invincible. He urged me back into his frame, holding my hand to his chest, the other wrapped around my waist.

"The love of your life, huh?" I repeated, his earlier statement filling me with contentment.

"My forever." And in case I needed further reassurance, he dipped his head and kissed me. My hand broke free and slid up his chest to join the other at his nape. The hand that came to the back of my head held me in place as the innocent meeting of lips turned more amorous. My tongue flicked out, mapping Nate's full lips, searing them to memory before losing them as he opened his mouth. His tongue was quick to find mine, the sweetness of black cherries coating the heat of his kiss.

Love overflowed between us as Nate staked his final claim of me. Everyone and everything around us disappeared.

"I can't believe we just did that in front of everyone. In front of your family!" I buried my face in his neck.

"They're lucky it's all they witnessed."

I pulled back. His face was flushed, eyes bright. He gazed at me like I was all that existed in his world. All he could see—all that mattered.

I needed us to be alone, away from the distraction of guests and music. I didn't want to share him, or our precious time, with anyone else. For a little while, I wanted him to be mine.

I took a deep breath. "Can we go somewhere quiet?"

Chapter 34

Nate led me through the courtyard and into the hotel. He pushed through the private staff doors into the kitchen, bidding the surprised chefs and wait staff a good evening without stopping. Holding his hand, I hurried behind him. As we passed the wine cellar, he grabbed a bottle of champagne.

"Where are we going?" I asked excitedly.

"You'll see." We exited through a fire door into the darkness of night. "This way."

The sounds of laughter and music faded as we left the hotel behind us. The three-inch heels of my shoes were not ideal for the gravel pathway crunching beneath us. I stumbled more than once.

"Here." Nate handed me the bottle then turned and crouched. "Hop on."

"I'm butt naked. I can't hitch up the dress to climb on your back."

The lazy smile spreading to his dark gaze when he faced me seared through me like a scorching flash of lightning. "How could I forget?" he purred, scooping me over his shoulder like a fireman.

"You're crazy!" I yelped, clinging one-handed to the tail of his jacket.

"Hold tight." He smacked my backside and started off again into the inky blackness. The crunch of gravel quickly gave way to the silent tread of grass. When Nate eventually set me back on my feet and turned me around, I gaped with wonder. The stillness of a vast lake was illuminated by the full moon shining in the clear night sky.

"Okay, now you've *really* excelled yourself." Whilst I marvelled at the beauty in front of me, Nate shrugged off his jacket and lay it on the ground, then loosened his bow tie, leaving it hanging around his neck.

"You bring out the best in me." He took the bottle and made quick work of opening it, giving the base a twist until the cork popped.

"We don't have glasses."

"What? You've never drunk champagne from the bottle before?" He grinned and passed it over.

"Not one costing hundreds of dollars, no." With an impish smile, I took a sip. Bubbles fizzed on my tongue as I swirled the pink liquid around and swallowed.

"Taste just as good?"

I shook my head. "Better."

Nate sat and pulled me onto his lap, leaning me back to his chest. The organza layers of my dress fell around our legs, the tiny sequins catching the moonlight. "I knew this dress was perfect for you the minute I saw it."

"When exactly was that?"

"The Saturday after our first date."

I glanced at the side profile of his face as he stared straight ahead, taking a swig from the bottle. "*Two* days?"

Lifting a shoulder, he placed the bottle to my lips. "I knew we were gonna happen, even if you hadn't quite figured it out."

Resting my head to his, I swallowed the champagne, letting his words sink in. Everyone—Nate, Mai, even my father who'd never met him—had seen what was right in front of me. I was the last person to get it.

Surrounded by the trappings of luxury, both of us dressed head to toe in designer labels, we swigged vintage Moët like it was a bottle of Coke. Yet at the end of the day, it was merely expensive packaging. Underneath, Nate was completely down to earth, not loud and brash, but sensitive and kind, appreciative of everything he had.

A mirror image of my soul. The other half I hadn't known was missing.

Until now.

With a small twist, I faced him. I ran my fingers through his hair, taking the uninterrupted time to really look at him. He did the same. My fingertips caressed his cheekbone then traced his soft pouty lips. Lips that kissed me like no other had before, or ever would again. Lips that always found the right words to say. Lips that I knew had never lied.

The way Nate's eyes sparkled with love in the moonlight made my heart constrict. All seeing eyes confirmed what I already knew, giving me the courage required to open my heart. This was a moment where nothing else needed to be said.

Except one thing.

"God," I sighed on a long exhalation, "I'm *so* in love with you."

Nate sucked in a breath, eyes widening, his grip on my hip tightening. He set the bottle down beside him without taking his eyes off me. I'd caught him completely off-guard with my declaration of love.

"Like, it's ridiculous how much I am." I cupped his jaw. "I wasn't prepared for any of this, but with your patience, your encouragement and honesty, you've opened my heart again and earned my trust. I'm a different woman to the one I believed I was. You've swept me off my feet. My world will never be the same again, and for that, you deserve *all* of me. All of my love."

Nate's mouth parted, his breath coming in a long sigh. Cradling his face with both hands I moved closer. "I love you, Nathan Blake," I whispered, brushing my lips over his. "I always have, and I always will."

Our mouths met. It began slow and teasing—an exploration—grazing, tasting, biting and licking. Nate's arms banded around my back and hauled me to his frame, chest to chest, squeezing hard. With a sigh, I opened my mouth to welcome him inside.

With lush, unhurried strokes intended to ignite the fires in our stomachs, it was the most heartfelt, all-consuming kiss I'd ever experienced. A hint to a long night of tender lovemaking between two lovers. Nate's love coursed through my blood, filling the empty void that had resided there for too long. When I broke free, my head was spinning, my brain starved of oxygen. Never had I been kissed that way, so deeply I lost my mind. The times before had all been a prelude to this one life-changing moment.

"You have no idea how long I've waited to hear those words," Nate breathed, dropping his forehead to mine.

"Do you believe them?" I asked cautiously.

"Without a doubt." His chest continued to thunder against mine. "And I love you, too. More than anything." Gradually, his mouth curved then widened into the most stunning smile to ever light up his beautiful face. He fell onto his back, taking me with him, his arm under my shoulders keeping me off the ground. "Tell me again," he murmured, brushing my hair behind my ear.

I grinned, touching his face, revelling in the deeper connection between us and the freedom I now felt. "I love you."

The kiss we shared again was as emotional as the first, only sexual intention singed the edges. By the time we came up for air I was burning for him.

"I don't want this moment to end," Nate admitted softly.

"Every chance I get, I'm going to tell you and show you. You'll be so sick of hearing it, you'll be begging me to stop."

"If that happens, you have full consent to check me into a mental institution because there's no way in hell I'll ever tire of it with a sane mind."

NATE carried me back the same way, hoisted over his shoulder. The party was in full swing, most of the guests dancing, including his parents. The rest of the family were sat at the table.

"Here they are!" Will exclaimed. "What happened to you guys?" He had a smirk on his face like he'd done the maths and figured it out.

"We're calling it a night," Nate said, drawing me to his side. The smile I'd put there was still lighting his face.

"We are?" I asked quietly.

He nodded. "Time to lock ourselves away in our suite and not show our faces until morning."

"You can't bail now!" Will shoved his chair back and stood. "The grey brigade will be heading to bed soon," he moaned, pointing to the older generation of guests, "then the party can really start."

"Got my own private party to attend, thanks." Nate reached out a hand to Will, who reluctantly shook it as Nate spoke in his ear at the same time.

"Could've told you that, bro," Will replied. Then he frowned, put his finger to pursed lips and said, "Oh, wait, I already did."

Simon collared Nate, so I quickly said goodbye to Bethany. Will turned to me, genuine happiness in his eyes, and tugged me into his arms. "Remember his age, Kara. Don't wear him out too much." He winked and planted a kiss on my mouth.

"Night, Will." Laughing, I stepped out of his arms, straight into Mel's. It took a while before I responded to her unexpected embrace.

"We got off on the wrong foot," she admitted in my ear, "but I see how much Nate loves you."

I prised myself free but kept hold of her elbows.

"I've never seen him so caught up in a woman before," she went on, hands lightly gripping my biceps. "Dad calls it the love light, when your eyes light up.

Nate looks at you exactly the same way."

"I'll look after him," I promised. Nothing would give me greater pleasure than to stand on the table and announce to the world that I was crazy in love with the brilliant man making his way around the table. But I wanted to keep our private elation sacred for a little while longer.

"I know." Mel glanced over her shoulder to Nate. "You're good for him," she said, turning back. "Just don't hurt him."

"I'm taking her back now." Nate joined us, kissing my temple as Mel's eyes rolled skyward.

"You guys have fun," Mel ordered, returning to her seat rather ungracefully. "I'm gonna have one hell of a hangover tomorrow," she giggled and emptied her glass.

"Just my parents left," Nate said, leading me to the dance floor, "then I'm taking you to bed." His warm breath tickled my ear, his words sending a wave of heated anticipation through me.

"Your tuxedo! Your beautiful dress!" Sadie cried, interrupting her dance to inspect us. She took my hand, fussing over my gown. "What happened?"

"We took a walk by the lake and sat a while. We're fine," Nate assured, "it's only dust."

"Ah, that's where your father proposed," she sighed, turning her adoring gaze to her husband. "My favourite spot."

"It is beautiful. I can't wait to see it in daylight," I told her. I said goodnight to Thomas whilst Nate wrapped Sadie into his arms, kissing either cheek.

"Enjoy the rest of the party," Nate said to his parents.

"Thank you, honey," Sadie replied. "Now, get this gorgeous girl out of that dress."

Nate hugged Thomas with a smirk. As he led me inside, he murmured, "You heard what mom said."

"Are you always a good boy who does what mommy tells him?" I smirked back.

The cerulean blue of his eyes flashed then thinned, overtaken by the black dilation of his pupils. His nostrils flared, his grip on my waist tightening as we climbed the stairs. *"Always."*

AWARENESS and expectation hummed through my body. I was breathing fast, pulse racing. Nate hung the *Do Not Disturb* sign on the door and kicked it shut. Sinful ideas played in his eyes. He led me to the bedroom and switched on the antique table lamps, casting a pattern of shadows on the cream walls.

"Finally," Nate growled. He threw his jacket on the chaise and prowled towards me. "I've got you all alone." He caught my chin, keeping my head raised to meet him eye to eye. I wouldn't have looked away—I couldn't. This man was mine and I was his. I wanted to see that ownership reflected in his blazing eyes.

"You have full permission to smudge more than just my lipstick," I encouraged.

His mouth twitched as it neared mine. "And I fully intend to."

My sigh was lost in his kiss. I shoved my hands into his hair and pushed my body flush against his. He lured me into near unconsciousness—how he always could—with precise strokes of his tongue in a blatant mouth-fuck. Because that's how it felt to kiss him.

"First," he panted, "I need to get you naked." The tips of his reverent fingers sent shivers over my heated flesh as he slowly unzipped me. "It won't take long," he breathed, teeth grazing my shoulder blade, "not like you have much underneath, is it?"

Pink organza and silk pooled at my Louboutin'd feet. I took his proffered hand and stepped out. Crouching, Nate removed my shoes and gathered up the dress, draping it carefully alongside his jacket. Seeing him before me, hair mussed from my hands, black tie loose around his collar, all gorgeous and prime male was like visual Viagra for women. My hands flexed, restless at my sides, itching to touch him.

With eyes riveted on me, Nate removed his cufflinks. I waited until he'd set them on the dresser and started on his shirt buttons before moving. "Stop," I ordered, brushing his hands away. "If you think I won't enjoy undressing you equally as much, you're crazy."

"Crazy for you." He grinned.

Smiling, I slipped the shirt over his shoulders, my palms sliding over hot skin and lean muscle. Then I started on his belt and didn't stop until I'd stripped him naked, too. I clasped his neck and blinked when the light hit the bracelet. "Thank you for my gift."

He walked me backward to the bed and sat on the edge, pulling me between his parted legs. Raising my hands in front of him, he fingered the bracelet, examining it, then bent my arms behind my back. Holding them firm with one hand, he placed the other over my heart. "Thank you for *my* gift," he murmured, "I'll keep it safe. I promise you."

I nodded, needing nothing more.

He started pressing tiny kisses over my stomach, paying special attention to the spot below my navel—a favourite of his, it seemed. Slowly, his hand moved from my heart, over my puckered nipple, trailing over my hip and groin, settling between my legs with a gentle push. The pad of his middle finger circled my clit. "I'm not gonna fuck you," he growled, timing the slide of his finger inside me with the moment our eyes met. "We're going to make love for a very, *very* long time. Possibly all night. You'll know I've been here." Another finger joined the first in a tantalising rhythm, seducing my mind with words and touch. "But you'll still want me there again and again."

I sighed, my head falling back so the tips of my hair tickled my hands. He worked my body like a gifted artist, licking and sucking, nibbling and kissing, worshipping me with his talented mouth and hand to create the perfect picture. Locked by his legs, trapped by his hand, he forced me to surrender all power and allow him to take me another step on our journey.

My hands dived into his hair the second he released me, pulling his head to my breast. The heat of his mouth as it covered my nipple made my stomach clench. For as long as I could, I gave him what he needed, allowed him to revel in my body until the urge to cherish his virile body with the same veneration consumed me. I shoved his shoulders, urging him back onto the bed, going with him until I lay flush over him, skin to skin.

"I love you," I murmured against his jaw, sliding my mouth down his neck. My fingertips grazed his abs as I shifted down his body, rippling over the cut ridges, mapping a trail for my lips to follow. I loved how his muscles tensed, how tiny goosebumps chased across his skin with my caress. "And I love this," I confirmed when I reached his rigid cock, now ready and waiting.

"Fuck," Nate hissed, a strangled mix of urgency and pleasure as I took him in my mouth. Hollowing my cheeks I sucked him in, then let him slide out almost to the head, teasing and taunting with my tongue and lips.

"I love sucking you off as much as you enjoy receiving it," I breathed, pumping him with one hand before taking him to the back of my throat.

"Christ! Keep talking like that…I won't last long." His hands dived into my hair, pushing it off my face and gathering it all at my nape. I knew he was watching, creating an unobstructed view of his cock sliding in and out of my mouth. Encouraged by that visual, I gave him the show he wanted. Raising my eyes to his, I opened my mouth wide and traced the head with the tip of my tongue, then gradually swallowed him back with a moan of ecstasy.

"Keep doing that." His mouth opened with a soundless moan. "I want my cum in your mouth—in your body."

I continued driving him to the edge, his muttered words of love and praise scorching my ears. Never in my life had I remotely entertained the idea I could come from words alone, but suddenly it seemed a real possibility.

Nate's hips bucked, his cock pulsed. "Fuck." With his fist in my hair, he yanked my head back and reared up, watching me swallow the hot semen filling my mouth. His eyes were wide and ablaze with passion, trapping me in their focus and holding me hostage. I swirled my tongue over the tender head, not wanting any of his lust to go to waste. I didn't think I'd ever have enough of him.

When his legs relaxed, I kissed the sexy V of his groin, filling my lungs with the musky scent of testosterone and pure male satisfaction. I had to admire how he was still firm. "I want to do that again."

"No chance," he panted, flipping me onto my back. "My turn." Gently, he spread me open, and gave a long groan. "You get so fucking wet for me, baby. So wet." His tongue seared me. "You're gonna come any minute."

There was no time for the steady build-up to orgasm, every decadent lick and taste making my body jerk and tremble. I'd been craving this since this morning. From the last time Nate had touched me, I'd been counting down until I experienced his touch again.

"Nate." My orgasm crashed through me in sharp bursts of pleasure. I clamped my knees to his head, the covers scrunched in my fists, his name falling repeatedly from my mouth. "Make love to me," I begged through the spasms still wrecking my body.

Nate crawled up my body and slammed his mouth to mine. I'd never have enough of his kisses, each one like a drug, a potent force that numbed the mind and made the heart race wildly.

Without pausing for breath, Nate shifted us until he sat in the centre of the bed, his crossed legs the perfect cradle for me. I rocked my hips, seeking him out, and lowered onto him with mutual groans of relief. Nate's arms were wrapped firm around me, holding me against him. There was no space between our stomachs, Nate's cheek pressed to my chest, mine to the top of his head. I don't think I'd ever been held so tightly.

It was an act of pure, intense, unequivocal love.

In a steady even pace, not wanting the night to end, we made love. Slow and deep, with little friction from the minimal movement, I felt like I had days of lost time to make up for and didn't want to miss a second of our love.

I tilted back his head. Dark, azure eyes, endlessly expressive, were filled with adoration and wonder. "Are you all right?" I whispered, curling the hair at his nape.

"More than," he breathed, leaning me back so the angle of penetration shifted. "Why?"

I moaned as his cock stroked deep inside me, the sensation rippling across my stomach. "You're quiet." Propped up on my hands, I allowed his one hand at my hip to support and guide.

Nate groaned and reached an arm behind him for balance. The sting of being this stretched was delicious. "I don't wanna talk. I want to listen…to *feel*." He gripped my waist, dictating the pace as I started to reach the peak again. It all became a sensory experience—the touch, the taste, the sound of heavy breaths ringing in your ears in an alternate rhythm to the heartbeat.

A thin film of sweat covered us both, making it harder to hold on. My impending orgasm weakened my arms, making me tremble. "Do you feel that?" Nate rasped. His chest heaved, his face glistening, damp hair clinging to his temples.

I nodded. Overcome by how deeply I truly loved him, I drew him close, wrapping my arms around his neck.

"This is real love, Kara. This is us."

Nate came the exact moment my orgasm rode through me in a tender wave. Never had I experienced a more intense connection with a person. The pulse of exhilaration flooded every part of my psyche, throbbing over and over, taking me somewhere I'd never been before. With tears of happiness, I whispered, "I love you so much."

"Kara." My name spilt from his lips with a rawness that cut me to the core. That's when I got it. The extent of just how hard he'd fallen for me, when those three words weren't enough. All of that power, that meaning, that soul-claiming obsession was there in the simple whisper of my name.

We collapsed onto the bed, limbs twisted until we were one. I nuzzled into his neck, his pulse racing against my nose. Nate stroked my spine, soothing until my breathing slowed.

My eyes fell closed with the words, "I love you" falling from my lips.

Chapter 35

"You always know the best way to wake me." Laying side by side on the bed, I ran my fingers through Nate's just-fucked hair and placed a kiss on his smiling lips.

He took my hand and placed it around his waist, shifting closer. "You look a little sleepy still. Think you need another alarm call."

I threw my head back, laughing. He took advantage of the opening and worked his mouth down, cupping my breast to meet the wash of heat from his mouth. Laughter turned into a gasp, then a purr of content when he sucked harder.

The doorbell to the suite rang, followed a second later by the holler of "Housekeeping!"

"What the fuck?" Nate bolted upright. "Can't they read?"

"I thought you hung the sign on the door?" I cried, hoisting the crumpled sheet up from the foot of the bed.

Nate swung his legs off the bed, cursing as he stalked towards the chaise. "I did."

"Hey." I lunged for his hand and pulled him back. "You can't go out there like that. *With that.*" I pointed to his erection. "I'll go." I jumped out of bed and fished out my panties from his jacket.

"Hello? Housekeeping." The voice grew louder.

I slipped them on and grabbed his shirt, buttoning it up as I rushed to the door. "That body is for my eyes only," I warned. "Stay there."

"Going nowhere, sweetheart." I turned at his playful drawl. Flat on his back, propped by a mound of pillows, he fisted his cock. The large hand wrapped around the base, barely covering half up, slid smoothly up and down in practised strokes. I was riveted to the spot, mouth open. Nothing was going to move me. Until the door handle turned in my grip and the door opened, hitting me on the back.

I spun so fast, using all my strength to keep it from opening further and giving the maid an eyeful of my man.

"Oh, I'm so sorry." Beetroot red, the young girl backed away from the door. "I thought the room was empty."

Careful to close the door behind me, I followed her out, conscious I'd only managed a few of the buttons. "We're checking out later. Can you leave it until then?"

"Sure." Relieved, she darted out the main door and rushed off with her laundry cart.

When I checked the notice, it was *Please Make Up the Room* side facing out. I flipped it around, shut and dead-bolted the door.

"Some idiot switched the notice," I said, re-entering the bedroom. Nate hadn't moved an inch. Ravenous eyes devoured me as I began stripping off. He met mine just as I realised the culprit.

"Will," we both said together. I collapsed onto the bed in a fit of giggles.

"His dues are gonna have to wait," Nate murmured, hauling me on top of him. "I need taking care of."

AN hour later, all the family had gathered in a private dining room for a buffet brunch. Sadie and Thomas were deciding on the right time of year to take their all expenses paid trip to Paris, courtesy of Nate's generosity. Will was close to finishing his second plate of waffles and bacon, covered with maple syrup, but the seat beside him was empty and Bethany was nowhere in sight. Mel sat beside Simon, white as a ghost, nursing a mug of steaming black coffee.

"Sure I can't tempt you with some food, Mel?" Will shoved his chair back and strolled to the back of the room for more food. He smacked the shapely backside of a petite blonde waitress as she bent over to replenish a tray of fruit. She wasn't offended, in fact she seemed to enjoy it. Not wanting to mix business with pleasure wasn't a standard shared by the two Blake brothers, that was for sure. As he passed Mel on the way back, plate piled high, he shoved it under her nose. She heaved and smacked his hand away.

Smiling, I sat back to let my brunch digest. I don't know why I'd been so worried about fitting in with Nate's family. They were all gracious and welcoming. I imagined my own, and the family meals we used to take together. Precious times I could never get back.

"You okay, baby?" Nate asked quietly.

I stopped twisting the eternity band on my finger. "Just thinking about my family, my mother especially. She would've really liked you."

Nate's eyes softened. "If you're anything like her, your dad was a lucky man."

I nodded and gave a small smile of gratitude.

"I know it's not quite the same," he said, stroking my hair behind my ear, "but they're your family too now. I can't do anything about Will, but the rest of them aren't so bad."

My future flashed before me, life with Nate, something I never imagined happening. "You are." I touched his smiling face and brought him closer, brushing my lips against his. "Thank you."

NATE took me back to the lake so I could see it in daylight. This time, my choice of beaded flat sandals paired with an off-white chiffon sundress was far more practical. Light and airy, it stayed cool against my sun-warmed skin. My hair, still wavy, was loosely pinned half-up in a knot.

"Will has some great plans for this place." Nate stood on a rock beside me, skimming stones across the tranquil surface of the water. His tanned arms stood out against the white of his shirt, and the navy shorts let me see his calf muscles flexing each time he stepped back to throw another. "Over there" —he pointed to the far side where the land had been cleared— "will be organic fruit and vegetables. We can bottle juices and sell the produce. It'll also supply the hotel kitchen."

"Why didn't you tell me you own the hotel?" I glanced up, unsure if he'd realised his slip of the tongue.

"Does it make any difference?" he asked, not taking his eyes off the view as he sat.

"No, it just surprised me when I read it in the room brochure the other night." He had a sizeable property portfolio, but it hadn't crossed my mind this was part of it. I just assumed it belonged to his family.

"I bought it a few years ago to work in partnership with the vineyard."

"So Will manages the hotel, too?"

"He does it all," he confirmed, turning towards me. "I'm a silent partner."

It wasn't a big deal, so I left the conversation at that. "Who does the farmhouse on the hill over there belong to?" The shell of the building was intact, but there were a few vans and a bulldozer parked up at the side. It had a bright red terracotta tiled roof and was set back a few hundred feet from the edge of the lake.

Nate smiled fondly. "It used to belong to my grandparents. I spent all my summers as a kid there."

"Really?" I smiled, gleeful at the discovery of a childhood memory.

"See the big oak?" He pointed out the massive tree standing all on its own near the waters edge. "We used to have a swing on it. One day, I climbed it to shake Mel off. She'd been on it way too long and wasn't sharing." His grin widened. "I crawled along the branch, then my foot slipped and I fell ten feet to the ground."

I winced at the visual of a naughty little boy getting injured.

"I was lucky. All I got was this," he said, touching the hairline scar I'd noticed a few weeks back. Then he shrugged. "Well, that, and an ass-kicking from dad."

I laughed at his boyish smile. "Ah, poor baby." I leant my head on his shoulder. "Is it being demolished to make way for the farming?"

"It's being renovated."

"Who by? It looks like the development will be right next door. Are they okay with that?"

Nate smiled mysteriously as he swung an arm around my shoulder. "They're good. Not gonna be a problem."

AFTER ARRIVING back at the condo late last night, neither of us woke until mid-morning Monday. Fortunately, it was Labour Day, so I didn't have to work. Nate, of course, spent a few hours in the home office preparing for the busy week ahead. I called my father and caught up on his news. We were both excited by the prospect of Liam visiting. A little after 7 p.m., Nate found me in the media room on his iPad, catching up on some personal emails.

"I've been neglecting you." Wandering in, dressed casually in black sweatpants and matching t-shirt, unkempt hair and two days worth of scruff on his face, he stopped in front of me and held out a hand. "Let's go work out."

Tilting my head up, I met his warm gaze and smirked. "Are you inviting me to have sex?"

A corner of his mouth curved. "I was thinking of showing you the gym, but wearing those glasses, I can be persuaded otherwise."

I set the iPad beside me and unfurled my legs, taking his hand and allowing him to pull me into his arms. "The gym could be fun. I feel like I haven't exercised in days."

"No?" he asked, steering me through the apartment to the stairs. "Maybe we do need to have sex then. Remind you of my favourite way to burn off calories."

With a quick change of clothes, we headed down to the Ground Floor where the private fitness centre was located. The air-conditioned space had all the latest top of the range equipment. Treadmills were lined up to face outside to the pool, behind them elliptical trainers and rowing machines. There was a space cleared for floor based activities, with light grey mats and cushioned benches, and weights and dumbbells stacked in front of mirrored walls. Then there were assorted weight machines, stability balls, resistance bands and skipping ropes.

Nate grabbed two towels from the freshly stocked shelves and two bottles of chilled water from the mini fridge. "Looks like the place is ours," he noted, glancing around the empty gym. "What are you hitting up first?"

"Think I'll do a few stretches then use the free weights. Finish off with some cardio."

"Okay."

I followed him to the mats. Whilst I browsed the different weighted dumbbells, he laid my towel on a bench and set a bottle underneath. "What about you?"

"Me?" He grinned, backing up to the leg press facing the mats. "Think I'll set up right here and watch."

And he did. There were no focused repetitions of his leg raises to suggest serious effort. Every time I dared face him or caught sight of him in the mirror, he was staring, occasionally lifting and straightening his legs. The sexual tension filling the air between us made me brave, uninhibited.

We sparred back and forth trading moves. For every grunt of exertion he made, I made one louder. Confident eyes never left mine as he did push-ups on the mat while I straddled the bench and lifted weights. I balanced on the ball and did crunches, legs spread direct in his line of vision. I put more effort into my post-weight stretches. When I bent forward and pressed my palms to the floor to stretch my hamstrings, I made sure I faced away from him. With my backside thrust in his face, I knew heat would be firing the sapphire hues of his eyes when I straightened.

He didn't disappoint.

Invigorated and high on endorphins and female supremacy, I grabbed my towel and water, ready for the treadmill.

As I passed Nate, long fingers wrapped around my elbow, clasping and tugging me close. "You think you're gonna win this game we're playing?" he purred. He pressed the heat of his body against mine. In trainers, I was a few inches shorter and had to blink up to his face. The few times I'd teased him like this, his dominant nature had invariably won out. But I was more confident now and knew how to play him.

"Yeah." I pushed onto tiptoe and kissed him briefly, then took my time walking to the treadmill. A flash of doubt hit me when Nate casually sidled over and stepped onto the machine beside me.

"I reviewed my schedule earlier," he mentioned coolly, concentrating on selecting his workout settings. "I'm heading to Rhode Island while you're away."

The belt on my machine started moving. His indifference threw me until I realised he was intentionally trying to put me off stride. I'd picked up the pace to a small jog by the time his kicked in. Unfazed, I replied, "Oh? What's happening there?"

"The new Faculty of Arts at RISD has been named in my honour."

My eyes widened as my breath accelerated. "Wow! That's fantastic."

"I made a hefty donation for the privilege," he said dryly, settling into a fast but steady pace. "They're having the official unveiling next weekend."

Nate was a proud man who played down his successes. This was a significant milestone in his career. Nothing would have given me greater pleasure than to be on his arm that night, sharing in his remarkable achievement. "I'm really sad I'll miss it."

"I established a scholarship fund last year." Using his towel, he wiped his sweaty brow and puffed out some air. "I grew up fortunate to have an education that allowed me to realise my dreams." He shrugged and increased the running speed and gradient. "Some kids aren't as lucky. Investing in the Design School is an investment in our future, and subsequently my children's future."

His enthusiasm for education and giving back was admirable and typical of his generosity and kindness. We ran for another fifteen minutes flat out. In typical mischievous style, Nate pushed me, challenging me to match his pace.

I could barely breathe, my heart thudded loud. The waistband of my cropped leggings soaked up rivulets of sweat trickling between my breasts and down my back.

A man entered and gave us a nod hello before making a beeline for the heavy weights, intent on honing his already beefed up physique. I watched him load the discs onto the metal bar. Unlike Mai, I didn't find the muscle-man appearance attractive.

My gaze slid to the man beside me, his attention now focused on me, his sexual desire clear. There was a line of sweat marking the front of his plain white tank. His face was flushed with heat and exertion, his hair now resembling dark glossy rivers of chocolate. This was more my type. In four days, we were to be separated.

My thoughts briefly returned to last week. "How did you propose to get there," I puffed out, "if I had the jet in London?"

With no embarrassment, he panted, "In one of the others."

I hit the emergency stop button and grabbed hold of the handrails. *"Others?"*

Nate's eased his treadmill to a gradual halt. "So, now you know there's more than one, does it increase my chances of getting you to use it?"

"No," I reiterated, drying off my face as I stepped off with shaky legs, "so forget it." It was a clear violation of company property. Even if the boss agreed it. I downed my water. "Tell me more about RISD."

After wiping clean the machines, we tossed our used towels into a laundry basket and pushed through the glass doors into a small foyer to wait for the lift. "It's an accolade I'm immensely proud of." He followed me into the car and pushed in the keycard to gain access to the condo.

"And number two on America's Sexiest CEO's List isn't?"

"That's just scandalous," he shot back with a wicked smile and a naughty glimmer in his eyes.

"I know, right?" With the cool glassed interior against my back, I tugged Nate closer by the wet hem of his tank. "You should be number one if you ask me."

"If I ask you, there shouldn't be a list." His hands came up and pressed firm on my shoulders, eyes assessing with a touch of possession. "So did you win our little game?"

"Actually, I reckon I did."

He pressed into me, his erection stroking the exact spot where dark heat swirled low in my belly. "Yeah?"

Angling his head, he traced my jaw with his tongue, his breath hot on my skin. My eyes closed on a long sigh, my tired body surrendering. Then he was gone.

He backed up into the opposite corner. Like a caged animal desperate for freedom, he raked me with feral eyes. Grabbing the hem of his soaked tank, he peeled it over his head. "Come here," he growled.

The doors slid open, the contemporary piece of art on the console spotlit by overhead downlighters. Nate didn't move an inch, his heaving chest glistening, pumped and ripped.

"Here?" I mumbled, losing my bravado. My tongue darted out to moisten my lips.

He caught the hem of my tank, yanking me forward. Then, with consummate ease, peeled it from my sticky skin and dropped it by my feet. His eyes glittered as dark as his soaked hair. I panted.

He snaked a hand around my back, and as the hook on my bra snapped at the same time his mouth caught mine, I realised I hadn't won at all.

TUESDAY, I woke with a start. The abrupt jolt stirred the man whose arms I was firmly nestled in.

"Shh," Nate whispered sleepily, his arm around my shoulder tightening.

With a contented sigh, I stretched my body alongside his, taking a deep breath. I thought coffee was a great aroma to start the day, but nothing could beat the enticing scent of Nate's warm skin.

"Is it time to get up?" I rubbed my eyes awake, trying to gauge the hour of morning.

Blindly, Nate reached for his phone beside him and held it in front of my face. "Seven-forty!" I yelped. "Shit!" I wriggled free from his possessive grasp and leapt out of bed.

"Come back," he murmured, sending me reeling with a lop-sided lazy smile and my first glimpse of those brilliant blue eyes. God, how was it possible to be so attractive first thing in the morning?

"You're supposed to be talking to London in twenty minutes," I reminded him. "Ross is probably downstairs already, not to mention Maria." I dipped my fingertips in the small amount of water remaining in my glass and flicked it at his chest.

He didn't flinch. He ran a hand through his hair creating an even sexier look. "I've given Maria strict instructions not to come upstairs until we've left." Throwing the covers back, he patted the space beside him. "Now get your delectable ass back in this bed."

Shaking my head at his playfulness, I grinned. "No time for that." I darted to the bathroom before he could persuade me otherwise.

Ten minutes later I was showered and quickly slathering moisturiser over my still damp skin when Nate strolled in. I stopped, struck motionless by the magnificent sight of him naked.

"Don't mind me." With eyes keenly fixed on me, he reached up and gripped the doorframe. The pose displayed his ripped physique in all its glory. For a man who spent most of his day behind a desk, he had amazing body strength. My thoughts scattered back to last night, and the frantic fucking that had taken place in the lift. I'd never be able to ride in one again without blushing.

Recovering my equilibrium, I wrapped a towel around me and moved to the basin to brush my teeth, desperate to suppress a smile. He moved in, pressing me into the counter as he pressed into my back, nipping my shoulder. "Ross won't mind waiting a bit longer."

It took all my willpower not to concede, but Nate was already late, and I wasn't about to allow his reputation to suffer because of me. I rinsed my mouth and dried it before turning around. "You should start setting your alarm earlier if we're going to have lazy morning sex."

"Who said anything about me being lazy?" Slowly, he untucked the towel from my breast and peeled it open. I allowed it to fall by my feet and put my palms on his chest.

"Who said anything about *you* being in charge of it?" With a swift kiss, I ducked under his arm and ran out the door. His laughter made my smile widen. He was acting like he didn't have a care in the world and I loved his carefree spirit.

I picked up his phone and called Riley. I told her Nate would dial into the teleconference from home and asked her to arrange for the other attendants to phone in from the office. Once that had been organised, I called Ross and gave him the update. Feeling pleased with my organisational skills, I went to the closet to dress. My few items of clothing had gradually been on the increase, and I now had a small selection to choose from. I picked out a set of pale blue lacy underwear and slipped on the Brazilian knickers. I'd just hooked up the bra when Nate appeared.

Tiny droplets of water clung to his skin. His hair was a rich chocolate brown, he'd shaved, and he smelt so good I wanted to eat him. I fought the urge to lick the beads of water off his abs as he opened the tiny white towel from his waist and dried off.

"You can call London in half an hour from home," I told him, wiggling into a pair of light grey tapered trousers. "I've brought everyone up to speed."

"You have?" he asked, retrieving some underwear from the drawer.

"Couldn't have the boss slacking on the job, could I?" I smiled sweetly as he pulled on a pair of silver-grey trousers. It amused me how we often complimented our outfits unintentionally. "Of course, it wasn't just to save your sexy arse. Now I've time for my favourite morning wake-up."

"Really?" Nate purred, fastening the last button of his white shirt. He stalked towards me as I slipped a cornflower blue silk secretary blouse over my head. "Then shouldn't you be getting *un*-dressed?"

My lips pursed. "Correction. My second favourite."

Nate looked puzzled as he turned me away. He brushed my hair to the side and fastened the two buttons on my shoulder.

"Coffee," I explained with a smile.

He finished tying a neat bow at the side of my neck then squeezed my waist, tickling. Laughing, I happily allowed him to pull me back into his frame and nuzzle by my ear. "God," he sighed, "you smell too good. How is it possible to want someone so badly even though you've already given me so much more than I deserve?"

I faced him, hating how doubt still lingered in his mind over what he was or wasn't entitled to, presumably because of his ex. I wrapped my arms around his neck and kissed him, a long, heavenly kiss that could've easily led to more if I allowed it. Leaving him stunned, I straightened my blouse and casually walked away.

"You drive me insane!" Nate called after me. "Tie me up in fucking knots!"

When I reached the open space of the bedroom, I laughed when I heard him curse again.

GUILT over spending such little time with Mai the past week won out and I decided to take her out and treat her to lunch. It had taken all my feminine wiles of persuasion to get Nate to agree to it. He'd been busy moving heaven and earth to make space in his schedule, wanting to spend any time he could with me.

After lunch, I sat with Mai outside Pinkberry eating frozen yoghurt and finished our conversation about our respective weekends. I was a little mad—actually, really pissed off—with Mitchell. Saturday, he'd gone out with friends for the day leaving Mai home alone. Nothing wrong with that, everyone needs time to themselves. Only it was with a mixed sex group of friends, and he hadn't returned home until Sunday lunchtime.

The icing on the cake? He refused to provide any explanation for his whereabouts.

"Think we've run our course," Mai muttered dejectedly. She had no concern for the mango yoghurt she was poking with the tip of her spoon melting and spilling over the sides of the cup. Her eyes were staring off into the distance, her mind lost in troubled thoughts.

"What do you think he was doing?" I pulled a napkin from the dispenser to wipe the mess from the table.

"Honestly?" She licked her spoon, shoved it back in the yoghurt and pushed everything away. "Probably got loaded and passed out on someone's couch."

Once I'd cleared up and deposited the rubbish in the bin, I returned to my chair and took her hand. "You don't think he cheated?"

Mai shook her head but said nothing as we stood. I linked my arm through hers and we set off for the short stroll back to the office. The sun was beating down and the pavement busy with a mix of tourists and professionals on their lunch breaks.

When we first met, Mai was deliriously happy in her relationship. Her free spirit and zest for life was infectious. It was gut wrenching to watch her grow so despondent and sad. "Sorry I haven't been around much lately," I offered, feeling my heart leap when the NTB Building came into sight. "It's bad timing I'm going away Friday, too."

"Not your fault." She shrugged. "It's only taken me ten months to get you laid. I sure as hell aren't dragging you away from the sun now."

"The sun?"

Mai glanced up and grinned. "So hot your retina's burn if you stare at it for too long?"

I laughed loudly, shaking my head.

"To taming Nate Blake." Mai clinked her bottle of iced tea to my water bottle. "Told you he was the one."

"Talking of your talented eye for hot men, guess who's paying me a visit next month?"

Mai yanked me to a stop outside the revolving doors and lifted off her Jackie O sunglasses. Her deep brown eyes were wide and hopeful. "Not your hot-ass of a brother?"

"Got it in one." I pushed the door and entered the cool lobby. My eyes scoped the open space the way they always did, eager for any opportunity to catch sight of my man.

"Gah, what I wouldn't give to do a bit of Tarzan and Jane with him. He is seriously hot. Those bulging arms could throw me around like a rag doll."

"Don't need to hear this," I whined, covering my ears.

"Has to be fate. No other explanation." With a wave of her hand, she followed me through the security turnstiles towards the lifts. "Break up with Mitch, then hello Liam."

My poor womanising brother didn't stand a chance. I wouldn't exactly call Mai a man-eater, but being witness to her flirtations whilst in a committed relationship, I could only imagine what she'd be like as a single woman. "Do you really think it's over between you two?"

We were the only occupants of the car and headed straight to level eight. Mai leant back, shoulders slumped against the glass, her shocking pink belted dress all the more vivid under the bright spotlights. "Who knows? We'll see what the next few weeks bring. It's not what I want, but I'm not hanging around if I'm not what he wants. Simple," she stated, lifting a shoulder.

Except things were far from simple for her. She lived with Mitchell, and together, they shared almost two years worth of memories. That had to be considered.

"Just remember I'm only a phone call away. You're welcome to stay at my place anytime, too. If you need me, call me. Okay?"

Mai gave me a tight smile, exposing her not-as-strong as she liked to appear nature. "Sure."

We turned right out of the lifts and headed to the bathrooms. I admired the grown-up attitude she'd adopted to handle the demise of her relationship. If it were Nate and me, I'd be a quivering mess, utterly devastated after only a few short weeks. We'd gone through a lot in that short time and come out better and stronger because of them.

I followed, counting my blessings at how fortunate I was to have met Nate, and how happy and enriched my life was because of him.

NATE and I arrived at the condo not long after 7 p.m. Neither of us bothered to change before we sat on the barstools at the counter and ate the delicious meal Maria had left warming in the oven. I'd cancelled all gym visits and social activities for the remaining few nights. Nate had done the same.

I glanced sideways, catching him watching me as he ate. The sparkle in his eyes, shadowed with stress and fatigue, still made my pulse leap. No words were required as his hand settled on my knee. The small but purposeful squeeze, followed by a gentle sweep upwards all I needed to understand his intentions. Once our meal was over, we'd be heading upstairs and wouldn't be coming back down again until morning.

I moaned quietly and shifted in my seat. His phone started ringing, breaking the building tension between us. "Clark," he answered shortly.

I remembered the name from the conversation in the car when Nate had arranged security for me. "And that's confirmed?" Nate asked, setting his cutlery neatly down on his cleared plate. I took it over to the sink and rinsed it off with mine, then stacked the dishwasher. "What actions do you suggest I take?"

He was beginning to get agitated, the tone of his voice carrying a slight hint of frustration. Nate liked control, needed to understand and be conversant with every incident to enable informed decisions to be made. He was reasonable, but asking advice from someone else in business matters wouldn't have been easy for him.

"I have the information in my office." He stood and came over. Eyes that seconds before had glittered with sexual desire had now cooled, even as they gazed at me. He nodded to whatever Clark said, pressed a kiss atop my head then turned away. "Let me get the paperwork in front of me," he muttered, disappearing into the breakfast room and out of sight.

It had been quiet on the security front for a few days. Carl and Joe had been AWOL since last Thursday lunchtime, mostly because I hadn't been apart from Nate since then. I'd thought it was all behind us, but the niggling doubt creeping into my thoughts made me reconsider my assumptions.

I took a long shower. Afterwards, I slipped into a thigh-skimming rose-hued camisole, sexy but demure. I dried off my hair, brushed my teeth, then went on the hunt for Nate. Approaching the home office, I heard him talking. My entire body tensed, my instincts switching to high alert. I paused in the hallway, taking a minute to regroup and understand the strange reaction that had come over me.

After a few deep breaths, I took a couple of steps nearer to the half-open office door.

"Goddamnit," Nate hissed. "Just back the fuck off and leave me alone."

My spine stiffened and my legs turned weak.

"This is a private number. Who the fuck did you bribe to get it?"

Still riddled with unexplainable tension, my legs gave way and I slid down the wall until my bottom hit the parquet floor. Hugging my knees to stop my legs shaking, I was too wrapped up in my own bubble of confusion to notice the conversation had ceased. Or that the door had opened and two feet were now standing beside me.

"Baby?" Nate crouched to eye level. His dark winged brow was drawn in, furrowing above his nose. In the half-light of the hallway, he combed his fingers through my hair before brushing a thumb over my cheek. My gaze fell from his face to the mobile phone clasped in his other hand, the screen still illuminated, the call still connected.

I allowed him to pull me up when he straightened. I allowed him to lead me into the office. The daze I'd been in cleared. I let him lift me onto his desk before he reclined back into his leather swivel chair and rolled it closer to fill the gap between my spread thighs.

Nate placed the phone back to his ear. "Let me be clear," he said, calm but assertive. "I won't be taking any more of your calls. You have business issues? You raise them with the appropriate Execs. I don't need to hear any of this bullshit. That's what I pay them a small fortune for."

He ended the call without waiting for a response, and tossed it onto the desk beside me. The paperwork he'd mentioned earlier littered the surface and his digital camera was connected to the computer. He wrapped his arms around my waist and pressed his cheek to my chest. "You smell delicious."

I locked my ankles behind his back and began massaging his shoulders. "You're tense. Is everything all right?"

He sighed and rolled his shoulders and neck. "Turns out those guys we assumed were reporters are actually PI's."

"Private Investigators?" I pinched an especially stubborn knot of muscle between my thumb and finger, easing the stress away. "What do they want with you? With *me*?"

Nate reclined back in his chair. "Clark has already run you through the system. No red flags have come up to suggest you're the target. He's determined you've just been collateral damage, caught in the crossfire. A failed attempt at using you to reach me."

"That's only half a reassurance." And it was, in so far that I was in the clear, but Nate was still being targeted. I leant back on my hands for balance. His gaze drifted from my face, setting a blaze of heat on my skin as he crossed my chest and stomach, settling on where the camisole was barely covering the tops of my thighs. "Why you?"

"I have no fucking clue."

I did my own bit of eye-fucking, sliding my gaze over his shirt, still as crisp as when he first slipped it on this morning. The tie had gone, tossed onto the iron bannister with his jacket when we passed the stairs after arriving home. I scooted forward and dropped into his lap. "You really have no idea?"

He shook his head and rocked my backside forward and back in a slow, seductive rhythm intended to make me forget my line of questioning. Fighting the sparks alighting in my groin, I pressed on. "No skeletons in your cupboards someone wants to unearth? Business associates holding grudges, wanting to drag your name through the mud? No—"

His head snapped back. "Fuck," he muttered, running both hands through his already messy hair before clasping them at his nape. "How the fuck did I not see it?"

A burst of excitement filled me. Something I said had jogged his memory. "What is it?"

"I have to call Clark." He stood, lifting me with him as he straightened, and set me on the desk again before grabbing his phone. "This may take a while."

"Take as long as you need." I kissed his jaw and slid off. "Just don't burn yourself out."

Nate already had his call to Clark speed-dialled through and the phone to his ear. He didn't release my hand until I was the other side of the desk. "I love you."

My heart filled with devotion. I kissed the fingertips of both hands, mouthing I loved him as I blew him a kiss. With a sweet act only Nate could kill me with, he caught it mid-air and pressed it to his chest.

Chapter 36

"I'll come get you at twelve-thirty," Nate told me on my office phone Wednesday morning.

"I'm looking forward to it." I hung up and immediately set to work on moving some meetings to accommodate our impromptu lunch date. Nate was a changed man after talking with Clark last night. I hadn't realised how heavy the burden he'd been carrying was until that light of realisation had switched on in his head. Part of me felt guilty for not understanding, but he'd hidden his worries from me how he always did. With skill and the innate ability to put me and my welfare and happiness in the centre of his world. Having his attention solely on me made it impossible to think about anything outside of our world.

Ross ensured we were at the restaurant in time for our 1 p.m. reservation. Nate breezed us through the busy indoor dining to the quieter patio outside, turning more than a few heads. Not so long ago, I might have hated the attention he was receiving. Now, as I joined the female diners in their admiration, it was pride more than jealousy that filled my conscience. The Prada suit from the first time we met adorned his gorgeous body. I'd determined long ago, navy was by far my favourite shade on him. The darker hue drew out the cool blue of his eyes and made them shine.

With our hands firmly clasped together, I felt a rush of heat through my body. Knowing he really was all mine brought a large smile to my face as we reached our table.

"That's a beautiful sight," Nate said, holding the back of my chair as I sat. He gathered my hair off my shoulders and kissed the hollow of my collarbone.

"What is?" I asked through a long exhalation of air. Even that innocent display of intimacy had skyrocketed my heart rate. Nate hung his jacket on the back of his chair then sat.

"This." He touched the corner of my still upturned mouth.

"You make me so happy." I kissed the tip of his finger then settled our joined hands on the pristine white tablecloth covering the round wrought iron table. The chairs matched and were cushioned in white for comfort. The tableware was white, the small posy of roses in the centre were white. Only half of the tables were occupied, mostly by couples.

We ordered, then relaxed in the shade of the ivy-strewn pergola. I couldn't tear my eyes from Nate. Every word he said, gesture he made, I was reminded of how dreadfully I would miss being around him. I was looking forward to seeing my father, but struggling to reconcile the excitement and happiness that brought with the sadness and empty feeling over leaving Nate.

"We've been invited to social drinks with a client Thursday night." Nate calmly took a sip of iced water as the waiter served our lunches.

"Nate," I sighed. I shook out my cloth napkin and draped it across my lap. "That's the night before I leave. I was hoping for something a little more… private, for our last night together."

"You're still going?"

"Of course."

He stared at me with an impassive expression that hid whether he was being flippant or not. Since dropping the bombshell on him, he hadn't mentioned me leaving again. I'd assumed he was okay with it. Clearly, he wasn't. "Don't make me feel like shit for wanting to see my father," I moaned, poking at my ahi tuna steak, my appetite lost. "It's not fair."

"Sorry." Nate stopped slicing his steak and put down his fork. "I didn't mean to make you feel that way. I'm going to miss you, that's all," he murmured, giving my hand a gentle squeeze.

"So I suppose now isn't the ideal time to inform you my departure time has changed?"

"To when?" he asked, resuming his meal.

"Eight." I grimaced. This wasn't good information I was imparting. "I'll have to leave straight from work for the airport."

His cutlery clattered onto his plate, the noise garnering a few concerned glances from fellow diners. "Fucking unreal. Now do you get why I wanted you to fly private?" He shoved his half eaten lunch to the side. "This means I have, what, two hours less with you than planned?"

I reached under the table and dug my mobile from my bag. "I'll send you the email so you have the new details." I scrolled through, found the message and forwarded it to his private account. "There, done."

He wasn't happy. One hand covered his mouth, the index finger rubbing pensively across his pouting upper lip, his entire frame closed off from me.

"I do have a surprise that might ease your pain," I told him.

He glanced sideways, one brow raised. "Oh?"

"I changed my return flight. I'm back on the nineteenth."

"The day of the fundraiser?" His eyes glimmered with hope. "That mean you can come?"

I smiled but said nothing, allowing him time to figure it out. The hard lines of his face softened, a heart melting shy smile curling his lips. "That's why you changed it, isn't it?" he murmured in awe.

Nodding, I leant forward and kissed him. "I knew how important it was to you, and wanted to be there to support you. I just hope I'm not delayed."

He took both my hands and brought them to his mouth, brushing his lips across my knuckles. "You're incredible, do you know that?"

I laughed shyly, lowering my gaze. Nate could still render me bashful with a compliment.

"Can you leave on time tonight?" he asked hopefully.

"I'm leaving earlier. I haven't packed yet."

"Okay, I'll come to you. We'll stay at your place tonight." He pinched a French bean from my plate and popped it into his mouth with a grin. "You can cook."

My lips pursed. "I'll make you a sandwich."

"Deal."

"Eat that." I pointed to his lunch. "I've a feeling you'll be going hungry tonight."

"WHAT'S your afternoon looking like?" I asked Nate as we travelled back to the office. He had my legs draped across his parted legs, his hands were running up and down my calves. Legs I'd often considered a hinderance, especially in my formative years, Nate found incredibly attractive. He took advantage of every opportunity he had to touch them.

"I'm being interviewed for The Edge." The Edge was NTB's premium online magazine. Managed from the New York office, it covered style, fashion, travel, health and general lifestyle advice for the discerning modern man. There was also a private concierge service for members wanting the luxury items and experiences featured.

Being such a private man, it was odd hearing Nate was doing an interview. "Didn't think that was your kind of thing?"

"It's not." He smirked. "They approached me when this gorgeous blonde had just agreed to have dinner with me. I was in a good mood and feeling generous. It's a behind-the-scenes exposé on the owner. The man behind the suits."

"Well, a naked spread will certainly boost the subscriber count."

His mouth twisted wryly. "For your eyes only, baby. Remember?"

Grinning and comforted by that knowledge, I settled into his side.

"I'm considering something similar aimed at the female demographic. Those wanting to know the best places to shop for fashion, the latest styles, beauty and so on. You'd be a great contributor."

I snorted. "I wouldn't know where to start."

"Cut yourself some slack. Your style is effortless, you're consistently stunning in whatever you wear. You're intelligent, financially savvy, you understand what the career women of your age group want and need." He stretched his legs and leant back. "You can't cook for shit, but hey, few diamonds are flawless."

"Hey!" I dug my elbow in his rib. With his head back, he laughed, a rich hearty sound that made my stomach flurry with happiness. He put an arm around my shoulders and brought me back to his side.

"I haven't green-lighted anything yet, but consider my offer. It's the perfect role for you. We could base ourselves here or move to New York. You'd be Editor-in-Chief. Every decision would be yours to make."

This was a massive career change into unknown territory. I'd spent the best part of six years studying for a career in Finance. The opportunity to be involved with something I loved, almost to an obsession, couldn't be dismissed without careful consideration. "You'd actually take that big a risk on me?"

"Why not? I've risked everything for you once before. I'd do it again in a heartbeat."

I cupped his jaw and brought my face closer to his. The big, blue eyes, now mere inches from mine, had my heart. I'd taken a huge gamble on him, and the payout had surpassed anything I could ever have dared to dream possible. I brushed my lips tenderly over his. "I would, too."

"YOU'LL LOVE some of the donations," Nate assured me as he dressed for work the next morning. Using his connections, he'd secured items to auction at the fundraiser and raise additional funds for the charity.

"What did you get?" I called out from my bathroom.

"Caribbean holidays, Cartier jewellery. Hermès has even donated a one of a kind Birkin you'd love."

"Ah, well," I sighed, joining him in the bedroom, "a girl can dream."

His eyes ran over me with familiar appreciation. "I can't wait to show you off." He finished knotting his tie, a patterned golden silk, and tightened it around his collar. It was the only splash of colour against a white shirt and black pressed trousers. He held his hand out for me to use for balance whilst I slipped on my black heeled pumps. "I know it'll be a big deal for you. There'll be press there. Are you ready to finally make us official?"

I smoothed my dress, the same shift I'd worn on our first date. "Before, it would've been a big deal. But now, I honestly can't wait for you to escort me. Plus," I added, grabbing my bag, "it's another chance to wear my gorgeous Dior dress."

"Think again," Nate said smoothly, slipping on his jacket as we moved into the lounge.

"Why not? I wore it to a private party. No one has seen it before."

"My family will be there. They've seen it. Besides," he said, collecting two travel mugs of coffee from the kitchen counter, "the dress code is strictly black and white, so you can't."

He followed me through the front door, waiting at the top of the stairs whilst I locked up. "We should take another trip to the store. I'll call Audrey, see if she can fit you in before you leave."

"I'll get something in London." I took his arm and headed downstairs. "Let me surprise you."

We settled into the back seat of the Mercedes and drank our second cups of coffee. I mentally planned a girls shopping trip with a fashion-loving cousin and set about emailing her while the idea was still fresh in my head.

Nate called Riley, asking for his 9 a.m. meeting to be rescheduled. Arriving late and leaving early was taking its toll on Nate and his workload. I knew the pressure was mounting and once I was out of the picture, his head would be buried in work to catch up. I made no attempt at conversation, leaving him to plough through some emails on his phone instead.

"I'll meet you at yours tonight," I told him as we neared the office.

"We'll ride home together," he corrected, dropping his phone into his inside pocket. His palm, warmed from his drink, slid under the hem of my dress and squeezed above my knee. "This is our last full night together."

I loved Nate with such a passion it was frightening. This beautiful man was a massive part of my life. It was difficult to remember back to the time when it was only me, and I only had my own needs to consider. I teased the hair above his ear, loving when he leant into my hand and closed his eyes. "I need to do some shopping before I leave. Women's stuff. Catch up on some work. I know your schedule has been suffering because of me."

"Baby, you'll always come first," he murmured, glancing at me briefly. "Besides, I'll have fourteen days to catch up."

I squeezed the hand stroking obscenely higher up my thigh. "If I know you, it'll also take a fortnight of working out to relieve your sexual frustration."

The lips I could spend all day kissing curved wickedly. "You know me well."

"Just don't work too hard," I continued. "I'll see you at seven. Be prompt, I'll have a special treat for you that'll make it worth the wait."

He opened one eye, his sexy half smile tempting me with the promise of sinful pleasures I knew all too well were utterly justified. "Put like that," he purred, "how can I refuse?"

THE sweetheart neckline of the satin black basque pushed up my breasts, giving me a fantastic cleavage, and squeezed tight at the waist to form a classic hourglass figure. The matching knickers were tiny and cut high across my backside. With my hair tumbling loosely over my shoulders, minimal make-up and only the sweetness of my shower gel scenting my skin, I was Nathan Blake's wildest fantasy come to life.

A little innocent, subtly aware of the sexual allure of her body, all poured into one hell of a sexy outfit and ready to blow his mind. I snapped the last clip of the suspender belt to sheer black stockings, stepped into irresponsibly high stilettos and made my way downstairs to the kitchen.

I could be submissive, he could thoroughly overpower me, but tonight was all about Nate. This was the woman I'd always been, not the diffident creature hiding behind the armour. With pride of my figure at an all-time high, I was in charge, and I was ready to give him a night he'd be remembering well into the coming weeks when we'd be apart.

"Hey, baby. I'm home," Nate called out when he entered the condo. My stomach flurried with nerves and excitement.

"I'm in the kitchen," I shouted back. I positioned myself on a barstool and faced the doorway, crossing my legs and leaning back on the island.

He laughed. "Now there's something I never thought I'd hear you say."

When he entered the kitchen, he froze. "Hell." His eyes practically bulged out of their sockets, his mouth gaping. It was all I could do not to burst out laughing. "What have I done to deserve this?"

"I decided you needed a little stress relief, Mr Blake," I purred in my most seductive voice. In deliberately teasing movements, I slid off the stool and sashayed towards him, stopping a foot away. Twisting his tie around my hand I pulled him close. His neck pulsed, his gaze hungry.

"What makes you think I'm stressed?"

"Work has been distracting you the last couple of nights," I murmured. Our mouths were millimetres apart, but I made sure they didn't touch, heightening his anticipation.

His eyes flared slightly, his breath quickening. "Now you want me distracted with you?"

"Something like that." His scent, always such an aphrodisiac, sent tingles across my skin. I slid my hand into his and led him back to the island, ensuring there was enough space between us so he could check me out from behind. I knew he was. The sensation of being devoured by his lustful eyes ran down my spine and over my backside, a sense I'd grown all too accustomed to but would never tire of.

"Take a seat." I encouraged Nate onto a stool. Rounding him, I slipped off his jacket and tossed it aside. My palms glided over his back, visualising the ripped body beneath the white shirt. I stroked up and down his arms, wanting to touch him everywhere, then folded my arms across his chest, my heaving breasts pressed to his back. His breaths were shallow, his heart pounding.

Nate loosened his tie and top button, and ran a finger between his collar and neck. "Has it suddenly become very hot in here, or is it me?" he asked hoarsely.

"I think it's you," I purred, "although I'm feeling very, *very* hot right now."

His restraint was impressive. I wondered how long he'd allow me to play with him. "Dinner is in the oven," I murmured, temple to temple, "I've poured you some wine. All you have to do is relax." Using the tip of my tongue, I traced the shell of his ear and tugged the lobe between my teeth. "I've got everything…under…control."

"For now," he growled.

"You're going to let me have it for as long as I want," I warned, walking around him.

"You think you're ready to take us up a notch?"

"Oh, yeah." I placed my hands on his thighs and lowered my face inches from his. "I'm going to take what I want from you. Make you come so fucking hard. That might be in my mouth"—I grabbed his hand and pushed it between my legs—"or it might be here. I haven't decided yet."

God, I never realised being so brazen and dirty could feel so good.

He cocked a brow. "Is that your decision to make?" His mouth hinted at a smile, and his skin was flushed.

I stepped out of reach, allowing his dark desiring eyes to look but not touch. "Open your mouth." I took some chilled wine into my mouth then leant forward. I opened my lips against his and let the icy liquid trickle into his mouth. With force, he grabbed the back of my head and kissed me, moaning with pleasure. We licked and sucked, ate at each other hungrily, the built-up tension exploding into a fervent kiss. He'd overpowered me again. I pulled at his hair, writhed my hips into his groin to tempt him, frantic to regain some control. It took all my strength to shove his shoulders back and tear away.

"That was very naughty, Mr Blake," I gently admonished.

"Suck me or fuck me, Kara." He yanked my hand to his crotch, his large hand covering mine, making me masturbate his rigid cock. "I need my dick inside you."

Desire unfurled deep in my belly. My nipples puckered against the satin as my chest heaved. "Tut tut tut. You're forgetting who's in charge now." I removed his tie and opened a few more buttons. Nate watched with salacious eyes as he took a sip of wine. He swallowed, licking his upper lip slowly. I dragged his tie around my neck and tied it, intentionally leaving the knot nestled in my cleavage.

His mouth twitched as he carefully placed his glass back down. I cupped my breasts, smoothing my hands down my torso, over the curves of my hips.

Adrenaline pumped through me, making me fearless. “Maybe I don’t want your dick,” I murmured. I pushed my right hand down the front of my panties and found my sex, soaking wet. I whimpered at the desperately sought after contact, only experiencing half the satisfaction because it wasn’t Nate’s hand. “Maybe I’ll touch myself, make you come that way.”

“Not tonight,” Nate bit out, pulling my hand free. He yanked open his belt and buttons on his trousers and pulled down the zip. His cock fell into his palm, throbbing and hard as stone. “Last chance to decide, sweetheart.”

I couldn’t give up now, let him take me and fuck me. I sank to my knees. Nate exhaled harshly, nodding his approval, eyes on fire as I took him in both hands. I circled the head, teasing along the slit with firm flicks of my tongue. He quivered beneath me. I sucked, taking only the head into my mouth. Keeping still, I used my tongue to play. My eyes never left his.

“Goddamn it.” He cupped the back of my head. “Open your mouth.”

He pushed his cock deep into my mouth, hitting the back of my throat. I jerked, blinking rapidly as my eyes watered. He gave me a second to compose myself before bucking his hips, grinding without restraint as my lips created a seal around him and began to suck.

“Harder,” he ordered. The musky taste of his skin, hot and aroused, the satiny softness encasing solid muscle made me groan. I straightened my spine and wrapped my arms around his thighs, needing the support. Glorying in his need, knowing I could be his undoing, I increased the pressure and bared my teeth.

He scrunched my hair in his fist and yanked my head back. “I’m gonna come in your mouth,” he hissed, clutching to keep what little control he had. “Then I’m gonna come in your sweet pussy ’til I’m dripping down your fucking gorgeous legs.”

I groaned, his words almost sending me over the edge. I was a fool to think I could overpower him and not expect any retaliation. I sucked with everything I had, milking his cock until my jaw ached.

His eyes flickered, thighs tensing. “Fuck.” Semen flooded my mouth in hot bursts. I swallowed repeatedly, his legs shaking under my forearms. Both hands were in my hair, their touch gentling to reverent strokes as the last of his release pumped into my wanting mouth. My entire body felt on fire, my nerves and senses alert to the brink of climax.

Nate hauled me to my feet and crushed his mouth to mine. Hungry.

Needy. His hands cupped my breasts, soothing the heavy ache as he thumbed my nipples. “Turn around,” he demanded, pushing to his feet. He pushed me against the kitchen island. With one hand at my nape, he gently eased me forward until I was bent over it. “Hold on to the edge,” he whispered gruffly into my ear, “and don’t let go.”

The cold quartz did nothing to absorb my body heat. I was panting, my breath hot against my arm as I stretched above my head. Nate kicked my legs apart and stood between them. “Is this what you were shopping for earlier?” he murmured, trailing fingertips along the edge of my knickers, across my arse.

I nodded.

He snapped a couple of the suspenders sending a sting shooting right to my sex. “Nice.”

I gasped and shifted my legs, restless. The tip of his forefinger outlined the lips of my opening through my panties, then he shoved them aside and eased a finger inside me from behind.

I moaned. My grip tightened, my back arching. I pushed back, welcoming the warmth of his groin and the hardness of his cock as it fell between my cheeks. Nate groaned, a strained sound of yearning for something dark and forbidden. “I can smell your desire, Kara.” He spread my arse and moved closer.

I stiffened. My mind began to fog, his words, his finger, his touch all making me loose my grip on reality and what I wanted. “Be brave, baby. Tell me exactly what I’m going to do.”

He removed his finger and stroked the head of his cock over my opening, masturbating me back and forth. I wiggled my hips, desperate to have all of him, but with his hand at the base of my spine holding me still, nothing was happening until I said it.

Squeezing my eyes shut, I took a deep breath. “Fuck me,” I whispered.

“Fuck” —he pushed into me a little— “or make love?”

“Fuck.”

With a guttural groan, he rammed into me. He pulled out slow, then back in just as languid, but this was the calm before the storm. His fingers dug into my hipbone as he started to move. “Did you like being in control?” he snarled, his question broken by sharp intakes of air.

“Yes.” I panted.

“Did you forget I can keep going all fucking night?” he grunted, fucking me harder. “I’ll come inside you, then, when you think I’ve had enough, I’ll fuck you again."

I unfurled one hand and reached behind for him, needing a tender connection to balance out his aggression.

"But, you know I'd never hurt you?" he asked cautiously, slowing and gentling the decadent rolls of his hips. He entwined his fingers with mine and lowered, covering me with a blanket of solid muscle.

"You're everything to me, baby." Heat radiated between us, his love for me clear as he wrapped me beneath him and pressed gentle kisses to my shoulder.

"I love you," I whimpered, the last word lost as I came.

Chapter 37

I needed all my strength to get out of bed the next morning. Aside from having a hectic last day tying up loose ends at work, I just didn't want to leave the comfort of Nate's arms.

My predictions had been right. I'd been busy right up until two when I joined Michael in his office to update him on every project I was working on. "There shouldn't be any problems," I assured him, closing my tablet. "The rest of the team are fully capable of running with things for the next couple of weeks." I knew it was the right thing to do, but I couldn't bring myself to suggest he could call me if there were issues. I pulled off my glasses and stood.

"One more thing," he said, his chair creaking as he bounced it back. "The Star presentation in half an hour upstairs? I'd like you to go."

I opened my mouth to speak but quickly shut it. Michael wouldn't like what I wanted to say. *What possible use could I have to attend that?* "But," I spluttered.

"I have to leave early." He smiled sardonically and slurped his coffee. *So did I.*

"It shouldn't be a big one," he went on. "They're unveiling some of the new branding suggestions. The Senior Execs are all there. Think of it as getting that pretty face known."

It was pointless arguing, and only prolonged my time with him. Begrudgingly I conceded and left his office. He didn't even wish me an enjoyable holiday.

I skipped returning to my office, figuring Mai would catch up on my whereabouts. Instead, I headed straight to level fifteen.

I didn't have to make a sound for Nate to know I was there. From where he sat on the sofa, he glanced up. Sharply astute eyes held my gaze for a long minute. I rubbed at my chest, the sudden twinge reminding me how badly I'd miss him.

"I was just thinking of you," he said, signing the last of the papers in his lap.

I made my way in and sat beside him. I looked at the pen clasped in his hand. "I didn't realise you were left-handed."

"The ability to use both hands comes in very handy at times," he purred, setting the papers onto the table.

"Can't argue with that."

He turned towards me, drawing one leg up onto the leather between us. "It's a shame I can't demonstrate quite *how* useful. Unfortunately, I'm about to head to my meeting."

"I know. I came to see you before everyone arrives."

The hand draped along the back of the sofa came up and curled my hair around my ear. "Don't let Michael catch you. He's one of the attendees."

"Not anymore. That's why I'm here."

Nate stiffened, brow furrowing. "Why send you?"

The way he asked, so rudely, as though it was beneath me, was offensive. "I've dealt with ego-driven male executives before. I'm sure I can handle it," I bit out.

"That's not what I meant," he snapped. Before my eyes, he withdrew into his guarded businessman shell. My presence usually calmed him but right now, he looked anxious and thoroughly uncomfortable. Nervous even. The audience we were about to face were Senior Executives, influential people from both companies who wielded a lot of power. There was no room for private emotional attachments.

"Hey," I said, touching his thigh. "I won't pounce on you across the boardroom table. I'll be the consummate professional." I stroked playfully, edging up to his groin and back again.

Nate laughed nervously, a forced sound and stilled my hand.

"Oh, I'm sorry." We both turned sharply at the sound of a female who'd entered the office. Her gaze fell to our joined hands resting on his thigh. "Hope I'm not interrupting," she sneered.

"I'll be there shortly," Nate snapped, scowling at the now smirking redhead. Her grey eyes narrowed as she scrutinised me, looking me up and down. Wrinkling her nose, she grimaced. *Charming.*

In a blatant come-on, her arms crossed over her chest, pushing up average sized breasts so cleavage swelled through the opening of her emerald green blouse. Her tongue darted out to wet bright, red lips. Offended and annoyed, I was pleased with my restraint as I patiently waited for her to finish her performance.

"We're ready," she said breathlessly. She turned and sashayed out, her narrow hips swaying far too obviously to be natural.

"Well, I haven't impressed her." I turned to Nate.

"You have nothing to prove to her. I'm with you now. Don't forget that."

I found his reassurance at that moment strangely odd, but I had no time to dwell on it. "I better go in first." I stood, needing a minute to pull myself together ahead of what was shaping up to be an interesting meeting.

"Will you be ready to leave as soon as we're done here?" Nate asked.

"I've done my handover with Michael so I'm all yours." I turned when I reached the doors. The bleak shadows in his eyes worried me and sent a wave of unease crawling over my skin. The silence between us spoke volumes of the agitation building inside him.

"You know how much I love you, don't you?" he asked quietly. "That I'd never willingly upset you?"

"I do." I swallowed past the lump in my throat, thinking his questions strange and untimely. He still got on edge about how deeply he'd fallen for me, and worried I would never understand the extent of his feelings. That alone told me how much he did. "Do you know how much I adore you?"

Nate replied with a soft smile. Glancing into the lobby to check we were alone, I dashed back to him. "Give me a kiss," I pleaded, desperate for that reassuring connection. "Go on, no-one's looking."

"My forever," he whispered, sweeping luscious soft lips over mine.

I stepped back, still feeling off. "Don't keep us waiting."

The large Boardroom had been set up with concept boards for visuals, and two young men from the creative team were frantically preparing the laptop ready for the presentation. About twelve personnel, all male in business attire, were milling around the rectangular table and taking their seats.

"Can I help you?" A familiar voice asked behind me. I turned and found the redhead glaring daggers at me. "Are you the intern?" she went on, pushing past. "Take a seat at the back."

"Actually," I said, drawing my shoulders back, "I'm replacing Michael Cole." Taking advantage of being a good six inches taller, even in my ballet flats compared to her nude Jimmy Choo's, I extended my hand. "Kara Collins. Any financial queries can be directed to me."

She didn't take my hand. "Fine. Sit quietly, save your questions until last. Make sure you take notes." She looked me up and down with pursed lips. "I have no time to run through details with him because of your incompetence."

Remaining professional, I took the seat closest to where I stood. I felt more than a little out of place, sitting here in my grey skinny jeans. Her patronising dismissal of my intelligence riled me. I was glad to have no more dealings with her after this. The CEO for Marketing, Geoff, sat to my left and made small talk as I fired up the note app on my tablet.

The chatter descended into a hushed silence, signalling Nate's arrival. He walked with brisk, harried steps, phone clenched in one hand, to the far end of the table where the redhead sat batting her eyelids. He pulled out a chair, unbuttoning his navy jacket as he sat beside her. He looked uncomfortable, agitated even. Definitely not like someone about to unveil the culmination of months of hard work for the biggest deal in his company's history.

The redhead smiled, patiently waiting for him to begin. Her bright smile didn't even slip when Nate whispered something in her ear. The sight of them being so intimate spiked a pang of jealousy in me. It was silly, but I felt like my ear was the only one he should be whispering into. By the scowl on Nate's face, I knew it wasn't sweet nothings he'd said.

"First," he began, "I appreciate you all being here today in what should be an exciting moment for both of our companies." His eyes followed each attendee around the table, but completely skipped me. They also skipped the woman to his right. "I must apologise for missing dinner last night. Trust me, I didn't go hungry. And neither did you if the tab was anything to go by."

There was a ripple of laughter, but I think everyone in the room sensed something was off. I had no idea Nate even had a dinner scheduled, let alone cancelled because of me. I knew his hungry reference was aimed at me, but when I glanced up again from my tablet, he still wasn't looking my way.

"I'm sure you're very much in demand, Nate," the redhead purred.

"I am," he agreed, "which is why, unfortunately, I'm going to have to cut this meeting short." Calmly, he twisted the lid off the water bottle in front of him and took a long gulp. The attendees shuffled in their seats with murmurs of discontent and uncertainty.

"This is highly unprofessional, Blake." A greying man with a portly belly and rosy cheeks huffed a few seats down from Nate. He was right. This behaviour was so unlike Nate, but he didn't seem to care about the damage this could cause his reputation.

"Let me assure you, RED will continue to handle this project with the utmost care and professionalism, synonymous with the NTB Brand. I've seen some of the mock-ups, and I believe we've truly excelled ourselves this time with our innovation and forward-thinking. You won't be disappointed, Roger," Nate stated, addressing the man. "And as a gesture of good faith, I will fully reimburse all of your expenses and cover the rescheduled trip at a later date."

Roger looked a little mollified. The redhead placed her hand on Nate's arm. "May I say a few words?"

Nate shot her a look that would've had the mightiest of men withering in their seats, but she didn't flinch. "Nate and I go back a long way," she started, "and I'm certain there's an excellent reason for cancelling at such short notice. He's such a consummate professional, an expert in his field. There's no-one else I'd rather get close with again."

She failed in catching his eye, because now was the exact moment he chose to find mine. Wide-eyed with concern, he studied me carefully. He'd reclined in his seat, distancing himself from the redhead who had noticed where he was looking. The glare she gave me could've killed.

"Purely professionally, I mean." She giggled coyly as if her faux pax hadn't been intentional. Her fake smile said she was full of shit. "I'm sure everyone agrees, mixing business and pleasure rarely ends well."

That comment was definitely intended for me. My skin prickled and the knot in my stomach returned.

"If that's all, Miss Grainger, the meet—"

"Oh, Nate," the redhead giggled again, "you know you can call me Ashleigh."

Ashleigh. Her sickly sweet tone grated on me—her name even more so. *Why did it feel like it had been following me around, hounding my subconscious?* It only took the sheer panic flaring in Nate's eyes for me to realise it had.

Nausea flooded the pit of my stomach as it gradually dawned on me who this woman was. Nate had called her Ash, but there was no mistaking he was referring to the woman sitting across from me, cosying up to him without shame. Only she wasn't some ex-girlfriend tucked away in the past as he'd led me to believe. Ashleigh Grainger was here, large as life in the very same room, breathing the very same air.

The urge to vomit became so overwhelming I lunged for one of the water bottles in the centre of the table and promptly sent my tablet crashing to the floor. "Shit!" I cursed quietly, all shaking fingers and thumbs as I scrambled to retrieve it from under my seat. There was a small commotion and a very audible *tsk* from her.

"Are you okay, Kara?" Straightening up, my eyes found Nate. Leaning forward, concern etched into his beautiful features, he waited anxiously. I knew from his gentle tone he wasn't referring to the accident that just happened.

He'd got it. He knew I'd put all of the pieces of the puzzle together and made a very ugly picture. Ashleigh peered at me with a fake look of concern. "I'm fine, Nate. Sorry—Mr Blake." I squirmed as all eyes turned on me. My hand went to my neck, twisting the starfish back and forth along the chain. My face heated. My black sheer blouse felt like it was sticking to my skin, and my mouth was dry.

I didn't even hear the meeting conclude. The only indication it had finished was when everyone stood and the room began emptying out. Ashleigh pushed to her feet, her fingers steepled on the table. "Miss Collins? Could you wait a moment, please?"

Nate was buttoning his jacket, standing beside her. "You have nothing to say to her," he snapped, picking up his phone.

"Just want to ensure she has all she needs for her boss." She touched his chest and swung her eyes to me, a cruel smirk twisting her lips. Disgusted, I looked away, busying myself with gathering my belongings together.

The room had emptied by the time Nate reached me. His hand curved my shoulder as he bent down. "You don't have to listen to any of her bullshit, Kara."

A chill moved through me as his lips brushed my ear. My traitorous body had other ideas, reacting to the briefest of touches the only way it knew how—with heated longing and understanding of how good they felt when they swept over more intimate parts of my anatomy.

"I think I do." I pulled back my shoulders. "Maybe I'll finally get some answers."

I should have been preparing for a confrontation, but instead, I found myself scrutinising everything about her. Ashleigh was pretty—I'd expected nothing less—but she was nothing like me. I'd hazard a guess and say she was late twenties. She wore her blouse tucked into a knee-length white pencil skirt and expensive accessories. Impossibly thin, her face was immaculately made-up and framed by shoulder length hair cut in a choppy style that looked effortless but had probably spent hours to perfect.

Redheads were notoriously fiery and spirited. Ashleigh appeared no exception to that stereotype. Everything about her screamed bold and sexy. And the way she'd been chasing Nate? She wasn't afraid to use her assets to her advantage.

Nothing like me.

"So," she said, perching on the edge of the table a few feet away, "how long have you two been fucking?"

"That's enough!" Nate turned to me. "Let's go."

"Don't try to deny it. I've seen evidence proving it. My investigators were very thorough." Ashleigh pinned me with narrowed grey eyes designed to force me into submission.

"*Your* investigators?" I spluttered.

"This is so out of line, Ashleigh," Nate warned, his mouth thinned, eyes glaring. "It's none of your fucking business."

My mind raced, question after question jostling for position. Still, I found myself answering, "What Mr Blake does in his private time is none of your concern. Your association is business, not pleasure."

Ashleigh gave a conniving laugh and swung her legs off the table. "Kara, you seem like an intelligent girl, so it should come as no surprise to learn you're merely warming his bed for me."

"Jesus!" Nate raked a hand through his hair, the other on his hip. "You're so deluded it's sick."

"That's what you think?" I asked. Small and inferior because she was standing, I pushed back my chair and stood.

My sense of superiority was fleeting when she sneered, "It's what I know. We have history. Our families are great friends. It's a shame I was out of town for Thomas and Sadie's party, my parents had an amazing time."

The couple I met briefly… No wonder the atmosphere had been frosty. Then I remembered how protective Nate's family had been that night. "I doubt you were invited. I know you weren't missed."

Nate came to me. "Let's go, baby. She isn't worth our time. I'll answer every question you have, just not here. Not like this."

"Let her talk. I'm interested to hear what she has to say." I had no idea where my fighting spirit had come from, but I wasn't running this time. I was ready to confront the truth. Belief that I deserved better, along with a backbone to stand up for what was mine were the greatest gifts Nathan Blake had given me.

"You know she's gonna feed you a pack of lies?" he warned sternly.

"Am I lying when I say we've met for dinner in New York, and we had a very…*interesting* run-in at the vineyard a while back?" she pointed out sweetly.

I couldn't ignore that. I knew he'd seen her the other week, but not over dinner. And how long was a while back? "Is she?" I croaked.

"You make it sound like it was just the two of us," he corrected harshly, glaring at her before turning to address me. "This all happened weeks before I even met you."

"Kara." Ashleigh sighed, propping her hip to the table. "He'll inevitably return to his first love. Me." She crossed her arms, all the while maintaining eye contact, trying to put me off. "We were both virgins, but it was still good." Cocking her head, she giggled. "Well, as good as anyone's first time ever is."

Her revelation hit me like a punch in the gut. The bitch was goading me with moments I could never share with Nate. A memory forever etched into his mind.

"Enough!" Nate snapped. He stalked towards her, knuckles white with rage around his phone. "Didn't you cause enough damage the last time? Can you not get it into your fucking crazy head that I'm not interested? You have *nothing* over me anymore!"

"No?" she asked calmly, her smile sardonic.

"No," he hissed, a warning through gritted teeth. Towering over her, irritation and rage rolling off him in waves, he was a man on the verge of cracking and losing all self-restraint. "Now, I swear to God, if you don't get your goddamn ass out of here, this whole bullshit farce of a project can go to hell!"

Ashleigh balked and swayed a little, her head jerked back from the venom in his threat. She did what he said, hastily shoving her bound notebook into a beige Chanel tote. I picked up my glasses and tablet, shaking with anger. Pain lanced through my chest and I was on the verge of collapsing. I watched her leave when she stopped by the door and looked back. "I still wear the ring he bought me," she said dreamily. "Reminds me of his eyes." She flashed a rather gaudy sapphire creation on her right hand. So *not* like something Nate would choose. Then she laughed and waved her left hand. "Not on *that* finger anymore, though."

"Out!" Nate grabbed her elbow and marched her out.

My head pounded, overloaded with intimate revelations. The room grew small and stifling hot, stagnant bitter air circulating around me. My feet began to move, carrying me out of the room. From the corner of my eye, I saw Nate haul Ashleigh into a lift, but I carried on walking, stumbling my way into his office.

I left my tablet on his desk and went to the cabinet in search of a drink. He came in and shut the door a few seconds later.

"Why don't you have any alcohol?" I cried. "What good is water to me?" I poured a large glass, then twisted to face him. His chest was heaving, the stunning face I adored flushed and set hard and angry.

"I didn't fuck her," he seethed, his lips thinning.

"Jesus! It's not about that! Before we met, you could've fucked hundreds of women for all I care!" That wasn't true, but I had no claim on him back then. "You led me to assume you'd had a casual run-in with her, not that you're in business together."

I allowed my gaze to drift over every sophisticated, divine inch of him. My eyes snagged on the long, talented fingers flexing nervously by his side, the tensing making the throbbing veins glaringly prominent.

"You were engaged?" I whispered.

"Never," he assured softly. He tossed his phone onto the sofa and approached. "It's all lies, Kara. All of it."

"Stop," I snapped, my upheld hand warning him not to come any closer. I gave the tumbler a squeeze, imagining it shattering into a thousand tiny pieces when it hit the window behind him.

He sighed. "Ashleigh bought that ring years ago with my money and passed it off as an engagement ring to any fool who cared to listen."

"A fool like me?"

He cursed under his breath. "A fool who doesn't know the real me—who wouldn't know a man in love if he kicked them up their ass and shoved his heart in their faces."

I went to his desk, focusing on the two photographs taking centre stage. I lifted the newest one, the two of us at the anniversary party—a gift from his parents—and studied it carefully, searching for flaws. There were none. Our love was real and deep down I knew it.

"What happened between you two in New York?" I asked shakily, leaning back on the desk so I could face him. I had to know everything before I could move on.

"Ah, God." He scrubbed his face. "Ash thinks she has something over me. I have no idea what. She came on to me in my office, tried to kiss me."

I gasped, sucking in a breath. I squeezed my eyes shut, fists clenching around the photo, battling to stay calm and determined to let him finish before reacting. He didn't.

Nate took my mouth roughly. The pads of his thumbs smoothed along my jaw, easing away the tension until I willingly opened up. The second our tongues joined, the kiss softened but was nonetheless insistent.

I fell back, buckling under the force of his will. The photo frame hit the desk as I scrambled for balance. My mind was a riot of thoughts, my body a chaotic mix of love and resentment. His lips worked frantically over my face like he couldn't stop kissing me, whilst his hands began unbuttoning my blouse. "Nothing and no-one will ever change my love for you," he murmured gruffly between kisses.

"I know," I whimpered. My back bowed, my head dropping back, surrendering my neck to his mouth. I wrapped my legs around his waist and dragged him closer.

"I fucking need you," he growled, pushing my blouse open and cupping my breast. "You own me." A low rumble moved through him as his teeth grazed the swell of flesh. He yanked the cup down and sealed his mouth over my nipple, sucking and biting.

"Stop it!" I cried, shoving him off me. I scrambled off his desk, trying to salvage some dignity. "You can't gloss over this with a fuck! No matter how much I want you to."

Nate straightened. He wiped the pad of his thumb over his lips. "Don't mistake that for an apology or admission of guilt. I admit I've handled her, and you, in the wrong manner, but that's all it is. No lies. No cheating. Just misguided reasoning."

"I know you didn't fuck her! But finding out she had her hands all over you is something you should've told me," I stuttered, shaken as I buttoned up my blouse. Tears began to clog my eyes.

"I didn't think you'd trust me going forward if I detailed precisely what happened in New York. I couldn't bring myself to confide in you and ruin what we'd found in each other." He raked both hands through his hair. "I feared you'd give up on us and walk away from me because it was the easy way out."

Nate. I'd made him second-guess his own gut instincts. He'd always been truthful. I'd kept him at arm's length because I didn't want to get hurt, and he'd kept this from me because of it.

"I had no idea she worked for Star until it was too late." He disappeared into the bathroom. "Last I heard, she was taking time to herself to figure some personal issues out. By the time I realised, contracts had been drawn up and signed."

"And now she's going to be a part of our lives whether we like it or not."

"I meant what I said," Nate muttered, returning with some tissue. "I'll sever all ties, break the deal."

"I can't allow that to happen." He'd already made too many sacrifices. Any more, and his business would be jeopardised, possibly beyond repair. Nate had called me immature once before, but I'd grown since then. The ability to handle threats to my relationship was stronger than ever. "And I won't give her the ammunition she needs to break us up."

I'd stand by him and face whatever Ashleigh wanted to throw at us. He was worth it. *We* were worth it.

He smiled, carefully wiping my eyes. "There's the inner strength I fell in love with."

I sniffed, managing a half-smile. The same glow of adoration I'd seen so many times before danced in his eyes. First thing in the morning; the times I'd caught him watching me when he thought I didn't know. The same way he gazed at me when I was beneath him, covered with him. Mind, body and soul.

He checked his watch and gathered up our belongings. "We need to leave."

"I can't get on a plane now. Not with this hanging over us." I let him take my hand and lead me out of the office towards the lifts. Reception was eerily quiet, both Riley and Ramón nowhere to be seen.

"You can." We stepped into the waiting lift and travelled down to my level. "You're going to spend some quality time with your dad because he needs you."

"So do you," I murmured, loving him more than I ever imagined possible for putting everyone else before himself.

"And I'll be right here waiting for you when you come back." Nate dropped my tablet onto Mai's vacated workstation before continuing to my office. In a daze, I let him sort everything out. He shut down my computer, locked up my cupboards and tidied the place up.

Nothing had worked out as planned. The romantic meal we were supposed to grab en-route to the airport had gone out the window with no chance of salvaging it. I hadn't said goodbye to Mai. Now it was late afternoon, and the traffic would be a slow grind to the airport. I'd be lucky if I managed to get there on time and catch my flight.

"Got your passports?" Nate asked, helping me into my long grey cardigan.

I gave him a reluctant nod. "In here," I said, grabbing my tote. He wheeled my two suitcases to the door and let me take the smaller one.

With my hand firmly clasped in his, we made the long walk back to the lifts.

ROSS loaded everything into the boot of the Mercedes. I was about to climb into the back, when, "Can't believe you were gonna sneak off without saying goodbye."

Mai stepped from the shadow of the building, puffing smoke into the air as she stubbed her half-smoked cigarette out on the packet.

"I wouldn't dare." Relief danced inside me. "I'd never hear the end of it."

She scanned me up and down. "You okay? You look a little off."

"I'm a bit shook up, but I think I'm going to be all right." I squeezed her hands. "Are you?"

"Oh, you know me," she sang, shrugging a shoulder. "I'm always happy."

"And that is why I love you so."

One brow arched. "Are we having a moment?"

I laughed. In the most upsetting of times, Mai could make my heart fill my chest. I kissed her cheek. "Be good. Focus on your work, study hard. If you do, I'll bring you something awesome back."

"A hot man?" she asked eagerly, reminding me of her relationship woes.

"That's happening in a few weeks, remember?"

"Want me to take care of yours while you're gone?" She nodded behind me. I glanced over my shoulder to the car. Nate waited patiently. He always had, and he'd assured me he always would.

A tiny smile crept over his face, forcing me to realise how unsettled he actually was. Again, his focus in all this mess had been on me and my well-being. But what about him?

"Get in the car, K." Mai shoved me, breaking my thoughts. "You know he doesn't need taking care of. He's got you by his side. He'll be good."

I settled into the backseat, immediately grabbing Nate's hand when he joined me. I waved to Mai through the tinted glass and rested my head on his jacketed shoulder. He nuzzled into my hair, taking a deep breath, his body relaxing.

I dropped my gaze to his left hand clasped around mine. I began stroking his ring finger, smoothing my fingers over the long digit. My free hand toyed anxiously with the starfish around my neck.

The bright lights of Los Angeles passed in long drawn out metres as we moved then stopped, moved then stopped. It had been little over a year since I'd returned to a place I'd once called home. Aside from my father, and all the wonderful cherished memories of my mother, it held nothing for me anymore. Everything I wanted was right here.

"I treasure what we have, Nate," I said quietly. "You and me, you know?"

Glancing at me in the dusky light, something flickered in the eyes I found myself drowning in every day. I didn't know what it was, I'd never seen it before.

An unravelling of the soul…a power exchange…a surrender…an admission of defeat?

The demons he'd helped me battle and destroy were creeping into his soul, reminders of his past returning to haunt him. I swallowed the lump in my throat and lifted his hand to my mouth. "I love you," I whispered, kissing the spot I'd been stroking moments before.

He sagged into the leather, closing his eyes on a long exhalation. "We're going to be okay," he promised.

As my salvation, I was depending on it.

Epilogue—Nate

What was good about a goodbye?

Not once, during the entire course of our relationship, had I ever said goodbye to Kara. Even now, standing in the International Departures Terminal at LAX after watching my girl disappear through Security, I hadn't uttered the words. It was too final. Like an admission that the moment was ending, never to be experienced again, and that I was happy about it.

That would never be true with her. In the blink of an eye, the strikingly brilliant essence of my life had gone. It would be fourteen long days, even longer fucking nights until I could hold her in my arms again.

Deep in her heart Kara hadn't wanted to leave. If I'm honest, I didn't want her to go. But family was as important to her as it was me. Her dad needed supporting through this rough time, and she needed him whether she admitted it or not.

The kiss we'd shared seconds ago lingered on my lips, the taste of her still coating my mouth. I touched them, never wanting the feeling of her sweet mouth on mine to leave me. Ever.

I wished I could get back every minute of the journey to the airport. Hell, I wished I could get the past goddamn six weeks back. Do it all again. Differently. Not the time spent with Kara—I wouldn't change that for the world. Not even the times fraught with tension, the misunderstandings or the arguments that had been few and far between. My girl challenged me, half the time testing my patience without even appreciating she was doing it. I thrived on the difference it made in me as a man.

But this whole fucking mess with Ash hadn't been handled well. She'd damn near wrecked me once before. I gave her the benefit of the doubt back then. She was sick, not herself. Grief made normally sane people behave in strange ways. Fucked with their heads, tested their resolve, pushed them to their limits to see how long they could last before breaking.

I should know. I'd been there.

That's why I allowed what happened to happen. I was damned if it was happening again.

I shoved my hands into my pants pockets and rocked back on the heels of my wingtips. A gaggle of flight attendants breezed past, placing me in the centre of their group as they flowed either side. There used to be a time when I'd flash them a smile, give them what they were hungry for, maybe even invite them for drinks with a few friends. Now, I didn't even bat an eyelid. When you've tasted the finest life has to offer, why chase anything else?

Reluctantly, I turned to leave, imagining what Kara was doing. Hopefully, though I doubted the likelihood, she'd get something to eat in the First Class Lounge.

Yeah, I changed her ticket. Hell if I'd let her travel that distance in cattle class. Her wellbeing was in someone else's hands and it was gonna be at least eleven hours before I heard from her again. If only to appease my own anxiety of waiting for that call before knowing she was safely back on the ground in London, I'd make sure she was being taken care of while travelling there. She was mad when she checked in and found out, but her indignation hadn't lasted long. It never did.

I stepped outside into the warm night air. The thrust of aircraft engines assaulted my ears. Cabs lined up, offloading passengers who wielded trolleys like possessed animals. Maybe if they didn't load the damn things too high, they might push it in a straight line without running innocent bystanders down.

My cellphone vibrated next to my chest. I dug it from the inside pocket of my jacket: **MISS YOU. LOVE YOU X**

Love warmed every cell of my frustrated body. My dick twitched. Not gonna lie, it happened every time I thought about her, was worse when I saw her. When she talked? Hard as stone damn near every time.

I quickly tapped a reply, ignorant of the chaos around me as I strolled to the Valet parking lot where Ross waited: **MY FOREVER X**

I reached the Mercedes and climbed into the back seat. "Thanks for cancelling our dinner reservation."

"No problem, Mr Blake." Jayden Ross was one of my best employees. Discreet, reliable and trustworthy. A man who had become a friend as much as anything. He swung out of the space and headed back to the city. "Shall I take you home?"

Home? My home was about to take off, be flown further away from me with every breath I took. If she wasn't with me, I was homeless. A drifter, with nothing to anchor me. Only one place could ease the discomfort in my chest, fill the hollow space in my soul. I rolled my head back to the headrest and shut my eyes on a deep sigh.

"Take me to Kara's place."

Nate and Kara's story will conclude in Book 2 of the Heal Me series.

Acknowledgements

Where do I start?

Family. Goes without saying. To my husband and children — thank you for your unconditional love, and for happily coming on this wild, crazy ride of writing with me. I would never have been able to write this book if it wasn't for your support, encouragement and patience. This story consumed me, and you just went with the flow. You put up with the piles of laundry, uncooked dinners and an untidy house without any complaint. You sacrificed wife and mummy time without any grumbles (okay, maybe a few, but that's allowed). I love you. And yes, husband, you can now finally read my book…

I have to thank the rest of my family, even though they have no idea I've been writing this. One day you may find out my alter ego…if that happens, please don't be too shocked. Behind every innocent looking face is a naughty person waiting to escape.

To my wonderful beta readers — thank you for providing such insightful feedback, for reading my rewrites, and for doing it all in such a timely manner. You were the first people in the world to read this story, and I'm so pleased that you loved it as much as I hoped you would. You helped shape Salvation into the novel it is today.

Special thanks to my two cover designers. To Emmy at Cover Me Designs for creating the ebook version and inspiring the full wrap for the paperback. You summed it all up perfectly when you said, "It's like choosing a wedding dress. When you see it, you'll know it's the one." Well, you were right. I loved the image we used for the ebook cover the second I saw it. Thank you for your hard work. To Ida at Amygdala Design for creating the paperback cover, and for doing it so quickly! When I was at the point of believing Salvation would never go to print, you rescued me. You are a life saver and I thank you from the bottom of my heart.

A massive thank you to Paula at Passionate Promotions. You went above and beyond what I expected when I approached you. Proofreading, editing, synopsis writing, cover choosing, promotion — you helped with it all. When I was full of doubt, your words of encouragement and support were invaluable in picking me up. I know how crazy busy you are, yet even with injuries and a thousand other commitments, you worked tirelessly to get this book out there. I look forward to working together again and hope we remain friends for a long time. In the meantime, I'll see you in that line for Nate, right behind me…

To all the amazing authors, writers and bloggers I've connected with through social media, thank you for being such an inspiration. On days when I felt like throwing it all in, you lifted me up with silly quotes, virtually shared cocktails and countless pictures of sexy men. That never fails. Please send more (sexy men, especially).

Finally, the biggest thank you to you — yes, you — for picking up this novel (or 1-clicking, depending on your preferences) and taking a chance on an unknown author. I hope this story consumes you as much as it has me. I thank you from the bottom of my heart.

About the Author

Most days, you'll find Stephanie John on a yacht, wearing a very skimpy bikini, drinking champagne, eating chocolate and never gaining weight.

When she isn't asleep and dreaming, in real life you're more likely to find her at the school gates, wearing whatever she dragged on that morning, drinking copious amounts of coffee. She still eats chocolate, though — everyone has their vices, right?

Somehow, amidst the chaos of full-time mummy duties, she manages to write. Contemporary romance has always been her favourite genre to read for as long as she can remember (age-appropriate, of course).

Never in a million years did it occur to her to write one of her own. Now, she couldn't imagine doing anything else.

Facebook - https://www.facebook.com/stephjohnwriter
Twitter - https://www.twitter.com/stephjohnwrites
Website -https://www.AuthorStephanieJohn.com
Pinterest - https://www.pinterest.com/stephjohnwrites
Goodreads-https://www.goodreads.com/author/show/6294518.Stephanie_John

Made in the USA
Columbia, SC
16 October 2017